Painted Fires

Nellie L. McClung

Afterword by Cecily Devereux

Early Canadian Literature

Wilfrid Laurier University Press acknowledges the support of the Canada Council for the Arts for our publishing program. We acknowledge the financial support of the Government of Canada through its Book Publishing Industry Development Program for our publishing activities.

ONTARIO ARTS COUNCIL
CONSEIL DES ARTS DE L'ONTARIO
an Ontario government agency
un organisme du gouvernement de l'Ontario

Canada Council
for the Arts

Conseil des Arts
du Canada

Library and Archives Canada Cataloguing in Publication

McClung, Nellie L., 1873–1951, author
    Painted fires / Nellie L. McClung.

(Early Canadian literature series)
Originally published: Toronto : T. Allen, 1925.
Issued in print and electronic formats.
ISBN 978-1-55458-979-1 (pbk.).—ISBN 978-1-55458-993-7 (pdf).—
ISBN 978-1-55458-994-4 (epub).

    I. Title. II. Series: Early Canadian literature series

PS8525.C52P3 2014   C813'.52   C2014-901191-1
                                         C2014-901192-X

Cover design and text design by Blakeley Words+Pictures. Cover photo by Cyril Jessop, Library and Archives Canada, Acc. no. 1966-094, PA-030212.

Every reasonable effort has been made to acquire permission for copyright material used in this text, and to acknowledge all such indebtedness accurately. Any errors and omissions called to the publisher's attention will be corrected in future printings.

This book is printed on FSC recycled paper and is certified Ecologo. It is made from 100% post-consumer fibre, processed chlorine free, and manufactured using biogas energy.

Printed in Canada.

RECYCLED
Paper made from
recycled material
FSC® C103567
FSC www.fsc.org

Contents

Series Editor's Preface

Nellie Letitia Mooney was born in Chatsworth, Ontario, on 20 October 1873, the youngest of six children born to parents who had emigrated to Canada from Scotland and Ireland. In 1880, her family settled on a farm in Milford, Manitoba, on the banks of the Souris River. She learned to read only when she started school, at age ten. Eventually she received her teaching certificate from the Winnipeg Normal School and taught school until 1896, when she married pharmacist Robert Wesley McClung. By the time of her marriage, she had begun to use her gifts as a debater and a public speaker in her work with the Women's Christian Temperance Union. She spent her married life balancing politics, public speaking, writing, child-rearing, and domestic responsibilities, moving with her family to Winnipeg in 1911 and to Edmonton in 1915 and finally with her husband to Victoria in 1932. She died in Victoria on 1 September 1951.

McClung is remembered today less for her writing than for her political work: throughout her married life she continued to fight for a number of causes, including temperance, woman suffrage, the creation of a minimum wage, equitable divorce rights, health care in rural communities, and factory safety legislation. She was elected as a Liberal to the Alberta legislature in 1921, serving in that capacity until her defeat in 1926. Later that decade, she became known as one of the "Famous Five" who contributed to a landmark decision in Canadian politics, one overturning a statement included in the British North America Act that declared that "women are persons in matters of pain and penalties, but are not persons in matters of rights and privileges." On 18 October 1929, thanks to the "Famous Five," women were finally declared "persons" and as such could be appointed to the Senate ("Women").

As Janice Fiamengo notes in her entry on McClung in the *Encyclopedia of Literature in Canada* (2002), "From her early years she wanted to be a writer, to do for her people what Charles Dickens had done for England's poor" (723). Her best-known book today is her 1915 feminist manifesto *In Times Like These*, which Veronica Strong-Boag calls "a collection of suffrage and temperance speeches that remains a classic of the North American movement" of woman suffrage (351). Her first novel, *Sowing Seeds in Danny*, was a Canadian bestseller when it appeared in 1908 and was followed by two sequels featuring the indomitable Pearlie Watson, *The Second Chance* (1910) and *Purple Springs* (1921). As Clarence Karr notes about McClung and her contemporaries Ralph Connor and Robert Stead, "she used her fiction as a vehicle for the advocacy of reform, but unlike [Connor and Stead], she was primarily concerned with opportunities and rights for women. All three authors shared a liberal idealism that was prevalent in the society of the time; they hoped that, through their fiction, readers would learn how a better world could be achieved." Karr adds that McClung "related her stories in an easy, natural style with a language appropriate to the setting in rural and small-town Manitoba in the early twentieth century" (109). McClung also published several volumes of shorter works of fiction and non-fiction as well as an autobiography in two volumes, *Clearing in the West* (1936) and *The Stream Runs Fast* (1945).

McClung's fourth and final novel, *Painted Fires*, appeared in 1925, the year she was made president of the Canadian Authors Association. The maturation story of Helmi Milander, who leaves her native

Finland as an adolescent in order to make a new life for herself in North America, the novel has been described by critics as McClung's "angriest" novel (Coleman 147). While the novel was conceived as an attempt to present in the form of a novel the story of a young immigrant girl, McClung initially planned for Helmi to be a supporting character. As Karr reveals, "McClung experienced a character with its own mind when Helmi Milander took over and demanded a conversion from minor to central character," forcing her to discard eleven chapters of the manuscript and start over (52, 244n95). Fiamengo suggests that the novel's "series of improbable coincidences" reflect McClung's attempt "to address a variety of social issues, including drug addiction, sexual abuse of immigrant girls, the entrenched misogyny of social and legal structures, and the pious complacency of the middle class" (724). Noting that McClung's views about women's rights seem inconsistent from a contemporary perspective, Fiamengo adds that "[i]n the debate over whether McClung should be venerated as a feminist icon or excoriated for her class and race biases, the consensus seems to be that she was a leader who was also a product of her time" (725).

This Early Canadian Literature edition of *Painted Fires* contains the complete text of McClung's novel, originally published in Toronto by Thomas Allen in 1925. An American edition appeared the same year from New York publisher Dodd, Mead and Company, but the text was reset for that edition and contains a number of non-substantive departures from the Allen text (mainly involving conventions of spelling and punctuation) as well as some substantive alterations. The character of Major Gowsett appears as Major Dowsett in the U.S. edition, for example, and the mention of the "Allen Theatre" in the Allen edition (page 114 of the ECL edition) is replaced by a mention of the "Palace Theater." The novel was reprinted by the Ryerson Press (Toronto) and by Grosset & Dunlap (New York) in editions that are undated except for the original copyright notice, and these editions replicate the Dodd, Mead text. The novel was also published in Finnish translation as *Suomalaistyttö Amerikassa* ("Finnish Girl in America") in 1926. The Allen edition is frequently inconsistent in terms of spelling, hyphenation, capitalization, usage, and punctuation. While this edition corrects obvious errors, for the most part it lets stand the inconsistencies as well as alternate or archaic spellings.

BENJAMIN LEFEBVRE

Works Cited

Coleman, Daniel. *White Civility: The Literary Project of English Canada*. Toronto: U of Toronto P, 2006. Print.

Fiamengo, Janice. "McClung, Nellie Letitia." *Encyclopedia of Literature in Canada*. Ed. W.H. New. Toronto: U of Toronto P, 2002. 723–25. Print.

Karr, Clarence. *Authors and Audiences: Popular Canadian Fiction in the Early Twentieth Century*. Montreal: McGill–Queen's UP, 2000. Print.

McClung, Nellie L. *Painted Fires*. Toronto: Thomas Allen, 1925. Print.

———. *Painted Fires*. New York: Dodd, Mead and Company, 1925. *Peel's Prairie Provinces*. University of Alberta Libraries, n.d. Web. 10 Apr. 2014.

———. *Painted Fires*. New York: Grosset and Dunlap, n.d. *Library and Archives Canada*. Government of Canada, n.d. Web. 10 Apr. 2014.

———. *Painted Fires*. Toronto: Ryerson P, n.d. *Project Gutenberg Canada*. Project Gutenberg Canada, 2010. Web. 10 Apr. 2014.

———. *Suomalaistyttö Amerikassa* [Finnish Girl in America]. Trans. Väinö Nyman. Helsinki: Kirja, 1926. Print.

Strong-Boag, Veronica. "Print and the Promotion of Women's Suffrage." *History of the Book in Canada*, vol. 2: *1840–1918*. Ed. Yvan Lamonde, Patricia Lockhart Fleming, and Fiona A. Black. Toronto: U of Toronto P, 2005. 349–51. Print.

"Women Are Persons: The Famous Five and the Persons Case." *Alberta Centennial*. Alberta Government, 2002. Web. 21 May 2014.

Painted
Fires

Chapter I

I t all began with the rustle of silk.

When Helmi's Aunt Lili came back to Finland for a visit, after six years of the crowded ways of life in America, the older womenfolk of her family regarded her with mingled feelings of awe, envy and reproach. Her elder sister, Helmi's mother, said it was foolishness for a girl who had to earn her money hard, carrying trays, to put it all on her back and wear clothes that only queens should be wearing. At which Aunt Lili had laughed, showing her gold teeth, and said it was a matter of principle with her to spend her money so fast that no one could steal it from her! Helmi was the one member of the family who gave the visitor full hearted and unmixed devotion. She loved the rich sound of her silken skirts, it was so luxuriant, so *hieno*, it seemed to raise the whole family to a higher social level, and she marvelled how any one, even her mother, would dare to find fault with this wonderful person who wore silk stockings, had fur on the inside of her coat, and pink ribbons in garments that did not show at all!

Aunt Lili had not spent all her money on her own clothes. To Helmi's mother she had brought a purse which closed with a crack. It had a head on one side, and two claws which could be flapped on the other side; gold satin lining; mysterious chambers inside; and better than all was the delicate inference it conveyed regarding women and money. To Helmi's father she brought a silk handkerchief with welted roses on both sides, a sort of magic handkerchief, for no matter how hard it was squeezed in one's hand it would spring out again without even a wrinkle. To Anna, Helmi's big sister, who had her hair in bangs, she brought a square bottle of powder the color of skin, and a round downy thing to put it on with. Aunt Lili used a black sock herself for this purpose, but she said powder-puffs were certainly in style in America now.

Aunt Lili made many contrasts between America and Finland. "You work too hard here," she said, "and you never play. We work in America, but we have good times, too. This country is all right for men, but what is there for women but raising children and work? When a woman here is married ten years she is old, and her life is over. It is all just giving in, and giving up for women, until at last they give out. I wouldn't live here if you gave me the whole country. I couldn't stand it now after I have seen what a good time American women have!"

Her words, received in silence by the older woman and scoffed at by Anna, who was going to be married in the Spring to Emil Saari, who lived near and had built a two-roomed house, found a sympathetic listener in Helmi, who was then thirteen. Her mother and Anna might be content with Finland, but Helmi's eyes had caught the vision of the far country.

The resolve to see this wonderful country for herself was definitely taken when she saw the beautiful picture Aunt Lili brought her. It was a colored picture, shiny as ice and rioting with light and color, called "Aunty's Flower Garden." It showed an old-fashioned garden bursting with roses and hollyhocks and Canterbury bells. Down the brick walk came two lovely ladies, one in a crimson velvet dress, the other one in fairy blue; a little golden-haired girl ahead of them clad in white, carried a green basket brimming with roses.

Helmi believed the title literally, and wondered how her Aunt Lili could leave such an enchanted place even to come for a visit to the

4

old home. Aunt Lili had saved soap wrappers to get the picture, and had left it honestly enough in the pasteboard roll in which it came and where all concerned might see from whence it came. But to Helmi the name carried proof—"Aunty's Flower Garden." It was too thrilling a thought to lose, so she did not ask for confirmation.

Aunt Lili stayed for the Black Ice Skating, and then returned to her adopted country, but the picture she left with Helmi kept the fires of her imagination and desires burning.

Brighter still they burned after her mother died and the querulous, scolding grandmother came to direct the house until her son would find a stepmother for his family. Anna had married and entered upon the strenuous program of a baby a year.

With monotonous work and continuous scolding all around her, and before her the example of Anna, who was rapidly losing her red cheeks and her light heart, Helmi held to the vision Aunt Lili had given her of the Promised Land. The roses in the picture nodded approval, the Canterbury bells were ringing a welcome, the velvet clad ladies, still sauntering along the garden path, smiled into her eyes and whispered "Come and be one of us."

There are great moments in every life. When Aunt Lili sent the money and Helmi, now seventeen, held the letter in her hand, with its mysterious pale blue paper that the postmaster said was money, she was suddenly caught up into another world. Now all things were possible, for here were the wings with which she could fly away. She, too, would come back with silk skirts that creaked like a bag of cabbage, and purses and toys for Anna's children. Granny would be sorry then for the things she had said, but she would tell her that the past was gone. She was sorry for Granny, who would never, never see America.

Helmi made the journey to Saint Paul, Minnesota.

It was well that her young heart was fortified by so many pleasant thoughts upon the way, for bleak disappointment and sorrow were hers when she arrived. Aunt Lili, the dashing Aunt Lili, who seemed to defy sorrow and death just as she defied conventions and traditions, lay fighting a losing battle with a pitiless disease, in a cheerless little room in the hotel owned by her husband. Over the bar, in the noisiest room, lay the shadow of the great Aunt Lili, praying just one prayer between her spells of coughing, that she might live until her young niece came and then have breath enough to tell her what she must be told.

Letters take a long time to go to Finland, and although she had written as soon as she knew how serious her condition was, she feared her message might not arrive in time to save Helmi the journey. She must stay alive for Helmi's sake. Helmi had always been her favorite niece, Helmi with her golden hair, and eyes the color of the green brown moss in the bottom of the running *puro* at home. "Oh, just for enough time to see Helmi and tell her things—please . . . please . . . God!"

And so the frightened Helmi, who had expected to be met by the Great Person who had brightened her childhood, came into a dark and dreary room, whose only vivid spot was the white face on the soiled pillow with its two burning eyes.

"Don't kiss me, Helmi. Ain't it awful? It is a bad disease I have which goes from me. I thought it was just a cold like I often have, but it's worse than that. Anyway, I only wanted to see you and tell you. Don't stay with Mike. He says he will keep you. You do not owe him the money—it was mine. He wants you because you are young and pretty. The girls tell me he's acting bad already, and me not dead so soon. I have money enough to send you back, Helmi, that will be best. You know what is ahead of you at home. It might be worse. You will go back, won't you, Helmi?"

Helmi fell on her knees beside the bed.

"But isn't it a good country, Aunt Lili, like you said? Can't I get along like you did?" she sobbed. "I can work, Aunt Lili, like you did."

"It's a good country, Helmi," said Aunt Lili when she could speak, "just like I said, only men are so bad, and it's hard for a young girl alone, and I am so afraid for you. Men just want their own pleasure. Mike was good to me while I could sport around and dance, and while I did not say a cross word to him for what he did to men when they got drunk. He takes their money, Helmi; I can't stand that. I threatened him I'd go and tell, and then he struck me with a chair. He never comes to see me now, Helmi, and he made me take this room above the bar because when people pay for rooms they want to sleep. He says. 'You're awake, anyway, with your cough, so what's the odds!' Helmi, men are queer and all for self. The trouble started when my little Helmi was on the way. I had her named for you. Men do not like kids, they're too much trouble. He was mad and cross at me because I was not smart and was sometimes sick, and when little Helmi came she only lived a day, and he was glad. Then I hated him, Helmi—I hate him now, and that's bad. It's wicked to hate when one is going to die, but I cannot help it, Helmi, I wanted to warn you not to get mixed up with men—they break your heart."

"Are they all bad, Aunt Lili?" asked Helmi tearfully.

A long spell of coughing delayed the answer.

"They don't want to settle down in their home like we do; they don't like kids and a nice quiet life—though they will tell you they do. You are pretty, Helmi; that's why I am afraid. I don't want Mike to see you if it can be helped. He'll want you just like he wanted me. Kate, the cook, will keep you safe. All the girls are my friends . . . Remember what Aunt Lili said, Helmi."

Having received the extension of time she had asked for, and having delivered her message, Aunt Lili gave up the fight without a struggle. The silence of the room was broken by the stormy sobs of big Kate, the cook, and the two upstairs' girls. She had said good-bye to all the girls in the house the night before. Her last and tenderest words were for her young niece.

"If you could only talk English I would say stay," she had said. "It is a good country, but it's too hard for a pretty girl who has no English."

"I can learn, dear Auntie," said Helmi, kissing the thin white hand, "like you did, Aunt Lili," but Aunt Lili did not hear.

Mike Laine, the proprietor of the "Farmer's Home," learned in some way of his niece's arrival and asked to see her. He pinched her arm affectionately the day of the funeral and told her to call him "Mike" and cut the "Uncle" stuff. His burning eyes made her shudder.

One of the girls talked Finnish, and in big Kate's room, off the kitchen, a council was held. Helmi was firm in her determination to stay. Big Kate, who had one hundred dollars in trust for her, urged her to go home; the Finnish girl faithfully interpreting both sides of the argument.

For three days the discussion raged, Helmi during the intervals having washed her clothes and learned their English names. She also did her share of dishwashing and potato peeling. Her skill in these matters won the heart of the cook, who on the third day wrote a letter to her sister in Winnipeg telling her to meet the train from Saint Paul on a certain day and look out for a "Finnish girl with red hair and a green Tam o'shanter."

The day that Helmi left, Big Kate made the explanations to the bereaved uncle. Being the cook, she was not afraid to talk back to any one, and besides, she had certain information which quieted Mr. Laine's outburst of indignation. Miss Katherine Kenny was not so large that she could not kneel at the door and apply her eye to a keyhole in such a manner that the whole room and its activities were revealed. Mr. Laine could not reply to Miss Kenny's accusations and threats of exposure by hitting her over the head with a chair. Such crude methods of dealing with women can only be safely used inside the hallowed precincts of matrimony. He contented himself by telling the cook he didn't care what she had done with the girl; he had "had enough of these bad tempered Finns, anyway."

With this Mr. Laine shrugged his shoulders and went back to the bar. He would probably get the girl yet. She would be writing back for money and claiming relationship with him. A girl like that, right off the farm in Finland, with a pretty face and no English—Some fellow would be too smart for her.

On the Soo line, in the day coach, with her face against the glass, a box of sandwiches beside her, money in her purse and five ten-dollar bills sewed securely into the pocket of her petticoat, sat Helmi, watching the landscape slip past. It was a brilliant day in March; wild geese were flying north in V-shaped formation; cattle with blotchy coats were roaming the fields; black channels of water licked their way through the snow; fence-tops were showing like rows of fancy stitching around the fields. At one station, where the train waited to change engines, the boys and girls just out of school had come down to the station. Helmi was glad to see one girl wearing a cap much like her own—it gave her a delicious thrill of *monti*. A boy and girl walked away together—the boy carrying his companion's books and skates as well as his own. He leaned towards her as he spoke.

Helmi's eyes were wistful as she watched. "They are not all bad," she said in her own tongue.

The train bore swiftly on. Eagerly Helmi watched the racing, swinging, sliding fields. The sun went down in a crimson mist, shooting streamers into the sky, so warm and glowing that it seemed to Helmi like a welcoming fire, where she would find friends, home and happiness. Even after the sunset had paled and faded into the gray of night she knew that it was still burning and glowing and beckoning her further on.

And so came Helmi, young, strong and unafraid.

Chapter II

Margaret Kenny was wiping her hands on the bran-colored roller towel which hung behind the pantry door, preparatory to the opening of her sister's letter, which lay on the drain board. Not for a moment did the elder Miss Kenny take her eye off the letter.

"It's from Kate in the States," she said, "and so it's trouble. She's adopted a child, or killed a man for beatin' his horse, or something. She never writes only when she is in howlt of some kind. Gosh! I often wish she was in jail, where I'd be shut of her, bad cess to her impitence. I told her the time she sent me the dog that I was done with her. Well, I may as well open it."

As Miss Kenny read the letter, following each line with a red forefinger, consternation settled upon her like a tent.

"What the divil," she began, "A Finn girl, red haired and smart . . . had to get her away, it was not safe for her here . . . I remain your loving sister, Kate."

"Oh! So she remains my lovin' sister! Well, I'm no lovin' sister of hers. She always finds the trouble,—she can place it without a willow wand, can Katy,—and then hands it on to me. Well, here's a pretty how-do-you-do, a Finn girl, no English, comin' on the train. 'Please,

10

Maggie, find her a place. Easiest thing in the world, Maggie sorra a thing you have to do; anyway' . . . "

"See here, Anna Milander, you should be the one to look out for a Finn girl. Listen to this."

The head dining-room girl came languidly into the kitchen. "What's the row?"—she asked.

Maggie read the letter.

"She'll come in at five tomorrow, just when I'm up to me eyes in the dinner. Now, you go down—you can speak to her and be back in time to carry the dinner, too."

Anna's head was flung back. "I think I see myself—I didn't send for this girl—she's nothing to me—merely another wage slave coming to take a job. There's too many girls now for the jobs."

Maggie Kenny's face was screwed up in astonishment. "My God," she cried, "is that the brotherhood you learn at your meetin's?"

"We're opposed to immigration," said Anna firmly, "the Government dumps in people here, just to keep wages down. It's the capitalists again. You haven't sense enough to see it."

"For all the brazen, selfish lumps I ever saw it's you, Anna. When you came here two years ago all you could say was 'Yiss.' Who showed you how to make a bed and comb your hair and garter up your stockings? And now, by Gosh! you wouldn't meet another girl at the station, and her from your own country and all. Did you never hear of the Golden Rule, do as you would be done by?"

"Old stuff, Maggie," scoffed Anna, "no one believes that now. The idle rich sling that stuff round to lull us to sleep, that's all. It may catch you and your breed, but not us. We've gone a long way past that."

"What the devil do you want, Anna Milander? Haven't you a good job, good meals, good bed, better clothes than you ever had?—What ails you?"

"We have nothing to lose but our chains," said Anna loftily. "How long could old Spencer run this joint without us? The world belongs to the workers, but we haven't the backbone to claim it. Softies like you keep us back with your Golden Rules, and the Spencers get the profits. There's only two classes, those who work and those who live on others' work. Some people earn and some spend. If the workers would all organize we could dictate terms. Some day we'll do it. Then a new day will come."

"Get along with you, Anna," said Maggie soothingly; "you're crazy. Be thankful you have a roof over your head and good money comin' every month; and I'd advise you to stow all that wild talk or you'll get canned."

"Sure, that's the threat—shut your mouth or lose your job. We're slaves, every one of us. And you're one, too, but you love your chains." Anna was not to be appeased.

"Well, slave or no slave, will you meet the girl at the station?"

"No," said Anna, "I only recognize the claims of the Union. This girl is a scab so far as I am concerned. Your religious stuff doesn't go with me—it's soothing syrup, that's all. This is war, Maggie; we might as well name it, it's war. Now go, and tell on me if you want to."

Maggie Kenny, looking after the head waitress as she swept from the room, shook her head. "That's the divil's own talk," she said, "and there's no sense in it. Well, she needn't go to the train; I can get Mrs. Spencer herself to give me a hand with the dinner, and it's herself that can do it well, and will make no complaint of it, either. Slave owner she may be, but it's a grand woman she is, anyway."

Mrs. Spencer, when appealed to by her old friend and cook, readily agreed to cook the dinner. She had planned to go to a Tea at the Rectory to raise money for the Chinese, but she would send her dollar instead; and, indeed, she confided to Maggie it was grand to get her hands into the pie crust again, and maybe it was just as good to do a kind turn for a Finn girl coming into the country as for a Chinese, across the sea. The problem of the new Finn girl did not bother her at all. "Any girl that will wash dishes and scrub can always find a place, and if she's civil and clean and honest she'll get on, and," added Mrs. Spencer, "we can do with another now the Spring is here and we'll be for turning out the bedrooms."

When Margaret Kenny got off the Broadway car opposite the station a crowd obstructed the traffic, gathering, knotting, and swelling, overflowing into the street. Policemen on horseback shouted, whistles blew, impatient automobile horns gave back derisive answers, and every moment the crowds grew denser. Maggie, remembering her mission, kept on the edge of the whirlpool, wondering what was causing all the excitement. In a lull in the commotion a man's voice fell on her ear, a hoarse voice, rough with shouting. The words were strangely familiar.

"Wage slaves, when will you wake up? The ruling classes, the owners, bring us here to do the rough and dirty work, pitting us one against the other to get their work done cheap . . . Nothing to lose but our chains! . . . they send their paid policemen to scatter us. But the day will come."

Maggie turned away. This, then, was the place where Anna Milander was getting her education; and too bad it was, for Anna was a smart girl. As Maggie made her way through the crowd she came suddenly upon Anna; hardly recognizing her, for she wore an old cape and a heavy black veil. As Maggie jostled against her in the crowd her cape was brushed back, revealing a heavy stone in her hand.

"Cut that," whispered Maggie in her ear, "Don't be a fool, Anna. Do you want to go to jail? Remember there's law in Canada."

"Law for the rich," sneered Anna, "none for the poor only what we make for ourselves, and you're not helping us!"

A movement in the crowd swept Maggie on before she could say another word. She hurried into the station and saw that the big clock above the stairway pointed to the hour of the arrival of the train, and already the two living banks were forming in readiness for that troubled and palpitating stream which would come surging through the iron gates below.

"It's quare to be livin' in a country where the whole world comes to see us," Maggie thought to herself when two Hindus with their lightly draped head-dress walked haughtily by, followed by a colored man and woman with their little girl held by the hand.

"I'm glad I'm white," said Maggie to herself; "a white skin may be harder to keep clean, but it's worth the trouble . . . and even the poor child is as black as a boot,—that doesn't seem fair—but that's God's business and not mine, and I'm glad. Gosh! I hope Katie hasn't landed a lemon on me.

"'A red-haired girl in a green tam'—that's not much to go by— there's ten thousand shades of red hair—and every girl these days wears a tam—sloppy, lop-eared things they are, too."

They surged past her, women with shawls over their heads and endless troops of children, uniform only in weariness and mussiness. Maggie's tidy soul longed for oceans of soapy water and mountains of soft towels, and racks of clothes and troops of ministering angels with their sleeves rolled up, to help her. Absorbed in her gigantic plans she forgot her errand, rousing with a start when a voice beside her said, "Maggie Kenny." She looked around to see who had spoken and found beside her a tall young girl with soft brown eyes, red hair, and wearing a green tam.

"Maggie Kenny?" she said again, with a note of enquiry at the end, and an unmistakably foreign accent.

Maggie took her hand impulsively. "You're a smart thing," she said, forgetting that the girl could not understand; "how did you know me?"

Helmi had a photograph in her hand, an old one taken years before, when bangs were worn laid on straight and plastered down apparently with shoe polish. A stern tobaggan-slide of a hat, stiff and unrelenting, sat on Maggie's head like a helmet of mail, and the frozen look, which even the smallest kodak could inspire, was in her eye.

"Say, kid, you're smart!" cried Maggie in admiration, "I wouldn't know that myself."

Helmi laughed, showing a row of shining teeth; she knew she was being praised.

She touched the photo and then pointed to Maggie's eyes.

"You'll do," said Maggie approvingly, "Kate Kenny didn't hand me a lemon this time."

The head waitress of the Yale Hotel was absent; lawfully detained, too. Indeed, at the moment that the delicious odor of roast beef, gravy, fried onions and creamed cauliflower was floating into the dining-room from the kitchen table, where Mrs. Spencer, in a bungalow apron, carved and "dished," at that very moment Miss Anna Milander was locked in a cell at the police station, charged with having maliciously and with intent to hurt hurled a stone at a policeman. Anna did not deny the charge; she was well pleased with her afternoon's work. She had struck a blow in Freedom's cause. It was all rather vague in Anna's mind. She was rather favorably disposed toward policemen as a class, but having joined the Union she was determined to become "class conscious." Policemen were enemies; so were employers; every one was an enemy except members of the Union. So Anna, having a clear program in her mind, sat on her narrow bed in a warm cell, well content. Her picture would be in the paper; she would be praised by the speakers. She had risen from the dull, gray, dusty depths of obscurity, which the speaker called the base of the economic pyramid, and in the interests of her comrades in the submerged strata had heaved an honest rock. More than that, it had gone unerringly to the mark, and the pride of achievement burned in Anna's heart. In the fulness of her contentment she sang:—

"The banker calls it interest, and winks the other eye;
The merchant calls it profit, and heaves a joyful sigh;
The landlord calls it rentals, and he puts it in his bag;
The good old honest burglar—he just calls it swag."

Though not related, Helmi and Anna bore the same name and resembled each other in features and coloring—the same creamy skin, reddish hair, brown eyes and general type. But at the moment they were widely different in appearance owing to the different styles of dress. Helmi wore a coarse skirt, a print blouse, with leather belt, heavily soled boots and home knitted stockings. Anna, having been two years in Canada, had already acquired "style." She wore a narrow skirt, slit at the side, showing a flare of crimson petticoat, with a knife pleating at the edge; a belted coat, a red Windsor tie, and silk stockings always. The thought of having worn cotton stockings when she arrived in Canada gave her a smothered feeling now—they were the brand of servitude. "Bandages," she scornfully called them.

Anna dreamed pleasantly of the golden age of which the street corner leaders told, when there would be leisure and luxuries for the workers and confusion for the capitalists; when railways and street cars and theatres and all the sources of pleasure would be free as air; and tiresome, disagreeable drudgery would be gone forever.

Indeed, for Anna the golden age was already here. Some one would get her her breakfast tomorrow morning; someone would have to make this little stingy, stringy bed—if you could call it a bed. That was something, too. Instead of attending to other people and carrying trays and washing dirty dishes, someone was going to do it for her. Hooray!

So Anna sat on her narrow bed, a prisoner before the law, but not cast-down or desolate. She, too, had her own little painted fire, and she had not yet found out that there was no heat in it.

Chapter III

Meanwhile, Helmi washed the gold clover-leaf ironstone dishes at the Yale Hotel, made beds and carried trays and learned new words every day. English language in Helmi's hands became a simple thing. She took no account of its idioms. She did not see why the man who brought the bread should not be called the "loafer," or why if the cat licked up its milk Mrs. Spencer would mind if she said in answer to a phone call "Mrs. Spencer is out licking up tea!" It was rather bewildering; and how was Helmi to know that the meter man had to do with the electric light—she thought he must be the butcher!

Helmi's outbursts of temper gave Miss Kenny some concern. The first one was directed against Martha Draper, the bow-legged English girl who washed dishes, and to whom Helmi was now an assistant.

Martha had washed dishes in her own untidy way all her life, no one taking notice of her methods. The cook, concerned with roasts and pies and such important things, could not very well cumber her mind with the details of dish-washing. Martha always had the dishes ready for the next meal, and that was about all that mattered.

Martha believed in purification by fire as well as by water, so she frequently left the potato pot to burn on the stove until the burning smell caused some one to investigate. Helmi had many times shown her the better way, to which Martha had given but scant and scornful attention. Martha had the British tradition—foreigners were dirty and ignorant, and certainly "could tell her nothink."

Martha washed dishes by piling them into the sink without scraping them, turning on the hot water when she was ready, and subsequently rescuing the unhappy cups, saucers and plates from the seething and unlovely flood. Helmi broke into a storm of Finnish rage when she saw it, and let the water run away prior to cleaning out the sink. Then she scraped the dishes until even the clover leaves were in peril, set them in neat piles on the table; scoured the sink, and proceeded to show the lady who had been born within the sound of Bow Bells how dishes should be washed. Martha watched in cold and stiffening silence. She hated dish-washing anyway, and saw nothing in it but a means whereby she could earn money to buy herself some swell clothes. Martha had a "sweety"—a night watchman at the Parliament Buildings and she believed he meant business. Martha's way of breaking the news of her approaching nuptials was, "I wouldn't be surprised if we saw the finish of the whole business this summer."

When the next meal was over the dishes arrived as usual on the kitchen table in their great irregular, dizzy piles, slippery with gravy, pickles and meat. Martha proceeded to insult the sink again (which Helmi had polished into a state of whiteness it had not enjoyed for years) with the presence of the dishes and their unused contents. Helmi was serving the dessert for the evening meal and did not see what had happened until Martha had the sink dripping with dishes. When she saw what had happened she stood quite still, a black rage gathering in her eyes. With the empty tray in her hand she awaited the coming of Martha, who came gaily singing into the kitchen with another toppling load of dishes. Helmi waited until she had deposited them on the table, then brought her empty tray down on Martha's head with a metallic crash. Martha screamed in genuine terror and Maggie Kenny and Mrs. Spencer came running in.

Helmi pointed to the littered sink and tried to explain. Martha metaphorically wrapped the British flag around her injured person and called for justice. It was one of those easy cases where the evidence is all in plain sight.

It was Mrs. Spencer who made the abstract of the case.

"Ain't that just like a Finn, Maggie, clean and neat, but high tempered? Well, if she wasn't a tidy girl she wouldn't have done it. Martha, shut up or I'll give you something to bawl for; you're not hurt as bad as all that. Helmi shouldn't have clouted you with the tray. Do you hear, Helmi? Now, Martha, you can get off for tonight; Helmi will do the dishes alone. And I've a sort of notion she doesn't mind that a bit, so every one is satisfied, and it may be that Martha now knows it's a dangerous thing to be too messy with dishes when Helmi's around, anyway."

Helmi lost no opportunities of learning English, and counted the day lost if she had not added a few words to her vocabulary. She used the wrapping-paper which came into the kitchen on parcels for the purpose of keeping her lists, tearing it into squares and sewing them together with twine. Martha, who after the unpleasant event just recorded became a better dish-washer and a more agreeable companion, taught Helmi to say the words, resulting in her acquiring a cockney accent which the boarders found very amusing.

Helmi's love for the open took her out when her spare days came. One afternoon a week was hers and every second Sunday. Martha would not come with her even if they had been able to get off together, for she often said she hated the country and liked to see a bit of life when she got out. At 'ome, she always went to see the Guard change at the palace gates, "but why any one would walk out into the country to watch cows eatin' grass" was more than Miss Draper could make out; "but," Miss Draper generously hastened to add, "it takes all kinds." Miss Draper, however, could see some sense in going to see the dresses in the shop windows and picking out which ones you would get if you had a king's ransom.

Helmi had now been in the hotel four months. She had acquired enough English to take orders in the dining-room.

"Will you have 'am or bicon with your heggs?"

"Peach pie, happle pie or tapiocar?"

She often wondered why she was asked to repeat her orders, and why the boarders laughed, but it was all in the day's work to Helmi.

Helmi's great delight was to get out of the city on her Sunday afternoons, where there were no sidewalks, no pavements, no street cars and few people.

One day she determined to walk far enough to leave all the houses behind. Maybe she would find green grass, or a turnip field, or cows grazing in a meadow, or meet a friendly dog who did not know she was a foreigner. She soon reached the place where the sidewalk ended, and felt once more the good soft earth beneath her feet. It was familiar, home-like, her own. It spoke to her in her own language, it was not laughing at her. If she sowed a seed in it a little plant would come; even if she did not know its English name it would come just the same, and Helmi's heart grew warm with the thought.

The sky hung low that day, seeming to Helmi like a great glass cover over the earth, like the dome of glass that Mrs. Spencer had in the upstairs parlor over her seed-wreath. She lay down on a green slope to look into the sky. It was so like the sky at home it made her feel not so far away after all. Even if words were so very different, skies and grass and the ground were the same, and soon she would know how to call them. Aunt Lili, like her, had not known a word of English when she came out.

It was lovely to be away where it was quiet and green and all by herself. It did not matter if one could not speak English here; the sky and the grass and the little creek on whose bank she sat knew no English either. A fringed blue gentian growing in the grass peeped shyly at her as she peered about her. She called it by its Finnish name and wondered if it had ever heard it here.

From this distance Helmi could think of her work in the hotel with greater composure. She knew she was awkward sometimes, and maybe stupid, though she always tried hard to please. Anyway, it was good to have a job, even if she had to pick roots off potatoes in a mouldy, dark cellar, and gather up the rotten ones to burn in the furnace.

Helmi had the large, restless hands which generations of hard-working women acquire, eager, capable, hands ready for anything that has to be done. Even the cook Maggie Kenny, who wasted few words of praise on her assistants, admitted grudgingly that the Finn girl "has good smart hands and makes every move tell;—if she could use her head as well, she'd do."

Helmi from the little hill on which she sat looked back at the smoky city, lying like a great giant under its greasy, gray blanket of smoke. It reminded her uncomfortably of the blankets she had to spread every morning on the beds in the rear room of the hotel. In the front of the house she knew there were pleasant rooms, with white spreads and flowered wash-basins, but at the back a great yard of a room had what seemed like a hundred beds, spread with sweaty blankets, and it was this room, she had to sweep and tidy every day. Some days she found men still in bed when she went in, but having set out to tidy the room, Helmi held to her course, taking no notice of the storm of abuse which came from the late sleepers.

Helmi's dreams that Sunday afternoon as she sat on the bank were for the most part pleasant. Consciousness of youth and bounding health made her hopeful of the future. She could work and she could learn, and she too would one day go back to Finland with a velvet bag, a long white plume, and silk linings and fringe on her gloves; and all the young people would gather round her while she would tell of how she started, right at the bottom, washing ugly heavy dishes in a hotel.

Helmi always held the dream, too, that she might some day meet a prospector, maybe a young man from Finland who had found gold. Men can do such wonderful things. Women have to work hard, but pretty girls have a good chance. Lots of Finn boys had come away to Canada, and maybe she yet would meet some of them. She thought of the Prince who was in love with a poor girl and swore he would marry her and whose proud uncle sent him a lovely coat that had a great ugly patch of coarse cloth on it, meaning that if he married the poor girl she would be like the coarse patch. That was a dirty thing for the bad old uncle to do! But what did the Prince do? He got the patch all embroidered with pearls and lovely jewels and sent it back signifying that his lovely poor girl would be the grandest thing about the place. Helmi guessed that held the uncle a while, maybe.

Helmi was so deep in her dreams she was unconscious of the approach of two young men. They were close upon her when she looked up. She did not like their appearance, but she felt no fear. There was a strength in her right arm which brought assurance.

Helmi smiled and nodded to them as she would have if they had been two of the neighbors' boys at home.

They said something to her in English.

"Yes," she said, because it was the only word she could think of—and then added—"No talk—Finn."

The boys laughed at that and looked at each other meaningly.

Helmi's young heart was athirst for adventure. If the young men had been dressed more elegantly she might have thought they were the successful gold-diggers of her dreams. But with a calculating eye she appraised them correctly. She motioned them to go on, which they interpreted to mean that she desired to go back to the city with them. When she began to walk away the boldest of the two followed her.

Helmi quickened her pace. The young fellow caught up to her and took her arm. She shook him off and began to run. The running thing always invites pursuit, and, just as she expected, they followed. Helmi purposely let her pursuers gain on her, then, stopping and bracing herself, she gave the first one a powerful body blow which sent him rolling down the bank towards the stream below. While the other one stopped to see what injury had been done his friend, Helmi raced on. She was neither frightened nor angry,—it was all good fun to her,—but she knew enough to put as great a distance as she could between her and them for she suspected that the young man who had gone rolling down the muddy bank, might not be pleased with her.

A woman, driving a gray horse in a buckboard, saw her coming and waited for her, deeply concerned to see the flying Helmi, who had evidently been set upon by two ruffians. Helmi sensed her concern, and climbed into the seat beside her without delay. Again came the difficulty of language. "Yale Hotel," said Helmi in answer to the unintelligible inquiries, giving the name the accent and pronunciation used by the Swedish telephone girl at the hotel.

"Yell 'hotel'?" repeated Miss Abbie Moore incredulously, "Yell 'hotel'? Why should I? Why should anyone?"

All of which was lost on Helmi, who merely repeated the name of her present domicile.

Miss Abbie was distressed and greatly excited over the real adventure which had broken in upon her quiet Sunday afternoon meditations. She had been making her weekly visit to the Girls' Friendly Home, where delinquent girls of the City were lodged. The labors of the day were over. Miss Abbie had told the girls a beautiful story of a patient princess, held prisoner in a castle, who at last was set free by the ingenuity of her lover; and now as she drove home she was deep in a dream of golden romance.

Miss Abbie Moore was a maiden lady of forty-eight years, thin, neat and proper, her only extravagance consisting in the number of ornaments she would hang around her neck. On the day that Helmi bounded into her neat buggy Miss Abbie wore her Miller-gray suit of serge, with the chaste neck-piece of black fur crowned with a small hat of dovetyn and quills. All of this of course was most unobtrusive and ladylike; but hanging around her thin neck was a string of jet beads (her mother's), a gold chain (her father's), and a riot of miscellaneous articles suspended from the chain. There were keys and a kettle, a pencil which had never had lead in it, a little pig made of bog oak, with a silver ring in its back, and a pierced-silver urn.

In the little seven-roomed house where she lived the strictest order and precision prevailed everywhere save on the piano, where the same promiscuous spirit asserted itself. There, photos and vases, fans and shells, books and pictures, old stones, painted bottles, Easter eggs, a Buddhist idol, basket and candlesticks crowded and jostled each other for standing room.

Miss Abbie's life showed the same unevenness. Years of careful puritanic living would suddenly give way to unexpected bursts of wild extravagance. After living in one room in the house of a friend she horrified her select circle by building a house of her own. With equal suddenness she left the class of immaculate maidens in the First Pres- byterian Church to whom she expounded from Sunday to Sunday the International Sunday School lessons and began her weekly visits to the Girls' Friendly Home.

Certain members of the Ladies' Aid Society said Miss Abbie was very deep, and that these strange outcroppings were but indica- tions of her real nature. The minister's sister, who was something of a psycho-analyst, mentioned icebergs in this connection, with their small percentage of visibility as compared with their hidden volume.

Driving along the dusty summer road this Sunday afternoon, with the houses thickening on each side as they approached the city, Miss Abbie, roused from her dream, carefully studied her new companion. She suddenly felt that she was about to experience another outcropping. An extravagant wish swelled her heart; a daring, unheard of ambition convulsed her soul . . . She would do it, no matter what any one said. Let the minister's sister rave. She would show them. She would adopt the girl if she could get her.

Helmi had the quality Miss Abbie lacked; she was not afraid of anything. Miss Abbie read it in her eyes, in her carriage, in her poise, and for that reason she was attracted to her. All her timid life Miss Abbie had craved to be fearless and unconcerned about public opinion. That was the biggest thing in life, not to be afraid of anyone. Miss Abbie had heard it put very wickedly once. It made her shudder at the time, but it fascinated her too—"So live that you can look the whole world in the face and tell it to go to—" Miss Abbie could not even think the word. She struck the horse with the lines instead. He, believing her to be merely knocking off a fly, switched his tail appreciatively.

Miss Abbie would adopt the girl; yes, she would. If the girl was open for adoption she would be adopted by Miss Abigal J. Moore, Spinster.

Helmi directed her to the Yale Hotel, and Miss Abbie, tying Jasper to the ring in the sidewalk, entered. Tying Jasper anywhere, at any time, was what is called now a complimentary gesture.

They entered, Helmi striding through the front corridor down the narrow hall, where coats and hats of the diners hung, and so through to the kitchen. The "help" were not allowed the use of the front door, but Helmi reasoned that on her off day she had temporarily ceased to be help. Therefore the front door.

Miss Abbie, glowing with her new resolve, was brave even to recklessness.

"I found this young girl being chased by two young ruffians, and brought her home," said Miss Abbie to the cook, who stood in the middle of the floor with a long complicated can-opener in her hand. "I would like to know more about her if I may. She interests me; I am a worker among girls. She speaks no English, I see."

Maggie Kenny politely handed Miss Abbie the one vacant chair, and laid down the can-opener before replying.

"It's little I know myself, Ma'am, only that my sister in Saint Paul sent her to me to look after—and it's a handful she is, Ma'am, though a good girl as I ever saw in her work, and smart and willin'. She's a quare girl in the sudden way her temper rises."

"Do you think I might have her to come and live with me? I am all alone and have a little means." Miss Abbie blushed becomingly. "She seems so lonely here, not able to speak, that I feel sorry for her, and besides, I need someone. I would be good to her."

Maggie Kenny considered the petitioner critically.

"I can give you references," said Miss Abbie eagerly, "and I would be pleased to have you come yourself to see my home if you would be so good."

In all her long experience in dealing with the public it was the first time anyone had suggested that Margaret Kenny should look at references. She had been asked to produce them, but not to look at them. She wrinkled her forehead in deep thought. Maggie Kenny knew that a hotel with its comers and goers was no place for Helmi; besides she liked the genteel little lady who "offered references."

Miss Abbie won.

Chapter IV

Miss Abbie J. Moore lived in a neat little house in Chestnut Street, in an unimpeachable neighborhood, where everyone had a sleeping porch on the front of their house, with a square of grass at the back in the centre of which a clothes-line reel stood like a wind-inverted umbrella every day except Monday. On Monday the bare wires bloomed and fluttered in the breeze, running before it in vain circles. A sleeping porch in front, a square of grass behind, and a decent little mortgage covering all—but so arranged that one paid the interest in the form of rent. The building agency made that very clear. "Live in your own house and pay as you live," was a sentence oft repeated.

Miss Abbie kept two impeccable boarders, who came and went noiselessly, left their rubbers at the door, came in early, had breakfast at the same hour every morning except Sunday, when they had none at all; who shovelled the snow from the walk in winter; sent her a white lily at Easter, and a red cyclamen at Christmas; who paid on the first day of the month except when the first came on Sunday, and in that case made the payment on Saturday.

Miss Abbie referred to them as "Mr. A" and "Mr. B,"—but whether this gave any clue to the initials of their names remains a matter of doubt.

Miss Abbie's house reflected her excellent character. She believed in having things about her plain but good. The wood in her house was oak, the curtains net, the hangings a sedate brown, "snuff" brown to be more exact. The carpet on the living-room and on the stairs was of the dullest shades of brown and fawn she could get, and the pattern of geometrical design. Her pictures were steel engravings and enlarged pictures of grim visaged departed relatives.

"That's Mother, the winter before she died—it was working on her then, but we didn't know it. This is Father taken when he lay on his death-bed. The man came to the house.

"This is Aunt Mary. She ain't lookin' very cheerful, but you can't wonder; she went straight from the doctor's office when he told her he was afraid she hadn't very long to live. This is my youngest sister. She never was strong; her kidney floated all the time and killed her at last. She knew it was gettin' worse, so she got one of these for each of us the last Christmas."

In Miss Abbie's family it seemed that a photograph was something of an "intimation."

Her steel engravings were sombre in character, too—"The Stag at Bay," bleak, lonely, desperate; The doctor sitting by the sick child; Wellington greeting Blucher on the fields of Waterloo, with dead men under their horses' feet.

Helmi now for the first time in her life had a room to herself, and her own little bed, a gorgeous one in her eyes with its chaplet of white enamelled flowers tied with a bow of brass ribbon at both head and foot. The top quilt was a patched one of blue and white, in the pattern known as the "Pavements of New York," and for chilly nights there was a small eiderdown flowered in appleblossoms.

Miss Abbie was grieved to see in Helmi a growing tendency to stand before the mirror in the elm-wood stand. She was attracted by what she saw there, for it was the first mirror she had looked into which did not make her face look wavy. However, when the minister's sister, the psycho-analyst, pointed out to Miss Abbie that Helmi seemed to be growing conscious of her personal appearance Miss Abbie dismissed the matter loftily.

"One must not blame her, Miss Terry," she said in that sweet tone she always adopted when she was working toward a climax; "the curves of a young face are good to look at. There are certain privileges we must accord to youth, my dear. Now, with you and me the glass cannot exercise the same fascination, though, I fear it will not be counted to us for righteousness that we resisted."

Miss Abbie noted with some alarm the progress Helmi was making in adapting herself to her new life. Helmi's hair was no longer brushed straight back, braided and tied with a black ribbon. It came down over her ears now in the "buns" so favored at that time. The high collars on Helmi's print blouses had disappeared, and quite sufficient white neck was revealed; and when she took her down to see the stores she noticed how she lingered in front of the pretty dresses; and when they came to a millinery window Helmi stopped so suddenly that Miss Abbie collided with her and Helmi did not even know it!

Miss Abbie felt herself at a loss to know what to do about this. Evidently Helmi had a deep love for finery, and Miss Abbie trembled for her when she thought of the evils that are in the world. "And I don't blame her," she thought, "it's all men's faults after all! They want to see women dressed up like peacocks; they won't take much notice of them if they are not. I know I was always the homespun, flat-heeled, rainy-day-hat kind, and what good did it do me? Still, she will have to be guided."

When Miss Abbie went into the kitchen to tell Helmi what to get for dinner she found her busy polishing the tin dishpan so that she could see her face in it. So absorbed was she in her pleasant task she did not hear Miss Abbie coming.

Then and there Miss Abbie decided in favor of "snuff brown" for Helmi's gingham dresses. She had thought of henna and burnt orange.

Across the corner from Miss Abbie's prim little house a shingled bungalow with mullioned windows raised its symmetrical roof among the trees. Miss Abbie said it looked like a California house with its sun-porch in front and sleeping verandah screened from the world with green and white canvas at the back. It was set exactly in the middle of the plushy lawn with lilac bushes at intervals all around the fence; a Maltese cross of red and white geraniums; a hedge of blue delphiniums in front of the lattice fence which divided the front lawn from the back garden; window boxes of red geraniums, white daisies and blue lobelia, upstairs and down; a summer-house grown over with canary vine, a caragana hedge, neatly trimmed to that flat surface so much coveted by hedge growers. It looked, indeed, like the perfectly kept home of a substantial citizen.

Any neighbour would tell you that Dr. St. John had built this house when he got married, and if you had time to wait you might hear that the doctor would not have an office in his house because his young wife was not strong and the overflow of human misery from a doctor's office, even the coming and going, would be depressing to her. So the doctor had an office down town, where visiting patients sat in wicker chairs reading the selected magazines on the wicker table while they waited.

The doctor's wife had her own car, plenty of money, and all the time the day or night holds.

When Helmi had been with Miss Abbie three months the doctor came one day to call. It was not a professional call. Indeed, he, who advised in so many cases, now came looking for advice. He and Miss Abbie had known each other in Cannington, where they had lived on the same street, went to the same Epworth League, and were taught in the same stone school-house on the hill.

The doctor sat in Miss Abbie's golden oak rocker and stated his case. "You have a young Finn girl with you, Abbie," he said.

Miss Abbie nodded; there was no denying it. At that moment Helmi was scrubbing the back verandah and singing at the top of her voice a song of her own country.

"She's a bright girl," continued the doctor, "and attractive." Miss Abbie smiled and nodded again. "But needs more teaching in English. You send her to night-school, do you? Yes, well, here's my point. My wife needs more interest in life; she gets low spirited and upset, though I cannot find the cause. I think if you would ask her she might consider teaching your girl for an hour every second day or so. She admires the girl; indeed, made a sketch of her the day she dug your garden."

"She would do it," said Miss Abbie, apologetically, "I cannot keep work ahead of her. She wanted me to let her take in washing, at least enough to keep her busy, one morning. She does ours in such a little time, and she tells me she loves it. I wanted to hire a man to dig the garden but she coaxed me so that I gave in."

The doctor's face was wistful. "Don't spoil her, Abbie, let her work. Work and salvation are closely related."

Across the street the perfect bungalow dozed in the bright sunshine. Its windows sparkled, its flowers turned their faces to the sun. It looked like an abode of happiness and contentment.

The doctor's wife came down the steps in a long silk motor coat and veil. She had heard a horn pealing a signal, and went around to the side of the house, where a closed car was slowing down. A man sprang out lightly and opened the door for her.

"She needs something, Abbie," the doctor said sadly. "I don't know women very well. Women are queer now, Abbie, they are so restless and discontented. I believe the women who had to sew and knit and work early and late were happier. Women of this day, having little to do, do nothing. I fear I am a dull old stick for Eva. She is fifteen years younger than I am, and I'm afraid it is too much."

Miss Abbie's lack of matrimonial experience kept her dumb, but she knew her old friend was suffering, and her face spoke her sympathy.

"Eva is the kindest hearted kid in the world, and she would love to help any one," went on the doctor. "Will you come over to-morrow—she's out now—and ask her."

The first day Helmi went across the road for her lesson she spent an unusual time over her toilet. Her face shone from soap and water, her hair was tortured into crocheted curls, and as a final preparation she tightened her corsets until breathing became difficult. She had noticed the extreme slimness of the dainty person who went in and out of the doctor's house, and had grown critical of her own ample form.

The doctor's wife received her in the sun-room, whose magnificence completely overpowered Helmi. The sun came in through curtains of yellow silk, falling in pools of light on the green and white tiled floor. The tables were of wicker, with pockets of silk from which gaily covered books and magazines protruded. A black dish had gorgeous birds perched on its rim, apparently just going to slake their thirst from the water below, on whose surface wax water-lilies floated. Ferns with trailing fronds of green lace hung from the low ceiling, and birds in gold cages turned the air into a musical jangle.

Helmi stood at the door transfixed with the beauty of it all.

"Come in, pretty thing," sang the doctor's wife in a chanting voice. She was lying on a chintz-covered lounge with a box of chocolates on a low stand beside her. "Come in and let me look at you."

Though Helmi did not know the words, she knew she was being made welcome. She glided in with the peculiar walk she had when she was frightened, arriving as noiselessly at the couch as if she had come on runners.

"Creamy skin, green brown eyes and fiery gold hair—you should do well in this land of opportunity."

"Yes, Ma'am," agreed Helmi.

"No, don't say that!" Mrs. St. John was sitting up now, making a pretty picture with her flushed cheeks and rumpled hair. "Say 'Yes, Mrs. St. John.' 'Yes, Ma'am,' is gone forever with the hair-wreaths and petticoats and lots of other things I could mention. Say 'Yes, Mrs. St. John.'"

Helmi repeated the words correctly.

The lesson lasted an hour, coinciding exactly with the duration of the chocolates, and Helmi was invited to come every Tuesday.

To Helmi there seemed to open a new world, rapturous, rainbow hued and golden—something she had dreamed about. The subtle perfume of the sun-room, the air of indolence and luxury, of freedom from care or responsibility, the muffled sounds in the house, as if every one walked on carpets of plush—all this seemed a part of her dream.

When she came out into the sunshine and ran across the road Helmi, for the first time, was able to think in English, and the words that she said were, "Some class."

Chapter V

Young Methodist Church, though not set on a hill, was determined that it would not be hidden, in spite of that geographical handicap, and so resorted to the wholly worldly but nevertheless effective method of advertising. A black and gold signboard on the corner of Broadway and Balmoral acquainted the wayfarer with several facts in the hope of interesting that fickle person in his own welfare. It told the name of the pastor, the subject of his sermon, the name of the choir-leader, the soloist for next Sunday, the deaconess, the president of the Ladies' Aid Society, and in larger and still more golden type it proclaimed that this was the Strangers' Church. The stranger naturally looked around in an endeavor to locate his property, and if he would follow the indication of the gold hand which pointed up Broadway he would find it, sure enough. There it stood, solidly brick, an abbreviated tower and empty belfry, deep set windows, a few straggling vines holding to a network of wire that swayed in the winds and kept the vines in constant remembrance of the uncertainty of life!

Over the side door one evening, though it was yet early, a light burned, pale amber and faint because of the daylight. At first it looked as if the sexton had forgotten to put it out from the night before, but members, adherents and frequenters knew that it had a meaning. It simply meant that something was in progress—the house was in session. The sexton, a burdened man, with a lame leg and a short temper, who was rarely seen without a duster in his hand, was arranging and dusting the seats in the Tower Room. The Girls' Club was holding a supper meeting.

"It's a pity they couldn't eat at home," he grumbled, "it's a wonder they go home to sleep. I fully expect to find a bunch of them here some morning. The new man is bug-house on making the church serve the young people. If he had to clean up—and this new battleship linoleum shows every mark—he might feel different. There's no respect for the sacred edifice any more. I can't get used to rioting and mirth in God's house, an the cleanin' up after it is fearful; and my word! this swimmin' pool that he's goin' to put in is a wicked thing to me. The house of God is for the cleansin' of hearts. 'Cleanse your hearts and not your garments,' says Job. 'Whited sepulchres, makin' clean the outside of the cup and platter while the inside is full of ravenous wolves'—ain't it the livin' truth? But no one listens to me now—my ways is out of date. It's all youth, youth, and I wouldn't mind so much if he brought in only our own young people. I buried their fathers and mothers, some of them, and christened them, but this man brings in every tag end he can find—odds and ends—odds and ends—what does he care? This church had a name before he came. More cars and better cars stopped at our curb than at any church in town. What now? Baby carriages, mother's meetings, bean feeds. I find broken garters, tissue paper, table napkins rolled into wads, sandals, comforts, babies' bottles. 'Servin' the neighborhood,' he says. It's grand to be a sinner these days—there's so much done for them—and even at that he don't believe in hell! I asked him, and what did he say? Says he, 'I wouldn't like to take the responsibility of hell, Mr. Sims.' He says. 'Take away hell from our religion,' says I, 'and where are we?' says I, and he went out laughin' like an overgrown schoolboy—laughin' because he could not answer me.

"Religion ain't what it used to be. There's no way of warnin' the

35

wicked now. Where's the good old hymns we used to sing—'We'll hear the wicked wailin', wailin', wailin', we'll hear the wicked wailin' in that great day!' That was a grand hymn to bring conviction to a stony heart and to such as be of a perverse countenance. Now it's all 'Love o' God, Love o' God, Jesus the Friend.' Soft I call it, and too easy.

"These young ones that come here—tell me they are Christians? 'Did you ever repent?' I says. 'Lots of times,' says they. Is that religion?

"Well, here they come, rampin' down the stairs. 'The Merry Maids,' that's a silly name for a religious society. Where's the Christian Endeavour, the Epworth League, the King's Daughters."

"Good evening, Mr. Sims," cried the girls, swarming around the old man; "You have fixed the seats for us, haven't you? You're a good old scout!"

Someone began to sing:

> "How do you do, Mr. Sims,
>
>   How do you do?
>
> Is there anything that we can
>
>   do for you?"

"Shut up girls," said Lucy Powers, severely, "I want to talk seriously to Mr. Sims. He asked me the other day if I ever repented, and I want to tell him I've done nothing else all week. I've been kept in every recess for not getting my essay done in time, and I've had to watch the other girls playing while I sat inside struggling with an essay on 'Concentration' and the teacher was nasty to me all the time, and I've had such a bad time, I nearly lost my religion. Tonight I am going to ask for the prayers of the congregation for the teacher—she's so mean—that she'll either change or die or something. I'll leave that to the Lord."

Mildred Masters had a problem, too. "Say, Mr. Sims, isn't it fierce when no one seems to understand you? You know I resolved to try to smile this week and see if miles and miles of smiles would grow from mine, and when I smiled at teacher when she was scolding me she said to me right before everyone, 'Take that silly grin off your face.' Now what is a poor girl to do? Isn't life the bunk, anyway? What would you have said to her, Mr. Sims? They'll do the rest now, don't you bother; the House Committee has to get the meal ready, you just advise me."

Mr. Sims laid down his broom and considered the troubled soul before him, whose red cheeks and sparkling eyes plainly belied the sad tone of her voice. The rest of the girls swarmed into the kitchen.

Miss Rodgers, the leader of "Canadian Girls in Training," drank deeply from the Blue and Gold Book in her hours of need, for that wonderful book is a deep well, and no one need draw up an empty bucket who dips into it. It knows all about work among girls, and it can tell you exactly how to go about each meeting. Miss Rodgers, who had undertaken to lead this group of girls, would have perished long before if she had not had the Blue and Gold Book. It said that the meeting for this month would be social in its character, and the "activity" would be the entertainment of foreign girls. The small print said, "There are probably some girls of foreign birth in your neighborhood. Invite them to a supper meeting. Find out if they can sing or recite. Even if it is in a language unknown to you it will make them feel that they belong if they contribute to your program." (Do you see now how deep the Blue and Gold Book is?)

Miss Rodgers explained the project to her "Merry Maids." Consternation sat on their young faces. They had been able to follow the Blue and Gold Book on the "Curio" meeting, "Stories about Hymns" meeting, "Cooking out of doors" meeting, "Irish Stories" meeting, but where could they get enough foreign girls to go around? There were fifteen girls in the group. If they did get fifteen girls how could they all get time to do a piece? And it wouldn't do to leave any out. Maybe some wouldn't like some of the others, and with so many nations represented it might make trouble, even fighting!

Lucy Powers at this cried out, "Oh, gee, wouldn't that be fun?" She was of Hibernian extraction.

Dorothy Moss was afraid. "The foreigners quarrel so among themselves," she said, "and they're so fierce. Our washerwoman's sister killed her man up at Gimli, and when she was in jail at Stoney Mountain my mother went to see her and asked her if she wasn't sorry, and she said she was, and mother thought that was a good sign, and maybe she was going to repent and find pardon but she went right on and said she was sorry she had not killed him long ago. Mother did not know what to say. But Mrs. Karaski said she believed in God all right, if that's what mother wanted to know. 'God was all right, you bet,' she said, and she was thankful, too. God had been good to her and let her find the axe just when she was getting the worst of it. Mother came home all shaken up."

Hattie Butterfield had a bright wave. "Let's begin with one foreign girl—real foreign, I mean, just out from some foreign country—and I know one. Miss Abbie Moore has a Finn girl, and she smiles at me every time I pass, and she does her hair just like we do now, and she has white shoes and all, and she comes to church, and you wouldn't know it on her." Hattie did not specify just what it was that Helmi was able to conceal.

Miss Rodgers intervened. "Remember girls," she said, "foreign girls are just like us. They feel, see, are hurt or pleased, just like us. It just happened they were born in another country."

"I guess everyone would want to be born British if they could," said Hattie complacently.

Miss Rodgers shook her head. "Not a bit of it, Hattie; everyone likes her own country best. Here I am, an American, and I like my own country best. But we are making a new country here in Canada, and we will love it best of all because we are making it. We are making paths and laying foundations, and that is what makes life here so interesting. Now this Finn girl who lives with Miss Abbie Moore, she is a Canadian from choice. She has come to us. Most of you were born here and had no choice in the matter at all. So let us consider her a true Canadian by her own choice. I think we will just have this one girl, and we'll make it her party."

"Gee, Miss Rodgers," said Lucy, "that will be a rich dish for her—a party all for herself! Mother says you can spoil these foreign girls easy."

"Not many people are spoiled by being made happy," said Miss Rodgers gravely, "and an orphan girl, all alone, working for her living, is not likely to be petted overmuch. Well what do you say, girls?"

The girls agreed, and so it came about that Helmi Milander got her first invitation to a party. She was in the basement, cleaning out Miss Abbie's fruit cellar, when the invitation came. Two girls both dressed in the pleated skirt and middy she so much admired, stood at the back door asking to see her. Lucy Powers was the speaker, and the invitation was properly given. The only difficulty was in the fact that Helmi did not understand. Miss Abbie received the invitation and undertook to see that Helmi was present.

The basement of Young Methodist Church is the ordinary church basement, reached by a stairway that is worn silvery and gray by the passing of many feet, but to Helmi that September evening when two girls came for her and took her arm to conduct her thither it was a palace of enchantment.

They proceeded at once to the tower room, where small parties were held, and here, due to the decorating committee, opened a scene of loveliness that made Helmi catch her breath. Autumn leaves made of tissue paper ran in festoons from the electric fixtures over the table to each corner of the room. These were the Autumn decorations made by the girls at one of their meetings, and would later be replaced by the Hallowe'en yellow and black cats, witches and pumpkins. A stone crock filled with crimson and purple asters stood in the middle of the table, and from it there went out to each plate ropes of smilax from Lucy Powers' father's greenhouse. A broad band of Autumn leaf crepe paper ran down the middle of the table, and at Helmi's plate was a hand-painted card with the Beaver and Maple Leaf. On it was printed "Welcome to Canada." The streamers of Autumn leaves above the table made it easy for Helmi with her quick imagination to believe the table was spread in some sunlit glade under the golden and crimson foliage which in a frolicksome velvety wind, might come falling gently down.

The table sparkled with color—salads, ornamented with white and yellow daisies (hard boiled eggs); red flowers and green leaves (petals of beets and leaves of lettuce); platters of cold meat edged with nasturtium leaves, with velvety red blossoms peeping through, and jellies, amber and yellow, showing geometric designs of oranges and bananas securely and mysteriously suspended.

The crowning glory of the table—positive proof that it was a real party—was the high sherbet glass filled with iced orange juice, white grapes and grapefruit, with a red cherry on top riding at anchor! One at each plate!

Helmi breathed ecstatically as she gazed. Her cup of happiness was full. In addition to the gaiety around her, she had the exquisite rapture of knowing she was suitably dressed. The very day the invitation came Miss Abbie had taken her down town and bought her a pleated skirt, a middy and a red tie. She was dressed just like the others.

Helmi wondered if this is what Heaven would be like. She had some vague ideas on the subject of heaven which had come to her in her busy, crowded life as a child. She believed that in Heaven one's boots would always be new and squeaky; that one would sleep alone, and that one would always feel stylish.

Helmi felt very solemn about coming to the church to eat. It was queer to be asked to have supper at God's house. To Helmi, God was a terrible person, whom people only thought of when some one died, or in thunderstorms, floods, famine or sickness. The God she knew was not concerned about suppers or good times. He looked down with terrible burning eyes, seeing everything from His white throne in the sky, and could wither bad people with one scorching blast. Helmi knew that, for was not Peter Saari found blackened and dead beside his plow, though his horses were not touched, just because he had cheated the storekeeper? And it was a wonder He did not smite Peter's wife and children, too, because they cried so, Peter had been kind to them. Helmi had always thought God had been pretty quick and hard on Peter; but people must not say what they think when it is about God.

And now here she was in God's house for supper, and around her were fifteen girls of her own age, all making her welcome, and everyone as happy as if they weren't at church at all. And they sang some words at first to welcome her, that had her name in them, and they looked at her when they sang:

"How do you do, Helmi, girl, how do you do?
Is there anything that we can do for you?
We are glad you've come to stay
In this land of work and play,
And we welcome you today,
Helmi, girl!"

Miss Rodgers talked a little then, and the girls all put their heads down, and Helmi knew it was a prayer, and she had queer prickles all over her. Then they began to eat, and by watching the other girls Helmi managed very well. After the fruit cocktail with the cherry (and Helmi's had both a red and a green cherry in it) there came scalloped potatoes in a lovely glass dish, and a glass cover, too, with an acorn for a handle; and cold pork and beef, and pickles, and fresh biscuit that Lucy Powers had made herself at school. Lucy managed to get this over to Helmi through the medium of her meagre English, supplemented by signs. And for dessert there was ice cream, both pink and white, with nuts and cake and cocoa.

And the dishes were beautiful, with green ropes and pink roses, and somehow it seemed to bring God nearer than anything to know He liked pink roses on His dishes. They must have a nice God in Canada!

When the supper was over the girls all stood up and sang with hands clasped. Helmi stood between Lucy and Hattie. The music was strange, the words unintelligible, but the hand-clasp was warm and friendly. Helmi understood it and thrilled with a great new passion. In God's house she had been a guest and had found friends.

The leader presented her with a little Testament and a Blue and Gold Book which had her name in it, right on the front page. Lucy showed her some words and said them to her over and over again, and although Helmi did not know what they meant, she learned to say them, and because these words were vibrant with youth and hope and eager aspirations they fired her young heart with a great desire to live proudly and serve humbly. She belonged now, she had her own gang. She wanted to do something for God to show her love for Him, for her new country and these new friends.

Very early the next morning, when the crystal dawn, cool and sweet, was stealing into the sleeping porches on Chestnut Street, there came stealthily a young girl with a scrubbing pail and brush to the locked door. Trying it and finding it locked, she went round to one of the windows in the tower room, the one which had been just above her head. It yielded to her careful touch, and in a moment she and her pail had gone in.

That morning when the janitor came grumbling to his task a strange scene met his eyes. From the tower room arose the damp incense of a well-scrubbed floor, polished windows, shining wood-work—a hardy, honest smell, clean, soapy, satisfying.

"Maybe I was wrong about them youngsters; they've got some religion after all," he said.

As Helmi went around her work the next day she sang the tune of the song, but she could not quite get the words. Miss Abbie phoned to Lucy Powers to come over and tell her what it was that Helmi was singing. Lucy taught the words to Miss Abbie, who, when the Ladies' Aid met at her house the next week was very proud to have them hear

Helmi sing. "She has only been one night at the Club," said Miss Abbie proudly, "and look what she has learned!" Miss Abbie knew very well the minister's sister would think that the girls should have taught her "Abide With Me" or "Sowing in the Morning," or something like that, but she was prepared to tell Miss Terry that times were changing.

Helmi sang as she did everything else, without the slightest trace of self-consciousness. She stood in the doorway with her hands behind her, and to the gray-haired ladies who listened she seemed like the embodiment of hope and youth and aspiration as she sang in her deep voice,—

> "Keep on sowing when you've missed the crops,
> Keep on dancing when the fiddle stops,
> Keep on faithful till the curtain drops,
>   And you'll get there in the morning!
>
> "Keep on trusting in the cause of right,
> Keep on looking to the dawn of light,
> Keep on fighting till you've won the fight,
>   And you'll get there in the morning."

Chapter VI

H elmi's lessons went on. She could answer the telephone and explain in concise English that "Miss Moore is owett," or "Would you please wait one minute," followed by "Tank you very much."

"A civil tongue, Helmi," Miss Moore had told her, "may not take you as far as a pretty face, but it will take you along a safer road."

Helmi lived for the days she had her lessons. In the atmosphere of elegance and beauty she felt herself expanding like a Japanese water flower. Even the smell of her friend's house was luxurious. Miss Moore's house smelled of soap, clean clothes, moth-balls, and soup with onions in it, pleasant enough, too, in its common, coarse way, but the Doctor's house smelled—Helmi could not find one word to describe it. She had noticed the same delicious odor in a shop in Helsingfors before she sailed. It was of flowers in winter time, a rich smell, with that impalpable hint of luxury which was so dear to Helmi's heart. Some days she rode in the car with her new friend, reveling in the soft gray plush cushions and the sparkling glass vase at the side, which the Doctor kept filled with fresh carnations. Even the floor of the car had a velvet carpet, and a light came on in the roof by merely pushing a button! Helmi tried to write a letter home telling about it, but in the hard working world at home, with its meagre vocabulary, there were no words to tell of such magnificence. There was only one word to cover it all, and it was English, and if she had written home the Finnish equivalent of that word, it would have misled the people to think the car had sustained a bruise or had contracted mumps.

Helmi had to learn new words, for she was experiencing new thrills each day. Mrs. St. John took her once a week to the Moving Pictures Theatre, where Helmi sat spell-bound and dazzled. From the time she entered the enchanted place until she came out again into the sunshine she knew nothing of the real world. Watching the pictures she came up the aisle seeing no one, conscious of nothing, stumbling on the steps without knowing there was a step, or that she had stumbled, following her friend vaguely to a seat, and sitting perched on the edge until some indignant person behind her told her to sit down and let somebody else see, with an impatient "What is the matter with you, anyway?"

The world Helmi entered through the green plush doors, laid hold on her impressionable young heart. She saw lovely ladies in trailing beaded dresses and shining jewels, leaving their elegant homes to go with their lovers, and smart young stenographers wearing seal coats and hats they could clap on their heads and always look just grand, and who married the old man's wayward son and saved the old man's business from ruin by listening at the door when the bad men were plotting. Then and there Helmi determined she would be a stenographer.

Sometimes when riding on a street car Helmi would pick out some weather-beaten old business man with wiry beard whom she believed might be her future employer. It became her delight to give up her seat to such, rather to their discomfiture. She felt it only right that she should pay them this little attention. She wondered greatly about the sons of these men—so much would depend on the son.

After that her teacher could not keep enough words ahead of her.

Helmi kept a list of words pinned over the sink while she washed dishes, and in between her moments of attending to the real business of dishwashing she practised her sentences:

> The lady is beautiful.
>
> She has an elegant coat.
>
> Will you go for a drive?
>
> Have a chocolate?
>
> I adore chocolates.

Miss Moore, who tried to help on the good work of Canadianizing this young person who had come to our shores, wrote on her sheet:—

> "Honesty is the best policy."
>
> "Civility costs nothing."
>
> "Evil communications corrupt good manners."

And these Helmi faithfully copied, but they left her cold. Indeed, she told herself in good Canadian that Miss Moore's sentences were dumbells!

Further attendance at the pictures brought home another fundamental truth—the lovely lady is always forgiven—indeed, she can do no wrong. She may appear to do wrong, but someone else is really to blame. She found this to be true with the Doctor and his wife. The Doctor loved her even when she scolded him, pleaded with her when she pouted, laughed at her extravagance though pretending to be horrified, bore with all her moods and rages. Helmi knew it was because she was so beautiful. Everyone said the Doctor's wife was such a lovely lady.

No wonder Helmi now decided against stenography. She would be a lovely lady! And the words and sentences which appeared on the wall were tinctured with this resolve.

Helmi was struggling with the lesson on the beaver, in the Third Reader. "He is an amphibious animal," she read, "living both on the land and in the water." She looked inquiringly at her teacher, whom she knew, without looking up, was regarding her intently.

"Pshaw, Helmi, a girl with eyes like yours doesn't need to know about amphibious animals. Close the book—that will do for today. I want to talk with you. Life is a dull place anyway—we have to take what thrills we can. I get a thrill out of you some way, you are so young and promising. Now, I am going to have a party. The Doctor is going East in a week. I have my parties when he is gone, because my parties and my friends bore him to tears. So we set the dates to suit. And besides his mother is coming to visit us soon, and I want something new. You're the newest thing I know, and so I want you at my party."

"I have no clothes," began Helmi, "for style party."

"Listen, Helmi, I have the clothes, closets full, and I know just how to dress you. You won't need to talk, so don't worry over your English. You'll be a young Finnish lady visiting Canada, the Prime Minister's niece, and my friends in Montreal asked me to look after you. Your father is a shipping broker, and you are on your way to Vancouver to join him. We'll fool them, and when they are all raving about you, and wanting to dance with you, in your delightful broken English you will beg them to excuse you—you are so tired. You will slip upstairs, change back into your maid's dress, and come down and help Manda to serve. Now, come and let me try on your clothes. You are going to be a symphony in green, Helmi—there's no color so dazzling as green. Mauve dreams, red raves, but green sings. You're to be a singing goddess."

Helmi's eyes were dancing at the thought of such a thrilling adventure, and when in the region of enchantment upstairs in Mrs. St. John's room, the walls of which were of pale green brocaded satin, the hangings of the same, and the rugs so plushy green that they reminded her of the loveliest moss she had ever seen, she found herself looking into the glass at a beautiful girl in a creamy green clinging dress, silver

47

slippers, jade earrings and necklace, a marvellous cloak a shade deeper than the dress, and lined with flame-colored satin that glimmered and shone. It was all just like a fairy story.

"You'll come over early, get dressed, and I'll make you up a little; just a little rouge on your cheeks, and your eyes darkened a little. You will go out in the car with my driver, and at the proper time he will bring you in, and I will introduce you. You will dance with two or three and then come to me and tell me you are tired. There will be a great fuss then over you, but you will insist on going. Thomas will drive away with you and then bring you back to the back-door. Manda will be in the secret, of course, and she will see that the doors are shut. No one will see you, and you'll go to her room, slip off the clothes, put on your own, wash off the rouge and powder, and come down and help to serve. Won't it be fun?"

Helmi's days following this were passed in a golden glow of expectation. The whole air around her, the chaste, unimpeachable air of Miss Abbie's kitchen, trembled and glittered with visions. Her little world had been suddenly changed by the touch of clinging silks and the gleam of starry eyes—and those her own! Her young soul was intoxicated with the new wine of beauty and adventure.

At the next Ladies' Aid Meeting Miss Abbie complained of Helmi's absent mindedness. "I declare," she said, "that Helmi girl of mine is bewitched. She gave the milkman bread tickets this morning, let the toast burn, and I heard her talking to herself. 'I am so veree tired I beg leave to withdraw,' she said, and by the airs of her you would think she was a queen upon her throne. I asked her if the girls were putting up a play or something, but she said not. But she is in great glee over something. I hope she's not going to be taken down; she's a grand girl, only for this, and this has all come on so suddenly."

The day of the party came. Helmi asked Miss Abbie if she might go over early to help Mrs. St. John, a request which was cheerfully granted, and with a heart as light as thistledown Helmi ran over the road.

It was a spicy day in late September, when Indian summer hangs its banners on the trees. The asters and dahlias, now at their best, lifted their proud heads to the sun, revelling in the rich amber sunshine. Laura Slocom dahlias, creamy and waxen, with tips of burnt orange, bordered the path, so luxuriant in color, so utterly profligate and over-powering Helmi could not pass them without paying them the homage of her beauty-loving heart. They were so lovely they hurt her some way. She wanted everyone to see them. Next day would be the dahlia show and they would be taken to the big ballroom in the hotel, where prizes would be awarded.

Dressed in her neat gingham dress, with low-heeled brown oxfords, brown stockings, her golden hair in neat rolls, Helmi looked like a favored child in some well-to-do family. Her heart sang with happiness. She was getting on. Canada was very good to her. She was learning, too. She could now speak over the telephone, buy things at the grocery, and no one laughed at her accent. Miss Abbie was pleased with her and would pay her real wages next month, and all the girls were nice to her. Next meeting she was going to sing a Finnish song.

Helmi, as always, had come over early. Mrs. St. John would not be through with her sleep yet. So she loitered happily at the gate, with dreamy eyes. The birds in the golden cages were hung outside, and by their rapturous singing had attracted a flock of wild canaries that were fluttering now over the caragana hedge, trying to get a hearing with their aristocratic kinfolk. Helmi wondered what they were saying. She wondered if the caged birds grieved for freedom and the upper air when they saw their joyous brothers skimming past so light of wing, so happy in the sunshine. Yet there was no trace of sorrow in the caged birds' song, which mounted higher and higher. They were thinking perhaps of the bitter winds of winter, which held no terrors for them, for they were safe and warm, cared for, sheltered, fed, and yet birds were made for freedom, for unfettered flights, blue skies, mountain peaks. Cages brought safety; the open air held danger. There you are—choose!

Helmi stretched her strong young arms and breathed the perfumed air. "I will take the open air and danger!" she said.

Looking again at the riot of color the garden held, crimson and lemon and glittering gold, Helmi broke into her own tongue. "Here it is," she said, "my picture! Aunty's Flower Garden! It has come true! It was not only a picture drawn on paper; it was a promise—a true promise." Gratitude filled her eyes with happy tears. God was very good. A desire to speak to God was on her. She looked up to the sky and wished she could see Him just for one little minute. Then the words came, the words of the covenant she had made with Him: "Cherish health; seek truth; know God; serve others."

Then in her loyal little heart Helmi prayed to God to let Aunt Lili know. Surely He would. Aunt Lili was so good—and she would be glad to know Helmi had found the Garden.

Anyway, when she went to heaven herself she would tell Aunt Lili, and she would be sure to go to heaven now. She was going to be such a lovely lady no one could keep her out any more than they could keep out Mrs. St. John, and besides, she would be so good to poor girls, everyone would love her.

She would bring out Finn girls—a ship load of them—and make lessons for them on the boat, and show them how to make dresses and do their hair, make stylish coats and say stylish English words. She would drive her own car going to see her Finn girls, and would teach them nice yells like Canadian girls make, and have nice suppers and give them copies of the Blue and Gold Book.

Lost in the pleasant dream, Helmi did not notice that a cloud had come over the sun and a chill had fallen. A drab little wind, with an ugly jagged edge on it, came twisting across the road blowing dust in her eyes. She looked up. Aunty's flower garden had faded, and with it the vision splendid.

A sudden chill fell on Helmi's heart. Like most of her countrymen, she was superstitious, and she shuddered now with a sense of dread. Shiveringly she went into the house.

Seeing no one around, Helmi ran upstairs. Her friend was sick, maybe. That was the trouble which was coming.

In a darkened room, smelling heavily of some strange odor, Helmi found her lovely lady lying with face white and drawn, her eyes burning like Aunt Lili's had been. Helmi's heart was sick with fear. Was she to lose the flower garden again?

"Oh, Mrs. St. John, what is?" Helmi's English grew panicky.

"I will be all right, Helmi," her friend's ready voice reassured her. "You can help me. Will you go down town for me?"

"O yes, I go—anywhere," whispered Helmi, frightened by her friend's ghastly pallor; "I get doctor—he will get medicine."

Mrs. St. John's hand flew up in an imperative gesture. "You'll do as you are told, Helmi! I do not want the doctor."

The angry tone brought tears to Helmi's eyes.

Mrs. St. John's voice softened. "Don't mind me, Helmi, I'm so sick. The doctor wouldn't understand, and he would be cross."

Helmi grew more mystified.

"Listen, dear, you are my best little friend. I can trust you. Never tell, Helmi, I have a bad heart, and only one medicine can make me well." She paused a minute, and Helmi could feel her burning eyes on her face in pained entreaty.

"Can I get?" asked Helmi.

"Yes, dear, you can. Co down town—here's the address, ask for Sam. He's a doctor, a Chinese doctor, that's why we mustn't tell. Dr. St. John would be angry. Doctors often hate each other. Dr. Sam will give you a little box for me. Just say a lady sent you. Don't say my name, Helmi. And never tell—Oh, Helmi, I will love you if you'll never tell. I think he knows—the doctor—for he must have taken my box— who else—Sam always sends it with the laundryman, but today the doctor was here. I am so afraid, Helmi. Did you take my box, Helmi?"

Helmi's eyes went wide with terror.

"No, no, I'm crazy with pain. Go, Helmi, and be quick, and never tell. Helmi, promise me; if you tell I will die."

"No, no, dear Mrs. St. John, I never tell. See, I say my words." She held up her hand solemnly:—"Cherish health; seek truth; know God; serve others. Now, you see! I swear!"

Greatly wondering and distressed, Helmi went swiftly on her way. The address led her to the north end of the city, where, leaving the car-line, she went down a narrow old street where second-hand stores spilled their ruined wares all over the street. Dirt and dust, wounds and scratches were so thick on everything, Helmi shuddered with the thought that all the owners were dead and didn't care. Would her dear lovely lady's beautiful chairs and window hangings ever come to this?

The number Helmi sought was on a building that had been painted recently. The name was on the door in gold and red—foreign looking letters, with many sharp points.

Inside people were eating at narrow tables covered with white oilcloth, and all the waiters were Chinese. To one of them she went and asked for Sam. She was too distressed to be frightened.

"Upstairs," he said, "outside."

An outside door opened on a flight of dull gray, greasy stairs, which creaked and groaned as Helmi swiftly ascended them. She found herself in a dark passage at the top of the stairs, where dismal curtains of dingy brown obscured the rooms beyond. Fear held her then, and for a moment she stood irresolute.

"Sam," she called, "Oh, Sam!"

A face like a yellow pumpkin peered through the curtains at her. "Whatchawan?" it breathed.

Helmi held out the five-dollar bill. "For a lady," she said, "she is very sick."

Sam nodded. He pulled a curtain back, with a rattling of rings, and said, "Wait here!"

Helmi entered a room whose air sickened her, it was so strangely cold and dead, a sort of embalmed air which would never yield to sunshine. And although it was a very still room, everything she looked at seemed to writhe with a secret motion. A huge black glittering jar stood on the table in front of her, and coiled around it was a red snake with its head lifted ready to strike! Helmi would have sprung back but it held her with its cruel shining eyes, and although she knew its tongue would dart out like a red hot needle she could neither move nor scream! Then she saw it was not a real snake at all, and that there were many of them in the room. They writhed around the great bowls that stood on a shelf above her head, and gave her the unpleasant feeling that they might unwind any minute and come down. A bowl of goldfish made the only friendly spot in the room as they darted and turned and dove, catching a little gleam of light from the sky-light over head, but even they looked pale and dying as if their water had never been changed. Panels of embroidery were on the wall—crimson and gold and blue—stiff with peacocks and serpents and strange birds that she had never seen. One of the panels was of pale blue satin, on which stood out blood-red flowers. Helmi touched them wonderingly, and then looked at her finger-tips.

The old man came in with a little box, which he handed to her gravely. His ghastly yellow hands had claw-like nails that seemed to twist around her hand as she took it.

"You nice liddle girl—you come see pretty things—old Sam show you—maybe."

Helmi stared without comprehending, at his toothless gums and ghastly hands. "I'm in a hurry," she said, as she started for the door.

Just at that moment the outside door opened quietly and stealthy steps came up the stairs, one, two, three—then the stairs swarmed.

When Helmi reached the hall she found herself held by a tall burly policeman. The Shanghai Chop Suey House, long suspected by the police, was undergoing a raid.

Chapter VII

The newspapers the next morning carried startling headlines:—

"SENSATIONAL RAID ON A DOWN-TOWN OPIUM DEN! YOUNG WHITE GIRL FOUND IN POSSESSION OF THE DRUG! REFUSES TO REVEAL IDENTITY! APPEARS TO UNDERSTAND NO ENGLISH! SPENT THE NIGHT IN POLICE CELL."

The neighbors all were sorry for Miss Moore when it became known it was her Helmi—the girl to whom she had been so kind that was found in the Chinese den. They were sorry, too, for Mrs. St. John, who really felt very badly over it. "And fancy the deceit of the girl telling Miss Moore she was going for a lesson! She had been so good to the girl, too—really, it is too bad; but what can one expect from these foreigners with their standards so low?"

This was from the lady next door.

The minister and his sister called, the sister almost hysterical. "My dear!" cried the latter opening the door without knocking, as one would do if the house were on fire, "you might all have been murdered in your beds with an addict in the house! It is just another instance of God's protecting care. And to think you never knew she had the habit!"

Miss Moore sat down and leaned heavily on her broom. "I never saw a girl who loved work like Helmi," she said. "Surely a bad girl would not love work like that. But she deceived me—I cannot get over that. She made me think she was getting lessons from Mrs. St. John, and when I missed her that night and wondered about her, for she was always in in time to get tea, I phoned Mrs. St. John, who was sick in bed and hadn't seen Helmi at all. Then I asked Mrs. St. John about it, and I got it out of her that Helmi hadn't been coming for quite a while. That has been a terrible blow to me. Now, where was she when we thought she was over there?"

The minister's brows were contracted and his eyes narrowed. "I am going to see Helmi," he said suddenly.

His sister was about to remonstrate, but the thin-lipped expression of his face froze even her voluble speech. Edward was so obstinate sometimes, she told Miss Moore when he went out.

He went across the road and rang the bell. "Yes, Mrs. St. John is at home, but she can't see anyone, she is very much upset over the Finnish girl." The maid's eyes were red.

"What do you think?" he asked her.

"She helped me every day, and sang Finn songs, and was so happy—she couldn't be a bad girl, Sir."

The maid evidently believed there was a relationship between happiness and goodness. Here again was evidence of Helmi's love of work.

"Tell Mrs. St. John I called." He gave her his neatly engraved card:—

Reverend Edward Terry,

Young Methodist Church.

"I hope you can get her off, Sir, she's only seventeen," said the maid anxiously.

"I hope so, too. I believe she is an innocent girl."

Mr. Terry sought the Police Court, but found he could not see the prisoner—no one could see her until after the case was heard. From the matron he found out that Helmi was the only person arrested in the raid, and the most serious aspect of the case now was that she had resisted arrest and knocked Inspector Watt down the stairs.

The minister went to the magistrate's office to see if he could not obtain permission to see Helmi. After all, he was her minister.

Magistrate Windsor, a gray-haired, florid-faced old man, sat behind an oak desk and glared at his visitor from under bushy eyebrows. The minister had sent in his card.

"Well, Sir," said His Worship, testily, "What can I do for you? Sit down while you wait."

Mr. Terry took the round-backed, well-worn chair, vaguely conscious of the many anxious suppliants who had interviewed this fiery looking old official. "I am interested in the case of this young Finnish girl who is here under arrest," he said; "she attended my church."

The magistrate's face grew redder; his eyebrows bristled. "She's a young wildcat, that girl," he said. "One of our inspectors is laid up with a broken arm. I am afraid your ministerial efforts were not very successful in her case, Parson!"

It is strange what an insulting word 'parson" can be when uttered by some people. It seems to impute all the crawling unctuousness, the cringing dependence of the poor, starved incumbent whose wretched existence hangs on the whim of some drunken and dissolute squire.

What right had a parson, who should be meek and appealing and apologetic, to look like this young chap, who had the physique of a light-weight boxing champion? Magistrate Windsor, late of Stockton-on-Tees, having this conception, though perhaps unconsciously, in his mind, looked upon the Reverend Edward Terry with extreme ill favor. There was also the sudden antagonism of the administrator of the law, who resents civilian interference, particularly from the person he called "Parson." Let the church mind its own business!

Mr. Terry, reared in the new school of thought, would have stoutly insisted that he was minding his business as a minister when looking after the straying members of his flock.

"I am here to ask your permission to see her," the minister said; "the girl has no relations nearer than Finland; she is only seventeen, and she bears an excellent record."

"Well, Sir, she will have to learn to respect an officer of the law. These foreigners have no respect for the King's uniform, and I take it as my duty to teach them. I don't know or care anything about her record. She may have attended chapel three times a day and gone to the penitent bench, if you still use one; and maybe she can recite verses; but she can't knock one of my men down-stairs and get away with it—that's all. And besides, can you tell me why a girl with a splendid record should be found in the worst Chinese joint in the city, and have a box of heroin tablets in her hand when arrested? I would like to hear your explanation of that."

"I cannot explain it," said Mr. Terry quietly, "but I believe there is an explanation. I believe the girl is innocent."

"Oh, indeed!" the magistrate shot his eyebrows almost into his hair—"without hearing one word of evidence or considering the case at all your mind is made up? Well! And if she is innocent, why won't she talk? She has refused to utter a word. Can she talk English?"

"I am not sure—very little, I think."

"Well, we have an interpreter here, but she won't talk. She is a high-tempered, dangerous young anarchist—the sort I would like to see ducked in the river."

At this the minister's temper broke into a thousand pieces, but his voice was well under control. "Surely these are strong words to come from an administrator of the law," he said quietly. "Have we no law to deal with offenders that we must resort to mob rule? Your place, Sir, as a magistrate, is to exonerate the innocent quite as much as to punish the guilty. Yet here you are, prejudiced against the girl, before you even see her."

"Oh, I saw her, kicking like a wild steer and snapping like a mud-turtle. I saw her, all right. Well, I see no objection to your seeing her. Finns are naturally red, and I don't trust them."

"Surely, you cannot describe a whole country in one word?"

"Can't I?" the magistrate snapped. "Why not? Being a preacher doesn't give you much chance to know your fellowmen. I see them here in the raw; the veneer is all off when they come here. I know them, and in every case the women are the worst."

An officer was called to conduct Mr. Terry down-stairs and through a winding hallway, where their feet stuck gummily to the damp lino-leum. The light was murky and dim, filtering down through narrow squares of muddy glass in the floor above, and the air was old and dead.

Past many narrow doors they went, each with a round hole from which observation might be taken of the occupant, who was not even to have the poor solace of solitude. All the agony of loneliness and desolation was his, but not the dignity.

Stopping at the last one, the officer produced a key from his waistcoat pocket and opened the door. Helmi sprang from the pallet on which she had been lying and faced the intruders. Her eyes were red and swollen, her hair dishevelled, her gingham dress sadly crum-pled, and one sleeve was gone. But her eyes gleamed with defiance. When she saw the friendly face of the minister she seized his hand impulsively and kissed it—much to his embarrassment.

"Take me out,"—she cried, breaking silence for the first time since her arrest. Her eyes filled with tears. There was a sudden temptation to tell all to this man, whom she knew to be her friend. She was so desolate, distressed and bewildered. He would know. Then came a stiffening. Helmi choked back her sobs and stood erect.

"Won't you tell me, Helmi?" asked Mr. Terry.

Helmi shook her head.

"You are a brave girl," he said.

Outside, in the common room, the liberty of which Helmi would have had if she had been an ordinary first-class prisoner who had not resisted arrest, two frequent guests sat whiling away the hours by comparing their experiences in the great open spaces of life where they had carried on successful careers in their chosen profession.

Babe Summers was industriously knitting a sock of indistinct and neutral color. The sock had been a long time on the way, for Miss Summers worked at it only intermittently, and then only during her periods of incarceration. When the bright flower of liberty bloomed for her again, which it always did when she had paid her fine, Miss Summers' plans had no place in them for the dull task of knitting.

Miss Summers had been brought in the night before, slightly under the influence of liquor, but demanded that her knitting be brought to her first thing in the morning. Miss Summers declared she could not bear to be "hidle."

Not so her companion, Miss Fay Sharpe, who still occupied one of the three couches.

"It's grand to have a whoile to rest," she said, yawning luxuriously. "Good Heavens! what with this one and that one—'Fay here and Fay there'—I never gits a minute to meself only when I comes in. Good mornin', darlint,"—this to the matron—"Growin' younger you are—every toime I comes I sees it. Faith, ain't it good to be you, in a nice aisy job, and policemen all over the place to step out wid. Some women has all the luck. Some gits the roses and some gits the thorns, as poor mother often said—God rest her soul. A dacent woman she was, and never thought she'd see her darlin' Fay having to work her day's work."

Miss Sharpe turned her face to the wall and wept noisily.

"Woop'er up," said Miss Summers, unfeelingly, "it don't 'urt no one. Did you know there is a new one come in? Oh, Lor'—a 'igh stepper, young, fresh—resisted, mind ye—young as that—winged good old Watt, wot wouldn't 'urt a fly—sent him spinnin' down the stairs at the Chinks. She'll get time for that sure as she's a hinch 'igh. I did it first, too."

Miss Summers laughed reminiscently. "I was innocent that time, and fought, and they sent me down. They always fight at first. But, Lord! a person soon learns. She'll learn. Say, Fay, it's too bad for the little thing to be left in there lonely, and us waitin' to keep 'er company out 'ere, and givin' her lots of advice. Life is 'ard on the young ones, Fay, until they learn. It don't take long, either. Sit up, Fay, and dry your eyes, and tidy up a little bit. We'll get the old girl to let her out. A nice young girl, smart and spunky, would be 'andy for us now, and 'ere's the place to get them. I got Clara here, you mind, and she was a grand girl to me till the Harmy got 'er and turned 'er against me. Poor Clara, she's a roustabout now in someone's kitchen, and that girl 'ad 'er silks and 'er satins with me. There's always someone wot takes the joy out of life, as the good Book says; a person has to make the best of it and go on."

Miss Sharpe sat up uncertainly.

Her friend regarded her critically. "You do look seedy, my dear," she said, forced to be unpleasant. "Good Night! your heyes are ploppin' out of your head, and looks like two poached heggs. You're drinkin', Fay— no, don't deny it—and it don't do. We got to keep ourselves genteel in our business. Perhaps you better keep out of this—you're a little too pie-eyed today; a lot depends on first impressions, and I want the girl to like us. I likes to rule by love more than fear; it's easier, Fay. Now you lay over and rest your weary eyelids. I'll have a go with the new little girl and try to win her over if the old girl will let 'er out. It's a shime to keep her there like a little captive."

Every seat in the courtroom was filled. It is not every day such a thrilling case can be offered to the unemployed public. A young girl, pretty and well-dressed, found in a Chinese den with heroin tablets in her possession, who resisted arrest, fighting like a wild-cat, injuring an officer, and now refusing to say a word, is no ordinary attraction.

The gallery, reserved for the purpose, swarmed with anxious spectators. There was going to be a great show. Men with blue-black whiskers showing through the skin of their faces; and black shirts with a button or so gone, disclosing hairy chests; weedy youths, pimply of face; stoop-shouldered older men with veiny noses and heavy jowls, burned down to the butt like old cigars; eager-faced women, excited and strident, the boudoir-cap type, hungry for sensations to fill their idle days; flat dwellers, bargain hunters, can-openers, secure in their law-abiding virtue, they came crowding in, hungry-eyed and jostling. Their liberty was sweet to these women this morning when contemplating the prospect of another woman's possible loss. It gave them that pleasurable thrill of comparative virtue.

The Press table was full. It looked like a heart interest story,—real thrill stuff—lovely, but misguided youth.

Helmi's case was the first called. The police matron brought her in and sat with her. Her face was pale, but there was no shrinking or fear in her eyes, and the eager crowd, whose eyes were all fixed on her noticed that she anxiously searched for someone. Her friend would have come if she were well enough, Helmi thought, and again her rage kindled against the fate which prevented her from carrying out the very first favor her dear friend had asked her to do. She would know, though, that it was through no fault or carelessness of hers. Maybe she had died for lack of that medicine they had taken away from her. Maybe her dear friend had died—and there was no one she could ask. She must not ask—that was the trouble in her heart as she faced the crowd with its hundred eager, searching eyes.

Under a glass roof, suspended by chains from the ceiling, sat the magistrate, alert, eager. He would see if this Finn girl would refuse to answer questions. He would put something of the fear of the law into her. These Finn girls! He knew them; hadn't he had enough trouble with them?

The police officers gave evidence and identified Helmi. The one with his arm in a sling told his story. "The girl appeared to be very frightened, and did not understand that she was arrested, Your Worship, I think," he said.

"I am not yet convinced that this girl does not understand English," his Worship snapped, "that is a point to be decided, and she can save herself a lot of trouble now if she will tell us the whole story."

"What is your name?"

The interpreter spoke to her.

"Helmi Milander," she answered.

"Yes, that name is well known in this court—I had the pleas—painful duty not long ago of sending Anna Milander to jail for a similar offence, attacking a policeman. Have you a sister named Anna Milander?"

When the interpreter put the question, Helmi admitted that she had but not knowing what the magistrate had said, she did not know the implication. The interpreter did not give her all that he had said.

Miss Rodgers was on her feet in a moment.—"Your Worship—," she began.

The magistrate ordered her to sit down.

"I demand to be heard," said Miss Rodgers, "an injustice is being done this girl."

"All in good time," said the magistrate sternly. "You will get a chance to speak, but you cannot interrupt this court."

There were murmurs in the gallery. "Served her right to be set in her place!" "Gee, doesn't Magistrate Windsor know how to handle a case? No one can put anything over on him." The pimply faced loafers were having a positive thrill. They gloated over Helmi's pale face with its proud defiance. She would get jail as sure as she was an inch high, and when she came out she couldn't pull that stuff on them. Girls just out of jail were not so uppity; they were glad to have anyone show them around. They nudged each other.

"Now, I want you to speak," the magistrate said slowly, and

speaking in a long-distance voice. He seemed to think if he spoke loudly she must understand. "You are either an old hand at this business, young and innocent as you look, or you are hiding someone. You must speak. Just say the name of the person who sent you to Sam's for dope."

Again the interpreter spoke to her, and the crowd waited.

Helmi shook her head.

The spell broke at that, and the gallery relaxed. A rustle of whispers crackled over it, like a gust of dry leaves.

"Silence!" commanded the magistrate, and again the tightening came in the Court. The air was heavy now with unwashed humanity, perspiring feet, bad breath, scented soap. Outside, wagons rattled by, street cars clanged.

"Has any person anything to say?" asked the magistrate, looking wrathfully, at Miss Rodgers, who came forward.

"Give your name," commanded the magistrate sternly, "and be brief."

"This young girl has lived in our neighborhood for three months, and bears a good character," said Miss Rodgers. "She belongs to a girl's club, which she attends regularly; she has no bad habits, and is steady and industrious. She is an innocent, healthy, normal girl. It was not her sister whom you sentenced. She has no relatives here. Her sister is in Finland."

"She belongs to a girl's club, does she?" the magistrate seemed to bite the words off. "Well, I'll tell you and her, for I believe she understands every word, that I don't believe in girls' clubs or women's clubs either. Women and girls have too much liberty these days, and that's why they are going to the devil. They don't work any more—they just gad around to picture shows and get into trouble, and the women's organizations encourage them instead of trying to restrain them. The old-fashioned girl stayed at home and worked with her mother. But now the mothers are out reforming the world, and the girls are on the street or in their clubs. I blame the club women of this city for the devilment that goes on among the young people, for the home has gone. I tell you, there's no religion in the homes any more, no respect for law,—nothing but birth control clubs, political clubs, bridge clubs, while the young girls and boys steal cars, joy ride and snuff dope. There you are!"

The cliff dwellers were enjoying it. They did not belong to the women's organizations, so he didn't mean them.

Mr. Terry came forward and asked if he might give evidence.

"This girl's mother cannot be blamed," he said, "she is dead. Helmi has been here only a few months. If our society is in the state you say—"

"Give your evidence, Sir," interrupted the magistrate, "this is a court of law—you are not preaching, remember."

"The girl is doing an honorable thing," continued the minister. "She is suffering for some other person's misdeeds. She must have gone to Sam's place for someone. I know the girl; she is honest and innocent."

"Let her speak, then. No one is stopping her. Let her clear herself."

"It would be an iniquitous thing to send this girl to jail, where she will associate with evil women. I plead for mercy. She struck the policeman in her fright—he says so, too."

The crowd in the gallery were restless. They resented the preacher's coming into the play. The modern preacher who comes boldly into public life without apology is a jarring note in the complacent philosophy of their class. They had much the same conception of a preacher as the magistrate had. Preachers should be simpering, tea-drinking, bazaar-opening curates, pallid and dandruffy, with decayed teeth.

The magistrate proceeded to give judgment. "Stand up," he commanded again.

Helmi stood.

"You see—she understands—I thought she did."

Addressing Helmi he said, "You could have cleared yourself perhaps of one charge, but not of the other. So I have no option but to send you to jail. You shall be confined for three months at Stoney Mountain."

Miss Rodgers was on her feet. "I appeal the case," she said.

The court room began to empty. Only the regulars held their seats. The transients were going. Some of the women would go back to attack the dishes they left in the sink; others went to inspect the shop windows; two of them strolled leisurely down to the White Lunch to have a cup of coffee and a piece of pie. It was near lunch time, and as Mrs. Morrin remarked to her friend Mrs. Edgar, "When a woman has only herself to cook for, she never cares when or what she eats."

They discussed the case as they sat at the marble topped table.

"That girl was innocent," said Mrs. Morrin, "but foolish, I'll bet she's shielding a man."

"Oh, I don't know," remarked her friend; "I remember when I was her age I had an awful crush on a woman about ten years older than I was. I forget her name now, but she was my goddess for the time. There was something fine in that girl's face—something noble. It seems a pity to send her to jail, where she will have to see and hear everything that's vile and ugly. The whole thing is rotten."

"Well," said the other one, "why don't we try and do something?"

"What's the use?" Mrs. Edgar was breaking her pie with her fork. "Women never hold together. That's why people like Magistrate Windsor can insult the women's organizations and get away with it. The women's clubs are trying to make things better, and yet they get blamed for what goes wrong. You and I do nothing, and therefore are never blamed for anything. Great system!"

"Well, some of the women in the clubs are funny old frumps," said Mrs. Morrin. "I saw one of them the other day getting her money out of a pocket in her petticoat. She's one of their big spouters, too. Why don't they keep up with the times, visit beauty parlors and learn the use of cutex?"

The other woman considered a moment.—"Still, there's nothing criminal in keeping money in the pocket of your petticoat," she said, "when you come to think of it. She was lucky to have money anywhere. And life abounds in odd sights. I saw one of our foremost citizens trying to unlock the door of her suite with a button-hook last night. But so long as we are not doing anything to make things better we should not be critical . . . You won't forget this afternoon—don't be late—I am just having four tables."

Chapter VIII

The Girls' Friendly Home stands on a hill overlooking the city, a great bare, white building with glittering windows, which in the rays of the setting sun burn like the bush that Moses saw, yet like the bush are not consumed.

It seemed to be ever looking down with its many eyes on the struggling people below, watching them with kindly glances, ever beckoning to those who are sore beset in the struggle to come up and find safety. Indeed, some such conception was in the minds of those who built it, and in the dedication services many an eloquent speaker told of the seething, pitiless city, with its pitfalls and temptations, and rejoiced that here on this quiet hill-top the people of God had made an island of safety where the young things caught in life's cruel tangle could find sanctuary.

There were numerous references in the dedication speeches to the lost lambs of the flock, pierced by many a thorn; the white lily bruised and broken and crushed in the dust of life, the lost piece of silver which caused such a household upheaval. The speeches were made by the ministers of the city, who in large proportion made up the Board; the other members being of that type of middle-aged portly gentlemen who are usually alluded to as "solid business men."

The Board had its troubles, and sometimes even contemplated adding women to its numbers. Some of the ministers made that suggestion, speaking enthusiastically of the excellent help they received from Ladies' Aids and other societies in their churches. As a rule the solid business men opposed the proposal. It was felt that the presence of ladies might prove embarrassing. There were certain matters which were best discussed by men alone—besides, there was always a danger of women being too emotional. There was an Auxiliary Board, composed entirely of women, who held bazaars, teas, chicken suppers, made towels and sheets, looked after the girls' clothing, solicited donations and in general did all those little unimportant, yet necessary things which women do so well. It was felt by the majority of the Board that the women had their part, and it would be better not to confuse the issue.

The first difficulty the Board experienced was with a Matron,— rather a young person she was for such an important position, scarcely forty, who had come highly recommended from one of the Western States. She had many relatives in the city, and it was felt that her appointment might interest some more of the solid business men in the home, for her relatives were of that type.

She began by making some sort of a merit system in the Home, which was rather alarming. She unlocked the doors; insisted that the girls lay aside the mud-colored uniforms which the Board had decreed should be worn, and actually took the girls out with her in turn to the movies and to concerts and lectures. She also had her friends come with their cars every week to take the girls for drives. She planned picnics, corn-roasts, excursions, and indeed made the Home such a happy place that not one of the girls attempted to escape, although they had every opportunity to do so.

The Board looked on calmly disapproving, yet helpless. But the matter came to a crisis at a meeting where the Matron was present by request. One of the members (and one of the most solid, too) began by pointing out that there should be some differences in the way well-behaved girls and fallen girls are treated. Here the Matron interrupted to ask him to retract the word "fallen." She gave the Board members positive chills by the things she said about the double standard of morals which was made by men to shield men, and went on to tell them that many of her girls were innocent young things from the country who had come to work in the city to help the family at home, and had fallen victims to men's lust and hypocrisy. The very men who had led them astray, fathers of families some of them, and regarded as respectable men in society, no doubt now spoke of these girls as "fallen women."

It was most embarrassing. She also hinted that there should be women on the Board and questioned the ability of men to quite understand the problems of rescue work.

Anyone can see from this what sort of a woman the Matron was and why the Board dismissed her. The girls had loved her and had done their best to carry out all her wishes. They had scrubbed and washed and polished the Home until it sparkled; they had planted a garden and made flower-beds; they had sewed and crocheted and embroidered; they had studied, sung, prayed, and bravely tried to live a useful and happy life. The day she left the scenes were disgraceful—not a girl could eat a mouthful—they just sat and cried. The Board could see they had done well to get rid of her; she was having such a weakening effect on the girls.

The Board decided then and there to have a man for the head assisted by a woman of course. "There must needs be a woman," said the good old Dr. Smythe, "for appearance sake at least." So, after diligent care, Mr. and Mrs. Wymuth were found somewhere in the East where they were doing evangelistic work. Their letters of recommendation abounded in such terms as "earnest co-operation," "moral worthiness," "deep sincerity," "unfailing devotion," "passion for souls," etc. The Board was pleased with their joint and several appearance.

The Wymuths were of exactly the same type,—black-eyed, pale, anaemic, with lustreless thin, black hair, through which a bloodless scalp showed blotchily; false teeth—no, not false—everyone could see what they were—artificial, rather—so white they were almost blue. They believed in hell and spoke of the "world" in a tone which implied both horror and contempt. They knew that Christ was coming soon to take His own out of the world, leaving the other odd millions to their well-merited punishment.

Mr. Wymuth satisfied the Board that he believed in discipline for wayward girls—discipline, repentance, and after that a life of meek and lowly spirit,—"And," said Mr. Wymuth, "my wife will be guided by me entirely," at which Mrs. Wymuth bowed her head and drew her thin lips more tightly over her blue teeth.

The Board breathed more freely. "It will be better now," said Dr. Smythe, "and I think it would be well to have the pastors appeal to the ladies to have a series of teas to raise money for the additional salary. I am sure the ladies will take care of it."

It was to the Girls' Friendly Home (under the Wymuth rule) that Helmi finally was committed. If she had been of the full age of eighteen years she would have been sent to jail.

The police matron, a silent woman, who held her job because she was no talker, came with her on the car. Helmi, with her clothes in a little reed valise which Miss Abbie had given her, walked confidently down the path which led to the big oak door. The former matron's flowers bloomed at each side of her. They nodded a welcome to her, and she felt reassured and comforted. It must be a nice home where there were so many flowers. Helmi had put on her pleated skirt and white middy, which now had the monogram on it, just like the other girls. She wore it today, because it had always brought her a good time and was full of the vibrations of fun and fellowship. The Blue and Gold Book was in her valise, and her English learning book, too. She would be all right, and Miss Rodgers would come, and the girls, too.

Helmi had not yet given up hope that Mrs. St. John would come to her aid when she was better. She still thought of her as she had last seen her, heavy-eyed, distressed, ill, and told herself over and over again that this was why her dear friend had not come to her. She was still too sick to know what had happened. Helmi liked to picture the scene. Her friend in her slinky gown of black silk, with her pearls, would come; she would be wearing her green velvet cloak, the one that looked just like the ocean foam that had gone cutting away from the boat in creamy suds when she crossed the ocean, and her black hat with the silver arrow; she would come driving up in her big car and talk to the people in big swanky English words, making her eyes go snap like she could when she wanted the Doctor to do something. Everyone always did what Mrs. St. John wanted, and she would be so mad that people had been mean to Helmi, and she would call them names and stamp her foot, and maybe swear a little—just a few good ones. And then she would turn and say, "Come, Helmi, my poor, brave child."

Oh! it would be sweet.

As Helmi was the first case to be brought in since Mr. and Mrs. Wymuth came, the worthy couple were determined to show the Board the value of discipline. The history of the case had been given to them. The girl had refused to tell why she was in the Chinese den—It was evidently a stubborn case. Mr. and Mrs. Wymuth had dealt with stubborn cases before. The proud and forward spirit must be broken. And it could be. They were waiting eagerly for Helmi. The Board would expect results, and the Board would not be disappointed.

When the Police Matron and Helmi climbed the flight of stairs leading to the great front door and the bell was rung the lock was turned in the door and they were admitted into a dark hall. As they entered the door was shut again so promptly behind them that the corner of the Matron's cape was caught and had to be released. Then the big bolt shot into place, and in a whisper Mrs. Wymuth asked them to come this way, leading them down the hall to a gloomy room which she called her "Retreat." The door was shut and locked, and Helmi was told to sit down.

The Matron, living up to her reputation of being no talker, handed Helmi over with as much emotion as is shown by the ice man when he loosens his pincers from the square of ice and leaves it to drip its life out on your back step. His responsibility ceases when the step is reached.

"Good-bye, Helmi, be a good girl," she said, not without a degree of kindliness. Her last delivery to the Girls' Friendly Home had pulled a handful of hair out of her not too well covered head! so she felt kindly to Helmi.

Helmi wrote her name in the brown book Mrs. Wymuth showed her, quite proud of the fine big letters she was able to make. She wrote her address "c/o Miss Abbie Moore, 52 Chestnut St."

Mrs. Wymuth admired her writing, "And you can English speak?" she asked sweetly, feeling that if she transposed the words they would be more intelligible to the Finnish girl.

"A little," said Helmi, smiling back.

"You will learn more here," said Mrs. Wymuth; "all our good girls go to school. You like school?"

Helmi nodded.

"Now, dear I want to be your friend—I am a little mother to all the girls—I want you to tell me all about yourself."

Helmi told her about coming to Saint Paul—her aunt's death—her coming to Winnipeg—Miss Abbie Moore—the Girls' Club. Suddenly she stopped.

"Ye-e-e-s?" Mrs. Wymuth stretched the word out until it seemed like a sharpened pry which would be sure to lift another slab of conversation.

"That is all," said Helmi.

"Who sent you for the medicine, dear?" asked Mrs. Wymuth casually.

"I cannot tell," replied Helmi, looking her questioner straight in the eye.

"You mean you will not tell. Now, Helmi, trust me—I'm your little mother." She came over to the girl and laid her hand on her shoulder. Her touch made Helmi shiver, and when she bent nearer Helmi drew away from her.

"I will not tell," said Helmi again.

Mrs. Wymuth drew her lips tightly over her two plates. "We'll see," she said, and Helmi knew it was a threat.

That night Helmi met the girls at supper. The table had been turned diagonally across the room to get greater length, and it had a clean cloth, although it was not Sunday; Mrs. Wymuth had expected a visit from some members of the Board.

"Now, girls," said Mrs. Wymuth, in her sweet way, after a lengthy blessing had been called down from on high, "we have a new girl, Helmi Milander. She has come to us for a while, and I want you to be very good to her, and very kind. Let her know she is among friends here. Helmi and I have had a little difference already, which I wish to tell you about. In order to help her I must know her whole story, and this she refuses to tell me. I have coaxed her, but she remains stubborn. Isn't she foolish, girls? I am here to help every girl, but the girls must let me. Isn't she foolish, girls?" she repeated.

"Yes, Mrs. Wymuth," said the girls in chorus. But they said it listlessly. Their days of mourning for the other matron were not ended.

Then Mrs. Wymuth proceeded to tell the story, the girls listening open-mouthed. A new girl's story was always interesting.

"Now we will all pray that Helmi's stubborn spirit may be melted. You will all pray, won't you, girls?"

Helmi sat looking from one to the other helplessly. Had she not one friend anywhere?

Every night after the evening meal there followed this orgy of prayers, when every girl who wanted to stand well with the matron prayed. Much of it was meaningless, but as the prayers went on a certain excitement laid hold on them, and in their supplications they forgot that other ears than God's were listening, and unconsciously they revealed many things. The Matron was hopeful that Helmi would be swept into the whirlpool of excitement, and would tell what she wanted to know. Helmi sat still and listened, but refused to pray.

"I do pray," said Helmi, in her own defence, "but not loud, just me and God know. I don't like big row—neither does my God."

After that the matron tried giving Helmi more than her share of the work, but that plan was soon abandoned. Work melted before Helmi's clever hands. Then came isolation. Helmi's heart was so hard she could not have her meals with the other girls. Helmi bore this complacently. Anything was better than having the whole roomful staring at her.

Helmi had four happy hours each day, four hours that slipped by her on shining wings, when the dining-room table was cleared and lessons were given by Miss de Forrest. Always Miss de Forrest smiled when she looked at Helmi, and called her "dear." She praised her neat, clear writing, and gave her a beautiful shiny-backed note-book with green lines in it for her own. Miss de Forrest did not live at the Home, but came each day in her little car, her coming and going being events in the drab lives of the young prisoners to whom she came as an ambassadress from a happier world.

To the Matron, Miss de Forrest went one day with something weighing heavily on her mind. Mrs. Wymuth was in her "Retreat," and looked up questioningly when the teacher entered.

"Mrs. Wymuth, this system is all wrong," began Miss de Forrest, impulsively. "This young Finn girl who has just come in is as sweet and innocent as a rose, but she has to associate with all classes here. Rose Lamb has just come back from a terrible debauch, and she is full of the glory of her adventures—she knows every dive in the city. Lucille's baby is about due. Minnie is in the same condition, and the others are learning fast any wickedness they did not know. Many of these girls are mentally deficient. Certainly this is no place for a bright, lovely young girl like Helmi. I always have thought it a poor system, but since Helmi came it seems positively devilish."

Mrs. Wymuth's lips were thin as she replied: "We have nothing to do with the system, Miss de Forrest; that has been carefully thought out by the Board. You forget that under the softening influence of Divine grace, the hardest hearts may melt. Rose Lamb has had a wonderful conversion since she was brought back, and is a better girl this moment than Helmi with her proud and stubborn will. Rose is a brand plucked from the burning; Helmi is still a sinner."

Miss de Forrest protested stormily.

At the end of the month Miss de Forrest was dismissed. The letter from the Board said "it was deemed advisable to make a change."

During the rule of the former matron the hospital room was downstairs, located as far as possible from the dormitory. The Wymuths had other plans. They believed it was well for the girls to know the wages of sin. So on the dreadful night that Lucille spent in the hospital, the girls huddled together in agony, listening, listening. Poor Lucille, with her shining brown curls! Every girl but Rose Lamb cried in sympathy, and some in shrinking terror. The new girl who had come in that day came over to Helmi, who held her in her warm young arms all night. Like a stone she was, poor little Esther. Her teeth chattered and her heart beat wildly like a hunted hare's. Helmi did her best to comfort her.

Rose Lamb alone was calm. She sat up in bed and addressed the girls. "See here, kids," she said, "Lucille was a big fool, and it serves her right. She didn't need . . . "

The girls hushed their sobs and listened fascinated. Helmi covered her ears. Something inherently modest and clean in her young heart protested. She did not want to hear.

The Girls' Friendly Home had been built by Christian people. The men who sat on the Board were convinced that they were doing a noble thing. Faithful women sewed and baked and sold tickets to maintain it. O God! O God! what cruel things are sometimes done in the name of Thy Compassionate Son!

It was over Minnie that Helmi had her first quarrel with Mrs. Wymuth. Minnie's home was in the country, where the crops had failed, and Minnie had come to the city to find work. There had been no harvest to cut, so it seemed best for Minnie to come away. Only sixteen, and innocent and trusting, Minnie had come to the great city. She wanted money to get shoes for the little ones at home, and for her mother, too. Minnie's love for her mother was very deep and beautiful. Her mother had been so brave and sweet through all their bad years.

Minnie had worked in the home of a prospector, a man who had found gold in the north—gold running in the sands of a river—and he had traced it back until he found the deposits. He would be the richest man in the world some day. His wife went to the coast for the winter. "He told me," sobbed Minnie, "that he would stake a claim for me, and I would have thousands of dollars, and that I could do what I liked with it. I could pay off the mortgage and give my mother a trip. But only on condition that I wouldn't tell, and so I didn't tell anyone. The other matron, Mrs. Avery, was lovely to me, and told me if the time ever came when I wanted to tell she would stand by me. She explained to me how foolish and wicked I had been, but she knew it was for love of my mother and all of them at home. Oh, we would have been all right if she had stayed."

"She helped me to write the letter to my mother, and wrote herself so nice, too. It made me cry. That was just before they told her to go. I have her address—she gave it to all of us. Mrs. Wymuth made me burn my card, but I know it, anyway—she can't take that from me. She reads all the letters we write, and all the letters that come. Mrs. Avery never did that. But Mrs. Wymuth made me tell—she prayed it out of me. One night I got excited and said his name and now even if he finds the gold he'll be mad at me and never give me a cent."

Helmi patted the poor girl's heaving shoulders.

"But that's not the worst—I haven't got my mother's letter, and I believe there is one from her. I asked Mrs. Wymuth, and she said I would get it when I was a better girl and had stopped crying. I said I couldn't stop, and then she said I was saucy and she would punish me for that; and I said a letter from my mother would do me more good than anything. She said I would get my letter when she saw fit to give it to me and not before. I wish I could die—I hope I will die when my time comes."

"No, no," said Helmi, "don't die, Minnie, I'll get your letter if it is there. I'll take it. It is yours, and it is not hers."

"They will kill you—they thrashed Rose Lamb for running away—thrashed her right before all of us. It was terrible."

The next night when supper, which was always eaten in silence now, was over, the prayers began. Mr. Wymuth read the scripture, choosing a denunciatory psalm abounding with much malediction and woe. He spoke of Lucille, and drew a moral lesson from her sad story and her terrible suffering. According to Mr. Wymuth motherhood was the punishment which came to those who transgressed the laws of propriety (Miss Lamb dissenting, though not openly). The girls were strongly disposed to follow Miss Lamb's theory that it was not sin, but innocence, that had been Lucille's undoing.

Then came the avalanche of prayers, led most noisily of all by Rose Lamb. Some of the other girls followed, and Mrs. Wymuth as usual closed the meeting. She had a way of tattling on all the girls, telling

78

God everything she had noticed all day that was in any way unpleasant. "And oh, dear, gracious God, we ask Thee to forgive Mary, who came to the table tonight with filthy hands. Teach her that clean hands are pleasing in Thy holy sight. And soften Helmi's hard heart, dear Lord, we pray. Oh, bring down conviction like a rain of fire, so that her poor sin-stained soul may not be eternally lost and cast away to burn forever and ever. Teach Minnie to know that authority must be respected."

Mrs. Wymuth's eyes were devoutly closed as she swayed back and forward to her own intoning. Her voice whimpered and wailed and rasped like a rusty hinge.

Mr. Wymuth, who backed up his wife's petitions by hollow groans and exclamations of "Lord, save" and "God, have mercy!" was called to the telephone just at the moment that she was warming up to the real business of her daily report.

"O Lord, send down Thy chastening fire to convict and convert."

"Amen! Hallelujah!" shouted the girls, knowing what was expected of them.

Helmi, who was kneeling just behind Mrs. Wymuth, caught a glimpse of keys in the pocket of her black sateen apron. A sudden impulse prompting her, she cautiously abstracted the keys and crept quietly backward from the room. In the general excitement of the evening devotions she was not missed.

Helmi went at once to the Retreat, found the key which fitted, and then to the desk. She had been trusted to sweep and dust this hallowed spot, and so knew that one sacred drawer was always kept locked. It yielded to the right key, disclosing a pile of letters. Helmi found three for herself and one for Minnie. She hurriedly replaced the others, shoved her own and Minnie's into the front of her dress, and made the perilous journey down the long hall. If she had only told Minnie to keep on praying! Her heels seemed to suck at the linoleum, her knees cracked, the house seemed to scream with silence. Mr. Wymuth was still at the phone. She reached the door. They were still on their knees,

Mrs. Wymuth keeping up her supplications to the throne of grace. Some of the girls were crying. Helmi was on her knees in a moment beside them, and into her grateful heart there came an honest sigh of thanksgiving, Mrs. Wymuth, hearing it, redoubled her efforts—she would get Helmi yet.

"Oh, Lord, give us souls for our hire—unlock the stubborn door—break down the bars of silence;—O, Lord, we are waiting, waiting, waiting."

Helmi swayed nearer to her and neatly replaced the keys in Mrs. Wymuth's pocket, falling back on her knees in a rapture of thanksgiving and relief. And in the general responsive outcries of the girls Helmi, too, joined. But the words of her song were the words of one of the yells of the

"Merry Maids"—

> "Skin a mir inka! Skin a mir inka!
> Skin a mir inka doo!
> I love you!"

Fortunately for Helmi, Mrs. Wymuth attributed her strange words to her foreign birth, and in her joy at Helmi's apparent surrender she did not inquire closely into the matter. Helmi's silence was broken! Now for the full confession,—the stubborn will had yielded at last.

The other girls were sent into the common room, where they began their dreary task of making baby clothes in shamed silence. Although the Wymuths had been at the Home only a short time they had killed every spark of happiness in it. Mrs. Avery had imbued the girls with a certain gaiety and enthusiasm over their sewing which had lifted it out of all sadness. A baby was to her a sacred gift; it must be made welcome! and baby clothes must be beautiful. The girls loved the two hours after supper when the little garments were fashioned. Indeed, the beautiful things that Mrs. Avery had planned and the girls had made were used against her by members of the Board, who claimed that she encouraged the girls to forget that they were sinners, and had them actually looking forward to the coming of their babies, forgetting that they were children of shame.

The Wymuths let the girls forget nothing, and on this night they were as silent and sad, as bitterly cast down and ashamed, as any Christian Board could wish!

For an hour Mr. and Mrs. Wymuth struggled with Helmi. They prayed, coaxed, threatened. She must tell! Mr. Wymuth at last shook her roughly—he had often said this was the best way to deal with foreigners. They had to be mastered.

Something broke in Helmi then. The nervous excitement of the evening—her three precious letters that she had not yet opened—her anxiety for Minnie, and eagerness to know what her letter contained of good or evil—something broke in Helmi's heart with sudden fury. It was that flashing temper for which her countrymen are noted. One moment she had been perfectly calm, tight-lipped, composed, mistress of herself, determined to bear all things: the next moment she was a flaming fury, with murder in her eyes. She hurled Mr. Wymuth from her with a swinging blow that sent him crashing into the china cabinet, and the words she said were words she had not known that she knew. In the hotel in Saint Paul she had heard the cook say them to a persistent peddler at the door, "You go to Hell!"

Mrs. Wymuth screamed in genuine, honest fright.

Chapter IX

Girls! Oh, Girls!"

Mrs. Wymuth's voice was fraught with terror and brought the girls from the common room in a panic.

"Oh, you wicked, wicked girl, Helmi! You have killed the best man the sun ever shone on! He is bleeding to death, his life is oozing away!" Her voice, which always had a rusty whine, now fairly croaked.

The glass in the door of the cabinet had given Mr. Wymuth a cut in the cheek, and the blood ran over his pale face. Helmi, wide eyed and rigid, stood as if rooted to the floor.

"Murder! murder! murder!" Mrs. Wymuth's voice was rumbling now like distant thunder. "Oh, speak to me, Mr. Wymuth." Even in her excitement she remembered that it would not do to call him by his first name before the girls—in life or death, discipline must be preserved. "Speak, oh speak, pale lips!"

The pale lips spoke. Mr. Wymuth's thin veneer had been cracked by Helmi's blow. "Shut up, you fool, and get me something to wipe off the blood," he said.

"He raves," cried his wife dramatically. "Go, girls, go! When he wakes—if he ever does wake in this life—he must see no face but mine bending over him. Go!"

The girls drifted noiselessly up the stairs, deeply awed by what had happened. Helmi suddenly remembered the letters she had concealed, and ran upstairs to find Minnie, who had gone to bed early. When Helmi reached the dormitory she found herself the centre of an admiring throng. "Gosh, I'm glad you pasted him!" cried one. "Helmi, ain't you the best girl," said another.

"Serves him right, the big bum," was Rose Lamb's contribution. "I wish I had your nerve, Helmi. He walloped me for fair last week, and I was afraid to hit back. But Gee! he hadn't a look in with our husky Helmi."

Minnie had awakened with the noise and was sitting up in bed, very pale and frightened, when the girls swarmed into the room. Helmi put the letter in her hand.

The first flush of congratulations gave place to dismal forebodings. "Gee, Helmi, I'm glad it was you and not me that walloped him. I'm scared they'll half kill you." This was from Maude, a repeater who seldom spoke. "It's the Board I am scared of. There's a whole room full of them, and we get dressed up the night they come—and they ask us questions about are we happy, and we say 'We are very happy here and will try and repay all the kindness you have shown us.'"

"That's not a Board," said a young girl who had been brought in because she and her stepmother could not agree; "Board is what you pay when you eat out."

"Shut up, silly! Maude's right. Ain't she been here twicet? I guess she would know. I'm afraid they'll kill Helmi, maybe, or do something bad—expel her, maybe."

"That ain't the worst." Rose Lamb led the discussion now. "You can't get expelled from this place. I guess if any one could'a, it would have been me. This is a jail, really, only it's a jail where they're going to convert you or bust. It's best to get converted first thing. I've been converted lots of times; every time I run away I get converted all over again. Gee! I'm getting so fed up with these Wymuths! Ain't this a swell time we're havin' tonight! I'm all for Helmi,—she's as good as a show." Rose began to sing.

"Shut up, Rose—they'll hear us!"

"Hear nothing! He's dead—dead—the best man God's sun ever shone on—murder—murder—murder!" Rose wrung her hands dramatically in imitation of Mrs. Wymuth, while the girls choked with laughter. Then she cakewalked round the room, singing "I'm a little wrinkled prune, I am not stewed yet but will be soon."

Minnie held her letter rapturously in her hands. She could not open it before the girls. Waiting for a chance she stole out into the long, uncarpeted hall, where she ran along in her bare feet until she reached the linen closet. There she found the switch and turned on the light, trembling with excitement.

A great cry broke from Minnie's lips as she read—a cry of joy—her mother loved her still, loved and believed in her and would stand by her to the end. There was a dollar bill in the letter, and a whole row of kisses, and many a word of loving comfort. Minnie ran back to get Helmi, who was showing the girls what had happened. Her English had deserted her, but she shook Rose Lamb to show what had provoked her assault, and then showed with a menacing gesture how her hand had dealt the blow. The girls were deliciously thrilled and shivered with delight.

The sight of Minnie's radiant face recalled Helmi, and she followed her down the hall, where Minnie threw her arms around her, sobbing with joy.

"It's all right, Helmi! My mother knows. She is sorry but says I must not worry now. And it ends, 'God bless my poor little girl.'"

"That is good words," said Helmi gravely, "and I'm glad I got it for you. Will you read my letters?"

Helmi's letters were from the girls of the Club and one from Miss Rodgers. Lucy Powers wrote: "Dear Helmi:—We are at supper tonight and are thinking of you, we hope you are well and happy, too.

84

We have scalloped potatoes and salad, and rice pudding with a scab on top, and coffee, pretty weak, but with whipped cream on top that helps some. Mildred has a beau, but she won't tell who he is, and maybe she don't know, but anyway, we are teasing her, and Miss Rodgers says for you to read page eleven in the Blue and Gold Book, and you'll see what the little verse is we are learning today—it's the 'Upward Road,' and you can just think you are with us. Miss Rodgers will write, and we want a letter from you to read at our meeting. We have them from all our absent members. Lily is at the Coast and Eula is in California still, and Maud has gone to school. Miss Rodgers says you will be locked in at night, for she knows Miss de Forrest, who used to teach there. We often go riding now in the car, and I guess that is all. We all wish you were back,

"Your loving friend,

Lucy."

Helmi understood it when it had been read over again, and in her heart there was the joy of knowing that though she was in prison, someone was thinking of her, and someone wished she was again at liberty. Her gang were loyal to her!

Then came Miss Rodgers' letter, smelling daintily of lavender:—

"My dear Helmi:—Tonight we are meeting in the church, and we are all thinking of you, and when we knelt in our first prayer we had a few minutes when we all just prayed for you, and the girls said, 'Keep Helmi from evil—keep Helmi cheerful—let her learn English fast—and let her help someone every day—and keep hatred out of her heart.' I wrote them down so I could tell you, and then we prayed together, 'Dear Lord, do not let Helmi ever forget that she is dear to us and to Thee.' We know, dear Helmi, that you will always be pure and brave, and God will not fail you. Work hard at your English, and do not fret if your surroundings are not cheerful. Make the best of them, and remember the way to be happy is to help someone else. I am enclosing some stamps and paper. Write to me, or get some of the girls to write.

Miss de Forrest is living with me now, and she too wants to hear from you.

> "Ever lovingly your friend,
>
> Edna Rodgers."

Helmi's eyes were shining when the letters were read. Miss Rodgers, Miss de Forrest, her two friends! She was not alone, not a prisoner, not in disgrace—her friends loved her. Surely it could not have been wrong to steal the keys—she would write to Miss Rodgers and ask her. Maybe the Blue and Gold Book could tell. She and Minnie with their arms entwined were sitting on a pile of blankets. Helmi ran back to her little reed valise to get the oracle. Minnie turned to the page Lucy had mentioned and read the memory verse:

> "I will follow the upward road today,
>
>> I will keep my face to the light;
>
> I will think high thoughts as I go my way
>
>> I will do what I know is right;
>
> I will look for the flowers by the side of the road,
>
>> I will laugh and love and be strong;
>
> I will try to lighten another's load
>
>> This day as I fare along."

Minnie explained it to her. "See, Helmi, you've done all these. You lightened my load when you got my letter for me, ain't that so?"

Helmi nodded; that part was all right, but she was worried about Mr. Wymuth. Would page eleven throw any light on that? Would the Blue and Gold Book sustain her in knocking down the Superintendent of the Girls' Friendly Home?—that was the question.

Minnie searched the book again, going over each line. "No, it wasn't exactly 'looking for flowers by the side of the road'—but look here: 'I will laugh, and love and be strong.'"

"Helmi," cried Minnie, "It's here! You were strong when you hit him—that covers it. Helmi, ain't you glad?"

Helmi took the book and followed the line with her finger. "I sure was strong," she said.

The house was very silent—so still it seemed as if its heart had stopped beating. Helmi's mind was not altogether at rest over what she had done, alternating between the exaltation that the letters from her friends had brought to her, the happiness that had come to poor little troubled Minnie, the assurance of the Blue Book, and a deep sorrow for what she had done. Was it a very terrible thing? she wondered. She recalled the sudden rage that ran like fire through her veins when Mr. Wymuth had shaken her. Should she have just borne it and made no resistance? She would get Minnie to write it all to Miss Rodgers and Miss de Forrest. They would know. When she shut her eyes she could see the blood spreading on Mr. Wymuth's pale cheek, and hear again Mrs. Wymuth's queer words, and the glass crashing and splintering. She was sorry for that, and would write to Miss Abbie about breaking the glass. Miss Abbie would pay the damages.

The glass should be gathered up—glass was sharp to walk on and made quick cuts in feet. Helmi slipped stealthily from her bed. The girls were all sleeping now. Noiselessly she went down-stairs and into the dining-room, closing the door before she switched on the light. The chair which Mr. Wymuth had fallen against still lay on its side. Helmi lifted it up and set the room to rights. Then she began to pick up the pieces of glass, very careful to make no noise. At the blood-stains on the floor she shuddered—it was surely a dreadful thing to shed blood; she hoped Mr. Wymuth was not badly hurt.

Try as she would, Helmi could not make herself feel very sorry. The exquisite thrill of power which she felt when she saw him thrown from her was still like wine—it was glorious! Helmi could have written a psalm of elation! "Now is my head lifted up above mine enemies . . . they are as chaff that the wind driveth away . . . Thou preparest a table before me." She wanted to sing; to march; to dance. Suppose they did punish her, beat her, shut her in a dark room on bread and water like they had already done to Rose Lamb, she could bear it. She had the memory of this glorious victory, the joy of stealing the keys—and best of all, her letters.

Helmi turned the light out when her work was done, but lingered at the window to watch the city below, with its myriads of twinkling lights, row upon row, making weirdly fantastic figures as she watched them. She loved the city with its mellow hum of tramping feet, its purring autos and clanging, ragged train whistles, that seemed to rise in ever widening circles of sound. She loved to listen to the murmur that rose and fell, swelled and lessened. Something coming—coming—louder—louder—bursting—passing—fading—gone. The sleepless, restless, shifting city! She loved it; she was part of it. Away over there, where the reflection of big lights painted the sky, she had friends. There were people who thought of her and would be glad to see her. Helmi loved it; it was her city!

The door of the common room opened quietly. The light was switched on, and Mrs. Wymuth in dishevelled night clothes stood blinking like an owl at the light. Helmi stood at the window facing her, unafraid and calm.

Mrs. Wymuth had a sudden plan. Helmi had come back to the scene—she was frightened—now was the time.

"I came the glass to pick up," said Helmi, in a whisper. "I hope he is not hurt bad."

"He is dead," said Mrs. Wymuth, in a voice as hollow as an empty church. "Oh, Helmi, you have killed him, killed him by your blow. He is lying now cold in death."

Dead! The room swam past Helmi, table—chairs—door. Dead! The word beat like a drum with every beat of her heart. Dead! Dead! Dead! *Murha! Murha!*

The red word danced before her eyes.

"Helmi, the police will come for you. I will have to send for them—

I will have to tell them you struck him down. Listen, Helmi, tell me now who was it sent you for the dope? I'll save you, Helmi, even now, if you'll say the name."

Terror had frozen Helmi's blood. She knew how awful a thing it was to kill—people who kill are hanged! She locked and unlocked her hands.

"Just say the name, Helmi, and I'll save you—just the name."

For a moment Helmi could not remove her mind from the terrible present. Then she remembered. She began to speak mechanically.

"It was—" then she stopped abruptly. Her oath—she had sworn!

A deafening clanging outside drowned her words, the singing scream of a fire-engine that raced by rocking from side to side.

"Who was it, Helmi, dear—speak the name—I will save you." Mrs. Wymuth came closer, fawning terribly. "Helmi, I will tell them you did not mean it. Just tell me who sent you. They will hang you, Helmi, and you so young. But tell me, Helmi dear, and I will be your friend—tell me, Helmi."

Helmi drew back, irresolute. There was a step in the hall, quick, impatient; then a voice.

"What the devil are you doing in there at this time of night?"

Mr. Wymuth came into the room. With a small piece of court plaster on his cheek, the only sign of the accident, stood the alleged corpse in a faded brown dressing-gown, his big bare feet spread hideously on the floor.

Helmi looked from one to the other, and a dull red came into her eyes—a surging rage, which with difficulty she controlled. She addressed Mrs. Wymuth. "It is you who is one damn liar," she said, in careful English. She walked past them through the open door, switching on the hall light as she passed and making no effort to walk quietly.

After that Helmi was not allowed to eat with the other girls. Helmi was a girl of evil temper—Mrs. Wymuth explained this very carefully when the girls were at breakfast. Mrs. Wymuth loved to mix morality and meals, so she made quite a little ceremony of the casting out of Helmi. The girls were asked if they thought she had done wrong. Knowing what they were supposed to say, they said it—all but Minnie, who began to cry and was sent from the room.

Helmi was to be excluded from meals at tables, prayers and lessons until she apologized, Mrs. Wymuth rightly divining that she had struck a blow that would hurt deeply when she deprived Helmi of the lessons which she loved. She had her meals in the kitchen; prayers she could do without gladly, but the lessons!

Helmi was ordered to take her plate and cutlery to the kitchen. She did so, walking erect and calm, and looking straight into the eyes of the matron as she passed. The girls shuddered with fear for her when they saw how unconquered she was. At the door of the kitchen Helmi paused and looked back. Every eye was on her. They knew she was going to speak. She summoned her English as well as she could: "Your man," she said slowly, "Is he dead already yet?"

Chapter X

Eva St. John had many terrifying moments when she thought of Helmi, and in so far as she was capable of feeling sorry she was truly repentant. "Poor kid," she often said to herself, "if she weren't so pretty it wouldn't matter so much. Ugly women might as well be in jail anyway, for all the fun they can have, but this kid could have had anything she wanted. I believe she'll keep her promise, she's that kind. If she doesn't it will be my word against hers, anyway, and she won't have much chance. But I'd hate it to come to that—I hate scenes. How could I tell there was going to be a raid that day? And I believe that Home is not such a bad place—there's a teacher there—and maybe she won't mind it. Anyway, I can't help it. A girl as pretty as that was likely to strike a snag anyway."

Users of the drug are not much troubled with pangs of conscience. Yet the thought persisted, gnawing, nagging, cutting in upon her gayest moments. She could not forget Helmi with her worshipping eyes and her blind, unreasoning adoration—she couldn't forget her.

Then Eva tried another way. She had always been able by taking thought to justify her actions. She now justified her silence by telling herself that if she had come forward and confessed that she had sent Helmi for the drug it would have injured her husband's practice, and probably broken his heart. She told herself over and over again that she owed her first duty to him. He did so much for suffering humanity, eased so many people's pain, and did it so generously, that nothing must ever injure him. That was her first duty, to guard her husband.

Eva began to believe in her own wifely devotion. A woman's life should be submerged in her husband's anyway—she really had no life apart from him. She had been wrong to be so independent of dear old Humphrey—he was the safest port in a storm after all. An early Victorian spirit settled down upon her.

In her new-found enthusiasm Eva grew more thoughtful of the Doctor's comfort and more interested in his work. The Doctor, hungry for her favor, was quick to see the little attentions she was bestowing on him, and responded with the eagerness of a faithful dog. Eva, always analytical, and deeply interested in her own mental experiences, began to feel that the episode of Helmi was a providential thing, inasmuch as it was bringing her and her husband closer together, and under the stimulus of this belief she redoubled her efforts to please him. She went to church with him; she joined some of the women's societies. Eva was not unmindful of the benefit she would receive socially from these affiliations. It pleased her, too, to find what a flutter of pleasure her coming made in the societies. Any way, it was good policy to make her social position as secure as possible, and if Helmi did accuse her it would be easier. Through all of Eva's plans there ran one cool purpose, yet she managed to keep her conscience clear as the noonday sun. She had mastered the art of self-deception.

Following out her plan to establish a blameless record and an invincible social one, it occurred to Eva that it might be well for her to show an interest in the Girls' Friendly Home. It would show to the world that although the young Finnish girl had treated her badly there was no room in her noble heart for resentment. She glowed with the thought. Having put her hand to the plow she would not turn back.

Miss Abbie was delighted when she heard that Mrs. St. John thought of going out to see the girls, and not only that, but was going to give a tea for the Home. She reported this to Mrs. Wymuth the Sunday following, when paying her weekly visit to the Home. It was used by Mrs. Wymuth in her turn, not only to show the girls how grateful they should be for food, shelter, clothing, and the blessings of the gospel, but also for kind friends to think of them. Mrs. Wymuth's tongue dripped honey, when she made the announcement to the girls.

"And now, girls, for a lovely little surprise! There is a beautiful lady in the city who is going to have a tea in her own home for us. She thinks of us, living away up here on the hill, and wants to make us happy. So next Tuesday afternoon she will open her lovely home, and kind ladies will come and bring gifts and money, all for us. Shouldn't we be very happy over it, and very grateful?"

"Good eats! We'll go." It was Rose Lamb who spoke for the company, gathering up the feeling of the meeting with this one crisp exclamation.

"Oh, Rose!" Mrs. Wymuth's mouth almost trembled—"Rose, how could we be invited—all of us, I mean. You should not speak so!"

"Ain't she got room?" Rose persisted; "there's only twenty-nine of us."

"Go upstairs at once, Rose," Mrs. Wymuth commanded.

Rose started towards the hall, but stopped at the door to explain her position. "It's a swell way to hold a tea for us and not ask us!"

Miss Lamb's periodic excursions into the world of action made her a sort of social directory for the girls. At once every girl felt she had been slighted.

"Rose! At once!"

Rose sauntered leisurely up the stairs. Relieved of her disconcerting presence, Mrs. Wymuth resumed: "And, as is usual in these cases where teas are held in aid of a Home, there will be a lovely basket sent to us the next day and the goodies it contains will be given to the girls who have the most honor marks."

The tea was held. The morning paper featured it. "Wednesday

claimed Mrs. St. John for one of its most charming hostesses at a delightfully appointed tea in aid of the Girls' Friendly Home." The paper was quite correct—she was a charming hostess, and the appointments were perfect. The oaken door had a card on the outside which said "Please walk in." On a mahogany table reposed a sweet grass basket, tied with crimson ribbon, to receive the donations. The ladies came in gaily colored throngs, high-heeled, silk-lined, perfumed. Mrs. St. John, who stood inside the drawing-room door, received her guests, in an American Beauty cut velvet dress. The roses on the table, in a bowl sitting on a mirror and so doubling their number, were of the same shade. The table was garlanded with smilax and "the color scheme was carried out throughout."

Ladies came in swarms from the drawing-room to be served in the dining-room, and exclaimed prettily over the table. Very slim young ladies served, scantily clad in dresses which were low in the neck, high in the hem, and niggardly in width. There were stuffed olives, rolled sandwiches tied with baby ribbon, tiny biscuits,—faint replicas of the honest article of that name that we have known and loved—blanched almonds, more sandwiches, pimento filled, in harmony with the color scheme.

Then the ices! No one cut the ices—they did not need to be cut, they were moulded. Pink roses they were, set in the palest of green leaves. The guests were rapturous. Angel cake, white and of fairy lightness, and then white creams in disks, flavored with peppermint; rose disks, flavored with wintergreen, more almonds, more disks. "Really, I shouldn't—I am dieting—but these are so delicious! I don't believe it makes one bit of difference."

Then good-byes to the charming hostess, who was still at the entrance to the drawing-room, and away.

You see, the paper was right—it was "a perfectly appointed tea." There would not have been one jangling note in its perfect harmony if Miss de Forrest had not come. She had read of it in the paper and decided to come, and it so happened that she came at five o'clock, when the rooms were crowded. Miss de Forrest was a large woman, deep chested, deep voiced, dominant. When she spoke, her voice boomed.

"I am so glad you are interested in the Home," she said to her hostess, "it is high time someone became interested. I think it is a wicked place . . . innocent girls and guilty ones . . ."

Miss de Forrest's voice carried over the rising and falling chatter—hushing it at last as the women became conscious that someone was speaking.

"Now, take the case of that young Finnish girl, Helmi,— Some of you know her. She is an innocent girl, clear-eyed, truthful, lovely. Do you know the case? She is hiding someone and will not tell who sent her for the heroin. Rather a noble thing, too, in this dull, selfish age. But she's hounded to death by the matron to make her tell. It's just a question of how long she can hold out. Now, think of that lovely girl sleeping in the same room and eating at the same table with some of the worst girls in town. And when she gets out it will always follow her that she had been in the Girls' Friendly. I went to the matron and said some of these things, and so I got the blue envelope from the Board. The Board are all men—the solid business men we hear so much about. Some of you women should be on the Board and try to get some sense into its wooden head. I know now the origin of the word 'Board.' That's how to help wayward girls, though I admit it's a lot more fun to go to teas and eat olives on their behalf."

The women gathered around Miss de Forrest. Miss Abbie, in her excitement, left her post at the table. "I know Helmi is a good girl," she exclaimed, "even if she did burn the stew that I left simmering on the stove."

Eva St. John spent a troubled night. She hated Miss de Forrest, great hulking thing, with a voice like a fog horn,—what right had she, when everything was going so beautifully, to burst in like that and spoil everything? What good did it do a person, anyway, to try and do right? "Now, here I am," she thought, "more upset than ever, and if that big raw-boned valentine had only stayed away it would have been all right." Out of her troubled thoughts came one resolve—she must see Helmi.

"We are gaining a foothold, Edgar," Mrs. Wymuth told her husband that night. "People are beginning to realize that the Home is being placed on a new footing. Mrs. St. John is greatly interested in the work here, and asked so kindly about our methods. She pleaded for that dreadful Finn girl, and urged me to be patient with her. She seemed quite distressed when I told her that she had actually struck you. Perhaps we had better not keep her away from her lessons. Mrs. St. John asked if she might take her out driving some day, and I wouldn't like her to know. Yes, I think I shall reinstate her in her classes. Mrs. St. John spoke so very kindly of her. She said she would try to get Helmi to confess to her."

The winter passed not unhappily for Helmi, though she was troubled to account for Mrs. St. John's not coming to see her. There must be some reason for her friend's silence. Anyway, in a year she would be free. Rose Lamb had told her that when she was eighteen they could not keep her any longer. She would be eighteen in March, and then she would go back to Miss Abbie and the girls at the church, and take up again the happy life of the Club. In the meantime there were a lot of words to be learned and sentences to be written.

At Christmas Mrs. St. John brought presents for all the girls— twenty-nine white parcels, tied with red satin ribbon, held down with poinsetta stickers, each one containing a deeply religious book in chaste white and silver binding, with water lilies entwined in the letters of the title. She had made a face as she wrapped the first one, for the shuddering thought would intrude itself. "How would I like to get this when I was expecting a real present." The fact that she got a great bargain on them because they were slightly shelf-worn had turned the balance in their favor, for Mrs. St. John, like most people who can spend money lavishly on themselves, was a marvel of thrift and shrewdness where other people were concerned.

The white and silver book which went to Helmi was entitled "He is Faithful that has Promised," and the first promise, richly illumined by roses and violets and illustrated by a story of fidelity, was "I will take care of you." This she had underlined, adding "Never forget this, dear Helmi."

When Mrs. Wymuth unrolled the book (it was part of the discipline of the Home that all letters and parcels were to be opened by the matron) she was tearful with happiness, and declared to her husband that dear Mrs. St. John, though she really had not made a profession, was not far from the Kingdom.

It was in February that Mrs. St. John decided to take immediate action. Helmi would be free in March. It would be intolerable to have the girl under her feet all the time, with the uncomfortable feeling that she might upset everything. Helmi had a terrible temper. Mrs. Wymuth's stories of Helmi's outbreaks had been elaborately embroidered; indeed, the stories of Helmi in the Wymuth edition were positively exciting. And, true to type, Mrs. St. John began to find reasons for her desire to get rid of Helmi that had in them no selfish taint. It was better for the girl to go to a fresh place, new scenes, new resolves—the land of beginning again.

By the time she had resolved the idea in her mind a week, Mrs. St. John felt it was truly Big Sister impulse which prompted her to help Helmi to escape; the only disconcerting feature of it being that she could not tell anyone—which cheated her of the praise which was her due. But a calm sense of virtuous and heroic resolve permeated the region of her heart. She would do the noble thing, and she only hoped Helmi would be grateful. She would do it handsomely, too, and would give the girl an outfit of clothes that would surprise her. That tan suit which never fitted her properly—darn these home dressmakers! Her plaid motor coat—leather ones were newer anyway, and she really should have one to match the new car—and then a plain black travelling dress, severe as a nun's, black, straight and plain with stiff collar and cuffs.

She thought of everything, and prepared a perfect flight for Helmi. She took her for a drive and explained it all, overcoming Helmi's objections by telling her that she was to be kept another year. The plan was this: She would bring the "Merit Class" to see a picture at the "Grand." She had done this, so it would excite no suspicion. When they were all seated and the picture was absorbing everyone, she would whisper to the girl next to her that she had suddenly remembered that she must meet a friend at the afternoon train. Helmi would come with her. Her story after that would be that she left Helmi sitting in the car while she went to greet her friend who was passing through. When she came back Helmi was gone. She thought, of course, Helmi had grown tired of waiting and had gone back to the theatre, and when she went back in the darkness she did not notice her absence, believing she had found a seat in some other part of the building, she having arranged with the door-keeper for their return when they went out.

The play was over and they were getting into the car when they missed Helmi. Mrs. St. John ran into the drugstore and phoned to the Home. Was Helmi there? No, she wasn't. Then she told her story, rather breathless and incoherent in her excitement. Mrs. Wymuth at once suspected flight, and notified the police. Helmi could not be out of the city, for she had no money. Mrs. Wymuth expressed the belief that she had returned to her old haunts but a diligent search of the Chinese section of the city failed to find her.

It was two hours later that the conductor on Number Four walked through the train with a telegram in his hand:

"Finnish girl has escaped from Friendly Home, wearing gray coat, green tam, plaid dress, laced boots. Send her back on Number Seven."

Signed, "F. Brooks,
Chief of Police."

Conductor Bryce walked slowly through the train, furtively apprais-
ing his passengers. A woman with two children, a deaconess, an old
lady reading "The Christian Guardian," two young girls whom he knew.

Conductor Bryce shook his head. Then he went through the Pull-
mans and spoke to the porters, giving them the wire to read. They also
were puzzled.

"Only one flapper got on, Sir, at Winnipeg, all the rest were older
women—you know, stoutish,—with suits and veils and black bags. The
flapper is some swell—shiny black valise, heavy like stones—she's no
Finn girl running away. She's in the stateroom, Sir. No. A."

Nevertheless the conductor hurried to the stateroom and knocked.
The door was opened by a rather languid looking young girl, in a plain
black silk dress, with white collar and cuffs. In her hand she held a
Blue and Gold Book. She raised her eyebrows in polite and rather
haughty interrogation.

"Oh, I beg your pardon, I just wanted to see if the drawing room
was occupied," said the conductor. "Will you show me your railway
ticket, please. The porter will get the other one."

From the shiny new patent-leather purse which lay carelessly on the
seat, she drew a long ticket, which she handed to him without haste.

"You will go right through to Bannerman," he said, handing it back
to her.

The girl bowed her head and resumed her reading.

The conductor went back to the porter. "Why didn't you tell me,
you blockhead?" he said. "That girl is a swell. Can't you tell a thorough-
bred when you see one? She had already shown her ticket to the other
conductor. I felt foolish."

"Didn't I say she was a swell—didn't I? I said she wa'nt no Finn girl
clearin' out,—didn't I say that—I'll bet I did, and I'll bet you heard me,

too, I'll bet I did say it. Didn't I say she had a big valise and heavy—I'll bet I did."

"Shut up," was the conductor's reply.

The lady in "A" was no longer languid. She was regarding her new wardrobe with great interest and satisfaction. On a holder hung a handsome tan suit with silk embroidery; on another a motor coat. Numerous blouses and other articles lay on the seat beside her. In the black purse were four ten-dollar bills, and in her heart was great joy. A song came to her lips:—

"Keep on sowing when you've missed the crops,
    Keep on dancing when the fiddle stops,
    Keep on faithful till the curtain drops,
        And you'll get there in the morning!"

And so journeyed Helmi once more into the unknown—young, strong and unafraid!

Chapter XI

The hurried change of clothing in the motor car, the jumble of directions, and the excitement of her departure left Helmi breathless, but the quiet seclusion and security of the drawing-room soon restored her. She was here, the train was moving, she was entirely disguised in a new outfit of clothes, as far removed as clothes could be from what she had been wearing in style, color and texture. Her plaid dress, tam-o'-shanter, thick gray coat and coarse shoes were all safely in a valise in the back of Mrs. St. John's car and would within the next twenty minutes be smouldering in her furnace.

Helmi was dressed in a black silk, severely plain dress with a real lace collar primly held in place with an oxidized silver bar, a close hat of brilliant sweet-pea shades, under which her golden hair showed becomingly. Her coat was of dark blue cloth of raglan cut with leather trimmings, her shoes the pointed style so popular that summer. Mrs. St. John had eased her conscience by supplying Helmi with delightful accessories of travel, a handsome black suit-case fitted with ivory toilet articles, two of the latest magazines, a new novel, a box of chocolates, even a bunch of violets and a half-embroidered doily.

A wiser woman would not have supplied such expensive things for a girl who had to seek employment in some other woman's kitchen, but

Mrs. St. John had simply provided Helmi with the sort of things she would have liked herself had she been in Helmi's place. Besides, she had felt rather repentant for the stingy little Christmas present, the white and silver shop-worn book, which she had given to Helmi, and it was her desire to make amends now by showing Helmi how lavish she could be.

Helmi carefully studied her ticket—a pale mauve strip of paper with a yellow back, on which were strange words. She saw the names Saskatoon, Edmonton and Eagle Mines. Evidently this last was her destination. Mrs. St. John told her she was going to a lovely spot in the mountains where a lot of men worked in mines. Mrs. St. John had heard her husband speak of it, she said. Helmi shrugged her shoulders doubtfully. A mine where a lot of men worked did not sound very attractive. It would mean that she would have to cook, scrub bare floors, wash big white cups with ugly tea-stains, and have no good times at all. She would rather stay in the city, where she would find a girls' club, and go to suppers in basements, and play basket-ball in school-yards, and see lovely dresses in shop windows, and eat ice-cream cones, and perhaps have another chance at night school; then on Sundays she would go to church and hear a lovely organ with a sweet religious sound, and perhaps she might find another Miss Abbie.

Helmi now recalled Aunt Lili's advice and faithfully said it over and over again—"Leave men alone—they break your heart." She was determined that she would always remember this. Girls were best, nice girls like Lucy Powers and Hattie. She wished now that she could write Lucy and Hattie and tell them everything, but Mrs. St. John had warned her to write no letters. The Girls' Friendly would try to find her and bring her back, so she must give them no clue. It was a big disgrace for them to lose a girl, and they would set the police after her. Helmi shuddered when she thought of the police and the angry, red-faced old man who glared so fiercely at her in the police court. Still it certainly did not seem right to run away without a word to Miss Abbie and the girls,—but oh! it was great to be free! The joy of life and living enfolded her so closely as she journeyed that there was no room for resentment in her heart. At this distance she could even think tolerantly of the Wymuths. She would come back some day a very rich lady and buy out the Girls' Friendly home and run it herself. The first thing she would do would be to burn all the girls' uniforms and give every girl a new dress—pink, blue, mauve, and henna, according to their tastes—and she would drive a little car and take the girls riding with her in turns. They would tell her all their troubles.

Bubbling up through all Helmi's dreams came the joyous consciousness of freedom. She remembered the day she had watched the birds in Mrs. St. John's garden—that lovely September day of amber sunshine so long ago now. She remembered the dainty yellow birds in the pretty gold cages, with their little throats gurgling with music, singing to their little wild cousins, dark in color, harsh of voice, but free! Pilgrims of the upper air were they, who knew no law but their own desires; and now she was free again, too, just like the wild canaries, and was off again on the great adventure of living, with no one to please but herself. She had been one year in Canada, and, after all, it had been a pleasant year, too, and she had learned a lot of English. She would yet find the flower-garden of her dreams and live there forever and ever.

As night came down and the fields turned purple with twilight a momentary depression came over Helmi as she thought of the girls at the Home. Since the stealing of the letters Helmi had been a great hero with them, and had basked in their admiring glances. As night came on she suddenly missed it all and felt a shiver of loneliness go over her heart. The world was so big, and everyone else in it seemed to have friends.

The train came to a standstill at a little station, and Helmi could look right into the dining-room where the station family sat at supper. A rosy lamp with a wide umbrella shade threw a circle of mellow light over the table. Helmi could see the father helping macaroni and cheese from a large white bowl. A baby sat in his high-chair pounding impatiently on a blue enamel plate, a girl about Helmi's age, in a white middy, sat beside him; Helmi wondered if that girl knew it was nice to have a family of your own, even if you did have to look after the baby and clean the messy tray of his high-chair after every meal. As she watched, the scene slowly passed away from her.

The train with its load of human freight fascinated Helmi. Mrs. St. John had told her it would be best for her to show no interest in her fellow-passengers, but she lingered over her meals in the diner to watch them, wondering about each of them. Did they all know where they were going? Had they people to welcome them when they arrived at their destination, or were they like her, just going some place to be away from some other place? She wondered, if one kept on going, going, going, would every disagreeable thing fall away, every sin and every sadness? As she looked out over the melting fields, the air was so sweet and purifying—it would surely wash away everything that one did not like to remember—and how that train did eat up the miles— throbbing, pounding, beating, unrelenting and tireless! She tried to see if the telephone poles were all the same distance apart by counting on her fingers at the same rate of speed. Sometimes she could get to ninety, but more often a pole came in at eighty-seven.

Helmi felt the distinction of riding in the drawing-room all alone. It seemed to have about it a proud aloofness, with its own little wash-room and towels, and abundance of room, while the car outside was crowded. It flattered her, too, to notice how attentive the porter was, though she was shrewd enough to connect it with the generous tip which she knew Mrs. St. John had given him, engendering in him thereby that gratitude which shades delightfully into anticipation.

Mrs. St. John had told her that when she went for her meals it would be well to carry a book—a book keeps chance acquaintances at a distance, for it plainly means "Keep away! can't you see I'm occupied?"—and just now conversation was not desirable. Helmi's Finnish accent might betray her. All these instructions, hurriedly given though they were on the way to the station were strictly obeyed. She remembered to walk languidly, tip generously and betray no open interest in her surroundings. It was well to let her fellow travellers think that travelling was an old and tiresome experience for her. When she yawned she patted her mouth daintily.

A tired mother with a swarm of sticky children occupied a double seat half-way down the car. When Helmi came out of the drawing-room and passed them on her way to the diner, the woman looked after her enviously. "I hope that girl knows when she's well off," she said. "Gosh! it's me that ought to have that place to myself with this gang of mine, where I could wallop them in peace without having folks stare at me. But ain't it the way of the world? Them that has gets! People with big families have small houses; people in big houses have none at all. It sure does seem strange—but what can a person do? Maudie, I'll lay you cold if you don't stop teasing the baby."

When Helmi was on her way back the family was in a state of extraordinary commotion. Charley, the five-year-old, was getting a temporary cleaning up by the method known as a "spit-wash," the young man objecting noisily, not to the method alone, but to the whole basic principle. In addition to her operations on Charley the mother was trying to quell the riot that had broken out between Maudie and the baby over the finding of a nut-bar in the general turmoil of coats, hats, oranges, bags and toys which were wedged in between the children on the seat. "Maudie, stop! Don't take it from him—let him eat it." The baby had the nut-bar, Maudie hoarsely protested. Maudie's voice was hoarse with roaring. Maudie had to roar if she were to be heard above the family clatter. "Oh, leave him alone while he's good!" cried the mother in despair. "Let me have a moment's peace, even if it does make him sick, I'll give him castor oil tonight. Stand still, Charley, or I'll lay you cold!" Then it was that Helmi forgot her instructions, forgot that she was a fugitive from the law—she only knew that here were people who needed a friendly hand of the sort that she could supply.

The spirit of Helmi's hard-working, soap-making, dirt-hating grandmothers stirred at the sight before her. Her long, capable hands craved a chance to show what they could do with the travel-stained, tear-wet, much begrimed family before her, mother and all. The mother was at a low ebb—skirt crooked, belt wholly inadequate to cover the connection between skirt and blouse, hair in strands, hair net dragging from one hairpin, shoe-lace untied, stockings sagging; her shoulders drooped, and her voice wobbled.

"Let me have him," said Helmi, reaching out for the five-year-old, "I will wash." The family stopped all its activities; arrow-root biscuits were discarded; the seven-year-old, who was riding the back of a seat shouting "Ride 'em, Cowboy!" paused open-mouthed; Maudie in surprise relinquished the nut-bar, at least as much of it as would leave her hand. "I have a little wash-room of my own. There I will take him please," said Helmi. Charlie went with her without a word while the family looked on in dumb amazement. "Ma, ain't that the limit," whispered Maudie in wonder, "I thought she was a lady."

Charlie came back in due course shining from applications of soap and water. His garters were mended, his hair brushed, his ears pink as coral and shining inside and out. His clothes were straightened and brushed, and he smelled foreignly of toilet water and powder. He held a new five-cent piece in his hand, and his spirit was subdued and serene. The others were taken one by one, renovated and returned,—the mother last of all—while Helmi stayed with the flock, who sat very staid and dignified in their new state of cleanliness. Helmi sang to them in English, then in Finnish, the lullaby that had been sung to her by her overworked mother.

The conductor, passing, saw with surprise the change that had come into this nest of stormy petrels, and the same thought came to him that Maudie had expressed. "There's something funny about this," he said to himself. Then he listened. He recognized the Finnish songs, having worked with Finns in the lumber-camps near Port Arthur before he went on the road. His brows corrugated and one eye was shut tight. He went to the end of the car and sat down to think it over. He read the telegram again. Then he shook his head slowly. It was curious.

Just before Edmonton was reached the conductor knocked again at Helmi's door. She received him with the air of languor and the lifted eyebrows. Again she was the experienced traveller slightly bored, but his quick eye noted that all her things were packed away. "Here is your ticket, madam," he said politely, "will you please give me back the slip I gave you. Your ticket is for Eagle Mines, I notice. A funny thing happened yesterday. Just before we reached Rivers I had a wire from Winnipeg asking me to be on the lookout for a young Finnish girl who had escaped from the Girls' Friendly Home in Winnipeg. They seem to think she's on this train but I certainly can't place her. Well, if she's on board I hope she won't try getting off at Edmonton, for the police will be watching for her there, sure. She had better stay right on and get off at some little place. Now, that place you're going to would be all right, for it's on a spur-line quite away by itself, and it's the sort of place where there are a lot of people coming and going all the time, and there would be no questions asked there. I was out there one time shooting. It's a queer little backwash of a place." Their eyes met in a look of understanding. Helmi's were startled, wild and questioning; his were calm and reassuring, the level eyes of a kindly old conductor who has looked upon much human misery and trouble, and always to understand and help. His totally detached manner helped Helmi to recover her composure, there was something so protective and kindly in his face. In a moment she had back all her dignity and poise. "How very interesting," she said, turning to her book.

The conductor left the train at Edmonton, that being the end of his run, but he waited until the train went out. The lady in the "A" drawing-room did not appear, and the police who were waiting retired after a fruitless search among the passengers.

The conductor stood with his little valise in his hand watching the train, with its dull gray smoke-wreath laid well back on its shoulders, making its way westward through the yards. "She is a game little girl," he said to himself, as he laid down his valise, to light his pipe, "and I would just like to know her story. Well, I hope she gets a good man."

Helmi journeyed happily on, blissfully unconscious of the fact that a picture of her was in the evening paper and a short summary of her career as told to an eager young reporter by Mrs. Wymuth. It said among other things that she was a girl of violent temper who had given much trouble to the Home authorities.

Chapter XII

When the train slowed its pace above the Eagle Mines, Helmi looked down on a valley which lay like a shallow saucer, broken jaggedly but fairly down the middle by the river, which ran jade green and foaming to the plains beyond. The rim of the saucer was fluted by short lines of young evergreens running down toward the centre. The mines, three of them, looked like badger-holes of giant size, and were marked by long mounds of slag.

To the west rose the mountains, green at the foot where the forests grew, gravelly and bare above the timber-line, rising still higher into hard gray rock, seamed across like faded rag carpet, and at the very top an icing of snow which had run down the crevices as if it had been put on too soft by unskilled hands. The two great peaks stood staring at each other across the stream, seeming to dominate the whole landscape; and when the train stopped and the conductor called "Eagle Mines," Helmi could see nothing but the two giants towering high above her.

"I suppose, now, you think those two big gents are right near, don't you?" said the conductor as he carried her valise down the steps.

Helmi admitted that she did.

"Well, don't count on goin' over there before breakfast, for they're twenty miles away. Walking towards mountains is a thankless business in this country—a person don't seem to be able to get much nearer. In fact, you do well if you can hold your own."

Helmi thanked him, and, taking her valise, walked across the narrow platform. Looking up the river she could see far into the mountains, for the river channel is wide and its general direction unbroken.

Around the station buildings were huddled the miners' houses, all of the same pattern, all of new lumber and unpainted.

The bottom of the saucer, on both sides of the river, is a fertile plain of deep black loam, which in summer is covered with heavy grass and pea-vine, but with never a cow to eat it, for the miners are not given to domesticity. The company which owns the mines was seized by the desire to root their men in the soil when the first mine was opened, and to this end bought all the land in the saucer, which covers a full township of six miles square, and gave to each man who signed on for a year a tract of twenty-five acres; but so far not much success had come, for the miners when their eight hours were over had little inclination to plant or hoe. Even the mine manager, who could discourse nobly on the subject of giving the worker a stake in the country "to keep him from putting his foot through the plate-glass of civilization," had not laid spade or hoe on his own twenty-five acres of grass, nor indeed removed the pile of clay which had been excavated for the basement of his house. When a man can earn three hundred dollars a month and has a rent-free house, it hardly seems fitting that he should spend his leisure time manicuring young onions or confirming the feeble knees of spindly young cabbages.

The trouble with Eagle Mines was that no one expected to stay. A mine may give out and who knows where the seam may end? There were outcroppings, to be sure, all around the saucer, but there were foldings and cross faultings, and in some of the seams interbedded shale, which increased the ash and therefore raised the mining cost.

Three mines were in operation now, all owned by the same

company and all subject to the same conditions. Every one in the valley felt that his stay was but temporary, so no one called it home.

Facing the station stood the Boarding House, where the single men had their meals, a great weather-beaten building, square as a box, sun-dried and staring. The front of it bore a sign, printed in black letters on a white board:

> "Elite Boarding House,
> M. McMann, Prop."

M. McMann knew that Eagle Mines could never be her abiding city. Indeed, she had no hesitation in declaring that Canada would lose her just as soon as she made her pile. She would "go back to God's country," which in this case meant Lincoln, Nebraska. Mrs. McMann often wondered audibly why she had left. Certainly it was not for lack of friends. No woman ever had more friends, and though absent from them now she was not forgotten. To the boarders she gave verbatim extracts of letters she received. Her friends were very insistent for her return. "Why in the world do you bury yourself alive in that cold coun-try, where they have only three seasons, July, Autumn, and Winter—a woman like you, who can make her way any place?" or "Everybody is asking me when are you coming back—you sure would get a royal welcome."

Some of the boarders rather untactfully urged her to go and never mind them,—so warmly, indeed, that Mrs. McMann grew rather reserved on the matter. It is sometimes a decided social blunder to agree with everything that is said.

Mr. McMann had returned to his native land the year before, shaking off the rather cumbersome yoke of matrimony at the same time, and leaving a letter saying that so far as she was concerned he was dead—for it certainly was not her fault that he wasn't—and that he would leave her the farm and the insurance, too, if she would sign a paper saying she would never try to find him. He "hoped to God" she would marry again, though he realized it was a mean thing to wish on anyone; but in another way he would be glad for someone to know from actual experience what he had gone through. And he was "feelin' fine at present and hoped she was enjoyin' the same great blessing."

Mrs. McMann accepted the farm and looked forward to the insurance. She explained the letter by saying poor Mr. McMann had gone queer by the hardships he had suffered homesteading in this dreadful country. She talked about him now in the past tense, quoting largely from the complimentary things he had said of her.

"'There's one thing about you, Mercy Bell,' that poor dear man often said to me; 'you are never clean stuck when it comes to a hard place—you are certainly the beateree.' He thought it was wonderful when he saw me puttin' patches on grain-bags with flour paste. And really when any of the neighbors on the homestead was stuck they'd say, 'Go to Mrs. McMann.' I don't know why!"

The tactless boarders, riding for a fall, admitted it was odd.

Mrs. McMann was able to prove her scrupulous honesty by another quotation: "Mr. McMann used to warn me—he said I was too trusting, and in this world it does not do. 'Everyone gets ahead of you, Mercy Bell,' he said to me once; 'You think everyone is as honest as you are yourself; but my dear, you will have to learn.'" If Mr. McMann during his term of coverture was ever reproached or scolded he certainly was regarded as a man without taint and blameless in retrospect. He was a wonderfully tidy and particular man; he dusted his socks every morning, he arose in the early dawn to sweep front steps, verandahs, walks; he would not eat butter unless it was made by his dear wife's skilful hands; one look at an untidy kitchen drove him from his meat for days; he never could eat on a train, having once seen the kitchen.

Mrs. McMann took pains to go into these matters exhaustively the first day Jack Doran, who came from the East, appeared at her table. His city-cut clothes inspired her—this well-dressed young man must be given to understand that although he was in the West he could take no liberties. "So you see I am not used to people who leave their things lying around expecting me to pick them up," she confided to him. "Mr. McMann often said to me, 'No, my dear, certainly not—you must not pick up after me, I cannot let my little girlie do that—you work too hard as it is!' So you see, never having had to do it, I cannot begin now!"

Young Mr. Doran assured her he was quite accustomed to looking after himself, and having finished his meal, he made a neat pile of his dishes, carried them to the kitchen, set on a pot of water to boil, and declared that Mr. McMann had nothing on him in being handy around the house.

Mrs. McMann had picked the young man for an agitator by a simple process of reasoning. Why should a smart-looking young fellow, who speaks well and has white hands, come to a coal mine, even if he had a job at the pit-head? It did not look reasonable. One explanation presented itself—he had come to make trouble. Well, the mine boss would not be able to say she had not told him, for it was her intention to sound the warning note without delay.

But when the next morning this young man carried out a whole tray of dishes, piling them neatly on the table, she decided it was quite unlikely that he had any malicious intent. There couldn't be much wrong with a young man who carried dishes and sang "The Spanish Cavalier." It took her right back to Lincoln. Why, my land! she had sung it once herself at a school concert, her and Lib White, both of them dressed alike in very fixy dresses of that swell color called ruddy gore.

Indeed, it was not many days before Mrs. McMann had decided that Jack Doran was by far the nicest boarder she had ever had. Some people acquire popularity by saying the right word; Jack Doran had won the lady's heart by judicious and interested listening. He really listened. When she gave him bulletins of a more or less intimate nature on the state of her health he listened. When she told him what she dreamed of when under the anaesthetic, he even asked questions. And he did not retaliate by telling her a word about himself.

Young Mr. Doran was deeply impressed when Mrs. McMann hinted at some dark and mysterious disease bravely borne: "I am dying on my feet," she had told him the second day he was there, "but no one will know it till I am gone. It's my way. It's the proud Weekes way. I was a Weekes. Cut me in inches if you like, I will never complain. Poor Mr. McMann often remarked on it. 'Girl, you're a wonder,' he often said—he was a great hand to call me 'girl'—he said I was always just a girl to him."

"But see here, Mrs. McMann," protested Jack, in real concern, "why don't you get help here? You're foolish to work so hard. You have plenty to do when you do the cooking. Get a girl to do the dining-room work—there are lots of girls who would be glad of a job, for the summer anyway."

"No, I've tried girls. They get lonesome. It's too far from Jasper Avenue and the Allen Theatre. I don't know what's got into the girls nowadays—they won't work—all they want to do is to primp. They can't cook—they won't learn. They'll depend on canned stuff when they get married, and starve if they lose their can-openers. No I won't have another."

"But there's lots of good girls, smart and tidy and all that," protested Jack.

"Yes, maybe, but where could I get one of them?—You tell me and I'll tell you."

This conversation took place at noon. On the four o'clock train came Helmi.

The sun poured down with a pitiless glare on the confirmed ugliness of the little box-like houses. The kindly white snow which had covered the littered backyards, was gone, and now there came in full view the piles of cans, discarded clothing, old boxes, old boots, which the snow had mercifully hidden. Water stood in puddles on the one little street where the general store, the hotel, postoffice, mine office, and boarding-house, sat side by side all looking at the station, which, because it belonged to a system and was not dependent on local caprice, had walls of stone gray and a red roof. So far as could be seen, not another tin of paint had ever gained a foothold in Eagle Mines.

Helmi shuddered with the ugliness of it all, and looked wistfully after the train as it went on across the bridge to Mine No. 2. But when she looked up her heart was quickly lifted, for above her were the eternal hills of God, mistily purple, although the sun was so bright in the valley. They reminded Helmi that the ugliness of the scene below was a recent, temporary thing that could speedily be changed. The hills in their beauty, their strength and endurance were eternal. The rain and the wind had beaten on them for long centuries; the whole artillery of the skies had been marshalled against them, yet they had not been moved. The strength of the hills was in Helmi's heart when she walked across the narrow pavement and boldly asked for a job at the Elite Boarding House.

Chapter XIII

S pring had come with its carpet of flowers, its radiant days and velvety black nights, spangled with stars and musical with the sound of rushing waters, for the snow of the mountains filled the river's course with a foaming flood, on whose surface logs rolled, and sometimes broken trees.

The saucer was covered with thick grass, through which the anemones looked up blue-eyed and shy through their furry caps, shading in color from palest pink through mauve into purple. Helmi had never seen them before, and wondered if this was their first time to come. The buttercups which followed were like those at home, and so were the cowslips—and the wild roses! The women laughed at her delight.

"Gee Whizz!" said Mrs. Turner, who lived near the boarding-house, "it doesn't take much to please the Finn girl. A day at a circus would kill her for sure if she makes such a fuss over a few little wildflowers."

The coming of Spring with all its beauty brought no improvement in the littered yards, where the condensed milk tins mounted higher and higher. Blinds still hung crooked, boards in the verandahs were still broken.

"There's no use putting on curtains," said Mrs. Turner, apologetically, "this darned slag blows all over, no one can keep clothes a good color—so what's the use of trying. I ain't goin' to break my back tryin' to clean up the dump. Certainly no one tried to clean it for me; and if all goes well we'll soon be able to get out. You forget this stuff about cleanin' up, Helmi, and we'll all like you better. We've been here longer than you, you know."

When Helmi wanted to dig up some ground for a garden, she met sullen opposition. "I ain't goin' to put in a garden for someone else to eat—and that's how it may turn out." Mrs. Turner had come in to have her morning chat with Mrs. McMann. Calls were usually between ten and twelve, and this morning Mrs. Turner was determined to kill the garden idea once for all.

Helmi, with a towel on her head, stood on the kitchen table washing windows. "That's what I tell Helmy," said Mrs. McMann, patiently, "but she's got a notion that women should be all the time chasin' dirt or diggin' it out. I tell her she's tryin' to show off before the men. She's got that old country idea that if you want to make a hit with the men you have to show them what a great worker you are. I think Helmy is tryin' to get the idea over to this young Jack Doran—but that's not the way to get next to a boy like Jack. He's civilized enough to have the American idea that men make money and women spend it."

Helmi had been scrubbing the upper part of the windows and taking no part in the conversation. Just at this moment she had lifted the china top of a hen which had stood for a long time on the top of the kitchen cupboard, and found in the hen's interior an assortment of wax-ends, spools, a set of false teeth, a candle, and a watch-chain made of hair. "Did you know these were here?" asked Helmi, suspecting that the china hen had held her own secrets for some time.

"My stars, Helmy!" cried Mrs. McMann, "there's something to housecleaning after all. Mr. McMann blamed me for hidin' them very teeth, and we had words over it. He would leave them on the dresser and in cups, and I vowed I would hide them, but I really never did. One day they disappeared, and I was blamed. Fancy you findin' them when the trouble is over, and now I don't know where he is to tell him.

Gosh! ain't that the toughest part; it's the last straw that blinds the camel's eye every time. Now, if I just knew where he was! Just put them back, Helmy, and let the hen stay where she is—yes, wash it if you like, though I don't know as it matters now she's done her worst to me."

The front of the house was a big, bare room, where eight tables, covered with oilcloth, stood. The walls were of lumber, and bore only insurance calendars and posters of the Edmonton Fair, one showing a green child leading a red calf, another a bucking broncho with his heels aimed at the stars, his rider unperturbed and smiling, waving his hat at the audience. Two mottoes in frames of light wood, crossing at the corners under gold leaves, stared at each other across the space. One raised the question "What is Home Without a Mother?" the other one gave strange but definite answer, "Peace, Perfect Peace." It was here that the men ate their meals, carried in on huge trays, which Helmi handled with all the grace of the women of the East who carry their water-bottles on their heads.

After the meals were over and the tables cleared the men played cards on the tables. Helmi's manner was detached and aloof. She was remembering Aunt Lili's advice, which was easy to follow in every case but one. Young Jack Doran, who washed before each meal, flinging the water out of the basin with a circling motion, always looked so clean and fresh when he came in that Helmi could not refrain from looking at him. His hair was dark brown and marcelled itself in spite of its regular washings. Mrs. McMann had said it was a pity to see such lovely hair wasted on a man. Helmi was careful not to show her admiration, but it was hard to keep from looking at Jack. His face shone out so clear among the grimy faces around the table, and though he called her "Finn-girl" it never sounded fresh. He asked her to go with him to a dance one Saturday night at the hotel, and although she wanted to go, for she loved to dance, by some perversity of spirit she refused.

"Finn, you're foolish," Jack said, "you should take your fun as you go. It's the only way to get any." But Mrs. McMann commended Helmi by telling her the men would think all the more of her if she didn't jump at the first chance she got to go to a dance. Mrs. McMann quoted many instances in her own past life to prove it. "The seldom seen the most admired," she said was a safe rule for any girl. Helmi did not see that it mattered much about being seen once more when three times a day she was seen carrying trays, and, anyway, she didn't care whether the men admired her or not—but she wanted to dance.

Helmi spent a dull evening in her room, listening to the ribbony voice of the fiddles, which came through the open window, and wondering who Jack Doran was dancing with now—not that it mattered to her she told herself over and over. She wrote a long letter to her sister Anna in Finland, and put a five-dollar bill in the letter for her grandmother, and tried to feel she was a good girl to stay away from the dance—but failed.

Mrs. McMann told the other women that she was glad to be able to say of Helmi that she knew how to keep the men in their place; how when Bill Larsen, the bartender, who was a good fellow, too, tried to get fresh with Helmi because he knew her language, she threw a plate of soup at him—good soup it was, too—but Helmi was just that kind; the first thing that came to her hand she used. No one had tried to get funny with her since, "and," Mrs. McMann continued, "she's a great girl for her English lessons, off every night, as soon as her dishes are done, to the teacher over the river."

Helmi found life at the mines full of interest, too. From her window, which she washed clean the first day she occupied the room, she could see the mountains, and they answered to her every mood. When she was happy they lifted her up; when life was dull and gray, the mountains told her it didn't matter much—in a hundred years it would be all the same.

There was a flat stone by the river to which she often took her English book to read. For she loved the sound of the flowing water. It brought her back to the elemental things of life, and told her again the stories she had heard when she was a child—stories of man's long struggle with the wilderness, flood, famine and cold—and in its blithest murmurings Helmi could discern a warning note. It was trying to tell her that winter was coming, pitiless and cold, and that now was the time, when the grass was green and the water running, to build protection from the cold, and lay up stores against that long, white, desolate time. And although the river spoke only of the winter, Helmi knew it had a deeper meaning—and no matter how hard she studied her English book she could not altogether quell the voice of the years.

The velvety breezes of summer which went past her—some cool and fragrant with the wolf willow which grew thick around the edge of the saucer; some hot, like a blast from an oven—brought the same story and the same urge, filling her with a discontent and a vague restlessness that was new and disturbing. When she could bear it no longer Helmi always was able to drown the voices by a new orgy of cleaning at the boarding-house. She had never heard of sublimation, but she knew that something mysterious and uncontrollable drove her into activity, and in it she found peace.

Helmi was happiest when she saw a long day's work ahead of her, nerve and muscle tiring—a day's work that would send her to bed so tired and sleepy that the long black night would go by like a flash, bounded on one side by the moment her head touched the pillow, and on the other side by the first whirr of the alarm clock. She had done all she could for her own little box of a room up under the rafters. She had braided a mat for the floor, and hung blinds of flour sacking, washed white and rolled on a red crocheted cord. She had also made holders for her clothes out of rolled newspapers.

One day Helmi was on her way home from the teacher's house after a lesson in the proper method of letter-writing. She wanted to write to Miss Abbie. Miss Abbie would never tell she had heard from her, and yet if anyone asked her Miss Abbie couldn't lie. That was the worst about being a Christian like Miss Abbie, you couldn't lie, even when you should. Mrs. St. John had warned her not to write to anyone, but she did want to write just these words. "Dear Miss Abbie,—Helmi thinks of you every day." That couldn't hurt anyone, especially if she had it posted in Edmonton. Miss Abbie would know why she did not say more. She wished again she could ask someone. Jack Doran would be the best one—he was always so easy to talk to, and he did not laugh at her English.

As Helmi came close to the top of the street, on a knoll that had a balm of Gilead tree on it, she came upon a pile of lumber—new, shining lumber, fragrant in the warm air. She stopped to look at it, then, kneeling down, passed her hands over the satiny surface of the boards on which the drops of gum glistened like gold beads. It was a sultry afternoon at the end of June, and she was wondering how she would get along when the teacher went away. She carried a bag of laundry— she and the teacher traded work to their mutual advantage.

As Helmi looked at the lumber a sudden impulse came to her. She wanted to build a house—any sort of a little place that would be her own. Wasn't it provoking being a girl and not able to hit out for yourself—never able to step out and do big things, and here she was, working all day long for twenty-five dollars a month, while the poorest man in the mines had four dollars a day and only worked eight hours. It sure was the limit!

And she would just love to build herself a house. She would be content to stay in Eagle Mines if she had her own house. Then she put the thought away, summoning Aunt Lili again to her aid. A house meant an anchor, and she wanted to be free, always free. More English and more money, and then she would go to the city, learn stenography, work in an office, wear swell suits and have a wrist watch. Her plans seemed to end there in uncertainty. But here at her feet lay the material for a house, and it didn't do any harm to pat the lumber!

One sultry Sunday morning just before daybreak Helmi was awakened by a shuddering crash of thunder that seemed to burrow under the boarding-house, then burst upward with a terrific crash like the blasting on the mines. She ran to the window. A dull blue light was over everything, and great black clouds in commotion were advancing in the western sky. She watched them, fascinated, as they billowed, surged and twisted with an inward boiling motion. Then she thought of the lumber on the knoll—it would get wet and lose its lovely satiny sheen. When she looked she saw that a man was working there, sawing a board, as unconsciously as if the sun were shining. Then a flare of lightning ran blue along the blade of his saw, and Helmi shut her eyes in fright as another deafening peal shook the windows in their casings.

Helmi's mind acted quickly. Sunday morning—a man at work—and now a thunderstorm! God speaking to the wicked! God would not like to see a man building his house on Sunday, and yet Helmi knew how the man felt. It wasn't wicked—he could not help wanting to build—she knew how he felt—she felt it too. Now she was running down stairs and out into the storm.

The sky seemed to split wide open above her head as she ran; the heavens were lashed with knotted cords of flame swung by invisible giant hands. But Helmi ran on. She must get to this man and bring him in. She thought of Peter Saari, all blackened and burned beside his plough. She called to him above the storm, and he must have heard for he turned toward her, smiling. Then came a flash that blinded her and turned the world into blackest night. Something fell into her arms.

When Helmi opened her eyes a strange prickly sensation was in her arms and feet. She was sitting on the pile of lumber, holding someone in her arms, someone with face ghastly in the wan light, and whose eyes were closed. A cry broke from Helmi's lips.

"Jack Doran!" she called; "Oh, Jack Doran, is it you?"

She carried him into the house, his weight seeming nothing to her in her excitement. Her one impulse was to get him to shelter before the storm broke. Big drops fell on his face as she hurried along, and instinctively she leaned further over him to shelter him. There was no lounge or bed down-stairs, no place where she could lay him. To her own room she brought him and laid him on her bed. He moaned when she laid him down. Then she ran to alarm the house. The rain was coming down now in torrents, racing in a mad flood down the windows, filling the house with a steady, deafening roar, through which peals of thunder came bursting like cannons.

Mrs. McMann ploughed steamily up the stairs. "He ain't dead," she said, "nor nothing near it, but he's been stunned. You see there ain't a mark on him, but he sure has had a nasty wallop. It was lucky for him you saw him fall."

Helmi did not explain.

"He'd have been drowned to death like as not if he had been left lying there. Gosh! ain't that one awful rain. We can't send for the doctor just now, that's sure. Anyway, I don't think there's anything to do for Jack but just let him lie. He's breathin' all right, and his color is comin' back."

Helmi watched Jack's pale face anxiously. His cheeks were beginning to lose their ghastly pallor, and his lips were reddening. She noted admiringly the curly hair waved back from the high white forehead, the gracefully arched eyebrows, and the skin of the neck so smooth and white. Helmi touched Jack's forehead gently with her hand. There was something strangely familiar about his face as he lay before her.

For two days Jack Doran lay without speaking. Once he opened his eyes and seemed about to awake, but turned over on his side and went into another long sleep. The men came to see him and proffered much advice. "Lots of fresh air," they said, "and keep everything quiet, and just leave him alone." Helmi, rolled in a blanket, slept on the floor. The men had suggested carrying Jack to the bunk-house, but she had objected. She didn't mind keeping him, she said, and the bunk-house was noisy.

To Helmi it was all a miracle. The lightning, which to her was a definite personality, a real, living spirit, terrible in its workings, had given Jack to her. Straight and quick and sure it had come and struck him into her arms. Maybe sometimes lightning did kind things for people. It couldn't always be angry. Helmi felt the same thrill of something wonderful and vast, yet kindly, which swept her heart when she stood up to sing with the girls at the party in the church basement. She knew that God was her friend. God had spoken again in the lightning. Helmi was deeply awed, but deliriously happy. The lightning too, was her friend.

On the second morning Jack Doran wakened. Helmi was beside him in a moment.

"Tell me, Helmi," he said, "what happened? I remember the storm, and you coming running and calling to me. The lightning ran blue over my saw. Then what?"

A great shyness seized Helmi, but she told him as well as she could.

"I am all right now, Helmi, am I not?" he asked doubtfully.

She nodded.

After a long pause Jack seemed suddenly to realize what she had done. "You're a good Scout," he said, "how did you happen to come out through the storm?"

She told him all about Peter Saari and her fears for him. "I know how you felt," she said, "about wanting to work, even if it was Sunday. It is good to build a house any day, but I was afraid God might not understand and be mad at you, and so I ran out to get you."

"You're a good Finn-girl," Jack said drowsily. "Will you let me get up now?"

Helmi's eyes were very dreamy and tender when she ran downstairs and sent one of the men upstairs to help Jack to get dressed. The other men in the bunkhouse discussed the matter after she had gone, old Sim, the night watchman, leading.

"I wouldn't wonder if Helmi, for all her haughty ways, would fall in love with young Jack. A woman loves to take care of a man, and, after all, most matches are made by an old conspirator called 'Proximity.' Any girl, any man—put them together—Whiff!"

Old Sim made a sound which sounded more like the blowing out of a match than the making of one.

Chapter XIV

As the summer advanced through the hot days of July, redolent with sweet grass and wild roses, to the harvest haze of August, through which the sun shone with a golden glow of amber softness, the flowers began to show a bolder color. The timid blues, lavender and pinks of the small blossoms of early summer were replaced by the showy purples, deep blues and gold of the larger flowers. Plumy goldenrod; gorgeous gallardia in gold and brown; asters in purple and oxblood; wild sage in heavy purple, and odorous; fringed gentian as deeply blue as a mountain lake in a thunderstorm; and farther up the saucer's edge, the flaming fireweed, most brilliant, riotous and wanton of them all.

The mountains grew more wonderful and alluring to Helmi every day, for their beauty changed with the hour. The hard blue sky behind them in the early morning made their jagged tops stand out sharp like the blade of a knife, with a cruel, cutting brilliance that made her afraid to look at them; at noon, when the sun stood above them and wandering clouds trailed gray shadows over their slopes, they seemed to be more friendly and serene; but best of all she liked them when they twisted gray and violet mists around their heads, like dainty ladies before a glass, twisting and draping and never satisfied. From the kitchen window she could watch every change in the two great peaks, and when her work was done she often sat there wrapt in pleasant thoughts that could not be expressed even in her own language. The thunder-storms that raged upon the mountains, when black clouds spit out fire and thunder shook all the valley, were her delight, and seemed to sweep her soul with deep emotion.

One day Mrs. McMann found Helmi crying as she watched the raging skies, and scolded her for being such a coward.

"Leave me alone!" screamed Helmi, in Finnish, shaking off a hand which Mrs. McMann had really intended to be kindly; "I have a good time—I cry happy cry—Blixt is my friend—he knows me!"

Mrs. McMann decided that there is a queer streak in all foreigners, no matter how nearly like human beings they may appear. "Cry all you want to, Helmi," she said, "but that's no way for you to speak back to me."

Helmi apologized.

The harvest days brought on the breeze the smell of ripening grain from the plains, and many a miner had a sudden vision of the glad old life back East, and swore again he would go back to it as soon as he could. "This isn't livin' at all—there's no seedtime or harvest here—nothin' but pickin' black coal out of a bank, pilin' it in a car, and then when that one is full gettin' at another one—all in a black hole—and the sun shinin' and birds singin' back home. Gee! I sure am fed up!"

Helmi's days glided by on butterfly wings. She was so happy, it did not seem that winter ever could come, or any other unpleasant experience. She had grown more and more proficient in her work at the boarding-house, until now Mrs. McMann left almost everything to her. This had its drawbacks, too, for Mrs. McMann loved the centre of the stage. She loved to feel the world could not go on without her; and to have to admit that a young Finnish girl, only eighteen years old now, could come into her establishment and in six months be mistress of every detail, was not an easy thing to do. She explained to the boarders how carefully she had taught Helmi all she knew, and often sounded the pessimistic note, "and I suppose now, when I've spent hours and hours on her, she'll step off and get married."

"Watch Jack Doran, then," said one of the men, at which Bill Larsen's face darkened.

"Oh, Jack Doran," said Mrs. McMann scornfully; "Jack Doran will look a little higher than a foreign girl, and a waitress at that. His people are prominent citizens in the East, and although Jack is a wild young chap and likes his fun, he wouldn't go to the length of marrying so far out of his station. I know Jack pretty well, and I'm not afraid."

"Well, you know," said the man who had spoken first, "he wouldn't go so far wrong if he married Helmi. If you ask me, she's as good as he is."

This conversation took place on a Sunday afternoon in September. Jack and Helmi had gone for a drive to the English River, where, beside the falls, they had cooked their bacon on a fire of sticks. It was a dreamy day in the luxuriant Autumn, when the foliage was beginning to show like gold brocade against the darker green of the mountains.

Helmi had brought her English reader with her, and put it in his hand as soon as the meal was over. "Read it, Jack," she said, "this is the place."

> "By Nebo's lonely mountain,
> On this side Jordan's wave,
> In a vale in the land of Moab
> There lies a lonely grave."

Jack read the poem through. "Do you understand it?" he asked.

Helmi shook her head. "Not all—some—but I love it. One does not have to understand. It gives me such a happiness here," touching her heart, "that I want to cry. I know it is about a good man. He died— God buried him quiet. Maybe it was over there in that mountain—that would be good place. Read it again, Jack, please; I will watch close. Maybe I will see angels going into that cave!"

Jack laughed. "Helmi, you're a queer stick," he said. But he too, found himself lifting his eyes to the sunlit mountain, for never before to him had the solemn and moving measures throbbed with such majesty and power; and when it was done, and Helmi's eyes, shining with a hidden fire, looked into his, it seemed to him that the soundless feet of angels were passing by.

Helmi sat with her back against a tree, her shining hair catching the sunshine like the golden trees around her. Her eyes were fixed on the distant hills in deep adoration. To Jack she seemed like some beautiful spirit of the wood.

In the evening they drove home, almost without speaking, but with hearts curiously knit together.

Every second Sunday Helmi had the afternoon to herself, and, without any pre-arrangement, she and Jack took the trail to the Falls. Not a word of love had passed between them. They were just two good companions. Sometimes Helmi told him about Finland; sometimes he read to her; sometimes they sat still. But the day always held for Helmi a pleasure so keen, so piercing, it made her tremble.

The acutest part of Helmi's happiness centred around the little house which Jack was building. To please her he promised he would not work any more on Sunday. She loved to watch him from her bedroom window as he planed and sawed and hammered.

"He must be good man, that Jack Doran, to fit the boards so nice and make it all so well. He can't be bad like Aunt Lili said, or why would he want a house to build? In his spare time he works, while other men play cards and smoke and go to bar and drink. I think he must be good man, that Jack; I think I like that Jack Doran a pretty good lot!"

Jack's shift ended at four in the afternoon, and after he had changed his clothes he usually went to work at his house. Helmi often went over with him and helped to hold the boards while he planed them. Their conversation was limited. One day when he was putting in a window frame he said: "I don't mind working my eight hours while I have something nice to look forward to. I love making things, though perhaps if I had to do it, it would seem like work, too. Do you ever get fed up on dishwashing?"

"Gosh, yes," said Helmi, "but I try always to make them shine, and nothing is too bad if it can be well done."

There was a long silence then, broken only by the sound of planing.

"I don't know what I'll do when I get done with this," he said.

Helmi looked up in surprise.

"I believe I'll build another one down by the river. There's a big tree there on a high bank—I would like a house right beside it, and then I could hear the river all the time. I would like that."

"No chance," said Helmi quickly; "river is dangersome."

"Dangerous, Helmi," he corrected, "d-a-n-g-e-r-o-u-s," spelling the word for her.

Helmi wrote the word carefully in her book. "Yah, it's dangerous," she repeated. "This house is near the river—near enough—too near, maybe."

"Why," he asked, carefully sighting the edge of a board.

"Kids might fall in," she said.

Jack gave an exclamation of surprise and looked at her hastily. Helmi's face was grave and unabashed. Generations of child-bearing women whose business in life was the rearing and protection of their young had spoken through her.

"See here, Helmi," Jack said anxiously, "don't you say that to anyone. It is—well, people don't talk that way, that's all."

"All right," Helmi said simply. "I won't say it again, but it's true." Then she went on writing—"dangerous, dangerous, dangerous."

Jack went to the city for a week just before Christmas, and when he returned Helmi could not keep her heart from beating or her eyes from glistening when he walked in carrying his valise. He wore a new overcoat of black cloth, with an otter collar. The whole room seemed to be bursting with light and happiness when he came in. After supper he stayed behind until all the men had gone to the bunkhouse, and then came over to where she was setting the tables for breakfast and handed her a purple velvet box.

"For a good Finn girl," he said.

The lid opened with a spring, revealing a sunburst of pearls on a white satin lining, and a little card with a tiny house set against a snowy hill and flanked by evergreens, with these words printed on it in gold letters: "With love and best wishes for a Happy Christmas," and, written below, "For a good Finn girl called Helmi, who runs out in the storm and carries men in out of the wet."

Helmi gave an exclamation of surprise. "O Jack," she said, "it is so nice it makes my heart pain. Is it all for me?"

"Nobody else," he laughed.

Helmi turned to him with the rapt look in her eyes she had had the day she watched the mountain-side for angels, an adoring, worshipping look that transfigured her. She was always attractive, always striking, with her deep, dark eyes, high coloring and burnished hair; but now, with her eyes so tender, so full of devotion, she was beautiful.

Jack put his hand on Helmi's shoulder and drew her to him. "I think you should let me kiss you now, Helmi,—just once—I have never kissed you—or any other girl."

Aunt Lili's warnings were all forgotten when Jack's arms tightened around her. The river, under two feet of ice, was singing its old song; the sky was still luminous with the fires of sunset; the clouds had risen to form a Chinook arch, faintly green against the blue; already the western breezes were soft as velvet as they went past the eaves, murmuring something very sweet and satisfying, in which disappointment and heartbreak had no place at all.

Chapter XV

Mrs. McMann and Bill Larsen, the bar-tender, having a common grievance, had become fellow-conspirators. They were consumed with one desire, though from widely different motives. Mrs. McMann feared the loss of the best girl she had ever had, and more than that, she resented the sincere respect and friendship the boarders all felt for Helmi. Here she was, a girl who simply stepped off the train without a reference or letter, and in less than a year was the most popular girl in the valley. When the Anglican Church, desiring to raise money for their incumbent's salary, had put on a contest in Eagle Mines, Bannerman and Brule, running one girl in each place, Helmi had won in a walk. And there was something funny about the way she acted, Mrs. McMann confided in her friend Mr. Larsen, for when it was all over and the minister came to Helmi to find out where she came from, how long she had been in Canada and all that, she wouldn't tell him a thing, and begged him not to write anything about her in the papers. It was queer to see Helmi afraid of anything.

Bill Larsen looked as meditative as anyone could with Bill's cast of features. "There was a Milander girl in Winnipeg about a year and a half ago who raised a lot of grief," he said, "She was a hot socialist and got in jail, and all that. I remember the name, because I've had a lot to do with Finns one way and another down at Port Arthur. Of course it's a pretty common name—but Helmi wouldn't be afraid if she wanted to heave a rock." Mr. Larsen's mind reverted to the unpleasant episode which marked the beginning of his acquaintance with Helmi.

Mrs. McMann was for direct action. "I think we'd better put it up to Jack straight, and see what he's goin' to do. I don't believe for one minute he intends to marry Helmi, but she thinks he does, and if he's foolin' her, she may kill him or herself. I knew a Finn girl once who drank lye because her fella didn't come to take her to a dance. They're high tempered and quick with a gun or anything that comes to their hand."

Mr. Larsen admitted it.

"I don't suppose she's told him a bit more about herself than she tells us," Mrs. McMann continued. "You see, she never writes a letter only to Finland, and she didn't come straight from Finland here, that's sure enough. And where did she get the nifty clothes she brought here? It sure looks queer, and no one can get it out of her."

Mr. Larsen was unable to offer any advice. "She's a dandy girl, is Helmi," he said, "and I don't like to see her fooled. If she wants to get married . . ."

Mr. Larsen left the sentence unfinished.

"She'd be foolish to marry any man," said Mrs. McMann. "Here she is, pullin' down her twenty-five dollars a month, rain or shine, and lots of time for herself, and takin' lessons all the time. Gettin' married is a queer business, Bill. No one takes warning!—I didn't, and she won't. It's like the pigs that stick their noses in the hot feed and go along squealing, and another and another does it—no one learns,—But I think it's up to us to bring Jack Doran to a show-down, just to see what happens. I never was one that could bear suspense—I like to have a thing settled one way or another."

Bill admitted he was something of an out-and-outer himself.

Helmi was awakened next morning by the first beam of the March sun. It came around the corner of the factory cotton blind, and played over her pillow with a tremulous motion. It was a jolly little sunbeam that seemed to have a story to tell if there was anyone to listen. But Helmi's heart was too full of its own happiness to listen to any other story. She sprang out of bed and met the new day with a song, a strange song, that came bubbling out of her far-off childhood. Helmi had not thought of it since she came to Canada, and did not know that she knew it, but today it came unbidden. Six months ago or less Helmi would have sternly frowned on the old Finnish song with its old world ethics and customs. She would have been as scornful of it as she was of her sister's marriage and her placid acceptance of her swarming family. But now Helmi had a deeper understanding, so she sang the old chant, the "Kalevala" of her own country,—

> "Now the time has come for parting
> From my father's golden fireside,
> From my brother's welcome hearthstones,
> From my mother's happy dwelling;"

Weird and solemn and doleful, misty with years and the heart-throbs of another generation, the "Kalevala" had no place in this new world of action and realities.

But Helmi sang on as she got dressed, in a mechanical, toneless voice, imitating the old minstrel whom she had heard sing it years ago—laughing at it, yet bound by its strange spell. She was glad she remembered it; it would make Jack Doran laugh that big rolling laugh she loved so well. He would say again, "You are a queer stick, Helmi."

> "Do not harm the bride of heaven,
> Do not injure her thou lovest;
> Counsel with the bride of heaven,
> To the young wife give instruction."

Helmi rolled up the cotton blind and tied the red cord in a bow-knot. The warm March sun was filling the saucer with a ruddy glow, even brightening the weather-beaten little houses. Streamers of rose and orange were thrown into the upper heavens, indicating a windy day; curling smoke climbed up its stairless way, faithfully telling who was and who was not astir. To Jack Doran's house on the hill, faintly pink in the morning light, Helmi's eyes turned lovingly, and as she watched the first feather of smoke drifted aimlessly up into the waiting air. Some day that little house would be hers, and she would have her own little pots and pans, shining just like silver.

Helmi's light heart sang the old melody of love and mating, but the words, which never mattered much anyway, were the dismal lines of the "Kalevala." However, sung as they were by her in ragtime, no trace of the gloom was left.

> "Cut a rod upon the mountain,
> Or a willow in the valleys;
> Hide it underneath thy mantle,
> That the stranger may not see it;"

Helmi laughed at the concise instructions given to the young husband in the matter of keeping his wife in her place. It was all very humorous now, though she remembered how angry it made her when she heard it sung in Finland. She had once been severely whipped by her father for saying that if her man ever dared to strike her she would kill him with a bossa and throw his body into the flood. But the whipping had only confirmed her determination. She hoped her father would fall and break his leg or be struck by the blixt.

Helmi dressed as quickly as she could. Her bare little room, gilded now by the warm sunshine, was a paradise to her, because here she had dreamed her glorified dreams. Helmi's radiance of spirit covered every deformity, even as the sunshine warmed to life again the faded pattern on the stingy little quilt, falsely called a comforter, which lay on the bottom of the bed. Helmi's bed was a narrow white enamelled one, with so much of the enamel gone that its complexion was now that of an English coach-dog. The floor was uneven and splintery; a cracked basin stood on a box covered with red and yellow checked oilcloth; but today nothing mattered, for Helmi's heart was singing the old song. She went down the creaking stairs to the big kitchen below, where a solemn black stove, standing glum and cold on its four spread legs, awaited her. She had her kindling ready, her porridge already cooked. Helmi was what Mrs. McMann called forehanded—she was always on time.

Mrs. McMann usually slept until breakfast was over. She was glad of a chance to sleep in peace, and she did if the undulating snores which came from her room adjoining the kitchen could be depended on. Helmi fried the bacon in two great black frying-pans, and boiled coffee in two blue pots.

Mrs. McMann, having thought the matter over, decided to throw the "jolt" at the breakfast table. The table would be full, and it was as good a time as any. She arose as soon as she awoke, combed back her thin hair, speared it into a figure eight at the back of her head with a few iron hairpins, put on her best black sateen dress, which was beginning to "get to fit too snug," and came into the kitchen.

Helmi was carrying back the empty porridge bowls.

"Why, look who's here," said Jack Doran when she entered the dining-room. "Good-morning, Mrs. McMann, are you not sleeping well now?" Jack sometimes cooked his own breakfast, but this morning he was at the "Elite."

Mrs. McMann sighed. "No, I'm not sleepin' so good—I'm kinda bothered about some things. Maybe it's none of my business, but I can't help botherin' about other people."

Mrs. McMann had thought out a real plan, deep laid, daring, extreme.

"Why bother?" asked Jack, helping himself to a piece of toast from the pyramid which Helmi had just brought in.

"I suppose a person gets no thanks, but I was never one to look for thanks." Mrs. McMann was in the self-righteous mood which the boarders knew so well.

Jack Doran went merrily on. "Tell us your troubles, Mrs. McMann," he said, "boarders are human. Let us advise you."

Mrs. McMann saw she had the attention of the table. The time was ripe.

"Well, seein' as you're so anxious to hear my troubles, Jack, I will tell you—you should know, because you're the cause. I hear from a friend of mine in Edmonton that you are engaged to a girl there, and all this time you are stringin' Helmy along just for your own amusement— buildin' this house and all, and givin' us all to understand you mean to do the right thing by Helmi."

Jack stopped eating and looked up in surprise. Bill Larsen cut his mouth in his excitement.

Mrs. McMann continued: "I've seen young dudes from the city before, that came along and raised the deuce with decent girls, raisin' hopes in them that makes them scorn honest men in their own station, and it ain't fair, and I won't stand for it. A minin' camp is a rough place, but by Gosh! there's some things we won't stand for. Anyone would know a town-bred fella like you would mean no good to a girl who's only a hash-slinger, after all, and foreign, too."

A silence fell on the room. Helmi, who had a way of doing her work without bringing her mind to it, was aroused with the sudden jerk one feels when a train stops. The room, which a moment before had hummed like a factory, was now plunged suddenly into tense silence.

Mrs. McMann, having invented the story of Jack's sweetheart, proceeded to elaborate.

"There is some talk of your bringin' a wife here at Easter, and that it will be the city girl from Edmonton."

Jack Doran stood up and threw back his shining hair. His face was pale under his coat of March tan.

"You're a great guesser, Mrs. McMann," he said, "but you miss out in some things. I am going to have a wife before Easter, but it is not the girl from Edmonton. As a matter of fact, I do not know a girl in Edmonton, not one; but I know a girl in Eagle Mines that I think a lot of."

Helmi was passing behind him, and he turned impulsively and took her hand. "Helmi has worked her last day for you, Mrs. McMann, for today she is going to marry me, if she will. Will you marry me, Helmi?" he asked impulsively.

The men gasped. Wasn't Jack Doran "the queer divil to ask a girl right out before every one."

"Will you marry me, Helmi, today?" he repeated.

Helmi simply nodded.

A shout of applause broke from the men, in which Bill Larsen did not join. He suddenly hated Mrs. McMann for her interfering ways; she'd made a nice hash of things.

Mrs. McMann's face grew dark; she had been beaten, right here in her own house. Worse still, she stood to lose the best girl she had ever had. Jack Doran, with his big-feelin' ways, would never let his wife sling hash to miners. Mrs. McMann caught her breath on the intake.

"Well, at least you might have given us a little warning. What's all the rush about, I'd like to know. It don't look well—that's all I have to say."

Mrs. McMann resented youth more and more as she grew older. The slimness and agility of Helmi reproached her ponderous bulk, and now, looking at the boy and girl, so clean, lithe and wholesome, who stood before her, hand in hand facing the future calmly and fearlessly, she felt she hated both of them. They seemed to defy her; "crazy young fools—what did they know about life? She hoped . . ."

She blew her breath on her lips as if they needed to be cooled.

Chapter XVI

That afternoon Helmi and Jack drove to Bannerman, eight miles away, to find someone to marry them. Helmi wore the black silk dress which she had worn on the train, with the lace collar, fastening the latter with the sun-burst which Jack had given her at Christmas.

Mrs. McMann was horrified at the thought of Helmi being married in black. "I ain't superstitious, Helmy," she said, "but you know the sayin' 'Married in black, wish yourself back.'"

Helmi laughed—her little world was pulsing with joy; she hardly heard Mrs. McMann's doleful predictions. The mountains were bright with sunshine, the ice had gone out of the river, the world was very fair.

"Jack Doran is only a boy," said Mrs. McMann, "and I believe he asked you right out like that hopin' you'd refuse him, Helmy."

Helmi's eyes were pools of rapture. "I fooled him—didn't I? that Jack Doran? He'll know better next time than ask a Finn girl!"

Mrs. McMann looked at her and sighed. Helmi was too happy to yield to any discouraging suggestions.

Nothing dimmed the glory of the day for Helmi until they reached the top of the hill looking down at the little town of Bannerman, where a huddle of houses were grouped around the station. Then Helmi suddenly caught Jack's arm.

"Oh, Jack, I no like!" she said, "look at the little houses—they are like cats going to spring! It is not friendly."

Jack put his arm around her. "Don't be frightened, Helmi; nothing can hurt my Finn girl."

His eyes were tender when he looked at her, but Helmi's were full of tears. "It is a bad place, this,"—she said shivering, as she pointed down into the valley; "it is full of mad words and bad thoughts for us."

The river wound its wide blue ribbon below them, satiny and smooth, with no trace of haste or unrest. From where they stood they could see a smaller stream, which, coming down a wooded ravine, poured its waters into the larger stream with a musical murmur which came softly to their ears. They had stopped their horses at the top of the hill.

The arrival at the fateful spot and the solemnity of their mission gave eloquence to Jack's tongue: "We do not know each other very well, Finn-girl," he said, "but we love each other, and that's all that matters. Now, let us get one thing straight. We have to trust each other—that's all there is in getting married and making it go. I liked you, Helmi, from the time I saw you first, because you have such a straight eye. I believe you are square, and I am too. I've never had a girl but you. You are not afraid now, are you Helmi?"

Helmi wished she could tell him everything in her past life—Jack would understand—but it was so hard to get always the right words in English.

Jack continued: "We are like the two streams, Helmi dear, that join over there and run together to the sea. We are going to join, just like that, and run together all the way. Once we join we cannot separate. It is a long way to the sea, too, for us, and there may be rocks and rapids and rough water; but we'll always be square, Helmi. You are not afraid now, are you, dear?"

Helmi's eyes were misty with tears, as she turned and looked into his. "I am not afraid," she said.

They went first to the postoffice to get the license. An elderly man, with a long beard, filled in the form which gave John Ward Doran and Helmi Milander the right to be joined in the bonds of wedlock. For this the sum of five dollars had to be paid.

They asked for the Methodist minister, but found there was none. The Anglican minister was away, but the postmaster said the magistrate would be sure to be at home, and he gave them directions to find his house.

It stood by itself, inside a broken picket-fence, a dishevelled, untidy little house, plainly occupied by a man alone. There were no curtains, and the blinds hung crooked, with torn edges; the steps leading to the screened-in verandah were broken, and the wire screening was bulged as if football games were often played inside.

"This looks like rough house," said Jack, as they approached; "but never mind, Helmi, we'll get married all over again when we go to Edmonton, and in the biggest church there, with stained glass windows; and we'll have a car full of flowers, and bridesmaids and wedding-cake, and 'here comes the bride,' and everything. But in the meantime, if this old boy is sober, we will get enough of the law on our side to go on with."

The magistrate, J. Edgerton Blackwood, late of Stoke-Poges, opened the door. His manner registered deep annoyance, his appearance suggested fatigue. A soiled collar, held only by the back stud, flared jauntily from his neck, and the condition of his shirt gave evidence that there had been some disappointment over his last week's laundry. Tufts of hair, like small brushes, grew out of his ears; his eyes were bloodshot, his voice hoarse. Indeed, Mr. Blackwood looked and felt much like a dog that has barked all night.

"What the h— do you want?" he asked, when he opened the door. The words, though ungracious, were spoken in the well modulated tone of the cultured Englishman—the voice that one hears in the most remote and most unexpected corners of the earth.

Jack paused a moment before replying. "Are you a Justice of the Peace," he asked in surprise.

"I'm everything, damn it! I keep the pound, am clerk of the township, do book-keeping for the storekeepers here, and play poker. What can I do for you?"

"We want to get married," said Jack, smiling. No one could quarrel with Jack Doran on this day of days. He felt Helmi's hand tighten on his arm, and noticed she was pale and frightened, but Jack had no feeling save pity for this dirty and disgruntled old man.

"Come in," said His Worship, at length, "come in and sit down." He left them to solve the problem of sitting down as best they might. Every chair carried its own burden of clothing, papers, cooking utensils, and other bric-a-brac. A horse-collar occupied one; a pair of rubber boots another. A square red stove stood in the middle of the floor, its damper hanging drunkenly from one corner; ashes from its end door had dropped down and were tracked over the floor. A tumbled bed, visible through the open door of the room adjoining, gave the impression that Mr. Blackwood had but recently left it. The table in the room was full of dirty dishes and empty bottles.

Something prompted the Magistrate to apologize.

"There's a flock of women here, but they're too damned independent to do a day's work since the mines opened. I would like to see them slowly starving and freezing to death. Damned foreigners that they are, who never should have been let come into a white man's country, anyway. Bohunks and Finns."

"Go easy on the Finns, Captain," said Jack, laughing; "I am about to marry one."

Mr. Blackwood gave Helmi a long and insolent stare, before which her eyes fell. Were all magistrates cross old men? Were they angry at her because she came from another country?

"You'll need to keep her in her place, young man; she has the eyes of a broncho. They are a high-tempered, murderous lot, the Finns, fighting, stabbing, shooting."

"We're in a hurry, Captain," said Jack, still unruffled; "so if you will get along with the business now we will be very glad. I have the license here."

The old man put on a pair of smeared glasses and began to hunt through the incredible turmoil on his table, looking for the necessary papers, swearing as he drew out each handful that failed to reveal the proper forms. Someone had been interfering; he never could leave anything and find it again; they had been here yesterday or the day before. If people would only leave his things alone! . . . he would set a trap among his papers, and he hoped it would cut their damned fingers off.

Mr. Blackwood went to the cupboard, took out a teacup, poured himself a drink from a brown bottle, and made another attempt. After a second drink he found what he wanted.

Helmi hung to Jack's arm, terrified. "I don't like it," she said, "bad luck it will bring—it is so *smutsig*—dirty and bad. He is *drucken*, come away—we will go to another one—I wish we could get married nice way."

Jack tried to reassure her.

"Show me the license," the magistrate said, swinging around in his chair.

Jack unfolded it and put it in his hands.

The magistrate read the names aloud—John Ward Doran and Helmi Milander.

"Milander?—Milander?" He looked up suddenly and regarded Helmi more closely.

Again her eyes fell.

Then he turned to Jack. "I would like to speak to you alone," he said, "if Miss Milander will step outside."

Helmi went out, glad to be out of the foul air and away from the scrutiny of the old man's eyes, which reminded her uncomfortably of the only other magistrate she had ever seen.

"Mr. Doran, I take it you are a Canadian?"

Jack nodded.

"And an educated man—a college man, perhaps?"

"I put in three years at Queens," Jack said.

"Now you propose to marry this Finnish girl?"

"I certainly do," said Jack.

"Now, Mr. Doran, I want to point out to you the folly of this course. The girl is pretty, I'll admit, of a certain type of barmaid beauty."

Jack interrupted—"Now, look here, I am not asking for advice from you or anyone. I asked you to marry me to this girl—that's all. Will you do it?"

"Listen," said the magistrate, "and don't lose your temper. What I want to tell you is this. You don't need to marry this girl. These foreigners are not particular—this license will do her. They have great respect for a paper, and a man of your standing will soon tire of a girl who has nothing but a pretty face."

"So your advice to me, when I ask you to marry us, is for me to fool the girl, to make her think she is married to me. That is about the rottenest thing I ever heard a man say!"

"Wait, now—don't shout!" The magistrate was determined to be patient. "I wish to God someone had given me this advice when I was your age. Was this girl the waitress where you had your meals? I thought so—same old story. She took a shine to you—following you about. I know—the same thing happened to me, and now I live here, where the beldame can't find me."

"Why does she want to find you?" asked Jack, without any attempt to disguise his contempt.

"You'll know more of these things before you are done, if you marry this girl. Now, I've tried to warn you in general terms, but you won't take it. This is final, is it?"

"Yes, sir, I am going to marry Helmi Milander honestly and legally. If you do not want to do it we can go to someone else."

"I'll marry you, all right, but before that I want to show you something. You have been very impertinent to me, but nevertheless I want to be fair to you anyway—and I am doing for you what I would want someone to do for my boy if I had one. Perhaps you would be interested to look at this."

Without any difficulty at all in finding what he wanted, he went to the wall, where, on a huge spike, pages of newspapers were impaled. He searched through them for a moment and then returned to Jack and placed in his hand a page of a Winnipeg paper. Jack took it, wonderingly.

"Read this," said the older man, triumphantly, "and then tell me if you still want to go on. We keep a file of police happenings and find them very interesting."

Helmi's face looked at him from the page.

"Arrested in a Chinese den a year ago—escaped yesterday from the Girls' Friendly Home," Jack read the words aloud before he was able to grasp their meaning. He read every word of it, though the words seemed to be made of fire that burned him. Even the Magistrate was sorry for him.

"It's a damn lie!" broke from his lips; "it's a horrible mistake! See, it's the same name—that's all. If it were my Helmi wouldn't she have changed her name when she came here? She wouldn't be fool enough to go on under the same name."

Jack knew that Helmi did not talk of her life in Winnipeg, though it came out one day that she had been there a year; and the date of the escape recorded here corresponded with the time she came to Eagle Mines.

Jack's throat was dry and his soul sick within him, but to believe that of Helmi! He couldn't—he wouldn't. There were no dark chapters in the boy's own life. He had lived the clean, active life of a decent, fun-loving youth. He knew of the evils in the world, having worked with gangs of men who spoke of their carousals without shame, but he had always been repelled by the coarseness, the vulgarity of it all. It couldn't be—Helmi was as sweet and pure as a prairie flower. If she was arrested it was some rotten mistake. No, he would not turn her down.

"Is it her picture, do you think?" asked the magistrate, coolly.

"I am not sure," said Jack, "it's a young girl of Nordic type, dressed as they all dress. I never saw my girl wear these clothes."

Jack read the words again, and then handed the paper back. He had taken his resolve. "Now, you've done your duty," he said, trying to speak calmly, "I am going to marry Helmi Milander, and if you ever show this paper to anyone and try to injure my wife, I will come back and deal with you—old man though you are. Now, get your book, or whatever you go by, and come outside; the atmosphere of this house is hardly right for a wedding."

Jack had never felt such a need for fresh air—another minute in this foul place would smother him.

Outside, with the afternoon sun shining on them, and a wind from the pass blowing the leaves of paper the magistrate held in his hand, they made their vows according to the bald rites of civil marriage. Jack could not afterwards remember what he said. He only knew he had a great desire to take Helmi in his arms and protect her from every evil thing in the world.

When they began the drive home the sun had gone behind the mountains. As the early chill of evening came down upon them Helmi was silent and distressed. She knew there was something wrong. The magistrate was her enemy like the other one. Why were they all so cross to her? She determined to ask Jack.

"Why did he not want you to marry me?" she asked, when they had reached the top of the hill and stopped to look back at the little town, which would soon be blotted out by the purpling dusk.

Jack kissed her again. "Forget him, Helmi," he said; "he is a poor, dirty, miserable old soak, and he cuts no ice in our lives."

Helmi, who knew that weddings should be stately and dignified ceremonies, was deeply distressed. "Jack, I cannot feel that we are married by just those little no-good words; no prayers; no good wishes; no solemn words at all. It's a wicked way—I not like it."

"I don't like it, either," Jack replied, "but it is legal."

"I'll tell you, Jack." She was recovering her good spirits now. "I know what we will do—we'll make it good. When we come to little *puro*—what you call creek—on the way home, we'll stand one on each side and say good words across the running water, and then we will be married sure. I will feel better then."

"All right, Finn—anything you say."

They stopped beside a little brook that found its way down to the river, following one of the flutings in the saucer's edge, and there, with the horses looking wonderingly on, they held each other's hands across the running water and plighted their vows:—

"I take you, Helmi, to be my wife," said Jack, "and I will love you always." And Helmi said, "I take you, dear Jack Doran, for my man, forever."

And then, still holding each other's hands across the little stream, they repeated the words that Helmi had learned that night so long ago now at the Girls' Club.

"These are good words, Jack, I learned them in God's house. They are religious words that God understands. I'll say them first, then you.

"Cherish health; seek truth; know God; serve others."

Jack repeated the words after her, and then they kissed each other and stood silent for a moment. And for their witnesses, besides the angels in heaven, who surely were looking down, they had two honest bay livery horses that bore upon their shoulders the honorable scars of patient service.

And in the woods near by a robin, which really had retired for the night, opened one sleepy eye and sang a little song because it was the Spring-time and he, too, had a pleasant dream.

Chapter XVII

The tops of the mountains still held the glow of sunset although the valley was filled with mountain darkness. The lights in the curtainless windows of the little houses made bright holes in the platinum curtain of night. Helmi lifted her eyes to the hill-tops for some sign of encouragement—the hills had never failed her—and, flinty-hearted, stern and rock-ribbed though they were, they smiled back as even mountains smile at young lovers. The sky above them was clear and blue, with every cloud tidied away for the night.

As Helmi and Jack drove into the one little street of Eagle Mines there came to them the heartsome smell of frying bacon.

"Good luck, Helmi," said Jack, "it's good luck to smell bacon frying when you're hungry, isn't it?" He liked to laugh at her Finnish superstitions.

Helmi breathed deeply. It seemed to her that the magic hour of love would last forever, and that each night of her life would come to meet her as this one was coming, on wings of gossamer and gold.

Helmi and Jack together took the team to the stable, and while Jack paid the bill Helmi patted the horses' heads and talked to them in Finnish.

"Come on, Helmi," Jack called, starting to walk toward their house.

"Wait a minute," she replied, running after him. "Can't I say thank you and good-night to my two *morsiuspiikas*—what do you call them?"

When Helmi entered the little house all her fears fell away. Here was her home, and the gates of hell could not prevail against it. The lamp was lighted on the table, her new, shining kettle was boiling on the stove. These little attentions had been shown them by old Sim, the night watchman. Old Sim had had a checkered career matrimonially, but some old memory, which unfortunately he was not able to catalogue accurately, stirred in him when he saw Jack and Helmi drive away, and in a sudden rush of sentiment he had thrown after them his one gaiter for good luck. All the afternoon he had thought of them in his waking moments, and just before he went on duty he went over and lighted their lamp and fire, just to remind them that someone was wishing them well. As he settled down for his long night vigil at the mine Sim tried to decide once and for all whether it was of Maime, Lucy or Min that the Finn girl always reminded him.

Helmi pulled a chintz apron over her black dress and began to get the supper ready. Jack had gone to the postoffice to see if there was any mail—anyway, there would be the paper. Helmi stepped about lightly and happily in her new home. Oh, what a letter she would write home to Finland! Anna would be glad, and her grandmother, too. Now she knew what the river was singing—the river was right—home is best.

Jack came in then and hung his coat behind the door, and stood smiling at her. The bacon was frying—the kettle singing. Helmi drew the blinds on the three little windows.

That night, after Helmi had gone to sleep, Jack lay for a long time looking into the darkness. The fire in the stove had burned low, giving out but a faint glimmer through the mica windows. What a lot had happened since morning! He tried to forget the terrible ten minutes in the magistrate's house. Maybe Helmi would tell him after they got to know each other better. Anyway, he was glad he had her here right beside him, and even if he never should know the truth he would trust her. Then he tried to turn his thoughts to the great secret he had to tell her.

She thought he was a common miner, and had married him as such. Helmi, he knew, would be happy to live in this little house all her life with him. But better things awaited her. He tried to picture her surprise; and still he knew she would be anxious, too, when she heard he would have to leave her before long. That was the worst of it. . . . Hang that old magistrate!

The wind began gently in the mountain pass, coming in from the sea so far away, a soft Spring wind, sent to ferret out the last snow-banks hiding in river-bottoms and below trees—a sighing, singing wind, that went by the little house with gentle whisperings. But tonight Jack started at its voice, because it had something sinister in it and full of malice—a sort of double meaning for all it was so spring-like and so velvet-footed. He could hear in it the cackle of evil tongues, searing and stabbing, behind doors, in corners.

Helmi, knowing nothing of this, and having no sense of guilt or doubt, slept peacefully on.

They were married on Friday. On Sunday Jack told her his great secret.

He had been on an exploration party the year before, up on the Liard River, and had seen the gold in the sands, and knew there must be great deposits farther up. He had seen oil dripping into the river and running away, red and blue and green, and once had put his can below the drip and put the oil in a basin of the rock and cooked his supper on it. But the gold, it was the gold he was going to find. When he was in the city at Christmas time he had met a man whom he had often heard of in the North, a prospector who had been there fourteen years searching for gold, and now he had found it away up on the Nehanni River. He had found the motherlode, and had showed Jack specimens of the quartz with gold shining in it. Jack had seen it with his own eyes, and while he told her of it, his eyes gleamed with man's ancient lust for gold.

"That's our secret, Finn," he said, "aren't you glad? Oh, Helmi, there are silk dresses and diamond rings in this for you. I want my girl to have every good thing in life—English, education, poetry, music, fine pictures, all the lovely things her heart craves, yes, and a trip to Finland, and plenty of money for anything she wants to do with it."

Helmi's eyes were two deep pools of wonder and delight. Then over them swept fear, like a raw east wind.

"But Jack, have you to go? Will you have to leave me and go away to the north? I don't want gold, dear Jack, I just want you—big lot money makes only trouble."

Jack kissed her and laughed. "O Helmi, you will not mind my going. This man I am going with knows the North. He has lived in it for fourteen years, and he has the maps and all, and it's a great thing for me that he is taking me with him. There's hundreds of fellows who would wish they were in my place if they knew. But it is just the two of us and a half-breed guide. We have to keep it dark, because the oil syndicate are watching him. They know that he knows where the oil springs are. Helmi, he told me of a hot spring valley there where the rocks are always warm, and tropical plants grow, and the creeks come boiling out of the mountains. He is a wonder, this man, and to think he asked me to go with him, and he will let me stake my claim with his and give me a share in everything."

Helmi looked at him with deep trouble in her eyes. "I wish you had never seen gold in the sand, and never met this man," she said. "Now all our good times will be spoiled by thinking you have to go. Jack, I hate money—it is no good for happiness. I usta think I wanted money, plumes on hat, and big rings and trip to Finland—now I just want you—and my nice little house to work in—and make nice. Don't go, Jack—just stay with me."

"Poor little kid," Jack said, "I know how you feel. That was the reason I did not say anything about getting married when I came back at Christmas. I thought we would wait until I came back from the north, but it's better that we did get married, dear. I am glad we did, even if you are pretty cross at me for leaving you so soon."

"Not cross, Jack, but just sad. My heart is cold and heavy, just like a stone."

"Now cheer up, Helmi, and listen. I want to tell you what sort of a dress we will buy first when we get our money. The color for you, with that top-knot of yours, is green, and you shall have a clinging dress of green satin, with jade ear-rings and necklace, and a cloak of sea-foam green, lined with a sort of flame color that will show a little when you walk. Now, what's the matter?"

Helmi was looking at him in horror. She could see herself in Mrs. St. John's room before the glass. "Don't, don't," she cried excitedly; "that dress brings bad luck."

"Goodnight!" cried Jack, "what dismal old Finnish superstition have I jarred loose now?"

"No, no, not Finnish—but I will never wear a green dress, Jack, not even to please you."

Jack could see he had awakened a very poignant memory and again he wondered, wishing the magistrate had not told him. Was he always to be haunted by these evil spirits of the past?

If Jack had not been told anything he would no doubt have asked Helmi more about her past. As it was he avoided the subject. He hoped she would tell him everything, and to this end he told her all there was to tell about himself. His father and mother had died when he was five, and his sister, ten years his senior, and himself, were brought up in Toronto by his mother's sister. His sister had been very kind to him, and he adored her. When she was old enough she trained for a private secretary and got a position with a very wealthy woman, and travelled with her in Europe for several years.

"And then I seemed to lose her," continued Jack, "for when she came back she had such extravagant tastes my aunt was at a loss to know how to get along with her. She hated our way of living and all our little economies. She made no secret of the fact that she was going to marry a man with money—and she did, a very decent old scout, too, who worships her, I can understand that, too, for she has a way with her, I can tell you. She is so good to look at, and she is so frankly self-ish. She loves beauty more than anything on earth, and would sacrifice principle for it. Now, she may love this husband of hers—I hope she does—but I know this that if he had been poor she would not have looked at him.

"I must tell her about you, Helmi, and send her some snaps of you. She would love you for your beauty and I daresay when you meet her you will fall in love with her, too, as most people do. But I like to remember her best when she was such a good sister to me—before she went away. I am going to write to her right now."

This was Sunday afternoon, a dull, gray day, with a high wind and low hanging clouds. There was no pleasure in going out, so they stayed beside their own cheerful fire all day. The mountain-tops were hidden in the clouds, which seemed to be slipping lower and lower down their rugged sides.

Jack was writing his letter on the table. "I will read it for you when I am done," he said, "and I want you to write too. It is rather nice to have a relative to write to in case of marriage," he said smiling. "I want to show pictures of my lovely Finn girl to someone."

Helmi smiled back at him. Her mind was concerned with the one overwhelming thought that he would have to leave her some day soon. She could not think clearly because of this. Away in the North where there were whirling rapids, deep crevices in the mountains, and horrible roaring canyons; where there were bears and wolves, the possibility of starvation, and blinding storms and lost men going mad with loneliness! . . . Helmi cursed this man, this prospector who had put this wild scheme before her Jack. She wished the lightning had struck him dead. She interrupted Jack's writing. "What is the name of this man you will go with?"

"His name is Keith, Tom Keith. He has his home in Winnipeg, but is seldom there. His wife and family live there on the Crescent."

Helmi's eyes blazed with sudden Finnish anger. Keith—a prospector—gold on the Nehanni! Again she could hear Minnie, poor little Minnie, broken and ashamed, telling her pitiful story. "He said he would stake a claim for me if I would never tell."

"He's a devil—he's a devil and a liar!" Helmi screamed. "I know about Mister Tom Keith!" and she poured out curses in Finnish which made Jack shudder, even though he understood not a word.

"Helmi! Helmi! What is wrong? How do you know this man—where could you know him?"

"I knew Minnie," she said, quite off her guard in her excitement, "the poor little girl he fooled. He's a devil, I tell you and you are not to go with him."

"Come here, little wildcat," Jack laughed; "calm down and tell me what you know. Don't scream like that; Mrs. McMann will think I am beating you. I may have to yet, too—I can see that."

Helmi stood looking at him—she would tell him everything—she must tell him. She had sworn never to tell, but surely when one is married it is different. Jack would keep an oath, too, with her—it would still be kept! Oh, it would be such a relief to tell her dear Jack! He would be sorry for all she had suffered. Yes, she would tell him everything. Her anger was all gone now, and the happy light had come back to her eyes. It would be so good to tell him.

She came over to him and put her arms around him. "Forgive me,

Jack, I am a wild-cat; but it's all for love of you. Have you finished your letter? No! Well, I will wait."

Jack was just writing the address—

Mrs. (Dr.) St. John,

Chestnut St.,

Winnipeg.

"I forget the number," he said, "but everybody knows the Doctor. Now, come, Helmi, and tell me who Minnie is, and where you met her; in fact I want to know a lot of things."

Helmi stood staring at the name, pale with emotion. She choked back a sob by biting her lip until it bled.

"Oh, there is not much to tell," she said, as carelessly as she could with her heart beating so wildly.—"Minnie was a girl who lived in the same house in Winnipeg, and she said this man had said he would do big things for her, and he was just lying. He broke Minnie's heart—he is a bad man Jack—that is all." She did not look at him when she spoke; she was afraid he would read in her face what she must not tell.

Jack could see that Helmi knew far more than she was telling, and a miserable black suspicion, in spite of all his efforts, began to grow in his heart. After thinking the matter over he decided he would not tell his sister in Winnipeg about his marriage. It was just possible that she would remember the name of the girl who had been arrested in the Chinese place, and there was no use in having the matter stirred up again. He kept telling himself there was some mistake about it, and he was not going to let it trouble him. But none of us can quite control the thoughts that come to us. Jack threw his letter into the stove one morning when Helmi was out.

Chapter XVIII

J ack had told Helmi that his partner had stayed in Edmonton to raise money to buy their outfit, which they would ship to Peace River. People were investing their money gladly, and paying five hundred dollars for a claim. Helmi tried to reconcile herself to Jack's going, though she had no faith in the project. In her simple code of ethics, a man who would fool Minnie, taking advantage of her innocence and her poverty, would fool Jack and all the other people who paid him money. He was a bad man, this Keith, and there was no health in him. It was not possible that he could find gold—Why should God let a bad man find gold? But she knew she could not turn Jack aside from his purpose; he would go. That he would be disappointed she feared and in that she was only sorry for him; but he would come back then and settle down at the mines, and they would be happy yet.

All this time Helmi was wondering what Mrs. St. John would do when she got Jack's letter, thinking, of course, that it had been sent. She understood her character well enough not to expect that she would square the matter by a full confession. She would "let it ride," as she so often said about anything that was disagreeable. She always hoped that time would work for her and solve her difficulties. Mrs. St. John would never face a disagreeable situation squarely. As Helmi grew older she grew more resentful of Mrs. St. John and the easy way in which she had stepped from under the responsibility, leaving all the blame on her. Still she was Jack's sister, his only relative, and besides she had sworn by the good words she had learned in God's house not to tell—the same words she had got married by—and they were still more sacred to her now.

Helmi made great progress with her lessons, now that she had no work to do other than her light household duties, which were just fun, and with Jack to help her when his work was done. She could read every word in the Blue Book now.

One day when she came to the place in her speller where girls' names were given, she asked him which one he liked best. Jack replied he did not like any of them very well, for the best name of all, "Helmi," was not among them.

She said she liked Lela the best, but the way she would spell it would be "Lili," the Finnish way. "And which boy's name, Jack?" she queried.

Jack read the names and decided in favor of Charles. Helmi wrote, in her large, clear hand:—

Charles Doran

Lili Doran

Jack looked at her and laughed. "Now, look here, Finn," he said, "we do not want either Charles or Lili for some time yet. Wait till I get the gold, and then we will go to live in Edmonton, and buy a big house in Glenora, and have a Chinaman to do the work, and two maids and a car, and we can have a whole flock, all with fiery gold hair just like yours—Lili and Charlie and Emil and Anna, and we will put up a high board fence around the whole place, so they cannot run away and fall into the river. Do you remember what you said when we were putting in the windows?"

Helmi looked up at him, laughing with something in her face which made him kiss her very tenderly. With her face buried in his shoulder, he did not see the fear in her eyes, the cold, gaunt fear—for the face that she saw was Aunt Lili's, white with death, her great eyes burning, and Aunt Lili was saying: "Men don't want kids—and settle down like we do—they may say they do—but they don't—kids are trouble, men are all for self."

Two days after this the message came for Jack to go. Now that the time had come Helmi was cheerful and brave. She helped him to get ready, squeezing back the tears which were disposed to gather. He was going to leave quietly, letting people think he was just going to the Crossing. The plan was to go by boat on the Peace River as far as they could. Jack's partner knew every inch of the way; and he was so happy and excited Helmi knew he felt just the way she did when the money came from America.

"I will write when I get a chance to send a letter back, it is just possible we may not get a chance after we leave Fort Saint John, but I'll write from the Crossing anyway. Just say to yourself, Helmi, every day, your good words, and be a brave girl. I know you are that. There's two hundred dollars coming to me from the Mines. You can get that if you need it, I did not want to draw out everything and make them suspect I was going for good. For they've been watching me. Every one has his eye on Keith—he's the biggest man in the exploration world in Canada, Helmi!"

Jack was rolling his blankets as he talked. Helmi had his lunch ready, and stood watching him, her heart beating chokingly. There was something she wanted to tell him. Still, why should she worry him now? He had to go—he had promised—and besides, she remembered Aunt Lili's words: "Mike was all right with me until—" . . . No, no, no, she could not take the risk, and maybe it was not so. Jack was so gloriously happy, so confident—she must not worry him. Men cannot bear worry like women.

"Oh, I will be fine, Jack!" she said. "Mrs. McMann is all over her little mad, and she will be glad to have me back again. Her Chinaman made a pudding in the wash-basin, and the men not like it."

"I don't want you to work for her, or for anyone, Helmi. Just make your garden and do what you like. You have plenty to live on, even without the money at the mine."

"Sure," agreed Helmi. "It will be company for me—that's all. I like to work; but every night I will be home here, and I will say my words, and 'God bless Jack and keep him safe'—prayers help a good big lot."

"You're a good kid, Helmi," Jack said, giving her a hurried caress. The excitement of the chase was on him.

Helmi went with him that night over the hill and a mile beyond. Then he insisted on her returning. "It is just as easy to say good-bye here as anywhere," he said.

It was a mellow evening at the end of April. In a pond near by the frogs churred, and all the air was full of nature's awakening. There were strange creepings, rustlings and whisperings around them. It was a night of sweet odors and hushed bird voices.

"It may be a long summer, dear, but it will come to an end, and I think I can safely promise I will be home for Christmas. Don't expect me till you see me. Home for Christmas, with a gold mine for a present! How will that be?"

"I just want you, Jack," Helmi said, holding him in a close embrace.

Mrs. McMann welcomed Helmi's return to the boarding house. The Chinaman's way of muttering under his breath was disquieting to her peace of mind. She believed he was uttering Chinese curses. Helmi baked bread and biscuits, opened windows, scrubbed floors and polished glasses. She worked in a frenzy of energy which soon brought improvement to the disordered boarding house.

Mrs. McMann regarded her curiously. "Helmi is worried over something," she said, "maybe they haven't got along just as well as she thought. Good-lookin' men are notoriously hard to live with. Actors, musicians and preachers are perfect pills when you come to live with them. Well, she can't say I didn't warn her—I am thankful for that!"

Mrs. McMann prided herself on her faculty for eliciting information painlessly, and, as method one, used the familiar device of pretending to know all about the gold find.

"Ain't it wonderful the wealth of this country all hid away from eyes that pry, and yet revealed when people go to the right spot. My! you must be proud of Jack; he's a lucky boy."

They were in the kitchen, Mrs. McMann peeling a tub of potatoes for the evening slaughter, and Helmi dampening clothes for the next day's ironing. The latter lifted her dreamy eyes from the basket of clothes. "Ain't clean clothes beautiful?" she said, "all full of nice smells of good air and sun. I like clean clothes like flowers."

Mrs. McMann regarded her with a puzzled look. "Sometimes I wonder about you, Helmy, dear," she said kindly, "you seem so queer, and hardly all there. You don't seem to hear what people are saying to you—with your dreamy looks and the queer things you say."

"Were you speaking to me, Mrs. McMann?" Helmi asked politely, "I am sorry if I did not answer right. What was it you wanted me to tell you?"

Though outwardly pleased to have Helmi back again, Mrs. McMann's anger burned against the girl because of the fervent expression of joy her return brought from the men. Devout thanksgiving was expressed the first day she was there to wait on the table.

"Helmi at the helm again?" one little Jew cried out. "Don't leave us, Helmi—we missed you so! Don't leave us even if you did get married; we're willing to forgive you anything but desertion." "Gosh, I'm glad to see you," said the time-keeper, a man who seldom spoke.

"See here!" Mrs. McMann broke in, "what's the matter with you all? Didn't I feed you?—darn you! Didn't I sling grub here every day and hire a Chinaman to cook?"

"It's just we're glad to see her back—she's a pretty, young thing, and we like to look at her, Mrs. McMann," said the mine boss, whose special duty it was to keep peace. His wife had gone East and he was taking his meals at the boarding house. "The boys don't mean no harm to you."

Mrs. McMann's eyes narrowed. Helmi's agile movements, her boyishly slim figure, her perfectly rounded face, and the brilliancy of her coloring, gave her the same shock of bitterness the old actress feels when her theatre shakes with applause for the new star. Mrs. McMann, in her young days had "queened" in many a camp, where the youngest woman always travels next the pole. Now, by contrast with Helmi, she was merely a grindy-gray, stout old woman, withered and battered by time, in the sight of the men—and she knew it, and with the thought came a smouldering hatred of the unconscious cause of it.

One day when Helmi came in Mrs. McMann noticed the color of her cheeks was not so brilliant, and her eyes looked heavy and red.

"Frettin', are you Helmy?" she said; "married three months and frettin' already. That's not good—no man is worth frettin' over. By Gosh! I'll bet Jack's not frettin'. If there's a pretty girl in sight, Jack will be sparkin' up to her and makin' her think she's the only girl he ever looked at. Men are all the same—don't I know them! I should, I've had three men already. But I'm done—I wouldn't marry the richest man in the world, not if he went on his bended knees to me."

Mrs. McMann, with her hair in flaring curl papers, dressed in a faded and shrunken old wrapper which had lost some of its buttons in the course of its career, with shoes unlaced and the tongues hanging out, did not look much like the lady who would command abject homage.

Some such thought as this must have shown in Helmi's face, for Mrs. McMann went on. "I was good enough lookin' when I was your age, too, and had lots of fellows crazy about me. I made my first mistake when I got married and began to raise a family. Then I lost my looks and my figure. Lord! ain't the world hard on women. It's just like the potatoes that are planted in the ground—the old one has to die to make a new plant. The old one rots, while the new one springs."

Helmi shuddered.

"That's bad talk," she said hesitatingly. She wished she could have said it in her own language. "God made the world this way. It can't be as bad as you say. Lots of good men there are, and happy women, too, and it's all right for women to have families."

"Oh, you don't say so?" snapped Mrs. McMann. "I suppose the next thing we hear—"

Here the conversation was interrupted by old Sim's arrival. Having slept all day, he had come in for his evening meal, blinking at the light like a bear in the Spring.

Simeon Maskerville was a long, lanky man of uncertain age. His gray beard was tangled and knotted, but his eyes were young still, and, although generally half closed, as if the light hurt them, capable of seeing all that was happening. Simeon had the appearance of a flower that has grown stringy and pale for lack of light, or a potato that has lain in a forgotten corner of the cellar. He fell at once to talking, not wishing to lose any of the precious hours of conversation, remembering that the long night was coming wherein no man would be found to whom he could talk.

"Speakin' o' false teeth," he began, although no one had been speaking of them, "I lost my job with the C.P.R. over mine. I was engineer on the flyer when it happened, and happenin' to sneeze, out they flew into the grass. Just natcherly I stopped the train—Stars! I would have done as much for anyone—no man could do less than stop! and I hops down, for I had marked the place, and I walks right to them, dusted them off on my elbow, and puts them in. It didn't take no time.

But the company was sore. The chief heard of it and calls me in. Words passed that would have been better unsaid. I may have been hasty with the chief—anyway, I went. I often wish I hadn't been so hasty—anyway, I quit. I says to him, I says 'No man can talk that way to me and get by with it.' I spoke easy and gentle, like I always do, but it seemed to cut him to the heart. He just couldn't stand it from me. When I was goin' out, head up, I thought I heard him call. I never turned—maybe I should 'uv—I don't know."

"The C.P.R. seems to have got along all right since you left, Sim," said Mrs. McMann, testily.

"So have I, Mrs. McMann," said Sim, gently, "beautiful—never out of work—always a place for old Sim. I've had to rough it a little sometimes—eatin' at queer joints sometimes—associating with odd sticks here and there—that's the worst; but even at that I manage. I do not mind like some people; memory, my dear Mrs. McMann, of dear, dead days, though forever gone, can be very sweet, and I like to see the happiness of other people. Now here's Helmi and Jack, I'm that happy over those two kids, it seems like it brings all back to me. It was springtime when Martha and me went off and surprised everyone. Springtime in old Ontario, when daft little lambs were springin' up and down on their crooked little legs, and the air was full of that blue haze that trails on the trees like rags and the frogs in the ponds were saying 'Is tomorrow come yet?' You know the story, don't you, Mrs. McMann, of how the frogs was coaxed to go in for one day to the pond, and promised they would sure get out tomorrow?"

"Oh, shut up, Sim, and eat your supper—I can't be bothered to listen to you."

Helmi looked up quickly. "I like Sim's talk," she said, "he says good words."

"He's just an old plaster, Helmy, and would rather talk than eat if he can get anyone to listen to him. He's like the canal-boat back home—the engine always had to stop when the whistle blew—that's Sim."

"But I like it," Helmi said again; "He talks kind. Tell me about the frogs, Sim."

"Some day I'll come to see you, an' I'll tell you, Helmi." Sim spoke with dignity now. He had been assailed professionally and could not recover all at once.

"He's trying to bum a meal, Helmy," said Mrs. McMann brutally; "I know him."

"Come on Sunday for dinner with me, Sim, and then you can tell me."

Sim nodded gratefully.

"It is the long black nights, Helmi, black without a star, silent, empty, not a voice, not even a dog-bark. I have been a night-watchman for ten years—no wonder I have a cravin' for voices and friends. Yes, I will come, Helmi, and thank you for being so kind."

Helmi's heart grew tender as she thought of the lonely old man sitting alone in the long dark night, stark with silence; for although she had been only two weeks alone, she knew what loneliness and fear a night can hold when one lies open-eyed, staring into the black unanswering depths, wondering, wondering. One can imagine such terrible things of lost men in trackless wildernesses. And Christmas seemed so far away!

Chapter XIX

 One day in August, when the train came in, the conductor ran into the station and shouted to the operator, "Say Ted, there's a war in Europe! What do you know about that?"

Ted took his pipe from his mouth and spat at the red stove. "Quit your kiddin'," he said briefly.

The conductor handed him the paper. "What do you make of that?" he said, as he pointed to the staring headlines. "Maybe you'll believe me when you read that?"

The operator grudgingly admitted that there seemed to be more in it than he had at first believed. "Well, what's it all about?" he asked the conductor; "whose row is it anyway?"

The conductor tried to explain.

"'Tain't any of our business, is it, if someone shoots an arch-duke," said the operator. "Isn't it about all some of these arch-dukes is good for? Are they scarce of them?"

He was dusting off his desk with a large red handkerchief as he spoke, and that was a sure sign of mental activity.

"It looks bad, Ted," the conductor said, gravely; "there's lots of excitement in town—fellows joining up, bands playing and all. I know some of the boys that are just itching to go, but I assure you it isn't me. Well, so long, Ted; I guess we should worry—it's a long way from Northern Alberta."

Old Sim, the night watchman, took it more seriously than anyone in Eagle Mines. "Wars," he said to Helmi and Mrs. McMann when he came in for his supper that night "is inevitable. That's a big word, Helmi, and means can't be helped. They come ever so often, and kill a lot of people and maim and hurt a lot, make a lot of debt and trouble. Everyone in the war loses—no one wins—everyone blames someone else. No one knows for sure what it is about, but just while it is on no one cares. To these here fightin' men any war is better than no war. Then it gets done when everyone is dead or lame or blind or tired enough to talk sense, and the world tries to pay the debts, builds up the burnt cities, gets the sick fellows well, buys crutches for the one-legged men and glass eyes for the blind and provides for the widows and orphants! And then there's great councils and meetin's to find out who started the darn thing, and maybe they find out it was some stranger that no one ever knew was there at the time."

"The war I was in," Sim continued, "was started by the sinkin' of a big boat called the 'Maine,' and we was told to keep on saying 'Remember the Maine,' if ever we got chicken-hearted or soft toward the enemy, or tired, or homesick, or down in the mouth. That was to be what they called our slogan, and we stuck to it pretty well. It shook me up quite a lot the day I lost my leg—my best one it was, too—but ain't that always the way? I didn't do much remembering of the Maine that day. But dash it all! didn't they find out later that it wasn't the Spaniards at all that sunk the ship? There was great explanation and beg-your-pardons and excuses and after-you-sir, but no legs handed back at least not as came as far down as the privates. But that's war, Helmi."

"Do men have to go?" asked Helmi, with a sudden whitening of her face—"men like Jack, I mean—good men who don't want to kill?"

Helmi was getting the tables ready for the morning. Old Sim was always the last occupant of the dining-room.

"They do and they don't," replied the old man, cautiously, "The law don't make them, but you just can't stay when everyone is lookin' at you as if you ought to be there. I wasn't fussy about war—there's too much killin' in it for me. If it could be done by arguing I'd like it fine, but this thing o' contradictin' a man by runnin' a spear into him looks coarse and clumsy. Now that young Jack of yours, he wouldn't like killin' any better than I would, but I know how he'd feel. They get great meetin's and crowds and play bands, and by Gosh! when the bands played 'Dixie Land' or 'Marchin' through Georgia,' I never cared whether I got killed or not, and Spaniards wuz just like pizen bugs to me—that was just while the band with playin', though I always came to when it stopped."

"It is all wicked bad to me," said Helmi, as she held the dustpan with one hand and swept with the other; "I wish Jack would come home. I am afraid, Sim."

"War is hell on women," said the old man; "but it don't do no good to worry, Helmi."

"But it is far away, Sim—miles and miles of water—all gray and far! Oh, it's a long way! Why should we send our men to fight? We won't; it's the Old Country's fight—not Canada's."

It was a long speech for Helmi to make, and she had to stop her sweeping to do it.

"Anyway, Jack is safe up there on the Nehanni—he will not hear of it until it's over maybe," said Sim.

Helmi looked at him gratefully. "Will you have tea or coffee tonight in shiny bottle?" she said.

Eagle Mines, composed largely of Americans, was not greatly disturbed by the war. The mine boss, although a Canadian, expressed the general view when he said, "Let the people who started this thing finish it. It's not our funeral. We'll keep our heads down and mine coal—that's our business."

The men heartily concurred in this, and when the price of coal went up, and their wages had a corresponding increase, they were not disposed to quarrel with the cause.

"Good old war," said Peter Hamilton, the time-keeper, as he counted out the men's money at the end of October; "Long may she wave."

The first disturbing glimpse that the residents of Eagle Mines had, was the coming of an English homesteader from up the river. He was but slightly known to the people because he came in only twice a year to buy his supplies, and never lingered for a friendly chat like other people, and therefore was not liked by the few people who had seen him. Their diagnosis of his case was that he was just a little off. A man who lives alone, raises dogs, takes pictures, gets no mail, and talks to no one except when it cannot be avoided, has no right to expect that people will consider him a sane person. The residents of Eagle Mines when referring to him at all called him, "the crazy Englishman."

It was a dull gray day in early November that he came to town and drew up in front of Simpson's store. He sprang out of his buckboard and ran into the store excitedly. "The Empire is at war!" he shouted; "Did you know it? A man passing by my place showed me the paper. Did you know it? Why didn't you send me word?"

Jim Simpson wrinkled his nose. "How did I know you cared?" he asked, replacing a prune which had fallen to the floor.

The other man raised his voice almost to a shout. "Cared? Cared? Don't you know what it means? It's my country—your country—it's threatened—everyone cares."

"Well, I don't," said the storekeeper, positively; "she got into this without askin' me, and she kin git out the same way."

The Englishman stood speechless. Could it be that any man living in the Empire on which the sun never sets could utter such words and live? Something of the benumbed amazement which fell on Rip Van Winkle when he returned to find good King George gone, and no one sorry but himself, fell on him. Could it be that—but no, that was impossible. The Empire would endure as long as the sun held to its course.

The Englishman had been a resident of the neighborhood for over fifteen years. Long before the opening of the mines he had come and squatted on a piece of land in another fertile valley about eight miles further up the river, going in on foot with all his possessions, a gun on his back and a dog at his heels. Beside the crooked little stream (called English River, in compliment to him) he built a shelter of boughs and began to cultivate a piece of land for his garden with a wooden hoe of his own making. He had told the people at Bannerman, which was the nearest settlement, that any man should be able to wrest a living from the soil if he had a dog for company, an axe, a gun and a few seeds.

His house of branches was replaced by a little log shanty, with a home-made fireplace built of stones from the river, and into it he moved before winter. In the spring he returned to civilization with his season's catch of furs. After that his victory was assured, and if he had been more sociable and friendly he would have received the admiration of the settlement at Bannerman. As it was he did his trading almost silently, volunteering no explanation of his strange ways; and no man can gain the confidence of his fellow men unless he is willing to explain himself.

The year before the war, the Englishman had built a shingled bungalow, with glassed-in verandah, and hardwood floors. He had built-in cupboards and furnished it in such a manner that many a man living in the settlement was subject to drastic questioning by the wife of his bosom, who drew pointed comparisons between the house she was forced to live in and this one. Why was it that a crazy Englishman who lived alone but for his dogs, could afford such luxuries as these, while whole families were still living in congested quarters? Matters grew still more unpleasant when it was rumored that he was going to pipe the water from a lake in the mountains to his house.

The only explanation the harrassed husbands could think of, and it did not entirely satisfy, was that the man must be receiving money from home. No man could do all this on his fur catches.

It was Bill Larsen, the Swede, who conceived the idea of visiting this new house, and to this end organized a fishing party one Sunday morning in the spring of the year. English River abounded in mountain trout, and it was easy to get a party together to go out. They could ask permission to boil a kettle and in that way get in to see the house.

The party came back late that night registering complete success. He had not only asked them to come in, but had cooked a meal for them—roast chicken, canned figs for dessert, white cloth and everything.

"Did he ask you all to come again when you couldn't stay so long, or anything like that?" asked Jim Simpson, incredulously. Jim had opposed the fishing party.

"He doesn't need to ask us back when he fed us that well. We'll go all right—eh, boys?" replied Bill; "vittles like that speak for themselves—we're goin' next Sunday again. Gosh, Jim, you better come—he's tickled to see us, I believe. He's not quite all there—anyone can see that, he's so polite and ladylike—and we might as well punch a meal ticket on him as not."

The parties continued for several weeks, growing in number, and never did the hospitality fail. Fried lake trout, home-made bread and butter, eggs, and wild fruit were plentifully supplied and eagerly consumed.

"Gee! that fellow is easy," Bill Larsen was often heard to say; "he seems pleased to do it, and never seems to mind that none of us offers to help him clean up or anything. Well, some people like work, and I'm not the one to try to deny their fun. He don't even know when we're laughing at him!"

The next Sunday their host was as generous as ever, but when the meal was half over, apologized for his haste in clearing the table.

Usually he waited until his guests were gone, but today he was going out and if they would be so kind as to excuse him he would proceed to wash up while they were eating their dessert, which on this day was wild strawberry pie. The visitors winked at each other behind his back. Think of any human being asking leave to wash his own dishes! "Oh, sure they would excuse him providing he didn't rattle the dishes too much and disturb the speakers." This was from the barber, who was the humorist of the party.

Even at that their host politely replied that he would be most careful. He then gathered up the plates and laid them in a row on the sun porch, his visitors watching him with interest. They were in a radiant mood. This fellow grew funnier all the time. What funny work was he up to now?

The Englishman opened the verandah door and called. Four collie dogs came bounding in. He motioned to them to begin operations on the plates, which they did with eagerness. When they had made a thorough job of cleaning them he gathered up the plates deliberately and arranged them in one of his many cupboards.

"They save me a lot of work," he said, more to himself than to his guests, on whom a silence had fallen; "and they polish the plates very well indeed, and the pots and pans as well."

There was an understanding on the way home that no reason would be given for discontinuing the visits.

"Now, boys," said the barber, "that's what might be called tact. He didn't tell us we had worn out our welcome—just intimated it. I kinda wish he had waited until we had finished that pie! Wild strawberry pie! I never thought anything could turn me from wild strawberry pie. That fellow is not such a fool, after all."

"Well, I am going," said the Englishman to Jim Simpson; "I am going today. My only regret is that I did not know sooner. Will you buy my horses—the whole outfit as it stands?"

"What did you do with your fine house and all that furniture?" asked Mr. Simpson, cautiously.

"Left it—left it—locked the door and came out. Gave one dog away—shot the others. I couldn't shoot old Cleo, I tried but I couldn't."

"Good Lord, man, you're crazy! Them were dandy dogs! What in thunder did you want to shoot them for—I thought you were a real dog man."

"No one will ever abuse my dogs. I wanted to be sure, that's why. I gave the Ransoms a horse, and they promised to care for Cleo as long as she lives. What will you give me for the horses? Be quick now!" He had no time to argue—he going on the train that day.

"One hundred dollars for the whole thing," said one of the men.

"Very well," said the Englishman, "I'll take it. Be good to them."

He went to the boarding house for dinner, where he was the centre of curious eyes, for the story of his wild intention was known. When he had eaten a hasty meal he stood up suddenly and broke into speech.

"Boys, you are wrong," he began, "in going on mining coal and thinking you do not need to hear the call your country has sent out. The British Empire is threatened, her enemies are at the gates. Belgium, a little country, has been violated. While you sit here, villages are burning, women are screaming—and the Germans are marching triumphantly on. Have you no pride, no manhood? . . . I know the Germans . . . they have been getting ready for years. Lord Roberts told the Empire to get ready—it was coming—but they went on like you—'business as usual'!"

He paused here, overcome with emotion. One or two of the men laughed, the others regarded him stolidly. Crazy Englishman! Crazier than ever!

"Well, say, looka here," began Bill Larsen, "what are you gettin' so het up over, I'd like to know." Bill, although the proprietor of the "Grand Pacific," a hostel licensed to sell malt and spirituous liquor, and presumably a place of refreshment for man and beast, made no pretence of supplying meals even for himself, but took the monthly rate from Mrs. McMann. "What's bitin' you? Go yourself if you want to—who's holdin' you back?—but what's the call for abusin' us because we don't want to stand up and stop bullets. My old granddad fought in the American war, and he got his fill of it, I'll say!—lost an eye and a leg, and got four dollars a month of a pension from his grateful country! It don't look like a safe proposition. How do you know who's right? Your British Empire wasn't so darned right when she had the little run-in with the United States. How do you know she's right this time?"

The Englishman stretched out his arms dramatically. His voice quivered like a violin string. "The British Empire is my country," he said; "I was born beneath the British flag, and so were my people for generations back. I love it. The British Empire is in trouble and has called. I do not reason, I go. It's like your mother calling—would you wait to question if your mother called? If you knew your mother was attacked by a bully would you hang back to see first if she had been to blame in any way—would you? My mother couldn't be wrong—not to me. That's what I mean."

Helmi was coming in from the kitchen with the dessert on her big tray. She paused, arrested by the strange voice speaking with such terrible earnestness.

Bill Larsen had not stopped eating. Empires might rise or fall, but Bill believed in getting his "vittles" while they were hot. "Well no," he said, "I can't say as I feel that way toward any country. It's a case of show me—I'm from Missouri, first, last and all the time."

Helmi watched the Englishman's face. He was staring helplessly at the complacent big giant before him, who serenely buttered a slice of bread on his broad palm as he spoke.

"I ain't so fussy over your old British Empire, anyway," added Bill; "I don't know but I'd just as soon see Germany win."

Arthur Warner, walked over to where Bill sat. His face was very white and his eyes very dark. Helmi knew just what was going to happen.

"You cannot insult my country in my presence," he said quietly, and slapped the Swede's face with his open hand.

With a hoarse oath Bill sprang from the table.

Helmi screamed and darted forward, but the Swede's closed fist had already landed with smashing force on the Englishman's face, sending him reeling to the floor.

It was Helmi who was first beside him. "Oh, you big stiff, Bill Larsen," she cried, indignantly, "he only gave you a little slap, but you smash at him like a kicking horse. You're a big bum, Bill Larsen, that's all you are! Maybe you've killed this man, and he's a good man, ready to fight for women and children."

The men were gathered in a knot around the injured man, who lay very white and still, his head resting on Helmi's knee.

"Bring me water!" she cried, "and stand back."

Bill Larsen sauntered out jauntily, biting a disk from his plug of chewing tobacco. "No man can slap my face and feel as good as ever right after," he said. "Damn him and his British Empire."

Mrs. McMann was diplomatic. Bill Larsen was a boarder, regular and sure, paid in advance. Besides, he came from the States, and from Nebraska. "Bill, maybe, is too tonguey," she said, "'but sticks and stones may break your bones, but calling names won't hurt you.' The English man struck the first blow, so he will have to take what's comin'."

Arthur Warner certainly did not seem disposed to resist as he lay limp and bleeding, his eyes closed, one arm hanging lifeless.

"He'll never never make a soldier if he folds up like that with one knock," said Mrs. McMann scornfully.

"Big Bill hits too hard," said Helmi, bathing the pallid face. "Mr. English only hit a little slap."

The men had gone back to the table, helping themselves from the blue coffee pot on the stove outside. They were satisfied that the Englishman was not seriously hurt. Fights were too common to attract very much attention, particularly at meal-time.

"Well, here's a pretty how-do-you-do, I'll say," said Mrs. McMann, as she began to carry out the dishes. "Let the police hear of this and it gives the house a bad name. And who's to look after the fellow now, supposin' Bill has knocked him cuckoo! I guess maybe he didn't have far to go, but that won't make it any easier for Bill."

Bill had come back to the scene of his triumph and now stood leaning against the kitchen door, smoking a tranquil pipe. "Me?" he queried, "Don't worry about me—I always bury my dead!" Bill laughed a little nervously, not feeling quite so unconcerned as he appeared. The face of the Englishman was so corpse-like.

"Well, he can't stay here," said Mrs. McMann, decidedly; "I am providin' meals and beds, but only for well people. This is no 'ospital."

"He can come to my house," said Helmi, "he is a brave man, ready to fight for Canada, and I will take care of him and be glad to do it. He is not a coward, like Big Bill Larsen, who hits like a kicking mule."

"You chuck that gab, Helmy," said Mrs. McMann severely; "it ain't your place to interfere in gentlemen's politics, anyway."

Big Bill regarded Helmi with an angry eye. "Turning against your own country, eh, Helmi," he said to her in Finnish, "you turned me down for Jack Doran, that didn't take long to get tired of you and quit, and now I see you've turned against your own country."

"Canada is my country," Helmi replied, with flashing eyes, "and I would fight for it if I could. I wouldn't hang back like a big coward."

Arthur Warner was not able to leave on the train that day, nor for a week, during which time he was carefully nursed by Helmi and old Sim, the night-watchman.

Mrs. McMann discussed the matter in its social aspect with her boarders. "Helmi is a queer girl, but she's goin' to get herself talked about this time, takin' a strange man into her house when her own man is away. I told her—I've warned her all along—but do you think she'd listen? Her and Old Sim are hand in glove, and no one can tell them anything. She says it's her duty to care for a soldier who is goin' out to die for all of us. Well, he don't need to die for me—I'm an American citizen, and I guess Old Glory will always protect me. I wonder what Jack Doran would say if he came home right now? If I know men, and I certainly should, a thing like this will take a lot of explainin'. Poor Mr. McMann would have shot any man whom he found in his house like this. He was so impulsive where I was concerned. He didn't even like to have me left alone with the ice-man. I told him it was nonsense, but nothing could change him!"

But Helmi and her guest were not concerned over public opinion. Strangely enough, neither of them had thought about it. The doctor from Bannerman had set the broken arm, and advised him to lie still until the dizziness in his head had gone.

The time passed pleasantly for Helmi. She was glad to have someone to care for, and "Mr. English," as she called him, was so grateful. When he tried to pay her Helmi firmly refused to accept anything. "You are a good man," she said, "leaving everything to go to fight for us. I am glad to help you. I wish I could do more."

It came to the last day, and Arthur Warner was sitting in the rocking-chair watching Helmi as she packed his valise. She had taken out his things, washed his shirts and socks, mended them, and pressed his clothes. "By Jove, Helmi!" he said, in admiration, "you are a born nurse, so quiet and capable. They are calling for nurses over there—can't you come along? I have lots of friends there who haven't forgotten me, I am sure, and they would get you in. You are too smart a girl to be just a waitress."

Helmi held up a little garment which she had been making, and quite frankly told him why it was impossible for her to go.

The Englishman apologized humbly.

"Oh, no," said Helmi, "it's all right; I do not mind telling you. No one here knows yet, but I am not sad about it. I am glad, I am only sad about Jack being away."

"I love what you said about your mother," said Helmi after an interval of silence. "You would fight for her even if she were wrong. No, she couldn't be wrong to you. That is a lovely thing. Do all men feel like that? I would like to have a son who would feel like that for me."

"I think all decent men do feel that way," Warner said simply.

It was strange for Arthur Warner, after all his lonely years, to be sitting here talking so intimately to a woman who was a comparative stranger, and receiving from her confidences which she had given to no one else. He thought of his own lonely house—so precious to him, so eagerly acquired, so patiently worked for—how a woman like this would have brightened it and graced it with her presence. She was so calm, so brave, so gentle.

When their eyes met Helmi smiled encouragingly at him, though sadly too, as if the tears were not very far away. Were they tears because he was going?

"Helmi," he said, "we are both facing the elemental things of life, and it draws us together. We are facing the hardest things that men and women ever have to face. Your part will be to give life, maybe at the expense of your own. Mine is—God forgive me—to take life. Are you afraid?"

Helmi shook her head. "No," she said, simply, "I believe in God,— I believe He loves me. I love Him. Every day I say my good words. I learned them in His house. They are, 'Cherish health; Seek truth; Know God; Serve others.' Then I say, 'Please God, bring home my Jack.' It is good to pray, Mr. English, when one is afraid."

The first ragged whistle of the train came booming down the valley. "Tell me your name Helmi," he said, "I want to say good words for you and for your Jack."

Helmi took his hand and impulsively kissed it. "Helmi Doran," she said. "I am glad you will say good words for my Jack. Maybe you will see him over there—I know he will go."

"I hope for your sake that it will all be over when Jack comes home at Christmas."

He was standing up now with his cap in his hand. The train was whistling again as it came slowly down the grade. Helmi looked at him reverently. It was not merely a lonely, weather-beaten homesteader she saw standing before her; she saw a brave man who was willing to give everything he possessed, not withholding his own life for the cause of human liberty, and on his face she saw the unmistakable majesty which comes to those who are appointed to die.

Arthur Warner bent over and kissed her shining hair. "Good-bye, dear Helmi," he said.

"Good-bye, God bless you, dear Mr. English!"

When Arthur went out he met Mrs. McMann coming in. She had come presumably to ask Helmi what she had done with the tape-line.

Chapter XX

It was in December that Helmi decided to delay no longer, she would go to the city. Jack had told her to go to his mine boss and get the two hundred dollars which was due on his wages. She had not needed it until now, and had felt it best to leave it where it was. She had hoped her Jack would be home to her before this, and then he could go himself. Helmi had earned seventy-five dollars from Mrs. McMann, too, and she had often imagined the proud look which would come to Jack when she would show him the fifteen five-dollar bills in the pocket of her black valise. Helmi knew what she was going to buy with it, too. Had she not marked things in the catalogue? But the days had worn wearily on and there had been no word. It was often hard to keep from crying, but it must be all right—God would not let dear Jack be lost.

The Blue Book was a comfort, too. It was so full of happiness. The Blue Book was sure everything would come out right. She wondered if the people who wrote the Blue Book ever had their men go away so far and stay so long. She had found the Blue Book was right in what it said about gardens. It said a garden links one with God. Helmi had been happiest in her little garden, every sod of which she had turned herself. In the summer evenings she had worked there until it was so dark she could not see, and never did sad thoughts come to her then.

Helmi took it as a sure sign that God was pleased with her when her plants grew so beautifully and the hail-storm which broke windows in some of the houses did not touch her garden at all. Helmi was proud of her garden, too, because it was the first garden in Eagle Mines, and also because the women said nothing would grow. In that way her head-lettuce, radishes, onions, cabbage, carrots, and beets were something of a triumph. But best of all was the square in the middle, where stocks and asters and nasturtiums grew. Every day there were bouquets from her garden on the tables at the boarding-house, and although they were nothing like the flowers which Mrs. McMann herself had grown in Lincoln, Nebraska, either in color, size or perfume, yet even Mrs. McMann admitted they were very nice flowers as flowers go in Canada. Helmi did not mind what Mrs. McMann said. She and the mountains knew they were wonderful flowers. The mountains had looked down upon her so kindly all summer, she knew they were pleased.

There was no dearth of praise among the men, who were glad to have fresh instead of canned vegetables for their meals, and twenty-four dollars was the sum Helmi had in the pocket of her black valise to prove that her garden had been a success. Even after the vegetables were done the asters and stocks flared and bloomed, and Helmi hoped that by some chance Jack would come in time to see too. They seemed to grow more showy and brilliant as the night frost drew nearer and nearer. But one night, while she slept, the frost slipped down the mountain, without a sound, and laid low every stalk and every bloom in her garden, and having done its work went back the way it came. The morning sky was blue and bright, the sun was warm, and playful little breezes turned the dead flowers over, just to be sure that none were missed. When Helmi came out and saw the work of the night she wrung her hands—but only for a minute. That day she raked the dead stalks into a pile, and she burned them when they were dry and dug the garden for her next year's planting.

Helmi had not yet brought herself to ask for the two hundred dollars Jack had left. She wished the timekeeper would give it to her without asking for it, but the days wore on and she knew she must go soon. She would not let Mrs. McMann or anyone think she was grieving or distressed. Jack had told her that the greatest thing in married life was to trust and not be afraid, so she affected a gaiety she did not feel, which quite deceived the "elite" lady.

"These foreigners haven't got any fine feelings," Mrs. McMann told her friend Mrs. Turner. "Now one would think Helmi would feel a little shy, but pass her house any time you like and you can hear her singing, and as long as the days were nice she was either working in the garden or sitting outside sewing. And mind you, she went into the store and asked for white flannel from Jim Dawson—Mrs. Dawson told me. Well, of course, one can't expect much from these foreigners, their standards have never been like ours. Mr. McMann often told me I was too shy, but it was the proud Weekes way!"

Helmi waited until the middle of the month. Still no letter, no word. There was no use going to the post-office. The same answer was inevitable—"Nothing today." She could hear it all the time, beating, beating on a sore spot in her heart. But always she had been able to smile and say something, words she had prepared on the way down.

One day she went to the stuffy little mine office and spoke to the timekeeper about the wages Jack had not taken. The timekeeper sat in his shirt-sleeves making out his accounts. The place reeked of stale tobacco, and dust lay gray on the window-sill. Quite frankly Helmi explained her reason for going to the city.

The timekeeper looked confused and embarrassed. "I'm awful sorry, Helmi," he said, "but it looks as if there has been a mistake here some place. There was two hundred dollars owing to Jack when he left, but a man came one day with an order from Jack and I gave him the money. He said when Jack got to Peace River he found there were some things he needed. It was about a week after Jack left, if I remember—I have the order here, if you would like to see it. You see, I didn't know you would be wantin' it, or anything, or I would have refused this fellow, but he had the order and I couldn't very well do anything but pay the money over."

The nausea that came over Helmi made her sway uncertainly, but she caught the back of a chair and managed to say, "Oh! it is all right; Jack left me lots of money; I really do not need it. I just thought I had better take it with me." She was holding her lips very tightly so they would not tremble. She even smiled, winking very quickly to keep the tears back. "I expect to meet Jack in the city," she resumed. "He has just forgotten to mention to me that he sent for the money—but it is quite all right. I have plenty. Good-bye, Mr. Hamilton. It looks like snow, does it not?"

Helmi turned away quickly. The timekeeper called her back. "Say, Helmi," he began, awkwardly, "don't think I am buttin' in or the like of that, but I just wanted to put you wise. That old bird of a magistrate at Bannerman has been shootin' off his mouth. It seems he claims he knows a lot about you. He says—Oh, well, I don't need to repeat what he says—he is drunk most of the time, and nobody should mind a word he says; but he declares you and Jack ain't legally married at all, and he insinuates that Jack sort o' tipped him off. Oh, I don't know the ins and outs of it, but I just wanted to warn you to hang onto your certificate, and then in case of a frame-up you have the deadwood on them all. You have the certificate, have you not?"

Helmi nodded, her heart was beating in her throat so painfully she was afraid he would see it.

"Well, then, you're all to the good. But I just thought I would wisen you up on what was goin' round. We're all for you, Helmi—you know that!"

Helmi thanked him without knowing what she was saying, and got out of the office some way. The little street of houses seemed to be all eyes; all red-lidded eyes, staring and pointing at her; voices whispering and mocking. The mountains were closing in on her as if they would gladly grind her to powder, and the river—the river was the worst of all as it ran slithering by so green and deep and cold. A man had drowned himself at one of the other mines last week because his wife had taken his money and run away, and now Helmi knew that wasn't the reason at all—it was because the river had taunted him so, and mocked him, and dared him, and driven him to it.

Helmi reached her own house, and, going in, shut and locked the door. She must think! A basin of water stood on the box. She buried her hot face in it to try to stop the tears that were burning in her eyes. The heart-beat in her throat seemed to choke her.

"Oh, Aunt Lili! Aunt Lili!"

But it could not be. Her Jack Doran was a good man. God was good. She sought the Blue Book anxiously;

> "Oh! to be a girl and see
> Beauty in flower and bird and tree;
> To pass through, strong and pure and good,
> The gate which leads to womanhood."

She read it all with a heart that grew heavier and heavier. It was not for her at all. She was no longer a girl. She was a woman, with a woman's heartache, old as the world, black as night, and deep as the deepest sea.

And with all the hosts of heaven and all the ministering angels around the throne, there was no eye to pity and no arm to save—not one.

Yes, there was one. A dog whimpered at her door, and instinctively Helmi arose to let it in. A very thin and wistful looking sable collie, with a chewed rope hanging from her collar, entered timidly. It was the dog that Arthur Warner had given away and that had been kept tied up by her new owner, in the hope she would forget her old master.

Today she had made her escape and found her way to Helmi's door, demanding by her eager looks to know where her master was. Helmi tried to explain in both languages, but in vain. Then she offered her food, which she refused, still begging Helmi to tell her the truth.

The collie made no response to Helmi's attempts to comfort her, and having convinced herself that her master was not in this house, she asked only one thing, her freedom. She would take to the open road again. She would be on her way. Helmi knowing what was in her heart, and the hopelessness of the quest, endeavored to keep her, but she knew she was hating her for holding her back from her only chance. At last, with her heart sore for the dog's trouble, as well as her own, she tied a thick piece of bacon to her collar, knowing she would break the string with her paws when she wanted to, then opened the door and let her go. She ran straight to the station, whimpering excitedly. From there she ran yelping down the track with her nose to the ties.

Helmi watched the poor animal until a bend of the road hid her from sight. Then she turned back into the darkening room sobbing, "Poor dog! poor dog!—just like me, forsaken. Men who go away should shoot all of us who love them!"

Helmi hired a horse and buggy the next day and drove down the valley to Bannerman. She would know all there was to be known. She would find out what the magistrate meant.

It was a glorious day of blue sky, with a high wind that came booming through the pass in the mountain, roughening the deep pools of the river as it rasped over them. Helmi loved its cool breath on her hot face. She could not be cast down on such a day. Her Jack had not fooled her—no matter what any one thought. Helmi told herself again and again that her great fear was that something had happened to him— her dear Jack, so white-skinned, clean and gentle.

Anyway, she would be brave. Next day was train day, too, and he might come. Twice a week the train came down to Eagle Mines from the main line. Helmi had so often watched it coming in, her heart in her mouth, that she had grown to dread train days, for during the last few months at the first ragged whistle that came wearily piercing the valley a violent nausea had seized her. As she now drew near her destination it came again. She thought of the Wymuths and their awful philosophy. Was all this part of her punishment? Was it all wrong? Had she done wrong? But still, everyone who was in the world had come the same way. Surely God wanted people, and yet, why did he punish women so? She sat still a while, letting the horse feed along the side of the trail.

The magistrate was at home. No, he did not remember her. Helmi Milander, a Finn girl, whom he had married to Jack Doran last March? No he did not remember. He and his friend, Major Gowsett, looked at each other. The magistrate winked knowingly. "I think you are mistaken, girl," he said, sternly.

Helmi handed him her certificate. "You gave me this paper," she said.

The magistrate addressed his friend. "There's only one way to settle this, I'll look up the record. If I married her to this young man the record will show. A certificate tells nothing. Anyone can buy a certificate and fill it in."

He went to a dusty cupboard, whose open door revealed only a row of bottles, brown, with gold labels, gleaming evilly through the gloom of the room. With difficulty he found his record book and spread it before him on the littered table.

"You said March of this year?"

"March the twenty-first," said Helmi, breathing quickly.

The pages were turned slowly.

"I married no one on March the twenty-first," he said, looking around at her over his glasses.

"Look at other dates, then," said Helmi, trembling; "I may be wrong."

The two military men regarded her closely. "You are wrong more ways than one," said the magistrate, slowly. "Look—see for yourself—there is no entry of any marriage."

A sudden fury came over Helmi. "You were drunk that day," she cried. "You were red-eyed and staggering! You forgot to write it down. You sent me out. You spoke to my Jack here while I sat outside. You mind I said 'Come outside to marry us.' You were cross and swore."

Major Gowsett interposed. "Hush, girl," he said, "you must remember Col. Blackwood is a magistrate. Your condition makes you hysterical. We're sorry for you, but you must not speak like this."

Col. Blackwood said not a word. He went again to the cupboard, and after fumbling among the papers there brought back a newspaper slightly yellowed. "I'll show you something, you hellcat," he said, slowly, taking his pipe from his mouth and laying it carefully on the window-sill.

"Do you think I would marry you to a decent boy—a boy of good family—who was foolish enough to think of marrying a foreigner of whom he knew nothing, and of whom the police knew considerable? Look!"

Helmi leaned over and scanned the paper. Her own picture stared at her. For a moment she forgot everything but the pleasant memories it brought to mind of Miss Abbie's house and its kindly shelter. The picture was taken in front of the house; she had worn her white middy and pleated skirt. She remembered now that Mrs. Wymuth had asked for a photo—it was one of the rules of the Home.

"Helmi Milander, young Finnish girl who escaped from the Girls' Friendly Home. Arrested here a year ago in the worst Chinese den in the city." Helmi reeled, and would have fallen had not Major Gowsett sprang to her assistance and placed her in a chair.

"Do you deny this?" asked the Magistrate, when he thought she was sufficiently recovered to speak.

"No," said Helmi, faintly; "that's my picture, but it's all a lie."

"Of course, they all say that."

"Well, at least you can understand that I was not anxious to marry you to young Doran or any decent man. You have a record, you see, and every magistrate in Canada has a copy of this."

"Did Jack see this?" Helmi asked after a pause.

"Yes, I showed it to him while you sat outside," said the magistrate, "but he told me to go on. Like every other young fellow he wanted his own way. But now I advise you not to try to make trouble. You have no claim on him—remember that—and he's gone away, I hear, for good. You'd better go straight back to this Home that you ran away from. No doubt they will help you through again. I understand many of their girls come back two and three times. In fact," he said turning to his friend, "that is one great objection to these Rescue Homes—they make things far too easy for girls of this class."

Helmi was staring past them vacantly. The pallor of her face was deepening.

"Now, look here," said the magistrate, sharply, "no tricks, no faints. You're an old hand at this, although you are not old in years, and you can't make me believe you are an innocent young thing who has been deeply wronged. You're well able to look after yourself."

Helmi arose uncertainly. She reached out her hand for the certificate she had given him.

"This is no good," he said, "you may as well leave it here."

"Give it to me," cried Helmi, with some of her old fury, snatching it from his hand.

"Take it then, you tiger," he said, angrily. "It's no good to you. Take it and get out of here! I am not running a Girls' Friendly Home here."

Helmi opened her purse to replace the paper, and as she did so a card dropped out. She stooped and picked it up. It was a white card bordered with maple leaves, and in the centre were printed these words: "Welcome to Canada!"

The sight of the card brought Helmi back to the night she had got it. It was her place-card the night the girls gave her the party. They were good to her and would be sorry for all this trouble which had come to her. This man who had caused her so much harm would suffer for it. Canada was all right. God was all right. This man was a devil. In a moment all her faintness was gone, succeeded by burning rage.

The two men watched her uneasily. There was something terrible in her anger. She walked over to the table and stood in front of Col. Blackwood. "You are a bad man," she said. "A devil—an old dirty, drunken devil. I hate you, and I will kill you. If my man does not come back to me I will kill you." Her voice was low, but it filled all the room. "It will be your fault, and I will come back here and kill you."

Before either of the men could recover from the shock she was gone.

When Helmi drove into the yard at the Boarding-House old Sim, who had been watching for her, came to take her horse. Mrs. McMann came out, too, and the timekeeper, and the mine boss. They had been talking it over.

Helmi stepped out of the buggy and stood leaning against the wheel. Her face was white and lined, and her big eyes were feverish.

"Well, Helmi, what about it?" said Mrs. McMann, who could bear the suspense no longer. "What about it?"

"It is not in the book," said Helmi, wearily. "He says we are not married at all. He says Jack was fooling me. He is an old devil, that magistrate."

"Tough luck, Helmi," said the mine boss, "But we all know it wasn't your fault. He fooled you—that's all."

Mrs. McMann found her tongue—never a hard task for her. "Well, one thing sure, Helmy, you can't say I didn't warn you. I knew it means no good to a girl when one of these city dudes starts to go with her. They mean no good to any girl. I tell you, a girl has to watch her step all the time. I can't keep you here. I'd keep you on if I could, but there's so much talk of this, that and the other; and I've always tried to run a decent house, but with so many comers and goers, and now that Mr. McMann has gone I've got to be more careful. I guess you'd better go, into the city. There's so many people there no one asks questions."

Mrs. McMann went on talking.

Helmi stood up and faced the sunset and her eyes were looking far away. She did not hear what Mrs. McMann was saying. She was thinking of that sunset long ago—the night before she had crossed the Canadian border—how it glowed and gleamed and beckoned. She had been so sure it was a welcoming fire to warm and comfort her. She had come in full of hope and confidence—so sure she was of making her way, and finding friends. But these fires, these friendly fires, where were they now?

Her friend whom she loved had betrayed her into hostile hands. And now her Jack! Was Aunt Lili right after all? Was Jack a painted fire, too . . . and God, her God, who had seemed so close and dear and loving to her, was he just a painted fire, like the other, cold, and dead, and mocking, when she came to him crying and shivering, bitterly alone, and afraid.

The last glow of color faded in the sky and the night wind came whistling, cold and piercing, down the mountain pass.

Helmi was aroused by the collie dog licking her hand.

Chapter XXI

Dead gardens, littered with stocks from which the life had fled and the bright blooms had departed, with all the sadness of the silent places where throbbing life had been, hummocked over with newly earthed graves where the potatoes and turnips now lie buried; dead fields cleared out, swept clean and tidied away like the house of trouble where the neighbors gather and do this sad service for the one who is gone; leaden stubble whose golden hue has faded now to match the lowering sky; leafless trees that draw together moaning and complaining like toothless old women whose children have all forgotten them; no birds at all except the little graybirds who sing no song and whose coats are the color of dust; the rose-haws gone, driven out by the scouring winds of December that foam with rage at any spot of brightness; weary winds that rage all day and moan at night as if they had repented of their evil ways, but whose sorrow is only for the works of destruction which they were not able to accomplish. The harvest past, the summer gone, stark melancholy over all. So came that cold, gray, desolate time which we refer to as the "Turn of the Year."

There was only one hope for the sad old world, so gray and unlovely and lifeless—hope that the decent snow would come with its soft winding sheet to cover the unsightliness of the dead face. Surely there would be snow for Christmas. "A green Christmas makes a full church-yard" the old people said grimly, but no one could truthfully call this a green one, it was only gray and leaden.

In the City all the street sounds this Christmas Eve were harsh, cold and hollow. Street cars clanged and shrieked and roared through the Subway; horses' feet pounded on the pavement like blows on an anvil, and automobile brakes seemed to scream in fright and pain. Many a person turned hastily, expecting to see an accident, only to find it was just a car stopping. Cold, gray and hard lay the city on this day which should be the brightest of the year.

In the very grayest part of the day, when the sunlight was fading and the lamps were not yet lighted, the snow began weaving its changing patterns through the waiting air. The country people saw it falling, and said it had kept off well, and hoped for the sake of the cattle, that it would not fall too deep and cover all the grass. Snow was an old story to them, making them think of blocked roads, and paths to shovel to the stables, and, worst of all, hungry cattle looking for food. But in the city the snow got a royal welcome.

"Now it does look like Christmas," the people called to each other on the street through their wet fur collars, as they hurried along with their shopping bags dropsical with last-minute Christmas gifts. The red bells in the shop windows suddenly grew brighter, as if a candle had been lighted in them, and the Christmas wreaths sparkled through the splinters of frost that began to come on the windows, for with the approach of nightfall the cold increased. The hurrying bakers' wagons and coal-carts made frosty music on the snow, which in half an hour had covered the frozen ground. The Salvation Army captain on the corner slapped his red-mittened hands together to keep them warm, and blessed the falling snow because he knew it would help people to remember whose birthday it was tomorrow. As he rapped his cane on the pot and made it ring out its silvery summons, he called more heartily to all good Christians to keep the pot boiling.

"Help to provide Christmas cheer for all the lonely and homeless in our city," he cried, "Too bad for anyone to be hungry or sad tomorrow— Thank you, Sir—God bless you; and you, too, ma'am—Keep the pot boiling, remember our Blessed Lord! Keep the pot boiling! Christmas comes but once a year!"

A man in a coon coat walked hurriedly by, without contributing. The captain tried in vain to catch his eye.

"You won't get anything from me," he was saying to himself, "to feed a lot of lazy bohunks that would not take a job when it was offered to them. By Gosh! don't I know them? Everything comes out of the farmer these days—trimmed at every turn—but here's one place I won't bite anyway—I have all I can do to keep my own pot boiling."

He turned into the Dominion Cigar Store then, remembering that his stock of tobacco was low.

A crippled man on two crutches, back from the war, stopped to throw in the coin which he extracted with difficulty from his pocket.

"God bless you, brother!" cried the captain; "your legs may be on the blink, but your heart is all right—God bless you!"

"He has—He blesses me every day," smiled the lame man; "I'm lucky to be alive."

"You bet you are! Come on, good people, it will do you good to give; it will make your own dinner taste better tomorrow."

A young girl with hair of fiery gold, hat awry, flushed face and weary eyes, stood in a doorway across the street. She had laid down her heavy valise for a moment to rest her aching shoulders. The crowd of Christmas shoppers surged past her, some of them young girls of her own age, giggling, scuffling, incoherent in their gladness. She shuddered as she looked at them. There were young mothers, too, herding excited children who had been to see Santa Claus in the toy department of one of the big stores. Each of them carried a balloon, red, green and blue, bobbing gaily. The little children—the believers—were rapt and quiet with the wonder and glory of their visit—the older ones noisy, greedy, imperative, demanding.

Helmi Doran, not much more than a child herself, suddenly wanted one of the balloons, the like of which she had never seen; then as suddenly she remembered!

She must ask someone where to go, but no one even looked at her, they were so busy, so happy, so absorbed. The snow on the street muffled their footsteps, but the clanging of the street cars and their piercing steam-whistles were alarming to her, and the dual movement of the snow falling and the people passing was confusing. She began to feel dizzy as she once did when fording the McLeod River, the rushing water of which had turned her head. She seemed to be going, going, with the street and all the people. Then came a definite, horrible feeling of alarm. She seized her valise and went on.

The Army captain, relieved at that moment by the arrival of the adjutant, noticed her drooping shoulders as she went past him, and hurried after her. "May I help you?" he asked, with friendly interest.

Helmi's lips were dry and stiff, and she shook her head.

"Have you friends here?"

She shook her head.

"You can get a room at the North Star Rooming House, if you are looking for one," he said. "See, it is just ahead of us; shall I carry your valise?"

Helmi hurried on without answering. He noticed that one overshoe was unbuckled and the loose tongue of the buckle had caught in the hem of her dress and was tearing it as she walked.

In her dire need of haste Helmi did not even know it. Reaching the "North Star" she walked up the stairs to the front door and entered without knocking. Mrs. Maggie Corbett, wife of the janitor, who happened to be coming out at the same moment, met her and cried out in astonishment. "God love you, poor girl! Where are you goin'?"

Helmi's pain-twisted face told its own story.

Mrs. Corbett hurriedly put down the twine bag with which she had been going forth for a last shopping bout.

"I could see," said Mrs. Corbett afterwards in telling the story, "that the poor young thing would be worse before she was better, and so I shut me trap, for it was sure no time for an argument, and I took her up the stairs to No. 18, which, thanks be to God, was empty, and I roared at the top of me voice for Mrs. Kalinski, who was in No. 19, to come and help me, and we got her into bed; and then Mrs. Kalinski, who was expectin' her own trouble to come out in the crook of her arm, ran back into her room and like the good Christian she is, though she is a Jew, she brought in her own little basket with the dotted muslin over the blue sateen, and everything in it that we needed, the burnt linen and all, and in half an hour it was all over and the little beauty was lying on the foot of the bed with a smile on her face as if she had won a bet on some wan that she had a spite at!

"Sure, we thought first it was wind on her poor little stomach she had, and we got the nice little hot-water bottle that Mrs. Kalinski had ready for her own little Jacob, and put it in the blanket with her, but the more I looked at her pretty face, the more I saw she intended it for a grin and nothing more or less, and then I told her that with her poor mother so low, and probably not another friend in the world, and not a stitch to her back, she had blamed little to be smilin' at!"

All that afternoon, Helmi lay debating, considering, pondering. Would she go or would she stay. It seemed a good place to step out—perhaps she might get a chance to try life again, or maybe would be let just lie still like this. That would be the best, just to lie like this where everything was warm and quiet and nothing mattered. Though her eyes were closed tight she could see the snow falling—covering her up, weaving, rolling, eddying around her, and burying her deeper and deeper. She loved the feel of it on her face, which was so hot and dry and burning; and on her heart, which was so sore; and she hoped the snow would keep on falling until her heart would be buried so deep she could not feel it aching.

All the women on the second floor had been in to take a look at the pretty young thing with her golden hair spread out on the pillow, and at the radiant baby, who, pink, fat and fine, slept with her two little rosettes of hands rolled into her eyes.

"Her house is thatched—God bless her," said Mrs. Corbett, as she replaced little Jacob's veil on her face. "Poor little helpless mite, who wouldn't be good to her?"

Late that night a sound came through the three augor holes in the storm sash which had a meaning for Helmi. It was the ringing of a train bell as the delayed Canadian Northern train felt its way carefully out of the yards with its heavy load of belated passengers. People may be born or may die, but someone has to run the trains. The North Star Rooming House stood near the tracks, and the sound came distinctly and lonesomely to Helmi's ears. She raised herself on her elbow and listened, her eyes eager and straining.

When the train had gone behind the Great West Garment Factory, and the sound of the bell had grown fainter and fainter and at last was lost in the myriad sounds of the city, Helmi fell back on her pillow sobbing like a dog in a dream. "Home for Christmas! Home for Christmas!" she murmured. "Welcome to Canada—No! No! the snow is best—I will not go to train any more—I will go down deep under snow—snow is best place."

Away below the snow, in another world, Helmi's soul wandered lonesomely, torn with the old problem of whether to go on or stay. Life was too hard—it had been too hard for Aunt Lili, so she had stepped out and let life go on without her. God couldn't blame her for quitting. Why didn't He make life a little easier for women? God was all-powerful—He could make life as He liked . . . God was not quite fair. . . . Why had He let things go so wrong with her? . . . Why had Jack turned against her? Why had a baby come to her, when she had no home? . . . It would be lovely to have a baby if one had a home to keep it in. . . . The girls at the Home . . . she had wondered how they could be so foolish . . . Did they never think. . . . Now she knew it wasn't fair. . . . God was mean to women . . . Mean to babies. Rose Lamb was right, God was on the man's side every time. God was like the two magistrates, red-faced, mad, terrible . . . She hated God!

How could she mind a baby and work, too? . . . No one wanted a girl with a baby. . . . The girls had told her what awful things women say to a girl who goes looking for work. . . . God knew all this, and yet. . . . Rose Lamb had told her she left her baby at the Shelter, and it died in a week . . . Rose was glad. . . . Helmi had thought it terrible for Rose to say she was glad, but now maybe the Shelter would be the best place. . . . She could not help it, anyway—no one wants a girl with a baby. It would have to go to the Shelter.

Round and round in a red-raw circle went Helmi's mind, growing sorer and sorer with thinking, and yet unable to stop.

Suddenly the baby, from the folds of its blanket at the foot of the bed, began to cry, a frightened little eerie cry, like no other sound on earth, the weakest and yet the mightiest human cry.

From the region below the snow came Helmi at the sound—Helmi, strong, defiant, generations back of her speaking in every movement, ready to face the world. The Shelter was forgotten. She reached down instinctively "Lili, little Lili, don't cry; it's all right, nothing can hurt my little Lili; come to your *aili*."

Lili understood the words, and, lying in her mother's arms, went peacefully to sleep. The problem of the future ceased to trouble her. And Helmi, soothed by the presence of the little warm thing, so exquisitely dear and sweet, slipped gently into the kind gray mists of forgetfulness, where torturing hopes and choking fears were all held at bay by a kind gray wall in whose shadows her tired young soul found peace.

"She will be all right," said Maggie Corbett, when Mrs. Kalinski expressed her fears; "she is strong and healthy, and the long sleep will do her good. Ain't it God's mercy that she can sleep and forget her troubles, whatever they are, poor girl. No, I don't think there is any use in sending for a doctor. They will not want to be disturbed on Christmas Eve, when there is no need, and we need not call the inspector either, for he will ask her a lot of questions that will only worry her."

"She has no ring on," said Mrs. Kalinski, sadly; "I am afraid everything is not right."

"She has come from the North," said Mrs. Corbett, "and there's no jewelry stores there—that might account for her havin' no ring. We will say that, anyway."

After Mrs. Kalinski had gone to her own suite, Mrs. Corbett stood at the foot of the bed looking at her patient. Suddenly an idea occurred to her. She went to her rooms across the hall and made a determined search in the middle bureau drawer, which was known as the drawer "that has everything in it." Coming back, she lifted Helmi's left hand and put a ring on her finger. "If a little thing like a ring will give the poor girl back her character I will not be denying her mine, that has been too tight for me for many a day, and in case she should die it will save the wee one's good name. I will tell Mrs. Kalinski, for she noticed there was none, but there's none of the rest of them need know. It will save a lot of talk and wondering. Well, there's nothing wrong with the kid, ring or no ring."

Mrs. Corbett took the slumbering infant into her own rooms for the night, at the instigation of her daughter Rose, aged twelve, who offered the young stranger a share of her bed and personal service. On the Winnipeg couch she was placed, with a barricade of pillows in front of her to prevent any one from thoughtlessly sitting on her.

When John Corbett came home and found his family increased he expressed no surprise, nor did he offer comment when the events of the afternoon were related. But he did go to the couch to get a look at the baby, being warned by Rosie not to come too near for fear he would start a draught.

"She's a fine child," he said, and went back to his supper.

"Whether she is an honest woman or not, I do not know," Mrs. Corbett concluded her recital; "but I do know this—she has been treated bad. Ain't men the limit, anyway? To go off and leave a poor girl like that with no more thought or worry about it than a tomcat?"

John Corbett went on buttering his bread on the palm of his hand, and making no attempt to defend his sex.

"Oh, I guess they are all bad, right enough," he said pleasantly. "I often wonder myself why the Lord ever made them. It's a good thing there comes a war every wee while to kill them off—the divils!"

"Shut up, now, John, you sly old dog," said his wife, laughing, "you sure do like to get a rise out of me."

"And me just tryin' to agree with you, woman?" he said.

When Danny Corbett, aged ten, came in from delivering his papers, sheeted with snow, he was not allowed to look at the baby until he had taken off his outer garments and warmed himself carefully at the fire, and even then he was not allowed by the watchful Rosie to come very near. Danny offered no opinion.

After Danny had eaten his supper, Rosie made a proposition to him. "Sure, Danny, you and me could raise her if her mother dies, and she is not makin' a stir in there now no more than if she was dead. I could mind her, and you with your fine paper route now could get her milk. A bottle would last her a long time, and she would be a lot nicer than a kitten, and not any more trouble. You would get the milk, wouldn't you, Danny, and then we would go cahoots on her?"

Thus appealed to, Danny Corbett went over to the couch and carefully inspected the young thing that was likely to make inroads in his hard earned income. He put his chapped and dirty little hand very lightly on the glassy, smooth head, and felt its tiny beat. He gently touched the velvety cheek and found it soft as a rose-leaf to his fingers. He put his hand in his pocket and drew out thirty cents in change and looked hard at it. He may have been thinking of cold winds and aching legs—he knew something of them. But his answer was, "Sure Mike! I'll do it. Are you pretty sure her mother will die, Ma?" Danny's tone was eager.

"We ain't wishin' her mother no harm, Ma," Rosie quickly interposed, seeing the rebuke that was coming to her business partner. "We ain't wishin' nobody no harm." Rosie was very anxious not to prejudice the case. "But we know there is always a danger—you know yourself, Ma, that none of us knows one day from another,—we're here today and away tomorrow, as I have often heard you say—and Danny and me are just talkin' it over in case somethin' should happen—that's all."

The warm heart of Maggie Corbett was tender to her offspring at that moment. "Look at that, John, would you? Good little things, after all, and yet it was only this mornin' they were fightin' like drunken shantymen. I often thought if they had had a baby in the house it might have softened them. Well, don't be settin' your hearts on this wee one, for her mother is not goin' to die, I don't think; though you never can tell about a woman when her man has gone back on her."

Outside the snow was still falling. The evergreen trees were bending with the weight of it, their branches hanging down like great white bears' paws. Christmas Eve surged forward with all its infectious gladness as the crowds of belated shoppers increased. The electric fans in the windows were hard pressed to keep back the shooting frost ferns, which threatened to hide the season's offerings. Handsome cutters, with beautiful robes thrown over the backs of the seats, stopped at the curb to let out hurrying shoppers; delivery boys on foot, on wheels, in wagons, loaded with parcels, hurried to the suburbs of the city, sometimes pausing to look in at uncurtained windows where happy families gathered around sparkling tables—families so happy over the arrival of guests that they forgot to draw the blinds and so allowed some of their happiness to overflow into the street. Rosy shaded lamps threw patches of radiance on the glistening snow. Christmas wreaths tied with satin streamers glowed deeply red against the windows. The pulse of the city was beating with laughter and sleighbells.

At the corner of Second Street and Jasper Avenue a congested street car stopped to let out a flock of little girls and boys on their way to the Christmas tree in the First Baptist Church. Certain of the little girls, with their curls protected from the falling snow by being tucked safely away under their toques, were carrying mysterious pasteboard boxes containing sashes and bows and wings for the fairies. Others of them were darkly hooded and masked, their identity and sex entirely unguessed, for were they not cast for the dreadful witches of Shadowland? Accompanying them was a liberal sprinkling of parents, mostly mothers, with a few self-conscious fathers who had the appearance of having been dragged out. The mothers had an air of very conscious unconcern, as if they did not know their little boys or girls were going to take a part that was bound to be the very best thing on the program.

The Salvation Army Citadel blazed with light and pulsed with activity, for the big supper, where all were welcome, was going on, and the odors of turkey and sage and onions, drifting out into the street, compelled the reluctant ones to go in.

At midnight, when the bells were ringing, the snow suddenly stopped in that abrupt Alberta way. The city's lights were so many and so bright against the deep India blue of the sky, it was hard to tell them from the stars, but high overhead was to be seen the North Star, beloved of all bewildered travellers. Now it twinkled and gleamed above all these scenes of good fellowship and merry-making with unmistakable approval. Into the uncurtained window of the Corbetts' big room it peered with a deeper interest and kindlier understanding, for it could see that the Winnipeg couch was drawn out from the wall to make it into a full-sized bed, and in it there slept the unperturbed young Lili, with Rose Corbett on one side of her and Daniel Corbett on the other—her two new friends, who had covenanted in her presence and in the presence of each other to furnish her with shelter, care and sustenance in the event of her mother's death. Rose and Daniel Corbett—the underwriters!

Chapter XXII

It was Christmas afternoon when Helmi awakened—Christmas afternoon, the very sound of which brings pictures of children playing with trains on living-room floors, satiated with turkey and candy, starry-eyed with presents, numb with surprises and joy. Christmas afternoon! Of all the spicy, perfumed, sparkling glorious afternoons of the year the most dazzling and glorious; not merely an afternoon or a day that can be marked on a calendar or divided into hours like other afternoons—not that at all. Christmas afternoon is an atmosphere, a perfume, a sensation, a feeling, a spiritual experience.

It was Christmas afternoon when Helmi awakened. Number 18 in the North Star Rooming House did not suggest festivity, with its bare, buff walls, dull gray paint, elm dresser, iron bed, bare floor, with one strip of Japanese matting worn in the middle down to the threads. But Helmi was not left entirely without some gleam of Christmas, for Rose and Danny, who were going to the Salvation Army Cantata that night, went singing down the hall:

"Away in a manger, no crib for a bed,
The little Lord Jesus laid down His sweet head,"

and it brought to Helmi's mind the Christmas story; and because her own heart was more tender than it had ever been, owing to the rise and fall of the little white veil which covered Lili's face, she loved the little

Christ Child more than ever, and thought of Him and His pale mother as they lay there in the manger with the noise of cattle all around them.

> "The stars in the sky looked down where He lay,
> The little Lord Jesus, asleep on the hay."

Rosie, just outside the door, was singing as she "did" the linoleum in the hall with a dustless mop; Danny was working farther down the hall.

Helmi was awakened from her dream by the entrance of a little man with a slender black bag in his hand. He came in without knocking, and stood at the bottom of the bed regarding her critically. Before he could frame a question Mrs. Corbett had arrived, having seen the Doctor's car at the front door.

Mrs. Russell, who lived in No. 16 and did the cleaning in the City Hall, and therefore knew something of the correct forms of procedure, had notified the Department of the happening in No. 18. Dr. Symond came over at once. No one likes to be disturbed on Christmas afternoon, when the delicious sizzle of a turkey pulsates in the atmosphere of the house and one has just helped to put two leaves in the dining-room table. Dr. Symond was prepared to be quite stern. Indeed, as a representative of the city authorities how could he help being stern with these unregulated young women who leave their babies on the steps of the City Hall, so to speak. It was becoming entirely too common, and the Property Owners' Association at their last meeting were complaining about it; properly so, too, for they were the people who had to pay the bills. Everyone when in need rushed to the City— widows looking for help—unemployed—homeless—unfortunate girls—all come to the City.

Dr. Symond felt very stern about all this as he stood looking at Helmi. "Where is your husband?" he asked. His tone implied that he suspected foul play. She had probably murdered him and concealed the body. Dr. Symond's manner warned Helmi that it would be better for her to tell the truth. Roused from her dream, she stared at him with a frightened face.

"You must answer me," said the doctor, sternly. His manner was patient but firm.

Helmi did not know where to begin. How could she tell this man her fears?

Maggie Corbett came to the rescue.

"She has not the best English, Doctor, but I make out her man joined up early in the war and she got afraid and came in. It is all right, Doctor, she's married, safe and sound; she has the ring on her finger and has a valise full of nice things for the little one, and she's not a charity case, Doctor, at all. She has money to pay her way."

The doctor grew more cheerful. "That is fine, Mrs. Corbett," he said, "You see, I get so many cases where these foreign girls think they are married. Some fellow shows them a paper which he says is a license, and away they go with him. They have great respect for a paper, especially if it has a red seal on it. But almost anything will do—a tax notice or a water bill—even an unpaid one." Dr. Symond was quite cheerful now. Then he grew more serious. "I tell you, Mrs. Corbett, it is disgusting how easy these girls are!"

"Sure enough," said Mrs. Corbett, "easy is right. Ain't nature wonderful, doctor? Don't it beat all how she puts it over on us?"

"I tell you, Mrs. Corbett," went on the Doctor, not wishing to discuss this angle of it, "if the women of this city who meet in their local councils and women's institutes and a lot of these other organizations they are spending so much time on, would make it their business to get in touch with every foreign girl and warn her of these things—well, I wouldn't have so much to do; neither would the Superintendent of Neglected Children—and there would not be so much congestion at the Children's Shelter."

"You are right again, Doctor," said Mrs. Corbett, amiably, "and did it ever strike you that it might be grand work for the Rotary Club and Kiwanihans and such like to say a word to the men? They're doin' a fine work, buildin' Homes for these little ones, but maybe if they worked a little harder on the men they would have less need for Homes. But I see what you mean, Doctor, and I know it's a grand thing to always be able to lay all the blame on the women. You see the Lord lets her bear all the pain, and we see to it that she gets all the shame; so why not let the rest of the women bear the blame—there's no use spreadin' it any farther."

"You misunderstand me, Mrs. Corbett," said the doctor, quickly. "I have the utmost sympathy for these unfortunate girls, and that is why I would like the women to do something. Indeed, I spoke to the Local Council about it when they asked me to address them."

"That was fine and good of you, Doctor," commended Mrs. Corbett. "I'm a good hand at givin' advice, too. Don't it make a person feel grand to give out a good gob of advice; and then if anyone does go to the divil we can say, 'I warned you, anyway—you can't say I didn't.' But take the tip I gave you now, Doctor, get busy on the men. Leave the women to women—it's women who look after women, anyway."

The doctor interposed: "Now, Mrs. Corbett, I cannot agree with you there. You must have noticed that women are very hard on women." He was pulling on his gloves now, rubbing out the wrinkles carefully.

"No, I haven't noticed it, but I've heard it—I've heard a lot of men say it."

"Now, Mrs. Corbett, I see you are a great cynic, and I would not have thought that of you," Dr. Symond said, laughingly, as he shook hands with her.

"Don't let me keep you, Doctor," she replied, "and it Christmas and all."

When he was gone Helmi opened her eyes. "I can speak English," she said, lifting her head from the pillow, "I heard what he said. Did you give me the ring to wear?"

"Just so," said Mrs. Corbett, "and it's grand that you can speak so well. Swede girl, are you?"

"No, Finn," said Helmi, "two years in Canada. Do you know anything about me? You said my man had joined up—do you know anything about him?"

"Not a word, but you'll tell me when you feel like it," said Mrs. Corbett encouragingly.

Helmi regarded her kind friend gratefully. "You were good to me just now to say things for me and put the ring on my hand. I could not tell him when he asked me—he made me want to die."

"Sure Mike, I know, he's a good little man in his own way, but it's none of his business. He may be sure no woman goes knockin' round the country without her man at a time like this for the fun of it. Oh, well, you don't need to confess to him, or anyone for that matter, but only to God himself."

"God don't care," said Helmi bitterly, "I pray and pray, but God never hears!"

"Save us all!" cried Mrs. Corbett. "That's an awful way to talk about God, who is more anxious to do right by us than we are to let Him."

"Are you a Christian?" asked Helmi.

"My gracious, how do you think I could ever run a Rooming House if I wasn't and keep from committin' murder. If the love of God hadn't been shed abroad in my heart why do you think I would butt in and tell lies for you?"

"Is it always wrong to tell lies, even kind, good lies like yours? Will God be mad with you for telling a lie for me?" Helmi was afraid her good friend might get into serious difficulties over her.

Mrs. Corbett threw out her hands and laughed. "No fear! God ain't as touchy as lots of people try to make out. It isn't as if I lied to be mean or to hurt someone, and I'll tell you how I've got it sized up. It's a sort of treat for Him to hear someone lie for a woman instead of to her, or about her if you can get what I mean."

Helmi nodded.

"Don't be talkin' now, for tomorrow is the third day, and then's the time for the fever, if it is comin' at all. Rosie is bringin' your hot milk, and Mrs. Kalinski has your supper cookin' on her stove, and I must be runnin' now to see how the wee lamb is. She's done nothin' but sleep yet, and that's the best thing she can do with the long road of life ahead of her."

Chapter XXIII

Helmi stayed on in Number 18, taking her meals with the Corbetts, and trying to pay for their kindness by cleaning up their congested suite and making clothes for Rosie and Danny, who had become the baby's devoted attendants. Mrs. Corbett was full of encouragement when she heard Helmi's whole story.

"Your man has been delayed, that's all. Sure he'll come—never say die, Helmi, dear—and just think of how pleased he will be to find this fine little girl, the very picture of himself, with her lovely dark eyes. She must be the spittin' image of him, for she's not a bit like you. But looks don't matter so long as you are healthy, and a better child I never saw."

Encouraged by Mrs. Corbett's confidence, Helmi, as soon as she was able, began to go to the station on the two nights of the week the Peace River train came in, sitting huddled on a seat that commanded a view of the big moon-faced clock. Although due to arrive at four in the afternoon, it was often past midnight before the train drew in.

The station agent began to notice the pale girl with the big eyes who came each train night and who seemed so anxious.

One night an iron gray old man was met by his iron gray old wife, who looked so much like him she might have been his sister. Helmi watched them, noting their fervent kiss, their light steps as they walked happily away arm in arm, both talking. Helmi saw it all, and somehow it comforted her to know that some had found happiness in life, even if it had apparently passed her by.

Another night she saw a trim young lady, with many bags, a pair of snowshoes, a camera slung over her shoulder, a tapestry purse and a huge white fox fur, coming down the platform. She was met by a plain, hard working woman, with wisps of gray hair escaping from the hard little nub at the back of her head, a skirt that did not match her coat and needed to be pulled straight—evidently put on in a hurry; and with feet disfigured with bunions, hands red and bare, and shoulders bent.

Helmi watched the meeting. The girl was the last to leave the train, and the mother had almost given her up, and had gone to the wicket to see if a wire had come. While the mother was at the wicket the girl came bursting into the station. "Mother," she called, "Here I am, I was helping a lady with her baby."

The two women caught each other in a warm embrace, and as they were leaving the station Helmi heard the girl say, "The trustees paid me for the whole time, and now, old girl, you will have that fur coat— we'll get it tomorrow."

Helmi saw the mother's arm tighten. The girl's eyes were defiant and proud. She dared anyone to even think she thought her mother shabby.

Helmi wondered, wondered.

When the last person had come through and the doors were closed, Helmi walked slowly to the North Star Rooming House, lonely, tired and sad. She resolved she would not go again, but the next train night found her sitting in front of the clock, watching its tardy hands making their reluctant rounds. She had written to good old Sim, giving him her address—he would see Jack if he came.

At the end of two weeks Helmi began to look for a situation. Her money had lasted until now, but the little stock in the black, shiny purse had dwindled and dwindled. Fortunately her clothes, by careful brushing and pressing were still presentable. The kindness of the Corbett family, and the exquisite joy she found in caring for the little Lili, kept her heart from breaking with loneliness. The nights were the worst; even the regular breathing of the warm little treasure beside her, the feel of the velvety little fingers which clasped hers, could not entirely win her away from her sorrow. Why had God forsaken her? Or was He just doing this to try her faith, as he tried that of Job. Then she thought of Abraham, whom God commanded to sacrifice his little son. That was a terrible story, and Helmi wished she had never heard it, even if God did repent and say, "Oh, well now that I know you would do it that's all right—I just wanted to be sure." In happier days Helmi had decided the story wasn't true at all. God wasn't like that, someone had just made up that story. Now, she wasn't so sure.

Often in these long dark nights, Helmi thought of Aunt Lili. It had all seemed so easy when Aunt Lili came back for the visit to Finland, and now, Aunt Lili was gone, her little girl too. She had come to Canada so sure she could conquer all difficulties, and she had come on evil days. But little Lili here would have a chance . . . One might succeed out of four . . . surely God would let one Finn girl out of four do well in Canada! Maybe it was too much for her to expect to succeed and be happy—but she could be the ladder on which dear little Lili would rise, like the woman at the station, bent, shabby, tired, with the glorious, successful daughter, who loved her mother loyally in spite of her old-fashioned dress and knotted hands.

It was only when Helmi could get her thoughts out of the lonely, dark roads where disappointments and loneliness lurked, into the pleasant green meadows of the future where plans for little Lili could be made, that peace would come to her, and to her burning eyes the blessed dews of sleep.

On the day that Lili was three weeks old Helmi went to the Employment Bureau to look for work. She wore the blue motor coat, a black velvet hat on which she had transplanted the flowers from her summer hat, and her best shoes and gloves. She was still pale, and her cheeks had grown thinner.

"It's a question," said Mrs. Corbett, eyeing her critically, "how a person should dress when lookin' for work. If you're not well dressed they'll think you are needin' a job too bad, and that you must be shiftless and no good; on the other hand, if you're too well dressed they wonder why you need to do housework. Women are sure the limit, despisin' their own work and makin' every one else despise it too. A woman may forgive the woman who makes her dresses—she is even more likely to forgive the one that makes her hats, and who charges her three times what they're worth—but God help the poor dud that cooks her meals. No woman ever thinks well of another woman who merely does the work she could do herself if she wanted to. So, Helmi, dear, don't be hurt if they talk snippy to you—I know how you feel—the Finns and the Irish are blood cousins when it comes to temper—but just say what you want to, to yourself. You can come home and abuse them all you like to me. I know them—haven't I done washin's for them for years?"

Helmi, as usual, went early, but the room—a large one, with windows that ran to the ceiling—was already half filled. Her first thoughts were thoughts of discouragement—What chance had she among so many? But as she listened she learned that many of the women were employers, for the topic of conversation was the old difficulty of getting efficient household help. The conversation rose and fell like the fire in the chimney on a windy night.

"I am out so much," one woman said, in a loud voice, "I simply must have reliable help. The last one left on the electric iron until it burnt through the table." She was a worried woman, short of breath, as if she had been perpetually climbing stairs. Helmi wanted to talk to her, but she was surrounded by other women, all intent on their own grievances.

"It makes a difference when one has boys in the house; you see I have my own two, and Fred, my nephew."

"Well, I have just one rule—I must have a British subject. When I came home from the Red Cross the other day I found my house in a state. My German washwoman had the cook and the housemaid in terror of their lives. She had told them she was washing for me now, but I would be washing for her next year, and the Kaiser would be living in the Governor's house, and we would be begging jobs from the German aristocracy, who, it seems, are going to come over here to live. She flew when I came in, and she hasn't come back yet for her money. She never told me she was German, you may be sure. She was Russian—they are all Russians now."

Helmi at last got her chance at the desk. A kind-faced Scotchwoman, who called her "dear," asked her what sort of work she wanted, and had she registered. Helmi said she wanted housework by the day if she could get it. She could cook, yes, and wash, and make things clean.

The Scotchwoman called the lady whom Helmi had noticed first—the stair-climber.

"Here's a smart girl for you, Mrs. Angus," she said, "I doubt if you'll get better—she looks both clean and smart."

Mrs. Angus appraised Helmi critically. "Are you honest?" she asked at last. "I have lost so much by petty thieves."

"Yes," said Helmi, hotly, "I am honest, and I tell the truth, and I am square."

Mrs. Angus turned to the Scotchwoman angrily. "Is this the way you allow your patrons to be spoken to, Miss Ritchie?" she said.

"I doubt she meant no harm," said Miss Ritchie, soothingly: "she was taken by surprise—that's all."

"Have you worked before?"

"Yes, in Winnipeg—in the Yale Hotel—and at Eagle Mines in a boarding-house."

"Yes, I thought so," said Mrs. Angus, "you are certainly quite the hotel type, sharp and pert. Well, have you references?"

"No," said Helmi, when Miss Ritchie had explained.

Mrs. Angus looked sternly at Miss Ritchie. What did she mean by exposing patrons to the possibility of getting a girl who, by her own confession, had no references.

Miss Ritchie asked Helmi if she could send and get her references.

Helmi shook her head. "I would rather not," she said.

"Well, there's many a good girl has come to me before without references, Mrs. Angus. I'm not such a hand for references as I once was," said Miss Ritchie. "They are often written to get rid of a girl, you know."

"No, I do not know that," said Mrs. Angus; "I prefer references."

"Well, then, here you are," said Miss Ritchie; "here's an old country girl with letters from rectors and curates and local bodies and all— she'll do fine for you."

That morning Helmi was interviewed by four other women. She was viewed with favor by the first one, who enumerated her good points without ever thinking it might be embarrassing. "You look clean and smart," she said; "you know how to put your clothes on straight, and you look a person square in the eye. You are a foreigner, I see. From what country?"

"Finland," said Helmi.

"Goodnight!" cried the lady, with a harsh laugh; "then it's all off. My husband had one in his bridge gang, and a positive nuisance he was, a socialist and agitator. He would put me out if I brought home a Finn. I want a British subject, Miss Ritchie. We owe it to our own to give them the choice, though, dear me, some of the English girls have been a trial, too."

The next woman who talked to Helmi kept a boarding-house, and fancied Helmi on account of her height. "I like a tall girl—she can carry trays better. You've done it?—that's good. Yes, you are a likely looking girl, I must say—foreign, but still you have good English. I don't mind Finns—they're tempery, but clean and smart. What's that? You want to go home at night! Why? A baby! Nothing doing—you won't do me at all. No, sir, I had a girl with a baby once and it was always getting sick or dying or something just when I needed her worst. Never again! I believe in population all right, but I can't have a waitress with a baby, even if we never get the country settled. What in the world did you have a baby for, a smart girl like you?"

Helmi stared back at her haughtily. "It is not your business," she said, "I can have a baby if I want it without asking you."

"You bet you can, and welcome. Well, who else have you, Miss Ritchie?"

The fourth woman who spoke to Helmi asked her many questions about her past. "Where is your husband?" she asked.

Helmi replied that she did not know.

"Are you sure you are married?"

Helmi produced the certificate.

"Do you ever think he may have deserted you?" the woman asked, searchingly.

Helmi hesitated, and as the woman plied her questions she could only think of the brace and bit Jack used to bore holes in the boards. Helmi knew she had no right to question her, but she answered as bravely as she could, all the time praying, "Make her take me, God; make her!"

"Well, my dear, I wouldn't be too sure. Men are fickle, I know. My first husband left me."

"My man is a good one," said Helmi, firmly.

"Any family?"

"One little girl, one month old."

"Well, of course, that would be the difficulty."

"I can leave her with friends," said Helmi, eagerly. She was going panicky. Was there no work anywhere for her?

"Still, I have three sons, young men; it would not be nice to have a young girl who has a baby—you know what boys are like—inclined to tease."

"I like boys, good enough," said Helmi, eagerly, "try me—I am a smart worker. I have to get work, my money is nearly gone, and I must pay for my baby's care, my friends are not rich people."

"I would not suppose they were," said the lady, with emphasis. "I suppose they are Finnish people like yourself—simply working people."

"No, ma'am," said Helmi, "It is a Canadian family who have been very good to me."

"Indeed," said Mrs. Swallwell, "how good of them! I hope you are very grateful."

"I am," said Helmi. "I want to pay. Will you take me?"

"I will think about it. I do not like to decide in a hurry. My home is everything to me. I plan everything so carefully. People tell me I am foolish, but it's my nature. Give me your phone number. You haven't a phone? Oh, dear, how awkward! Let me see, you could phone me— No. 8333—that is easy to remember but I cannot just say when I will be in. Every day there is something. Really, I grow busier all the time, it seems, and one cannot refuse invitations when one accepts them. Friday evening at dinner-time—we dine at seven—I think I have no dinner engagement."

Sadly disappointed, Helmi turned away. How could she wait until Friday—she must have work. It was now nearly twelve—surely some-one would take her? She looked back and searched the faces of the women. Miss Ritchie nodded to her encouragingly.

"I'll phone about for you when I can," she said; "there is a rush on this morning."

Just at that moment the door opened and a dainty little lady entered. She came to the desk quickly, with tiny steps, like a mechanical toy. "Oh, Miss Ritchie, I am in such trouble," she began; "Mary has left me. She quarrelled with Robin, and wanted him to apologize. It is pretty hard for a big boy of seven to apologize, now, isn't it? He simply wouldn't. He had thrown a tomato at her—it was very naughty of him, of course—just a boyish prank—and she took it so seriously. Have you someone?"

Miss Ritchie called Helmi over. "Here's the very girl for you, Mrs. Brand," she said; "she has a baby of her own, and she'll be good to the twins, I know."

"Oh, I couldn't take a girl with a baby—it would be . . ." she hesitated.

"I can work by the day and leave the baby with friends," said Helmi. She was pale and tired now, and looked too ill to be an attractive venture for anyone looking for help.

"Oh, I am afraid you would not do," said the little lady, hastily; "I must have a strong girl."

"I am strong," said Helmi: "my baby is young, so I am pale yet. Try me—for a day even."

"Well, I must ask my husband—I always consult him of course"—(Mr. Brand would have been interested in this) "and I will let Miss Ritchie know. That will be the best. I couldn't very well let you bring the baby, and it's at night I need you most."

Helmi turned to Miss Ritchie. "I must go now," she said; "a little girl minds the baby—home from school, she stayed for me."

Miss Ritchie nodded. "Better luck next time," she said; "I shall keep you in mind."

In the afternoon Helmi came back. Mrs. Corbett was not going out, so she kept the baby. But no one wanted Helmi—she was a foreigner, and she had a baby.

Kind-hearted Miss Ritchie was distressed, and flared up in anger when one woman said to Helmi; "You should have thought of this about this time last year?"

"Having a baby is not a crime, Mrs. Coatsworth; the poor girl is honest and willing to work. She'd give service for every dollar, I'll go bail. She isn't asking charity or even sympathy."

All afternoon Helmi waited, while well-dressed women came and went. The seekers of employment sat together, and were easily distinguishable from the others. Their manner was humble and beseeching. The war with all its dislocations had thrown many women out of employment, and on the faces of many, gaunt fear was plainly written. This was particularly true of those who were the most refined and cultured.

Fragments of conversation fell around Helmi as she sat among the seekers.

Two women in seal coats were discussing the situation.

"My dear," said one, "it is our patriotic duty to save every cent. I cut down my cook ten dollars at once, and changed my dressmaker." Her voice fell. "My dear, there's a wonderful German woman on the south side—I will give you her address—and she made me a stunning little afternoon dress, with so much hand-work on it, for ten dollars. Madam Frouchette would have charged thirty-five. She is a positive find. She's frightened to death that she will lose her trade, and so has cut her prices away down. We're keeping it among ourselves, my dear. You know some of the I.O.D.E.'s would be up in arms if they knew. They say we should patronize our own, but, my dear, the German woman has to live."

When Helmi walked wearily back to the "North Star" that night she was beginning to wonder if to bring a child into the world were not the great transgression for which there could be no pardon. Only the thought of the blessed shelter of her room and the warm-hearted Irish family who had befriended her kept her heart from despair.

Mrs. Corbett had not thought it was so terrible. She had praised little Lili, and Rose and Danny were getting marbles now from the other children in the block for a look at the child.

The traffic was congested at the corner of First and Jasper. A Blue Line car waited for the rush of passengers homeward bound, and a coal wagon, lumbering past, narrowly escaped a closed motor which had dashed by disregarding the traffic law. A newsboy in an overcoat much too long for him shouted "*Evening Journal* all about the suicide."

Two men, waiting to get across, were talking about it. "She took a room at the St. Petersburg . . . left her baby there."

Helmi shuddered and hurried on. She wanted to feel the little warm cheek against her own, and to listen to the regular breathing, and get back the confidence she had lost. There must be someone in this city who would let her work.

The next day Miss Ritchie had an address for her. The lady there wanted someone to come by the day and go home at night. Helmi set out at once, taking a street car to save time. When she arrived she found that the lady had already secured a helper for the day.

After Helmi had gone the lady remarked to her friend that the girl whom Miss Ritchie had sent looked rather pale, and she wished she had given her a street car ticket. The friend advised her not to worry over it—"no doubt a brisk walk would do the girl good."

Helmi walked slowly over the long bridge, whose great iron pillars frowned coldly at her. On the river below men were drawing sleigh-loads of ice, glistening blue against the white snow. They looked so warm and happy in their fur coats. Helmi stopped for a moment to watch them, but soon hurried on, for it made her dizzy to look down, and yet it drew her back again in a horrible way that made her heart beat sickeningly. She compelled herself to think of little Lili's pink fingers, with their long, tapering nails, and the satiny feel of her little cheek.

Helmi knew there were kind women in the city; there were women like Miss Abbie and Miss Rodgers, and men like Mr. Terry and the Doctor. She would not give up—two days was not long to be looking.

When Helmi got back to the Bureau Miss Ritchie's assistant was there, a young lady with a metallic voice and stiff white collar which seemed to choke her. She motioned Helmi to sit down.

Helmi laid her purse on her knee and leaned back against the wall. Such a weariness came over her that even the hard seat could not prevent sleep. She was awakened by the metallic voice of the assistant and sprang up in confusion. It was near closing time and the seats were empty. Then she noticed that her purse was gone. The blood rushed to her head, and it seemed as if something snapped. She hunted wildly, talking in her own language excitedly.

The metallic voice was saying: "We cannot be responsible for property—you should have held on to your purse—was there much in it?"

"All that I have in the world," said Helmi, brokenly.

"Too bad," came from the stiff collar, "but you can't blame us."

Helmi walked down the street empty-handed and distraught. She had a desire to tear her hair—to scream—to break something—to kill some one. It couldn't, couldn't, couldn't be—all that she had—her seventeen dollars, her marriage certificate—God could not be so cruel.

A man was speaking at the corner of the street, catching the six o'clock crowd. Helmi could not make her way through the mob, and so found these words beating in upon her through the confusion of street sounds: "Canada calls you, as it has called me. Canada is good enough to fight for—don't fail her now in her need. How would you like to be ruled by Germany? How would you like to bow the knee to Kaiser Wilhelm? Think of our lives here in Canada, where we are free as the air we breathe, with all our wealth of wheat-fields, oil wells, mines and forests, enough for all, enough for ever—yours and mine. Canada, the land of plenty, is our country. Let us fight for it—the land of the maple leaf, where there is room enough and work enough for everyone."

A shift in the crowd revealed the speaker's face. Helmi remembered him—it was Major Gowsett, the man who had been with Colonel Blackwood. Black rage filled Helmi's heart. "Oh, the liar! how could he say there is work in Canada for everybody? There's nothing in Canada but heartbreak." Clenching her empty hands in an agony of hopeless rage—"He's a liar!" she cried aloud, "don't listen to him."

Someone tapped her arm. "None of that, my girl," said a deep voice.

Looking up, Helmi saw a big policeman shaking his head warningly at her. She turned and ran. Fear gave fleetness to her feet—she dared not look behind—it seemed as if the whole police force were in pursuit. Heavy steps pounded behind her. At the corner of Namao Street a sign in a window glared at her, a sign in black letters on a blue card. Helmi read it aloud in her eagerness, then darted in the door.

"GIRL WANTED"

said the sign. Pale and trembling, Helmi approached the desk.

"Do you want a girl? Will you take me?" she said, before she noticed the person who sat there.

A tall, old Chinaman rose from his high stool. "You washee dish, cook, waitee table?" he asked.

"I will do anything," said Helmi; "give me a chance."

"Sure, you nice liddle girl; old Sam give you chance. Want girl for night—seven till twelve every night. Nice liddle parties—lots of nice fellows come eat at old Sam's—like nice liddle girl carry chop suey— makea nice in white apron, liddle cap."

"I'll work hard if you'll give me a chance," said Helmi.

And so it happened that when Major Gowsett, who was recruiting for the Canadian Army, came in after a late meeting the next night for a cup of coffee and a sandwich, he saw Helmi carrying the trays from the kitchen. She was dressed very smartly in her black dress, with white apron and cap, and carried the trays with the old air of aloofness.

Deeply concerned as Major Gowsett was over the dishonoring of the Belgium women—and he spoke of them with deep feeling every

night in his recruiting speeches; indeed, with an almost fatherly solici-
tude—he did not hesitate to tell Helmi's story now to his young officer
friend.

"Our haughty looking waitress is a lady with a past—a real purple
past," he said, in a low voice. "I could swear to that head of hair any
place, and that Boadicea manner, though she was not looking quite so
haughty nor quite so svelte when I saw her last—she evidently has got-
ten over her trouble and is back to her old haunts. No decent girl works
in a Chinese restaurant at night. Old Blackwood, at Bannerman, had
the whole story in a newspaper and shoved it in front of her."

The younger man looked after Helmi as she walked noiselessly past
them with her tray of dishes. "She's a good-looking girl," he said, "and
certainly has not the face of a crook."

"Look out Jim," laughed the Major; "Go slow on this girl, she's a
wild cat."

"She would need to be," said the young officer, "if she wants to keep
straight. The girl is earning an honest living here now, anyway. Why
not let her past go?"

But in spite of this rebuke, which made Major Gowsett shrug his
beefy shoulders, he took time the next day from his arduous task of
recruiting for the 67th Battalion to write to his friend Col. Blackwood
at Bannerman: "I saw the Finn girl again. She is in a Chinese restaurant, working at night," and he underlined the last three words.

Chapter XXIV

I t was at Fort Simpson, in November, on his way out, that Jack
Doran heard of the war. They had floated down the Nehanni
River on a moose-skin barge to the Liard, and down the Liard to
the MacKenzie on a spruce scow, arriving in Fort Simpson one
raw November day when an icy wind from the North gave warning
of the freeze-up. They had brought with them a few furs, which
George, the half-breed guide, had got with his trap-lines, and from
the sale of these they hoped to be able to buy supplies for the home
journey.

Their summer had been full of adventure. They had seen the leaves
come on the trees, the flowers bud, bloom and fade, the leaves fall, and
now the lowering clouds of November driven by the cold winds; but
with their bags full of gold quartz to show what they had found, and
their little heap of dust carried in chamois bags and glass phials, they
were elated and confident.

Jack, with all the eagerness of the amateur, had been full of enthusiasm going in, and in the washing of gold from the sand of the river he
had enjoyed endless delight. To see the glint of yellow gold in the black
sands at the bottom of a pan fired his imagination. Keith had compli-
mented him on his success in panning.

"She's gettin' better all the time," Keith had said, "so we are gettin' closer to the deposits." He had a map of the country showing the exact spot where the claims would be staked. "You'll have some nuggets to bring home to that new wife of yours that will make her eyes pop out of her head."

It was in September they reached the place, and Keith announced the object of their search achieved. They staked their claims and gathered some rich pieces of quartz to bring back with them. Keith was exultant, and even George, the half-breed, grew garrulous with the prospect of riches. He was going to have three cars and a colored driver in a gray uniform!

Keith had the plan for mining all arranged. He showed them where the sluices would be placed, drawing a diagram to show the angle at which they would be set and how the riffles would be put in the bottom. He would bring the water in a pipe-line from farther up the river, and throw it against the banks of gravel in powerful jets. At the falls, up the river he would generate the electricity to run a stamp mill, where the crushed rock would be reduced to powder and passed through a sieve, and the gold collected on copper plates. "You'll see a bigger trek to this field than there was in ninety-eight," he assured his eager listeners.

The return journey, lacking the stimulus of novelty which had kept them from discouragement going in was toilsome and depressing. Their way lay through a gloomy, barren country, and the weather was cold and wet. The shortening days and lengthening nights, too, were unfavorable to travelling. But at length, ragged, unkempt, unshaven and dirty, they arrived in Fort Simpson just before the freeze-up.

The good-natured proprietor of the store bought their furs and outfitted them, giving them the news of the war as the transactions went on. "I wish I was younger, and I'd be off," he said, "I'd like to do a bit of fightin' before my time comes to step off."

"What is it all about?" Jack asked, as he tried on a pair of long boots.

"Well, I'm not clear on that, but sure it's a poor war that ain't better than no war, and you see war has to come once in a while to clear out the surplus population. We breed too fast—ain't that the truth?—so it's either pestilence, war or famine, and war's a lot more fun than the other two!"

Jack looked at him indignantly. "How many children have you?" he asked: He had noticed several little half-breeds around the store, moccasin-footed, noiseless, beady-eyed, looking inquiringly at the strangers.

The storekeeper did not resent the question at all. "I think there are six boys big enough to go," he said. "Three of them are out on the trap-lines and haven't heard about it yet, but the other three are going out. Their mother is cuttin' up a little, but she'll calm down; she's a good woman. We have eight others comin' on. It's a good chance for the boys to see the world."

The war did not relate itself in any way to Jack Doran until he arrived at Peace River. He had one consuming thought in his mind now, and only one, and that was to get to Eagle Mines as soon as he could, and to Helmi. He went at once to the telegraph office and sent her a wire.—"Mrs. Jack Doran, Eagle Mines;—Back safe, expect me in a week. Love, Jack."

Peace River was alive with excitement. Homesteaders walked the streets waiting for the train to take them to Edmonton. There was some delay, owing to trouble on the Judah Hill.

Jack, Keith and George got a room at "The Peace," and soon had the grime of travel washed away, and went to the dining-room for supper. Men in uniform sat at a table, eating noisily and drinking. The room was full of excited talk.

There was a meeting in the hall that night, advertised by a huge red poster in the stores. It said that Major Gowsett and Pte. George Crowe would address the meeting. Pte. Crowe had been wounded at Mons and been invalided to Canada. There were flags in the dining-room, and on the way in that day they had noticed flags flying from the houses and stores, fluttering bravely in the cold wind.

To the hall they went at eight o'clock, and were met at the door by women selling red roses for the Red Cross. A band inside was playing "It's a Long, Long Way to Tipperary." To Jack it seemed as though he had come back to a new world, a nervous, panicky, high-strung world, abounding in new phrases, new emotions. Fresh from the solitudes of the North, he could not at once grasp the meaning of it all.

Pte. Crowe, a pale lad, standing with a crutch, spoke first, and spoke simply and well. His superior officer had chided him for the mildness of his address at Spirit River the night before. "You've got to put more thunder into it," he said, "these people want color and action. Tell them about the children you saw with their hands cut off."

"But I didn't see any," protested the lad.

"Well, you heard of them—you might have seen them. Speed up a little—lay it on thicker, or you'll never get recruits."

But again the boy told just what he had seen—the mud—the hard-ships—the indescribable carnage—the comradeship and heroism of his companions of the trenches. There was no hatred, revenge or bitter-ness in his heart, only a great bewilderment. He appealed on behalf of his comrades—they were so brave, so cheerful and so fine—so willing to die.

Jack's heart was torn with the pity of it. Worst of all was the boy's twitching hands, never still a moment. What horrors that boy must have come through! His lips had quivered as he spoke, like a child's about to cry. "Don't leave those boys alone; send them reinforcements. The more we can send the sooner it will be over." That was the message of the quivering lips, coming from a heart that was clean and brave. He could talk without apology, could Pte. Crowe, he could ask any person to make a sacrifice and not ask them to do more than he had done.

Major Gowsett, who arranged the program, had left himself for the last. In the ordinary affairs of life Major Gowsett believed in being first, but, understanding what he would have called "mob-psychology," he believed the last speaker had the best chance. He began by damning the Germans with great spirit, reviewing their history, military aspirations, and their home life. He showed that they threatened the whole world. Major Gowsett had not been further than Boulogne during the present war, but one would never know it from his speech. It reeked with the stench of battle, it abounded in personal incidents. He dragged his listeners into shell-holes, dug-outs and across "No Man's Land"; he specialized on the treachery of the Germans—the hatefulness of their women—the bitter hatred they had instilled into their children. He had lived with them, he said, and he knew. It seemed that he and Lord Roberts knew the war was coming, but England had not listened to them.

Then he exalted war and military life. It developed the best in a man, and at this the Major beat his breast, directing his audience to that storehouse of accumulated virtues. Then he appealed to the young men to "get into the game." He painted the glory of it, the freedom of it; the army was the place where a man was a man. The nation's hero was the warrior—mollycoddles have no place in the world, especially with women. There was truth in the old song yet:

> "If a lad a lass would marry
> He must learn a gun to carry."

Then in a lighter vein the gallant Major hinted at the charm of the French girls and how they admired the Canadians. His manner indicated that but for the presence of the ladies he could tell more.

While he was speaking Pte. Crowe's hands were never still, nor did his lips cease from trembling.

The Major then called for recruits. "One volunteer," he said, "is better than ten conscripts. Conscription is coming, though"—he gloated over this—"we cannot desert our Army now. If men will not fight of their own accord, there are other methods." The Major unconsciously tapped his sword.

Suddenly it became apparent, even to the Major, that the spirit had gone out of the meeting. His audience sat stony-faced and rigid—the fires had gone out—the current was off. There was no response to his call.

The appeal had not gone home to the men of the north, who love the long trail, with its camp-fires and its peace; brave men, who do their duty from an inward sense, but to whom the thought of force brings not fear but rebellion.

The chairman tried to save the situation by calling for a song, but something had gone from the meeting. The people began to straggle out.

As Jack made his way back to the hotel he was deeply disturbed in mind. There was no moon, but the night was bright with stars. Looking up, he saw the North Star, like an old friend, looking so remote, serene and undismayed, though nations were rocking with war and hatred. The Major and his fiery eloquence were easy to turn aside, but Pte. Crowe, so pale and shaken, quivering with the horror of war, walked beside him in spirit.

The hotel that night resounded with jangling noise, shrill voices, snatches of song, bursts of harsh laughter. The Major was a prince of story-tellers. "Say, boys, did you hear this one? One of the boys who had been on leave . . ." Roars of laughter followed, then more beer. "Too much hard liquor is bad," laughed the Major "but too much beer is just right. No danger of being pinched for being noisy—we have both the proprietor and the policeman. Now, listen to this. There was a French girl . . ."

At one o'clock the party broke up. The Major had secured six names. He decided the next morning to let Private Crowe go back to the City. The kid was all right, but he lacked "pep." This was a job for a real he-man, and after all, the best little recruiter apart from himself, if it ever could be considered apart from himself, was the amber-colored bottle. It gave just the proper warmth and glow.

Jack made his journey around by Edmonton to Eagle Mines, arriving there on the first day of February. There had been no reply to his wire. He stepped off the train with a strangely beating heart. Helmi would be there, surely, but the platform was almost bare. Not a person whom he knew did he see as he hurried across the street and over to his own house.

The door was not locked, and he went in. A strange scene met his eyes—dirty dishes on the table, the remains of a slovenly meal; ashes from cigars on the plates; the bed showing that it had been slept in; the coffee pot was on the stove. The floor had been tramped by muddy feet and spat upon by tobacco chewers, and a forgotten pipe was on the window-sill. The air was heavy with tobacco smoke and the stale fumes of beer.

Jack's heart was heavy with apprehension. He went up to the loft by the ladder on the wall. The bed there had been used too, and a man's coat was thrown across it. There it was—the house he had built—defaced, defiled. What did it mean? He would know what it meant, he would go over to the boarding-house.

Mrs. McMann, a few minutes later, related the interview to her friend Mrs. Turner. "He bounded in at me," she said, "just when I was puttin' the potatoes on to boil. 'Where's Helmi?' he almost shouted at me, without even biddin' me the time of day. How could I tell him where Helmi was? 'She's not here,' I said, 'and I don't know where she is—she's been gone over a month,' I says. 'Where did she go?' he said. 'To Edmonton,' I said.

"'Why did she go?' he stormed! 'Didn't she know I was coming back? Where did she say she was going?' 'Well, Helmy never confided in me, as you know,' I said.

"Land! I couldn't tell him why she went. I never was one that could talk about those things. I don't believe any of my people could. The Weekes were funny that way.

"'Where's Sim?' he said at last, staring at me as if he didn't see me. 'Sim had an accident in the mine, and went out the last train.' 'Well, look here, Mrs. McMann, who has been stayin' in my house,' he says. 'Can you tell me that?'

"I knew very well a party of hunters had spent the night there—swells from town out deer shootin'—drunk as fools, too—I wouldn't let them in—'I certainly have no knowledge of what's been goin' on in your house since you've gone,' I said, very stiff. Mr. McMann always said there was no one could be stiffer than I could when I wanted to be. 'Do you know of anyone having stayed there?' he said. 'Yes,' I says, 'the crazy Englishman from English Creek was there for a week, about six weeks ago.'

"Lord, I thought he was goin' to strike me—but none of the Weekes was ever cowards, so I just glared back at him stiff as pork. I could give him eye for eye, let me tell you. He went out at that and over to the office. I think maybe he expected a letter from Helmy, but if she's writ- ten to him it's more than she's done for any of us. Gone over a month and not a word from her. And I was good to that girl, though I ain't the one to tell what I've done for anyone. Now, if Jack Doran had come in a better spirit he might have heard more from me. I'm funny that way,— anyone can lead me, but strong horses can't drive me."

Jack Doran went to the postoffice. He was moving automatically now. His voice sounded queer to him, and his tongue felt like a piece of rope. "Are there any letters for me, Mr. Armstrong?" he asked, hoping his voice was not beating like his heart.

"Two have just come for Mrs. Doran," said the postmaster, handing them to him. "Glad to see you back to us again, Jack. People come and go at Eagle Mines—come and go—it makes it hard for a postmaster."

Jack went back to his own house—he must get under cover—the eyes of the people he met hurt him—they bored into him, twisting, turning, screwing, gouging, red-hot and sharp as ice. He must get somewhere where he could shut the door.

In his own house, Jack sat with the letters in his hand. Helmi had gone, she had not waited. He was a month late, but Helmi should have waited. Where had she gone?

The letters might tell him—it would be better to know. He opened the first one and found it contained a Government cheque for fifteen dollars payable to Helmi Doran, and it said it was on account of Pte. Arthur Warner. Jack stared at it without understanding.

The other letter was from Montreal. "Dear Helmi," it said, "I have made over my separation allowance to you, and I hope you will accept it from me. You are the only person in Canada who has any claim on me. I have paid every other person in Canada for everything they have ever done for me. You, dear Helmi, I can never pay in money, for you gave me the most precious thing a man can have who goes out as I am going, a memory of something tender and sweet. I have made my will, leaving everything I have to you. I will never forget your last words to me. Nobody ever spoke to me like that before. Will you write to me, Helmi?

Ever yours,

Arthur Warner."

With the letter in his hand Jack sat looking at his polluted house—his poor desolate, violated house, the emblem of his own life. He had built this house with his own hands, lovingly, taking pleasure in driving every nail and fitting every board. And now—and now—so it had been with his life—he had lived it cleanly, decently.

Try as he would Jack could not believe that Helmi had forgotten him or been unfaithful to her marriage vow. If the worst he feared was true, it was some racial fault in her—Helmi had not sinned as an individual. What did he know of her traditions? He felt he knew her but little, although she was his wife. Nothing could alter that—she was his wife.

A dog came whimpering to the door. As Jack opened it the sable collie, thin and miserable, sorely neglected since old Sim had gone, looked timidly in at him. Jack recognized the animal—the crazy Englishman's dog. Mrs. McMann said the Englishman had stayed at his house six weeks before. Here was the proof, and this explained the letters . . . "Arthur Warner" . . . Jack had never heard his name. He had seen him though, a strange, uncouth, unshaven fellow.

Restraining a first impulse to drive the dog away, Jack coaxed her to come in, which she did, shiveringly. Her feet were sore, her nose hot. Jack went to the butcher shop and bought her some meat, which the hungry animal accepted gratefully. The dog was not to blame, whoever else might be.

The butcher told him about the dog, "The crazy Englishman had shot all his dogs but her. 'Cleo' is her name, and it seems he could not bring himself to shoot her. Old Sim looked after her until he got hurt and had to go to the hospital. Yes, sure, I'll give her bones. It's real good o' you to be providin' for her. The Englishman wasn't any friend of yours either, was he?"

One resolve Jack arrived at—he must get out. He could not spend a night in his little broken house, every inch of which was so dear to him—the little house that had lost its soul.

When Jack left it he did not think of locking the door, although there were things in it, the stove, chairs, table, beds, for which he had paid his hard-earned money. But it did not matter now. His little house, which he had built so eagerly, had been violated.

Jack sealed the letters and returned them to the Post Office, then hired a team at the livery stable and drove to Bannerman, where he would catch a train for Edmonton. On the way he met the time-keeper, who apparently did not want to speak, for although Jack drew up his horses the other one went on. Recognizing Jack, he feared embarrassing questions in respect to the money which had been owing. The time-keeper had one rule—if trouble seemed near make a wide detour and get around it. Something might happen before it again comes near,—some one might die—the world might come to an end—the coming of the war had made all things possible. So, instead of stopping when he saw Jack drawing up his horses, he hurried on.

Jack believed the time-keeper's reluctance to speak was because of what had happened, and his heart grew still heavier. A pale moon and starlight enabled the horses to follow the trail, leaving him free to pursue his own gloomy thoughts. He thought, with a stab of memory, of the words he and Helmi said across the running water. The stream was silent now in its fetters of ice, and the marks of their feet in the soft, sandy banks had been obscured long ago. He wondered if Helmi had forgotten it—wondered, too, if he would ever be able to forget?

At the top of the hill, when the flickering lights of the little town came into view, Jack remembered Helmi's fears when they had come there together. "It is not a friendly place," she had cried, "it will bring bad luck! See, the houses are like angry cats about to spring!" And he had laughed at her for her foolish fancy. He marvelled now at her premonition of evil! And, try as he might, he could not overcome his love for her. He wanted her, his high-tempered Finn girl, whose eyes were so tender. Helmi, with the lovely shining hair and the eager questioning mind. No! if he had lost Helmi he had lost everything. Life could not hurt him any more! If Helmi had deceived him he was proof against misfortune. He might as well go to the war, there was no reason for his staying behind, if Helmi were gone; and if he went he might meet Arthur Warner and pay off the score!

Having an hour to wait for the train, Jack wandered around the town. He did not wish to talk to anyone. The night was fine and clear, with Northern lights circling and folding in the sky with a crumpling sound like the rustle of silk. Pink and mauve, violet and amber, they advanced and retreated in endless manoeuvres, shooting, darting, rolling and unrolling, shimmering and dancing. He and Helmi had watched them with endless enjoyment from the north window of their own little house last year. A sudden impulse came to him to go and see the magistrate—he might know something. Anything would be better than this torturing uncertainty.

The magistrate was in and shook hands kindly—too kindly! Jack judged from his manner that he had some damaging evidence and that he was glad he had it.

"I came home today," Jack began at once, "expecting to find my wife, but they tell me she has gone to the city. I expected to be home a month earlier, but was delayed in the north. I can find no trace of her, nor any reason for her going. Do you know anything about her?"

"I did not know she had gone, until today," said the magistrate. "I had a letter from a friend of mine who saw her in the city."

Jack started eagerly. "Where in the city? I shall go there tonight."

The magistrate rubbed the bristles on his chin with a distinctly soiled forefinger, then with one thumb he pressed back the cuticle on the other until it hurt. He loved to do this. When he couldn't hurt anyone else he hurt himself. "I wouldn't try to find her, Mr. Doran, if I were you. She is in a place where you would not be pleased to find her."

"I don't care where she is—she is my wife, and I will never believe that she had done wrong unless she tells me so. I know her better than you do."

"I am sorry for you, Mr. Doran, and that is why I am patient with you. This Milander girl has gone back to her old associates, the Chinese. She is in one of the all-night eating-houses. I suppose you know what it means when a white girl goes into one of these places."

Jack sat staring at him. "Who was your friend who saw her there?"

"I would rather not tell—it is not necessary that I should—and he wrote in confidence. He knew I was interested. She evidently tired of the quiet life here—these girls crave excitement. There was some talk about her and the Englishman who owns the bungalow at English River. He stayed with her for a week before he enlisted. That is common talk at the mines. Men who are going out to fight, you know, like to take their fling."

He did not need to hurt his own thumb now—Jack Doran's face was enough. It had grown suddenly old and seamed and full of hatred. His nostrils quivered like those of a race horse.

He was about to go, but the magistrate waved him to a seat. "Mr. Doran, you were very indignant with me a year ago or a little less, when I dared to advise you. You were quite indignant, and of course I am ready to admit your feelings at that time were very creditable, very creditable—mistaken, but creditable. Since then you have had a bitter lesson, a very bitter lesson. I did not harbor any ill-will; on the contrary, I was still ready to be your friend. I was your friend, even though you scouted my friendship." Col. Blackwood leaned over, and his voice fell. "A man in my position does not expect thanks; we do not get thanks, but that is quite all right. We do not expect thanks, but I hope you see that I was trying to befriend you."

"I cannot see anything very clearly," said Jack, miserably; "I only know my wife has gone. Circumstantial evidence seems to be against her, but nevertheless I will do my utmost to find her. I will take her word against the world."

The magistrate laughed softly, but there was no mirth in the sound. "Have a drink, my dear young friend," he said, "and forget her."

"No, thank you," said Jack. "I do not drink, and I am pretty sure I will never forget her."

There was something in the young man's voice and in his face that made Col. Blackwood wonder if he had pursued the right course. Perhaps he should tell of her coming to him to find out about the marriage. Perhaps he should tell . . . No! the hell-cat!—she had been impertinent to him, and she had threatened him.

When Jack had gone the magistrate sat a long time, wondering. Then he went to the cupboard and poured himself a drink. Ah! that was better. Now he knew he was right; another drink, and he was sure that he had done not only a wise but a noble thing in leaving the marriage unrecorded. After the third drink, he sat in a mellow haze, musing pleasantly on the time that young Jack Doran would come to him with tears standing in his eyes and thank him for what he had done. "You saved me, Sir, you saved me, even from myself—you saved me, and though I should live a thousand years I shall never be able to thank you adequately, Sir." And he would reply—"Have done, my boy,—have done; one brave man must ever help another!"

So the night wore pleasantly on.

Chapter XXV

Not so pleasantly did the night pass with Jack Doran, who sat in the station waiting for No. 8 and listening to the wires telling their never-ending story—a dull, gray station, dusty even when the snow had covered all the dust. A red stove in the middle of the floor, egg-shaped, fluted, and either fireless or red hot according to the mood of the agent; torn posters showing palatial white steamers ploughing green seas and carrying pleasure-seeking Canadians to tropical lands, all for trifling sums "and return;" a bill of sale, where instructions had been given to the auctioneer to spare nothing, ill-health the cause of the owner's desire to sell; a stray notice re a bull pup answering to the name of "Buster," with a reward; a dance and raffle at Bannerman by St. Faith's Ladies' Aid, program and refreshments, and cordial invitation to all; "Save the Forest" poster—"The forest is ours, let us keep it always;" John Fernwaldt's announcement of his ability to mend shoes, Old Country methods and moderate prices—try me once.

Jack came back to his own bitter thoughts, to which the telegraph wires made a weird accompaniment, ghostly and grim. He could see the instrument from where he sat, muttering, tapping, clicking with its mysterious finger, silent for a few moments, then convulsed and shaken with the desire to be understood. He thought of all the suppressed emotions, the heartbreak, anxiety and fears the wires carried in dead silence along the miles, and how they break into strange tappings here, chokingly alive and articulate.

Life was like that, he mused, we all carry our load of emotions carefully hidden, but we cannot all throw it off at intervals in dots and dashes like the wires.

Reaching the city, Jack went to the Macdonald Hotel, where he met his partner, Keith, whom he had not seen since the night of the recruiting meeting at Peace River. They discussed their plans for the future.

"I am going to have our specimens assayed here at the University, and I will go at once to Victoria to file our claims," said Keith.

Jack told him briefly of his domestic trouble. "I believe she is here in the city," he said in conclusion, "and I want to find her. I will not believe a word unless I hear it from her."

Keith whistled softly. "This is bad work, boy," he said "and I sure am sorry. Women are the finest in the world or the worst—if they're not one they are the other. When you begin to break off the coupons from your gold mine stock you'll have a flock of them pursuing you, anyway."

Jack was looking out at the wide view of the winter landscape, with the magnificent river, covered with snow, winding away into the blue distance. "I don't want a flock," he said, "but I do want Helmi. If you knew her, Keith, you would know she couldn't be crooked. She has eyes that are like a little girl's, full of wonder and innocence."

"I don't believe there are any innocent girls these days," Keith replied, lighting his pipe for the twentieth time. He could never keep his pipe going, and when he sat for half an hour in one place he had burnt matches strewn around him like confetti around a bride. Keith was a low-set man of very dark complexion, tanned now to a rich mahogany.

"My own opinion is that you are well out of it, Jack," he continued; "but I'll admit I'm no judge of women. They can all fool me."

"Sometimes I think of enlisting," said Jack. "When I listened to that boy leaning on his crutch I wanted to go. The other old soak rather spoiled it, though."

"Gosh! I liked him," said Keith, grinning; "He told us some of the richest stories I ever heard."

"I couldn't stand him and his stories," Jack said with warmth, "he's the sort that make war, he loves it, you can see that—but you'll notice he will never do any of the fighting. It looks as if the thing had to be finished up now that we are in it."

Keith was watching Jack closely, even though he was so busy keeping his pipe going. "I'll certainly look after your interests, Jack, if you want to go. I'll file for you on everything I get while you're gone and I'm goin' to get right after the potassium deposits and the oil as soon as I get the gold cinched."

"I knew you would," said Jack gratefully; "I am not thinking about that."

"And I'll do my best to locate the Helmi girl and see that she has plenty."

Jack remembered Helmi's outbreak of rage when Keith's name was mentioned, and hastened to say, "I hope I'll find her before I go."

So, gradually, the thought of enlisting took shape in Jack's mind. It was with him when he stepped into the white bath-tub and enjoyed the luxury it afforded, with its shining appointments, snowy towels, foaming soap. But he couldn't forget what Private Crowe had told about the dirt, the mud, the lice, the scratchy underwear. He was glad to think of the wealth coming to him from the goldmine, for he craved all the luxuries of life, and he wanted to be able to give them to other people. He loved white sheets, smooth and satiny, and beautiful rugs with deep rich colorings, music, pictures; but especially did he want these things for Helmi, who had such a love for beauty.

No matter where Jack's thoughts began they would soon come back to Helmi. He wondered if she had got the two hundred dollars all right. At first he had thought that he would have to send for it when they were outfitting at Peace River, but Keith sold another share, and then they were all right. He had even written out an order for a friend of Keith's who offered to advance the money and get it when he went to Eagle Mines. What had he done with that order? Yes, he remembered—Keith got it back from his friend and destroyed it.

The first day Jack was in the city he made a thorough search of all the Chinese places, but without result. When he came to Sam's he was met by the wily proprietor, who had learned in a hard school that it is foolish to give information. Sam could lay down all his knowledge of English in a fraction of a second. "I not know," all at once became his entire English vocabulary.

Sam had been in our law courts. He had listened to many learned friends disagreeing with other learned friends, and he had become somewhat of a learned friend himself. He had one rule, "admit nothing—deny everything—remember you were not there when it happened." So, when a well-dressed young man came asking for a Finnish girl with red hair Sam knew nothing. In Sam's limited sphere the relations between men and women were elemental and simple. Maybe the police wanted his red-haired girl—that might be. Well, Sam did not want to lose her, she was a good girl, honest girl—she rang up the right change. Sam did not usually trust any white girl with change, but he was glad now that he had found one whom he could not catch, for it might be she was honest all the time.

"No," Sam did not know—Sam did not know anything. Sam did not tell Helmi, either. "Nice girl, Helmi—if wanta fella she could get plentee—no use gettin' nice girl all excite."

Helmi went back to the "Good Eats Cafe" one day to see if it would be possible for her to be given longer hours. The dollar a night was not going to be sufficient for her needs. Her room rent was fifteen dollars a month, and even at that she suspected the Corbetts were paying some of it. She would like to go to work at two o'clock in the afternoon if

Sam could arrange this. He had been away for a few days and another Chinaman had been in charge.

When Helmi arrived old Sam was at his accustomed place behind the desk, very elegant in a new black suit and a white tie. He wore a white flower in his buttonhole, and resembled a church usher on Mother's Day. Helmi remembered how they looked in Miss Abbie's church. He was very friendly with her, and bowed cavalierly over her hand. Helmi had learned to suspect polite men of being drunk, but old Sam was always sober. The cafe, too, was festive in its appearance. Flowers in bloom were on the tables. A drooping fuschia in the window rained its crimson and purple blossoms down like a spraying fountain, and squares of embroidery hung on the walls. Helmi wondered at the changes. It must be some Chinese holiday, she thought.

Sam came around from the desk to greet her, and she noticed further improvement—Sam had false teeth, with some gold ones. His nails were daintily manicured and his hands heavily perfumed. "Nice led-haired girl," he said, shaking her hand sideways; "good girl cally tlay. Old Sam got nice liddle white girl now all his own. Soon she come, my girl—grand girl—Mrs. Sam Lee—drivee big car—my girl."

As he spoke a big gray car with silver mountings drew up to the curb, and a lady in a scarlet suit came out. She came into the "Good Eats Cafe," filling the doorway with color, like some strange tropical bird. Helmi's eyes were so dazzled by the vision that in her admiring survey she had not yet reached the face.

A shout came from under the drooping black hat, and the beaming lady bore down upon Helmi. "Helmi, my love, come to me! I always knew I would find you."

"Rose Lamb!" cried Helmi, breathless with excitement. "Rose, are you out?"

"Hush," cautioned Rose, dimpling and drawing her shoulders up, "I was never in. You and I met at a Young Ladies' Seminary—no trades-man's daughters allowed—remember! Not that good old Sam minds—

he's been in jail, and it makes them broad to go to jail; but for the sake of my social position, mum's the word. Sam, tea for two please. Sit down Helmi, and let me look at you.

"Have you been converted lately? O Lord, do you remember how we were prayed over? I got to be their little pet lamb—pure as the driven snow—but I drifted! Well where have you been?"

Helmi told her.

"Married? That's bad. But I knew it. I saw it in you—you were that kind. And your man has sort of been mislaid, temporarily. He is only a miner—let him go—it's beastly poor pay, I hear."

"But I want him to come back," said Helmi, "I love him, Rose."

"Ain't that like you, Helmi? Of course you do, and you have a baby, and I suppose you keep it too."

"I sure do," said Helmi.

Sam Lee had gone into the kitchen, and Helmi leaning close to Rose, said: "Rose, did you marry old Sam?"

"Kid, you've said it," replied the bride; "I sure did—license, ring and all, Sam Lee, widower, Rose Annabel Lamb, spinster—Anglican clergyman doing the job."

"Rose, how could you? He is not only a Chinaman, but old, very old; he must be at least sixty."

"Sixty!" Rose almost shouted. "Don't kid yourself—he's eighty. I wouldn't look at anyone only sixty—he might outlive me. Sam is safe— he'll snuff out like a gentleman. Little Rosie, all alone—think of it!— with some forty thousand bones. How's that!"

"No good," said Helmi, shaking her head; "no good."

"Kid, I couldn't work. I hate dishwater and I couldn't scrub—it always made my nose sore. I hate work and what could I do? If I had lots of money I'd run straight. Old Sam is not so bad, and the gray car is a pippin.

"Come and see our house, Helmi; it's swell—rugs of blue and rose, with one little tea house in the corner; tapestries in gold blossoms, lamps of hammered brass—oh, come and see it. Sam, some more ginger! Thanks, old top. Lots of room for you, too, Helmi. I'll give you a room in rose and gray with fresh flowers every morning. Come Helmi, let's have a little run in the car. I've been pinched once for speeding, but I'm careful now. I want to tell you about what happened after you left."

Helmi went with Rose to the car and stepped in after her. The sudden rush of air, the delightful feeling of motion, the sensation of freedom, with these Helmi's fears fell away. Impulsively she hugged her friend's arm. "Oh, Rose, it's good to see you," she said.

Two men on the sidewalk regarded them closely. One watched them with wicked-wise eyes, cynical and hard, the only gleam of gladness in them due to his suspicions being verified. The other man's eyes burned with a great sorrow and a bitter disappointment.

"You see what I said," remarked the first, "that woman driving the car is well known in the underworld. Lately she has come here as the mistress of a rich Chinaman. The Finnish girl is one of the gang, as you can see. Mr. Doran, you are well out of it."

Jack leaned back against the doorway, sick at heart.

"Now I want to tell you something," said Major Gowsett, for it was he; "that girl has no legal hold on you. Col. Blackwood did not record the marriage. He knew her history, you see. She has therefore no hold on you, so do not worry about that."

Jack turned away without speaking.

The loom of life went on with its weaving, but from Helmi's life the golden thread had gone. But, of course the flying shuttles cannot stop to look for ends. The loom of life does the best it can with the threads its shuttles are able to bring, but it takes no responsibility for the pattern.

Chapter XXVI

Mrs. Kalinski and Mrs. Corbett were having a cup of tea in the latter's big room one afternoon when Mrs. Corbett had finished her duties as janitor's wife who could be got by the hour to "do out" rooms for the tenants.

"I've turned out Mrs. Rowan and Mrs. Snider today, given Mrs. Brown a lick and a promise, and put Mrs. Flickdahl off until tomorrow," said Mrs. Corbett, as she set the peanut butter and strawberry jam on the table and proceeded to cut slices from the loaf. Mrs. Kalinski was still "waiting."

"It's a long time—the last month," said Mrs. Corbett soothingly, "sure every day brings it one day nearer, and it's yourself has everything ready and fine and nothin' to do but to hop into bed and call the neighbours and good old Dr. Eckhardt. I never saw a woman any readier than you are, with the name and all."

Mrs. Kalinski looked very smart in her black satin tea-gown and gold embroidery that her Isadore had brought from the store. She took her neighbour into her confidence. "No matter what I could say, mind you! The woman said she paid seventy dollars for it once, and Isy got it for fifteen. She wanted thirty, but Isy told her it was the worst thing to sell. Who was wearing tea-gowns now?—they was out of date like leg o' mutton sleeves. And all the time Isy was thinkin' of me. I had a red cashmere one with Watteau pleats when our Rachel was comin', and his papa says little Isaac will be served as good, even if it did cost fifteen dollars and could be sold for thirty easy. He's that good a man, and spares no expense in reason."

Mrs. Corbett brought the tea from the kitchen and filled the cups. "You and me are lucky women," she said, "to have two good men like we have. Ain't some of them the easy goin' divils, though? I don't know what to think of Helmi's man, though she sticks up for him and is afraid he's been lost in a storm or drowned in a river. Poor girl,—it's a shame to see her havin' to work in a Chinks, but what could the poor girl do? Not one of those dainty ladies would have her, they all had some reason."

"If she were just a Hebrew girl, now," said Mrs. Kalinski, "one could go to the Hebrew Association of Women and they would find a place for her. We would not have any nice white girls of ours workin' in a Chinese shop and havin' to take lippy talk from every Harry, Tom, Dicken, and maybe worse. Mrs. Sternborg and Mrs. Swartz are grand on that, and good girls they have found for our people."

Mrs. Corbett paused, with her saucer half way to her mouth. "Look at that now! Ain't the Jews wonderful to think of things? We've got grand societies, too, and I never once took thought of them. Sure we've got societies. They're all up to their eyes in pneumonia jackets and many-tailed bandages now, and socks for the soldiers, but they're grand women, too. When I came here first I used to take care of the Club room at the 'Y' and I used to see them there millin' round, very civil spoken women, too, and tryin' to make the world better, and God knows it needs it: I'll go to Mrs. Bell, the old lady, and I'm glad you spoke of this, Mrs. Kalinski. Maybe we can get a decent place yet for Helmi, though if she takes the baby away I don't know what I'll do with Rose and Dan."

Mrs. Corbett went that evening, after Helmi had gone to work, leaving the baby to the watchful care of Rose, who sat in No. 18 to do her lessons.

Mrs. Bell was at home, and would speak of Helmi's case at the meeting of the Lloyd George Chapter the next day.

A week later a new place was found for Helmi. Mrs. Bell said it was an ideal place, and while ten dollars a month was very little, still it was not every place she could have the privilege of keeping her baby, and Mrs. Herriott would be very kind to her. Mrs. Herriott was young and inexperienced, and found her baby a great care. Helmi could mind the two babies and Mrs. Herriott would do the work.

Old Sam was sorry to part with Helmi, and gave her a feather fan. "You come back some day—old Sam be glad. Good girl—cally tray—teachee make chop suey—come back! You come see my girl too, and have chop suey."

Helmi paid her rent at the "North Star," and had three dollars left.

The Herriott home, was a six-room bungalow on 127th Street, three blocks from the car line on 124th Street. It was a little house, low-roofed, square, with but little pitch in the roof, and high pillars in front, much too high for the height of the house, giving one the sensation as Helmi thought of seeing a cow getting up hind legs first. Rosie and Danny conducted her to the place, Rosie carrying the baby and Danny helping Helmi with the heavy valise.

"I hope you don't like her," said Rosie, "and then you'll come back. I'll bet her baby cries more than ours, and just when you get little Lili asleep, her kid will wake up whinin'. Well, anyway, Helmi, you can always come back, and we'll manage some way."

Helmi kissed her two good friends at the back door, but Rosie refused to go until she saw if the lady were at home.

"Maybe she's changed her mind," she said speaking from her experience with ladies—"or has got help—or somethin' has happened. You can't depend on these women in the West End. Ain't that right Dan? They don't pay their debts, either, very good. They always say

'Come back again.' Dan collected for a tailor, and he knows. They don't remember anything less than five dollars, and when they're stuck for another excuse they peep out of one of the windows to see who it is, and won't let you in."

Mrs. Herriott was in and had not engaged anyone else, and so the escort had to go home alone, which they did regretfully.

Helmi found the house in a state of siege. Confusion reigned everywhere. The invader slept in a baby carriage which filled the greater part of the living-room, and when he slept all noises were muffled. The grandmother, who had been conscripted into service, padded about in her bedroom slippers. The telephone bell was stuffed with paper. No one was admitted to the house, not even the baker.

There was a little room off the kitchen where Helmi and Lili were to sleep. It had just room enough to take in the rubber-wheeled carriage.

"Oh, I will be so glad to have someone to take this old baby off my hands," said Mrs. Herriott frankly; "he spoiled last summer for me, but I don't mean to let him spoil this one. Isn't a baby awful? I hope yours is good. Anyway, I can get out now, and, believe me, I am going."

Mrs. Herriott, having shaken off family cares, resumed her place in her little world. She curled and played bridge, and went to the matinee with her friends and came home only when everything was over. She was a pretty, plump-faced girl of twenty-three who had the misfortune to be the only child of adoring parents. "Maudie is not fond of work," her mother often said; "but never mind, she'll take to it when she has a house of her own." Young Robert Herriott, who had married her with pomp and circumstance at the First Church believed the same thing.

Maudie had been in a terrible rage about the coming of the baby, but her mother fondly believed she would be attached to it when it came. "They make their own place, babies do," she said. "Maudie will be so fond of it she wouldn't take a million dollars for it when she has had it two days." But Maudie's friends agreed among themselves that they would hate to offer it to her.

The baby was now two months old, and the great fountain of mother love which the baby's grandmother had hoped for was still either non-existent or untouched. "She'll take to it when it gets a little older," she would say. "You'll see, when it gets cute Maudie will take to it."

Helmi knew that cats sometimes refuse their young, but she did not know that it could be true of human beings.

In a week the siege seemed to be lifted. Long lines of washing had been fluttering on the clothes reel; closets were tidied; floors polished, the "old" baby put on a regular way of living. Mrs. Herriott had won the Ladies' Points competition at the rink, and her friends had told her she was looking years younger.

One night, when the Herriotts were going for a drive, Mr. Herriott wanted to take Helmi, too, and her baby. "That girl hasn't been out of the house since she came," he said, "Ask her to come, Maudie."

Maudie laid a well manicured finger on a neatly carmined lip. "Hush, Bob," she said, "don't spoil her, leave well enough alone. Come on, we'll take the Bunnings—they have no kids to want to come. Hurry, Bob!"

When they were in the car, Maudie finished the conversation. "Helmi is doing well, but don't fuss her up by taking her out. They get to know too much. Now Mrs. Bell when she spoke to me said I would have to get some one to wash; Helmi wouldn't be able to do the wash-ing, especially the hanging out of the clothes, on account of nursing her baby—she might catch cold. But Bob, she does it and washes beautifully. I just kept quiet. So we're saving two dollars a week there. Now, how's that? Am I a good wife for a poor man? I'll say I am. Those foreign girls are strong as horses. Well, she's good to the baby, anyway, but don't spoil her, for Heaven's sake. The more you do for people the more they expect—take it from me!"

To which Mr. Herriott replied: "I bet she'd like a ride, though; she's only a kid. She's younger than you are, and I think she looks pretty pale and tired sometimes."

"Look here," said his plump little wife, asserting her dignity. "Who is running the house?"

And when she said it she looked so utterly sweet and plump and pink and white, so much like a spoiled but very pretty child, that her husband kissed her and forgot all about Helmi.

Helmi had a friend in the bread man, who gave her snatches of news from the outside world. The soldiers from out at the Exhibition Grounds were going away soon. They would go direct to England, to Salisbury Plains. His boy was with them—"as good a boy as ever stepped." But he would go—"a chip off the old block." He had been in South Africa in the War—was mentioned in dispatches, too—but nobody knows anything about it now. The world soon forgets. These soldiers will be forgot, too, for all the bands are playin' for them now.

Helmi was not unhappy. She had pleasure in her work and in caring for little Lili, who grew lovelier every day. The Herriott baby was a heavy jowled child who slept well and cried profoundly. "Has she taken to it yet?" the grandmother asked, each time she came.

From her room Helmi could look north to the railway tracks and see the Peace River train come in as it crossed the street, moving silently along, like a square, black, jointed snake. She found herself watching for it every Tuesday and Saturday . . . It was queer that Sim had not answered her letters.

One night in April, when Mr. and Mrs. Herriott were away to a dance, Roland, their baby, grew suddenly ill—the usual symptoms, little hot hands, fevered breath and restless tossing head. Helmi was walking the floor with him when the parents came in at two o'clock in the morning.

"Lay him down and let him cry," said his mother, as she threw her cloak on the dining-room table; "it's his teeth! All kids have it; you're spoiling him."

"You'd better send for the doctor," said Helmi. "See how red he is—I am afraid of *tulirokko*—the red fever."

"Nonsense!" Maudie Herriott had just come from "The Macdonald." She had danced every dance and the exhilaration of it was still in her brain. The idea of this Finn girl saying the doctor should be brought!

Helmi was frightened. The baby's eyes were burning and rolled uncertainly, and the night was heavy with the sudden heat of spring. "Please do get a doctor, Mrs. Herriott," she pleaded; "it's bad, this sudden sickness; sometimes it brings on convulsions and babies die."

Mrs. Herriott took another look at the baby and felt his head and his hands. "Oh, he's all right—his head is a little hot, but his hands are cool—feel!"

The finger tips were cold.

"Well, I am going to bed; I've had a hard day, and there's another ahead of me tomorrow. I don't see that there's any sense running up a bill with a doctor when there's no need. All kids get sick sometimes, and the less notice you take of them the better."

The next day Lili grew hot and restless and Helmi sent for a doctor. In three days the doctor declared it to be scarlet fever, and the Herriotts decided that both children should go to the Isolation Hospital.

"Let me stay and keep them," pleaded Helmi; "I cannot let my baby go—she will fret for me—she will die among strangers. Please, Mrs. Herriott, let me stay, I will work for you for a year—for five years—for nothing—if you will let me stay here and keep her. And I will nurse Roland, too." Helmi was rocking herself from side to side in her anguish.

Mrs. Herriott did not hesitate a moment. "No, Helmi, we can't do that—they'll be all right at the hospital—it's the right place."

"But my little Lili will die! I nurse my Lili."

"Well, you'll have to wean her—they'll look after that. I can't help it anyway, so don't stare at me."

Helmi sprang to her feet and shook her mistress fiercely.

"I care! I love my baby; you do not love yours. You can send yours.

If he dies you will be glad. If my Lili dies I die too. Let me keep both, please, please!"

"Say, Bob, listen to this—wouldn't it jar you! Helmi, you have your nerve. Now, listen, they are both going. I guess if the Isolation Hospital is good enough for Roland Herriott it will do for Lili, so cut out all the fireworks and get them ready."

Plump and pink and white, with a baby smile, was Maudie Herriott, the petted child and wife, but hard and cruel as any toothless old crone.

Both mothers rode in the ambulance to the hospital, and, strangely enough it was Mrs. Herriott who became hysterical when the nurse took her baby from her.

The brown-eyed nurse who had received Lili read the misery in Helmi's white face, and patted her shoulder kindly. "I do not think your baby will have it very hard—she is a lovely little thing and looks quite strong. Don't worry over her, because we have splendid success with our babies here. She will have every care, I promise you. No, she will not fret much."

Helmi kissed her hand with a rapt look in her eyes, but she could not speak. Her heart would have broken when she saw Lili carried into the fever ward—away from her, with a door shut between them, if the kindly touch of the nurse's hand had not been laid on her shoulder. The hand was warm, human and strong, and its touch went with her when she went down the dark stairs to the ambulance which waited at the door.

Mrs. Harriott was weeping violently, but Helmi sat tight-lipped and pale, but tearless. The red cross on the frosted glass of the ambulance door held her eyes with gruesome fascination; to her excited imagination it seemed as if it were painted with blood.

When returning they were stopped at First Street by the closing of the black and white gates, for the afternoon train was going out—a special, carrying the soldiers. The station platform swarmed with people, and a band blared its music. Helmi hated the sound of it. How could any band play when there was so much trouble in the world and her Lili so sick? Once when she was a child at home she had drawn her hand across the plastered wall, and some of the plaster had caught below her finger nails, making her sick with a horrible sensation. The band music brought the feeling back to her again.

There were flags on the train, hanging out of the windows, fluttering like little red wounded things licking at the side of the car with red tongues. Helmi shivered as she watched them. From the window of the ambulance she could see the swarming crowds, but the train hid from her view the farewell scenes.

As the train moved slowly out, Helmi could see the faces gliding past her. Most of the soldiers were at the windows on the side next the station platform, waving to friends. Just as the last car went by, gathering up speed now, one man sat moodily looking out of the north window with eyes that saw nothing. Helmi from where she sat in the ambulance was not more than six feet from him as he passed. When his face came into view, she beat upon the glass like a mad thing, screaming: "Jack! Jack! look at me!" But though she saw him so plainly, he did not see her, and the train went on its way. Helmi's voice, like the sobbing of many others, was lost in the blare of the bands.

The next day Helmi went to the North Star Rooming House, walking wearily up the stairs to No. 19.

Mrs. Corbett opened the door to her as she had four months before, and again the anguish in the girl's face told its own story.

"My God! Helmi, is she dead?" asked Mrs. Corbett.

Helmi sat down before she answered.

"Is that all? Sure that's nothin'; every child takes scarlet fever. They're grand at the Isolation Hospital. I know big Miss Shaw up there, as grand a girl as ever went on rubber heels. Cheer up, Helmi, the little pet will be all right, please God. I thought the gypsies had stolen her by the look on your face, and I'm glad it's nothin' worse than scarlet fever."

"My man has gone to the war!" said Helmi brokenly; "I saw him on the train. He did not see me—he does not care about me."

Mrs. Corbett paused. This was a harder complication than the illness of little Lili, and for a moment even this determined optimist was floored—but only for a moment.

"Well, sure, when he's there you know where he is, and it's noble of him to go, Helmi—remember that. Now here, dear, take a cup of tea. Yes you can; a person can always take a cup of tea, no matter who's gone, and it makes life look a little brighter. Drink it down, dear, and have another. You look better now. Don't get down to mourning, Helmi; there's nothin' happened yet that can't come right, remember that; and your darlin', blessed child, with God's blessin', will come through the fever just the way we all did, and your man will come back again."

"But he doesn't want me any more. . . . I know now. The magistrate has turned him against me. I said I would kill that man, and I will."

"No, dear, no; you mustn't talk of killin' anyone. God will deal with the wicked in His own good time. You come with me to the Army and you'll find comfort in God's love. No killin', though, Helmi, that's bad. And see, dear, I was forgettin' there's two letters for you—just came yesterday."

Helmi took them eagerly and opened one. "It's a mistake," she said, listlessly. "See, there's money in it. No one would send me money. It has been opened too, and sealed up again."

Mrs. Corbett took it out of her hand. "It's for you, right enough," she said; "here's your name on it. It's a separation allowance for fifteen dollars from Arthur Warner, Eagle Mines."

"I do not know anyone called Arthur Warner," said Helmi.

"Well, he knows you, and that's better—anyway, he wants you to have the money, and you're a fool if you don't take it. Read the other one—maybe it will tell."

Helmi opened it and read. It was the letter Jack had opened at Eagle Mines. Helmi read it aloud to Mrs. Corbett. "I know now," she said. "He is a good man, that Mr. English. I will take the money—he means good by me."

"Sure he does," agreed Mrs. Corbett; "he seems like a good fellow, a good Englishman, and there's nothing finer in the world. Now Helmi, dear, I want you to lie down in Rosie's bed and have a good sleep, poor child. Now you'll be havin' trouble with your breasts, cuttin' off the baby so suddint, so I'll run in and borrow Mrs. Kalinski's breast pump—she's the grandest woman that for a neighbour, for she has everything from a boot-jack to curtain stretchers. You see in their business they get all sorts, and he gives her the run of the store—but have your sleep now, honey."

But Helmi's thoughts were not of sleep. She had a duty to perform, and which she had no desire to evade. One great purpose dominated her heart and cried aloud for fulfilment. The money which had come to her had made it possible. When Mrs. Corbett came back, Helmi was gone.

Chapter XXVII

D r. St. John lay one evening on the chesterfield in his den, before a cheerful wood fire. Eva was entertaining her Wednesday night "Bridge," and tinkles of laughter, high-pitched and nervous, shot through the velvety murmurs of conversation.

The doctor had listened to such conversation many times, and knew the little razor-sharp points of antagonism it held and which seemed to pop out like needles from a squeezed pin-cushion, thin, sharp, unexpected, for the temper of the guests was uncertain. They had no community of purpose—they were pursuing no particular trend of thought, they were time killers, sensation hunters. He knew the very odor of the room—sachet powder, cigarette smoke, flesh of women too scantily clad, perfume heavy and exotic, a sweet smell, yet not whole-some—like good apples wanting air.

The doctor could see it all like a picture. The dark brown back-ground, shot through here and there with little flashes of pale lightning that began in nothing and ended in nothing, led nowhere. Eva's friends met, chattered, parted, met again. No one any wiser or better, more inspired to nobler living. They were doing nothing wrong—it was even worse than that, he thought—they were doing nothing.

The doctor recalled that it was Wednesday night. His mother always went to prayer-meeting on Wednesday night. How Eva would laugh if anyone mentioned prayer-meeting. And yet human nature was the same. But somehow it was getting off the track. His mother had spent years on a treadmill, her days laid out for her in regular lines. Work stared at her from morning till night, and she did it, and held her head above it all. She was always sweet-tempered, interesting, sympathetic. Eva having nothing to do, did nothing, and doing nothing, degenerated, grew shallow, selfish, cross-grained and hard.

In his struggling days Dr. St. John had dreamed of having a house like this and a wife who would help him by her sympathy and under-standing. But something had spoiled his dream. He had the house and the practice, and some one to spend his money, but—.

In some ways he had been to blame—he had been too easy, indul-gent and foolish. Eva and her friends laughed at him, he knew. The ease with which Eva was able to deceive him furnished many a good story for the lively company which sat at the bridge tables.

It was when his mother came to visit him a year ago that the doctor began to see Eva as she was. He had tried to imagine what she would be like when she was as old as his mother, who at sixty five was as alert and eager-minded as ever, doing many of the things she had wanted to do all her life. To Eva she was a puzzle. How could anyone get such joy from going to the New Year Rally of Sunday School Children? Or why did anyone get up early on Sunday morning to go for a walk? Eva's studied politeness toward his mother irritated him, and it was a relief when his mother went over to Miss Abbie's to finish her visit. So passed another dream. He had so often thought of what a pleasure it would be to have his mother visit him. She was such a good sport, his mother.

Another matter was weighing heavily on the doctor's mind. More surgeons were needed at the front. Why should he stay here at ease? Dr. Brown, his young partner was seriously considering the matter. Dr. Brown had a wife and children—a wife who loved him. Dr. Brown had said that he would go, he being the younger man. That did not matter. Dr. Brown was needed here more than he, who had no one depending on him. Eva would be happier without him so long as the money held out.

These thoughts occupied the doctor's mind as he lay listening to the commotion across the hall. The first year of their married life, when he began to see that Eva had no intention of entering into his life seriously, he was sorely hurt. He had had dreams of domestic happiness since he was sixteen, and it is the loss of a dream that hurts the most. Now he was still hurt, but he was critical. When criticism begins to fill the mind the tenderness of love is over.

Dr. St. John would not have been critical of his wife if she had chosen to follow some profession. He would have liked that. He did not believe that every woman had to be run in the domestic mould, making the coffee and ironing shirts—anyone could do that! But the companionship—the good fellowship of a wife—how he craved it! And now that craving was slowly turning to resentment. Other men had wives—he had a queen of chatter, a hoarder of trinkets, a bridge player, a tea drinker!

The telephone rang.

"Yes, it is Dr. St. John. Who is speaking?"

"Jack—Jack Doran."

"Eva's brother? On your way through! Come along, yes, we are at home—I'll drive down for you—only thirty minutes. Grand Trunk? I'll be there—yes, Eva will come, too."

The Doctor hurried into the living-room and spoke to Eva. "Jack is at the station. Get on your things," he said, "my car is at the door. Leave the crowd here."

"We will all go," cried one girl, with very bare shoulders; "I want to see Eva's good-looking brother. Let's give him a regular send-off."

The crowd arose flutteringly, all chattering. There was something particularly irritating to the doctor in their idleness, their gaiety, their lack of seriousness. "Stay here," he said curtly; "Jack Doran has no desire to be met by a crowd of strangers for whom he cares nothing. He wants to see his sister."

Eva turned on him indignantly. "Well, I like that," she said. "Remember, a station is a public place—anyone can go. Come on, kids, every one of you."

The doctor took his wife's arm with a suddenness that surprised her and said, "Hurry Eva—have you no sense?"

"You have no right to be rude to my friends," said Eva peevishly, when they were on their way to the station; "you acted abominably just now!"

"Oh forget it!" the Doctor said, "and try to get a serious thought in your mind for once. Your only brother is going to war, and the chances are against your ever seeing him again. Have you nothing to say to him? Forget that cackling gang for half an hour. Their feelings are not hurt."

Eva looked at him in speechless amazement.

Jack had hoped that he might see his sister and the doctor alone. He wanted to tell his sister about Helmi. The boy's heart craved companionship—he must tell someone. But the whole crowd swarmed around him with their incoherent gaiety, their senseless chatter, and the few minutes went by uselessly. The Doctor was furious, and it was against Eva that his rage was directed. Here was her only brother going away, and she had not a serious thought in her head, not one loving, personal word for him.

The Doctor took Jack's hand at the last as they stood at the steps of the train. "I am going over too, Jack," he said; "it is going to be a long fight, and we will all be needed. I cannot stand back and see other men go. I am proud of you, Jack. Can I do anything for you?"

A great impulse to tell the Doctor came to Jack but the conductor was calling and the train bell was ringing.

"I wish I could have had a good talk with you," Jack said, as the train began to move.

That night when her company had gone, Eva came into the Doctor's room. His light was still burning, and she knew he was not asleep. Eva, sinuous and graceful, in a light gown of cream satin, was determined to check what was the first sign of insubordination in her husband. Her married friends assured her that if a man is "let away" with an exhibition of temper or crossness he will be worse the next time; so Eva had her mind made up to be very haughty and coldly proud. She would forgive him, but only after a distinct understanding.

"Well, what have you to say?" she asked him, with the queenly manner that had never failed.

"Nothing," he answered, "only that it is time you were in bed."

"Do you mean to say that, after insulting my guests."

The doctor laid down his book. "If your guests had any sense, which they have not, they would have stayed here and let you and me go alone. They don't know Jack and care nothing for him. They raced to the station because it was something to do, something to relieve the dullness of their vacant minds. I told you to hurry if you wanted to see your brother. Now you can be as hurt over it as you like. I am tired trying to understand you, and have come to the conclusion that there is nothing to understand, in fact you have ceased to interest me."

Eva had not expected this. "What do you mean?" she said at last.

"Just what I said! Selfish people pay for their selfishness in the end, though they may be able to run on credit for a long time. The world is at war, Eva, but you do not know it. While you and your overfed friends were eating and drinking downstairs, boys were dying in mud and cold to save the world, brave boys like Jack. Nurses were binding up shrapnel wounds while shells fell around them; refugees were pouring into England to be cared for by the women of England. No, Eva, your type might last a long time in peace, but it shows up badly in time of war."

Eva was looking at him now through half-closed lids. Dull anger burned in her eyes.

"You are no longer a child, Eva, though I can hardly say you are a woman. You are a perfect form to hang clothes on, and a very graceful dancer, and a very free spender—on yourself—and if you thought you could get away with it right now you would give a violent exhibition of anger. But something tells you it would be quite useless. You will never be an old woman, Eva; don't be afraid of that. Old women are patient, kindly, motherly people, ready to help, ready to warn, anxious— perhaps too anxious. You know the type, and utterly despise them. You were quite ashamed of my dear old mother when she came to visit us, she was so old-fashioned and quaint to you and your friends. No, you will never be an old woman, Eva; in another fifteen years you will be a stale novelty."

She turned and left him without a word. Reaching her room, she flung herself across the bed and wept tears of sheer vexation.

The next day the Doctor told his wife that he had enlisted for service overseas. Eva hoped and expected right to the last minute that he would apologize and beg to be forgiven, but she was disappointed, and the hardest part of it was that he did not seem to care.

Chapter XXVIII

The people of Bannerman have not forgotten April 25th, 1915. The day began peacefully enough, with only a reddish tinge in the sunshine to mark it from other days, and that blinding heat which seems more oppressive in April than in July. The Spring had come early in Northern Alberta and now the budding of the earth was advancing with feverish haste. The red tassels of the poplars were paling into feathery gray, and already some were to be found littering the woodland paths, their work was done, they could take their rest.

Of all the spring birds that had come back to gladden the land the crows were most in evidence, for they had come in thousands from the south, filling the air with their clamor. In every flock that came, a noisy minority seemed to dominate, sometimes dividing from the company to seek their own way, and then, finding their following not so great as they had expected, returning noisier than ever to demand that another vote be taken because the first one had not been constitutional. Vastly entertaining is the crow, and full of a caprice that marks him for a blood brother of the human family. But he is welcomed by the northern dwellers—not because of himself or his habits, which are reprehensible, but because he is a portent of the Spring.

The willows that grew beside the river were blushing as the sap rose, green, yellow or red according to their kind—and the roads began to whiten with the fuzz from the aspens.

But, on this twenty-fifth day of April there arose out of the west a sheer black cliff of cloud into the boundless blue—a thick, deep cloud, in which silent lightnings played; and as the day went on, it shoved up higher and higher into the sky until at three o'clock it was ready to cover the sun.

During this time the heat had not abated. The air grew heavy and oppressive. It was the sort of a day when horses break into foamy sweat and people feel cross-grained, clammy, irritable, and full of aches and pains which they attribute to the weather.

The edge of the cliff had a whitish color at four o'clock, when the sun had gone under, and all the trees were standing still expectantly, as if bracing themselves for something which they were unable to help.

In the gathering gloom the houses in Bannerman, grouped around the station, looked more than ever like cats about to spring. The clouds are rolling now, with white lines on their billows, and there is a distant rumble of thunder, like the roar of a far-away city.

All day the rain clouds threaten and thunder growls, but it is not until night has fallen that the change comes. The crows that have been sitting like birds of ill omen, humped up on the trees, fly further back into the bush, as if in dread.

On the train coming to Bannerman sits Helmi, very pale, very determined, with a purpose so terrible she does not look at her fellow-passengers, for the fear is on her that they might divine her errand and try to dissuade her from it. She has made a vow of vengeance, and she will keep it. Why should she spare the man who has wrought so much evil in her life? There is a burning, torturing pain in her heart that only revenge can ease, and as she sits at the window looking out into the gathering storm, she gloats over the scene. She will come in upon him as he sits at his littered table—the dirty, grimy old man, who kept so safely the lying newspaper, guarding it, hoarding it, to do her harm. Other things he lost in the confusion and untidiness of his ugly den, but this he treasured safe, and showed it to her Jack—poisoning his mind against her—and now her Jack had gone overseas, angry and bitter—to be killed,—and little Lili, when the fever came on her, had no home where she could be nursed back to life—no home, poor little precious Lili, with her silky brown hair and soft little caressing lips.

The fever in her breasts when she thought of Lili burned like a thousand red hot needles, until the perspiration broke in beads on her face. She would see the color fade from her enemy's face when fear gripped his wicked old heart. She had thought of it often since she saw Jack's face gliding, gliding away from her . . . she would see the color go in patches from his face, and he would beg for mercy when he saw the gleaming barrel of the revolver—beg and whimper and call upon his God.

Wild strains of blood in Helmi's heart were crying to her to strike and be avenged, to strike and not to spare; and the pain, the horrible drawing, twisting pain around her heart grew more maddening every moment, and in every pang and spasm that tore her was a tongue that cried "Revenge!"

Once Helmi thought of God, when a flare of lightning lit up all the countryside, revealing farm houses ghostly white, and bending trees that crippled before the rushing wind. God? a lot He cared; God was with the magistrate and let him live secure while her Jack went out with a bitter heart to die and little Lili tossed in her fever with no mother to comfort her!

Helmi had ceased to reason and ceased to fight—she only felt. The primitive passions were ablaze in her. She had been robbed of her mate and her child. Red murder gleamed in her eyes.

When the train stopped at Bannerman the storm was at its height. The wind had the whine of stretched wires in it, and whistled across the deserted platform with a horrible hissing sound. The night was inky black, with bursts of lightning blinding her eyes, and continuous bellows of thunder, like a hundred fire-engines roaring past, shutting out every other sound. Helmi knew her way as if by instinct. In the lightning's revealing flashes the house she sought was easily found. She was breathing now like a person with pneumonia, her nostrils quivering like a wolf-hound's when he has his quarry at bay. The revolver was in her hand, and in each flash of the lightning it gleamed like a blinding searchlight. Each chamber was loaded, for Helmi intended to do her work completely.

She reached the verandah steps, remembering the one that was broken, carefully making no noise, and stood at the uncurtained window looking in. The man she sought sat at his table with a glass and bottle beside him. A roar of thunder made the bottle tremble on the tin tray and rattled the bricks in his chimney. He started and looked toward the window, though Helmi had made no sound.

Helmi moved a step nearer and tapped on the glass. She wanted him to know—to see. She wanted to see the cringing fear—she wanted him to beg—to plead. He came over to the window, and he must have seen her face, white and awful in the darkness, for he reeled back in fright with a scream of horror . . .

Then came a crash—a shuddering, sickening crash—with blinding blue lights that seemed to strike at Helmi's eyes like a thousand furies. There was a sound of crashing timber and a confusion that flung Helmi to her knees. When she opened her eyes and looked through the window she saw her enemy lying dead on the floor—his face livid, his eyes wide open, full of terror . . .

When Helmi came to herself she was running through the storm on feet shod with fright—running as if all the fiends of the night were in pursuit, the sky opening and shutting with dazzling lights and blinding darkness; night voices screaming, and louder than all, her own heart pounding in her ears.

Sometimes she fell, rising to her feet again; sometimes she felt a sudden blow, as if a crashing tree had struck her as it fell; but always her fear drove her on.

She had no sense of fatigue as she ran on and no plan of flight; but a strange homing instinct led her in the direction of Eagle Mines. Even in her hysteria and frenzy her feet carried her toward the little house where she had been loved and secure.

Then came the rain, a furious pelting rain that seemed to fall in drowning sheets of water. Every time the heavens opened with the bursts of thunder another downpour drenched the earth.

Suddenly Helmi was aware that some animal was running beside her, and in a flash of lightning she saw the sable collie, her breast showing ghostly white against the blackness of the night.

The nearness of something warm and living gave Helmi courage, and, falling beside the dog she clasped her arms around it in a sudden passion of weeping. The animal licked her hot face soothingly, whimpering softly, and with strange comfort, in its almost human tenderness. Her wet clothes hung on her now like heavy weights. The dog ran on ahead with encouraging barks and Helmi following begged the animal not to leave her alone in the darkness.

A great weariness came over Helmi now, and a growing fear that her strength was leaving her, but the dog was bounding back to her every few moments and urging her as plainly as a dog could to come on a little farther.

Suddenly at the mouth of the cave, black and terrible, the dog stopped and pulled her by the hand. Helmi followed blindly into the midnight blackness, into which even the lightning could not penetrate. She found something soft beneath her feet, and, stooping down, found a bed of hay, dry and comfortable, and on it she fell, grateful to be out of the lashing fury of the storm.

The storm still roared in her ears, and the fury of the rain filled the cave with a sound like a roaring cataract.

Helmi slept the sleep of utter exhaustion, for when she awakened the gray dawn was showing at the mouth of the cave. She looked around for the dog, but she was gone. The pain in her breasts was like a thousand knives twisting and torturing her, and a cry of utter anguish broke from her lips.

Then she remembered the horror of the night before and the terrible deed she had done. She saw again that face of fright and heard the scream.

She went to the mouth of the cave and saw below her the river, running so fair and peaceful and serene. The early morning light, platinum gray, was lying gently on the river's bosom, from which soft little veils of mist were ascending. Helmi shrank back from it in fright, remembering the man who had buried his troubles in its treacherous depths. She clung to the side of the cave, pleading with the river not to tempt her. Watching its current she seemed to see Jack's face again gliding away from her. Then came little Lili's face, so cool and peaceful and smiling, with no more fever or pain, and an irresistible impulse to cool her burning, tortured breasts, in the quiet green waters of the river drove her forward.

For one brittle moment she swayed toward the stream . . . Then something bounded against her, throwing her backward to the grass, and her friend of the night before was beside her, whimpering, whimpering, with a tenderness that Helmi knew, for it spoke a universal language. She crawled back in the cave, wide awake now, but writhing in her misery. Then came Cleo the dog, with something in her mouth which she laid in Helmi's arms—a little furry, cuddly puppy, with a fat little body and cool, soft, eager, questing lips . . .

When Helmi awakened, with a brain cleared of her midnight terrors and a body eased of its pain, she noticed the revolver, which through all her mad flight she had clutched in her hand. Horribly it recalled to her the madness of the terrible night and the loathsome deed that she had done. And yet—and yet—now that her brain was clearer, she could not recall that she had really fired the weapon. Her hand had been on the trigger when the lightning came.

She sprang toward it eagerly, for it could tell her what she wanted to know. Opening the chamber with trembling hand, she found every cartridge was in its place!

Then the soul of Helmi was born anew in thankfulness to God, and in a faith in His goodness that never again wavered, for God had saved her from sin. God had intervened to save her when her heart was farthest from Him. God was her friend. He loved her—He would not let her sin! With His own arm He had saved her.

Helmi went to the opening of the cave and drank in the beauty of the morning. The sun had just come over the edge of the earth, sending a sheen of gold and rose along the top of the mist that filled the valley below. As she watched, enraptured in her new-found gladness, the mist began to form into wisps and threads that curled and rose over the surface of the river, their upper ends twisting and thinning into the air.

A song burst from Helmi's heart, a song of gladness and love and faith—a song that the Blue Book had taught her:

"When the mists have rolled in splendour from the beauty of the hills,

And the sunshine falls in gladness on the rivers and the rills."

There was a whimper beside her. Cleo had come out of the cave. Helmi fell on her knees beside her, and kissed her honest forehead. "Cleo! Cleo!" she cried, "the dog God sent!"

Chapter XXIX

Helmi reached her own house that morning before the people of Eagle Mines were stirring. It was a sweet morning, without a trace of the storm of the night before, only that the air was washed clean and tasted cool in the mouth like a drink of spring water. She walked with her old sprightliness and without a single trace of fatigue.

Cleo followed her with one pup in her mouth, and Helmi carried the other two. The door of the house was not locked, and Helmi soon had a fire burning and a pot of porridge cooking for herself and the dog.

The house showed the traces of the hunting parties that had made it their abode, and from the fact that they had left the house dirty and littered, Helmi knew that they were not real hunters, but only city men out looking for game. The true hunter will leave everything as he finds it; this is the law of the wilderness. But in Helmi's heart this morning there was no resentment as she swept and scrubbed. She had received so much from God that she could easily forgive any of His children, and as she worked she sang.

When the porridge was cooked and the condensed milk poured over it, she called Cleo, who had stayed outside until she was invited to enter. "Come in, Cleo," she said, "my house is yours. You and I will never part, and your pups are welcome, too. Come on!" Cleo came in, with a pup in her mouth, smiling as broadly as she could without altogether dropping the pup.

The dog's hunger was pathetic. All the more because it tried so hard not to appear ravenous. This was evidently her first good meal for several days. The puppies, tired out by their adventurous night, were soon fast asleep in a box in which Helmi had placed an old coat of Jack's, and in which they curled up into an indistinguishable mass of sable and white wool, with only one little round head showing.

When Cleo had eaten her breakfast she stood at attention, her eyes fixed on Helmi's face, as if she were trying to read her mind.

Helmi patted the dog's head. "Take a sleep, Cleo," she said, kindly; "when I get my house cleaned up and my clothes dried I will tell you all my plans. I do not know where we are going to live, you and I and our families, but I know we are going to live together. I heard many times in the city that no one wanted a girl with a baby, so I suppose a girl with a baby and a dog and three pups is not wanted either. But still I have faith in God, Cleo—He always helps. Now lie down and be happy; we have enough here for a few days."

Life had changed for Helmi. The demon of revenge which had embittered her heart had been laid to rest by the hand of God, her friend. In her simple theology God had actually reached down His hand through the blackness of the storm and struck the magistrate dead because he had brought such evil upon her, and to prevent her from committing the crime of murder. God would be her friend for evermore; she would trust Him now whatever came. She had now no more fears for her baby. Lili was in God's keeping—God and the brown-eyed nurse who had spoken so kindly to her.

After a couple of hours of vigorous work Helmi had her house spotless again. Then she lay down to sleep, for a delicious weariness had come over her, and with it a sense of security and peace such as she had never known in all her life before. "Home and God," she murmured to herself drowsily, "Now I can sleep."

It was the middle of the afternoon when Helmi wakened. Cleo was sitting beside her, watching her. The pups were still sleeping. She sat up, shaking out her golden hair. The fire had died down but the house was pleasantly warm.

Outdoors the sun shone brilliantly, and Helmi went out to inhale the delectable odors of spring. How she had missed this in the city! But here it was as poignantly sweet as ever. The wind from the river brought to her the medicinal tang of the Balm of Gilead, pungent and healing, and Helmi's heart responded to it with a throb of love, for she remembered the salve her mother used to make of the buds, boiled with clean white lard on the stove, strained through a white cloth and put away in little glass pots for use all the year. As she breathed in the odor reminiscently, from the woods behind the station came the liquid notes of the meadow lark.

The heavy rain had washed the roots of the old dead grass into the ground, leaving the bold young shoots showing, and the air had such a balmy mildness that Helmi was content just to sit and breathe it and watch the clouds, clear and white, like lamb's wool, sailing overhead in the limitless blue.

She wanted to sing a song of the passing winter, with all its strength of frost and weight of snow, its frozen rivers and leafless trees, for every budding tree and springing flower and carolling bird was singing it, too. She remembered a song Mrs. St. John used to sing, which she said was an old-fashioned thing, but she sang it to please the doctor, who liked the old songs best:

> "Blue bird, true bird, bird with the golden wing,
>
> Do you bring me a letter or do you bring me a ring?"

Helmi brought out a chair, and sitting on it, nursing her knees, she sang in perfect happiness. She had four dollars in her pocket; a sick baby in the Isolation Hospital; a dog with three pups to whom she had promised food and shelter; a husband who apparently had deserted her; not a relative nearer than Finland; but she sang a song of hope and love and spring, looking into the blue sky above her, for in her heart there was the peace which passeth all understanding!

Mrs. McMann, on her way to the store, saw Helmi sitting at the end of the house and heard her singing, and forthwith forgot that she had left an oven full of pies.

"Helmy," she called, as she came nearer, out of breath in her hurry, "What is wrong with you? Have you come back?"

Helmi quickly rose up to greet her. "There's nothing wrong, Mrs. McMann. I'm all right—I'm fine—I'm happy that's all."

"But Helmi, where is your child?" Mrs. McMann was prepared to show a strong if somewhat belated interest in Helmi's baby.

"She is all right, too," Helmi said; "She is in the Isolation Hospital with scarlet fever, but is doing well and will be out in a few weeks."

Mrs. McMann heard the news with doleful forebodings.

"Oh, Helmy, don't set your heart on her if she has scarlet fever. It always leaves something behind it—deafness or blindness or something."

Helmi resisted an impulse to laugh. "Oh, I don't think so," she said, "she will be all right. I feel sure she will be well. I am not worried."

Helmi's cheerfulness seemed most untimely; nor could she explain it to Mrs. McMann—there was a greater bar between them now than even that of language.

"Well it's grand to take things as easy as you do, Helmy, I must say. Now when my children were little they had the fever, too, all together; not very bad, but I worried. Mr. McMann—no it was Mr. Bush I had then—scolded me for crying all the time, but I couldn't help it. My, how I cried! He could not understand a mother's heart, of course. But no doubt girls are different now—I was so conscientious. I suppose in a way you are glad to get away from the baby for awhile? Well it was different with me—I slaved for mine. But it doesn't pay. Are you goin' to stay? No! Goin' back are you? City life is too much for girls these days. Picture shows attract them. Well, in the midst of life we are in death, remember that, Helmy, and don't put your trust in worldly pleasures. Did you hear what happened to the magistrate at Bannerman last night?"

In her happiness Helmi had not been thinking of the magistrate. Startled by Mrs. McMann's enquiry she could only say "Do you mean Col. Blackwood?"

"Yes, the same one—the one that forgot to put it down in his book. He won't forget no more—he was struck with lightning."

"How do you know?"

"He was found lying on his back, stone dead, and his chimney all knocked down, and his eyes wide open."

Helmi shuddered—she knew just how the eyes looked.

"It gave me such a turn when I heard it, and I ain't been so well anyway. My stomach's up on me again, Helmy; I believe I'll have to go home and see a doctor. I can't trust any of the doctors here—they haven't got the papers like they hold in the States. All my trouble is inward, Helmy, and I don't believe these doctors could ever understand it."

"I am sorry," said Helmi; "I wish I could help you."

In her new found happiness Helmi could understand Mrs. McMann and her pitiful little striving for praise and applause. Her sordid life, her little meannesses, her petty jealousies, her dull gray outlook, smote Helmi's heart now with pity.

"You're a good girl, Helmy, no matter what you've done or haven't done, and I've a good mind to take you back, no matter what anyone says."

Helmi laughed as she patted her visitor's arm. "Where is good old Sim?" she asked quickly. "Is he still here? He did not write to me."

"Oh, didn't you hear? He had an accident in the mine and hurt his leg. He is still in the hospital, so I guess that's why. They say he'll never be able to night-watch again. You know I miss him, too, and wish now that I hadn't been quite so sharp on him. Well, won't you stay, Helmy?"

"No, I am going to the City," said Helmi, "but I want you to feed Cleo and the pups for me. There's plenty of scraps from your table, and they can sleep in my house. I'll ask Bill Larsen to shut the door at night and open it in the morning, and when Lili is better I will come back. You will like my Lili, Mrs. McMann; she can smile now and play with her hands."

Mrs. McMann sighed. "I am always sorry when I see a girl baby—life is so hard for us women."

Helmi got another letter at the post-office, a letter from Arthur Warner enclosing another fifteen dollar cheque. He was over in France now, on active service, and the letter was written as he sat waiting for the signal to go over the top in an attempt to capture a German position.

"It's good to have someone to write to, Helmi, someone who cares; and I want you to do something for me. It worries me to think of my house and garden lying idle there and going to ruin. I wonder if you would go there to live. The garden has raspberries and currants and strawberry plants too, and there are provisions in the house for a year. If you go there I want you to take Cleo, too, and give her a home. She is a wonderful dog. I cannot tell you what she has been to me. And my horse, Sailor, that I left with the Ransoms would be handy for you to drive to town. I would feel better if I knew you were there, dear Helmi, and I hope you will go. It does not seem reasonable to believe that I shall ever come back, but if I do, the place will be in better shape for your having occupied it. So you will be doing me a good turn. Write soon and often, Helmi, please."

At the bottom of the letter there was a postscript. "You will never need to be bothered with these meddlesome prospectors hunting for coal, for I bought all the mineral rights; so if the bank of the creek is solid coal, and I rather think it is, they can never come in without your consent. If you want to plant the garden this spring you will find the seeds in the root-house, all labelled. Maybe I had the wrong slant on life, Helmi, wanting to build a wall around myself. I've had time here to think it over, and I can see it was a mistake. One cannot live that way. Now I want you to do what you like with everything that is there. I have made my will and left all to you. My lawyer here will arrange matters fully if anything happens. I enclose his address. Now we are going. A.W."

Helmi was in her own little house when she read the letter, Cleo whimpering at her feet as if she knew her master had written. "He is well, Cleo, and he wants you and me to live together, and so we will. We had decided that already, and now I see God has sent me a home as well as a dog to keep me company. I do not know how we will make a living there, eight miles from any settlement, but we should worry over a little thing like that. God will provide for us some way, Cleo."

When Helmi returned to the city she went to the hospital for news of Lili, and she went without fear. She had the assurance of Lili's safety, and as she sat in the small, dark waiting room it did not occur to her that she was a lonely girl in a big city, with a sick baby and no money. Helmi was already planning her summer and counting the days until little Lili could go with her.

The nurse who had so kindly received the baby came to speak to her. "Oh, I remember you," she said smiling, "you are looking much happier. I told you she would do well, and she has. She was very ill the second night, but a change came about daybreak. The fever left her then and she went to sleep and has been doing well ever since. If you will go out and stand on the north side of the hospital I will show her to you through the window."

Helmi's face beamed with the prospect. "What will I have to pay?" she asked the nurse.

"Nothing, dear, not a cent. The City provides this hospital, everyone pays for it, so do not worry over that."

"It is like a dream," said Helmi; "everyone is so good."

When the nurse came with little Lili in her arms and Helmi saw the beloved little head of brown hair and the little face like an exquisite flower, her heart was full of love and gratitude, and when the nurse lifted the tiny hand and waved it toward her, Helmi could not see any more for the rush of happy tears. She came back into the office again to ask for Roland.

"I almost forgot the other baby," she said; "is he doing well?"

"You are more concerned than his mother," said the nurse, "though his grandmother has been here several times. He will get better we think. He is a strong baby, but a baby needs to be loved. Care is not enough—there is something more."

"I know," said Helmi.

To the North Star Rooming House Helmi went to explain her absence to her good friends, the Corbetts. Mrs. Corbett was alone, and over a cup of tea Helmi told her story. It was easy to tell Mrs. Corbett; she knew about God and how good He can be.

"Thank God, you're alive, Helmi! You gave me an awful scare clearin' out that way with the wild foreign look in your eyes. I did not know what you were up to, but I could only pray God to take care of you, for vain was the help of man and me not knowin' where to look for you. My Gosh child, what have you done to your boots?"

Helmi told her about her flight through the woods, the coming of the dog, and everything.

"Look at that now! Ain't God wonderful? That's what Christ said over and over again, only the people couldn't sense it. Well, I'm glad you've found peace, Helmi; it's the greatest gift God has sent to us. And you got the money, too? Well, get a new pair of boots, child, good strong ones. If a person has good boots and a good bed they're all right, for you are in one or the other of them all the time. And will you go to the Englishman's house, Helmi? But how can you live there alone, eight miles from the mines? If you were near enough you could run a boardin' house."

"I am going," said Helmi, "as soon as Lili is well enough. I am not a bit afraid now, and, Mrs. Corbett, in the holidays won't you let Rosie and Danny come? We'll get a cow somewhere, and there will be wild berries; and I know there will be lots of flour and oatmeal in the house, and it will be just like a picnic all summer. You will let them come, won't you, Mrs. Corbett?"

"It will be a lot easier to let them go than try to stop them when they hear of it—they're fair witched over you and the baby. Well, well, well, Helmi dear, ain't it wonderful how things come out?"

When John Corbett was told the whole story that night he sat for a long time smoking a meditative pipe, its gentle put-put making the only sound in the room. Helmi was going to stay with them until Lili could be taken from the hospital. No. 18 being occupied, Helmi was to share Rosie's narrow bed, the lack of space of which would be amply overcome by the warmth of Rosie's affection.

Helmi sat on a couch which later would be turned into a bed for Danny, and enjoyed the luxury of having such a welcome as the Corbetts gave her.

"I am thinking," said John Corbett, after a long pause, "that maybe the Englishman is the best man of the two."

"Oh, no, no, Mr. Corbett!" Helmi cried, distressed. "Mr. English is my good friend—I like him—he is so good—but I love my Jack. He is my man—there is a big *kiista*—what you call difference—isn't there, Mrs. Corbett? You tell him!"

"Tell him!" said Maggie Corbett, scornfully. "He knows, the sly old dog! He knows. I have often told him I'd rather be fightin' with him than agreein' with any other man. That's love—and he knows it!"

Chapter XXX

Vehemoor German prison camp, known also as Cellelager Six, was built on a peat bog from which the peat had been removed, leaving a sour, raw mud, on which not even a plank or log was laid. When the prisoners stepped out of the door they went to their knees in the indescribable muck. The condition of the camp inside may be imagined. A crowded room of miserable men; two smoking stoves burning the smouldering peat; double rows of berths where greasy blankets on planks furnished the beds; despair written on young faces—despair and bitter hatred.

Here sat Jack Doran, on this wet night in January, 1917, listening to the sleet slithering down the small windows. He had been in three prison camps before this, having attempted to escape from Geissen and from Callelager One, been caught and strafed, the last time in the dark cells at Oldenburg. He was dressed in the garments supplied by the Red Cross for prisoners, and carried himself with something of his former erectness. A white V was showing in his brown hair, and there were hard lines around his mouth. Two years of war had told on him. Still there was something about him that suggested hope. Many of the prisoners had the beaten look of men whose spirits are broken, the condition of soul desired by the German guards for the men under their care.

Jack Doran, thin, pale, determined, sat planning another escape. He had often wondered at himself for his tenacity. Life had not been so sweet that he should so earnestly desire it. In the days of his freedom he had not found happiness, but the fires of youth still burning in his heart urged him on. He had been captured in the night attack on Gavrelle, May 3rd, 1916, when part of his platoon lost their way in the darkness and found that they had the enemy behind them as well as ahead of them, and suffered under heavy artillery fire. Jack ran back to try to save his captain, who had fallen wounded, and they were both captured and separated, his captain going to another camp.

Jack had made his two other attempts in company with a Canadian, who was captured the same day, but when punished the last time in Oldenburg, his friend was sent to some other camp, for the German O.C. believed that separation would make it easier to hold these two adventurous ones.

Soon after coming to Vehemoor, Jack had been fortunate in finding a compass under a pile of peat in the bog where the prisoners were sent to work, probably left there by a prisoner who was fearful of having it found on him, and had abandoned it along with his hope of escape. The possession of a compass, being proof of the desire to escape, was in German prison camps an indictable offence. But Jack had found a loose board in the wall beside his bunk, and there he now kept it.

There were two other men in the camp who had attempted escapes, and between them and Jack a certain freemasonry existed. They met as often as they could to discuss their plans, and on the coldest days volunteered for work on the bog in order that they might have a few hurried words together. They knew that if they showed any unusual friendship they would be suspected of laying plans.

Only desperate men would ever have dreamed of such a plan as theirs. The camp was fenced with eight strands of barbed wire, and every sixth fence-post carried an arc light. But with the aid of a file which one of the men possessed, they would cut the two lower strands, at dusk, just before the lamps were lighted, and crawl through. At the last moment the other two men grew panicky.

"It is sure death," said one; "they'll catch us. I can see how they are watching us. I'd go, and take a chance only I have a wife and kid—I've got to think of them."

The other man declared the plan a foolish one on account of the weather. "January in Germany is too much like the corner of Portage and Main," he said.

A new batch of prisoners had come in that day, and one of them, who was standing near enough to hear, came to Jack and asked if he might go. He was a grizzled man of about thirty-five.

"I have no one depending on me," he said, "and I have already tried twice."

"Come along,—sure," said Jack, "three times and out."

"Thank you so much," said the man heartily.

Jack was startled by his politeness. A prison camp does not always foster the social amenities.

"Your name is Doran, is it not?" asked his new friend. "Mine is English—at least that is my nickname. We are both from Canada . . . We might as well try it as die here . . . there is always a chance."

While the prisoners were taking their exercise just at nightfall walking up and down the enclosure listlessly, aimlessly, Jack lay beside the fence filing away the two lower strands of wire. This done he crawled through, English following. The prisoners, who were all in the secret, kept a sufficient number directly in front of them to hide them from the camp.

Out into the bog went the two desperate men, fighting for what we hold so lightly because we have never lost it. Their enemies were cold and hunger and the pitiless rains which seemed to fall every day. They journeyed only by night. Jack found his new friend's knowledge of the country to be remarkable. He seemed to know every village, and he spoke German as well as a native. In this way they were able to travel after dark on the roads, and once they got a lift from a kind-hearted waggoner, with whom English carried on a long conversation, eliciting the information that everyone was tired of the war, but it was considered the wisest course to give the English a proper beating and teach them not to start another. He asked them to come in to his house for supper, but they were afraid to do that, their Red Cross clothes would betray them. The kind-hearted man gave them some sticks of liquorice from a bag he was taking home to his children.

"This man is the true German," said English that night as they continued their journey, "genial, simple, hard-working. The Germany that I knew when I lived here was a land of music, fairy tales, and a certain child-like simplicity. There was an inherent desire to make things beautiful, to turn desert places into gardens. But I was always afraid of the Prussians and their cast-iron methods. That, combined with the simplicity of the Germans, has made the war possible."

The fugitives had need of all the advantages English's knowledge of the country and language gave them, for the season of the year was unfavorable. The leaves were gone from the trees, making shelter difficult; there were no vegetables in the gardens, no cows in the field to furnish hungry travellers with a handy meal, and they could not be sure of finding a spruce thicket or a wood of Scotch fir just when daylight was coming, but there was one advantage in winter travel—the nights were longer.

A hundred times Jack blessed the happy chance which brought English to camp that day. His knowledge of wood-lore was wonderful—he seemed to carry everything that was needed—a sort of Robinson Senior from "Swiss Family Robinson." He made a fire each morning in the gray dawn to dry their clothes, explaining to Jack that a fire was almost invisible then. In daylight the smoke shows, at night the flame, but in the steely blue dawn a fire can be enjoyed in comparative safety.

In two weeks they reached the river which would determine their fate. Beyond it lay Holland and safety. The first night they stayed in the woods on the bank, trying to think out a plan. The river was in flood, so swimming was out of the question. Uprooted trees floated in its current. Vainly they hoped for a boat or a raft. The magical happenings which come to travellers in books did not come to them—not a boat, not a raft, not even a rope.

From their cover in the trees Jack and his companion could hear the sounds from the other side of the river, the ringing of bells, the shunting of cars. There seemed to be only one way, and that was to attempt the bridge. It probably would be guarded heavily, but English's knowledge of German might help. It looked to be the only chance.

All day they waited for the night to come. They had two good German smocks, stolen from a clothes-line, and Jack had a warm pair of stockings. To get these English had gone boldly into a garden as they came through a village. He had a way of quieting the dogs by a peculiar whistle and this gave him a distinct advantage. The dogs who came out barking fiercely, changed their attitude when he spoke to them, and even showed a disposition to follow him.

"If the dogs could bring us food we would have plenty," he said that day, as they sat in the spruce thicket. "The chances are against us, Jack, but one of us may get over."

"One of us!" exclaimed Jack, "It must be both or none!"

"No!" said the other, "it does not matter much about me. No one cares so very much, and it happens that the one person who cares a little bit about me, cares very much about you."

Jack looked at his companion—dishevelled, dirty, long-haired and long-whiskered, his eyes bloodshot—and wondered if his mind were going. "And who is that?" he asked gently as if he would humor his poor friend's mood.

"Your wife, Helmi."

"Helmi!" Jack repeated, "My Helmi!"

"Yes, yours—she is the only woman except my mother who ever cared whether I lived or died."

Then he told Jack of his quarrel with Larsen in Eagle Mines and of Helmi's kindness, and of the week he had stayed in her house.

"She asked me to pray for you, Jack," he concluded, "and I kissed her golden hair. She told me she was sure you would go to the war, and asked me if I met you would I be your friend. That is why I came—it seemed as if I must come—when I found you at Vehemoor."

Jack's voice trembled as he spoke. "Then you are Arthur Warner, and I have been doing you wrong in my thoughts. No one told me you were hurt—they only gave me half the story. When I got back I found Helmi gone—gone without a word. She had been gone a week—I was a month late—but she might have waited."

The trees were throwing long, cold shadows over the sweeping current of the river.

"Did you not know there was a good reason for her going?" Arthur asked, after a pause.

"I knew nothing," said Jack. "What reason could there be?"

"She went to the city to a hospital to give birth to your child."

Jack's face grew white with pain. "How do you know?" he whispered.

"She told me. I wanted her to come to England and train as a nurse, and when I urged her, she showed me a little dress she had been making, and told me, and she told me she was glad. Her only sorrow was that you were away and the adventure you were on was dangerous."

"I did not know." Jack groaned.

There was silence then, when neither man could speak.

"Here are Helmi's letters," at length said Warner; "they belong to you now. They will tell you everything. If we both get over I will take them back, after you have read them. I think if I had had a wife like Helmi I would not have doubted her. I don't think I would. However I am not saying that to hurt you—no one knows what he would do. Anyway I am glad I met you, Jack. And your wife is well and so is little Lili.

"And so you see you must get through. I may, but you must, and if you do you will tell Helmi. Come on—our chance is just as good now as it ever will be."

Jack took his hand and pressed it. "Arthur, I can't tell you what I want to say—you have been a better friend to Helmi than I have."

The bridge was a fine iron one, with heavily studded pillars. Every second light was burning. The road leading to it was not much travelled, and as they walked up the long approach their feet made a strange echoing sound. They had left their blue overcoats open, showing the gray German smocks. Jack knew what he was to say in German if accosted, but their hope was that no one was on the bridge. Every step brought them nearer, and the lights ahead of them on the Holland side twinkled like the lights of home.

Jack's heart was in a strange turmoil over what he had heard. . . . On, on—they were halfway over now . . . steps echoing, echoing . . . no sound but the gentle murmurings from the other side, gentle sounds . . . dogs barking . . . cow-bells . . . they must not hurry . . . on, on . . . ten feet from the end now!

Suddenly from behind the last pillar stepped out a German guard, who thrust a flashlight in their faces, blinding them with its sudden gleam. At the end of his rifle a bayonet gleamed in the light.

"Halt!" he cried.

"Why do you halt us? We are honest men," said Arthur quietly.

"Give me your passports, then," said the guard, putting away his flashlight, but not lowering his rifle.

Pretending to search his pockets, Arthur moved a little, then like a tiger he sprang on the guard, grasping him around the neck.

"I'll hold him, Jack!" he shouted. "Beat it! you're safe! Beat it!"

Jack found refuge in the trees on the other bank. There was a queer singing in his head, something droning like a swarm of bees. Then came a sudden pain in his shoulder like a knife thrust, and looking down, he saw the blood running off his fingers.

But he must see what happened. He crawled to the edge of the trees and looked back. Three guards were standing together, talking excitedly. He could see nothing of Arthur, but the smoke of rifles still hung around the pillars of the bridge. He crawled back into the trees and lay on the damp leaves, sobbing like a child. He was free; he was safe; but the loss of his friend was heavy on his heart.

Chapter XXXI

I t was a hot night in London in the early spring. The lights shone ghostly blue through their painted globes, and across the starless night search-lights stretched their spectral fingers, crossing, passing, converging, crossing again. Through the streets, in spite of the sombre gloom and the dangers of the night, an endless stream of people drifted, making a brave show of unconcern. The theatres were crowded, the dance halls echoed with rhythmic feet, and tinkled with laughter; and although grief, fear, and a sense of loss walked with every soul in London, the sound of their ominous footfalls were drowned by laughter and singing, true to the brave old British tradition.

At Victoria Station the V.A.D.'s were assembled with their waiting stretchers, for a hospital train was coming in. There were the usual noises of a great station—hooting of sirens, blowing of horns, calling of railway officials—all the sounds multiplied by the vaulted station roof. There was the usual variegated and cosmopolitan crowd, though the dominant note was the khaki of the thick-set, calm-faced Englishman; here the slim Canadian, independent and alert, actually looking for some one, and not ashamed of appearing anxious; there the blue-uniformed French officer, darting through the crowd like a gorgeous bluebird.

They are removing men on stretchers now, and the V.A.D.'s are busy. Very skilfully they manage to roll the bed-cases to the stretchers and carry them to the waiting ambulances—pallid faces, all of them, some bandaged, but most of them smiling bravely, too, and glad to be home.

There is one V.A.D. looking very slim in her blue serge uniform who works feverishly. She is returning with an empty when she meets the walking cases coming out of their coach, some on crutches, some being helped by companions, arms in slings, bandaged faces, but all on their feet.

She stops with a cry of gladness. "Jack, oh, Jack!" she cries, as a young man with his arm in a sling is passing. "Jack—it's Eva—don't you know me?"

She threw her arms around him. "It's my only brother—my only brother," she says to her companions, who wait for her. "Jack, are you a hospital case, or can you come with me? I have a flat, I can put you up. All right, wait for me inside on the first bench—I'll be through in half an hour."

Jack sat on the bench inside watching the crowds endlessly milling around him. He was surprised to meet his sister here when he believed her to be safe in Winnipeg. He wondered what had brought her to London—Eva, the luxury-loving, indolent Eva. It was strange to see her in plain uniform, carrying stretchers. But there was a high look on her face that transformed her. She looked more like the Eva he had known long ago.

Eva came for him at last and led him to the rear of the great station, where endless cars were parked, and put him into one which seemed very small and low.

"We pay a license according to wheel base, you know," she laughed; "and anyway, a car is a car, no matter how small it is. Oh, Jack, it's good to see you, and I have a bed ready for you. I've kept lots of the boys— I've been here six months."

Eva brought him to her flat in Maida Vale, and switching on a light, revealed a luxurious living-room, all in black and silver.

"Do you like it, Jack?" she asked with evident pride. "I work all day in misery and horrors so I have to have beauty at night."

A large black velvet divan, with round black cushions occupied one side of the room, the rug was black with a faint silver border—the fireplace black and white tiles, and on the mantel were silver candlesticks and a silver wrought image of the Madonna. On the black lacquered table stood a silver basket with American Beauty roses.

A slim maid appeared with coffee and sandwiches.

"We'll have a real meal later, Jack," said his sister. "And now tell me where you have been."

"First," said Jack, "tell me how you happened to come over?"

Eva laughed. "You will wonder, I know, but I couldn't stand it after the old crowd broke up—and I guess I missed Humphrey, too, though I won't admit it, because we had a row before he left, and he said things to me I shall never forget. But anyway, everyone was knitting and making bandages, and I couldn't get into it. So I rented the house and I can live easily here on the money. I really like the work I am doing, and I love the boys—they are so brave. I bring them home with me sometimes and write their letters and listen to their stories. I have one little extra room—and really, Jack, I never was so happy in my life. Now tell me your story."

Jack told her of his capture, imprisonment, escape, his friend Arthur Warner and his sacrifice.

Eva's eyes were filled with tears as she listened. "Oh, Jack, wasn't he brave? But why did he do it—why did he love you so?"

"It was not for me—it was his love for my wife!"

"Why, Jack, I didn't know you were married. Now begin at the beginning. Wait, do you want to go to bed first? You look pretty white. I mustn't let you tire yourself. You see I am a pretty good nurse now, and I know how to take care of people."

"No, I am fine," said Jack; "my shoulder is nearly well again. I have had two months in the hospital with it, and I want to tell you all about it."

Jack began with his meeting with Helmi at Eagle Mines; their marriage by the magistrate; the magistrate's objections, and his showing of the newspaper report.

Jack was lying on the couch while Eva sat beside him, the light so shaded that he could not see her face. She sat motionless through it all. He told of his return from the north and finding her gone; of his suspicions, confirmed, as he thought, by seeing her in Edmonton; of his sudden resolve to enlist; and lastly of his meeting with Arthur Warner. "I don't know," he concluded, "what is the explanation of the Winnipeg affair, but I know Helmi is innocent. She was sent to that place by someone and is shielding that person. Look at her letters, Eva—read them—and to think I doubted her and left her alone when she needed me!"

Eva took the letters in her cold hands, but she could not read a word.

"I got the news of my baby from another man," said Jack brokenly, "and it was his money Helmi got instead of mine to help her. Helmi had to beg for work and suffer insult. See what she says there—'No one wanted a girl with a baby.' Wasn't it damnable, Eva? I rage when I think of it. I blame myself—I shouldn't have believed anything. I knew how sweet and good and true she was—I knew! But the person that sent her for the dope and then slid out is the person who should be shot, and I'll sift it to the bottom when I go back. . . . Poor Helmi, bearing it all because she was too honorable to tell!"

In his excitement and deep emotion Jack did not notice that his sister had not spoken, but sat with bowed head, like a broken lily.

It was one of the soft nights when the blossoms are just beginning to scent the breeze, when there are those indescribable stirrings and whisperings of spring. Even if nations are at war and planning the destruction of each other, trees leaf and blossoms open. The streets seemed quiet to Jack; but for the heavy rumbling of the busses no one appeared to be abroad.

Suddenly the silence was broken by a weird, spitting noise as of giant fire-crackers; a sound of deadly import to the people of England, for it gave warning of the approach of enemy air craft.

"What is it?" Jack asked, starting up. The street resounded now with the racing feet of people hurrying to shelter.

"It's an air raid," Eva answered, without stirring. "They run to the tube stations; but I never go—I feel safer here—I have a dread of being smothered in those terrible places. I've been through three air raids already. So I am not afraid."

Eva spoke with a composure which was not assumed; anything was better than the maddening remorse that had swept over her as Jack told his story.

Jack went to the window and looked down into the street. Through the open window came the drone of the enemy's Zeppelins, malevolent, horrible, like the buzzing of some poisonous fly. Then came the continuous cannonading of the anti-air craft guns, like wildest days of battle. The searchlights combed the sky with their ghostly fingers, and people came tearing out of their houses and raced through the dark streets.

Jack had often wondered how people would act during an air raid. He felt no fear for himself—it didn't occur to him that he could be in danger here in London—his fear was for Eva. "Hadn't we better go, Eva?" he asked anxiously; "it seems to be almost above us. Is the tube far away?"

"Not far—but I never go. Come away from the window. There— that's a bomb—not far away . . . we're in for it, Jack, they're coming nearer. . . . Come here, Jack, I feel dizzy—come to me—I want to tell you something. I knew your Helmi in Winnipeg. She is not to blame—

I sent her, Jack. Forgive me—I sent her to the Chinaman's! Ask her to forgive me, too. I have been sorry ever since . . . "

A bomb burst in the square. There was a shattering of glass and a crashing of masonry; a horrible confusion of noises, tearings, screamings, concussions, clanging fire-engines.

By a strange chance the house in which Eva had her suite stood, though many houses in that vicinity fell. All the windows were shattered, and on the window sill of the room in which they stood was thrown the body of a little dead dog.

On the floor, where she had fallen, Eva lay, a piece of shrapnel buried in her cheek.

Jack stayed in London until Eva was out of danger. She would recover, the white-uniformed doctor at Guy's told him, but of course she would be badly scarred.

Behind her bandages, Eva smiled feebly. "It's all right, Jack," she said wanly, holding his hand; "better women than I have been blown to pieces. Maybe God is giving me a few more years to atone for what I have done. I have been a poor sport, Jack—I needed a smash of some kind—I am not complaining. Life is queer, Jack, isn't it? I wanted to show Humphrey I wasn't as selfish and shallow as he thought. He told me in the last quarrel we had, and the only one, that I would never be an old woman—I would only be a stale novelty. I was determined to show him I had some thought of doing things for other people, so I came here and got into the V.A.D. work. What I really wanted to do was drive an ambulance in France, but I was afraid, not of death, but of disfigurement. I hate ugliness so—far more than sin.

"It was my hatred of ugliness, not of sin," Eva continued, "which cured me of the drug habit. I had learned to take dope just because it gave me a thrill—it saved me from dullness; but I saw an addict—one of the doctor's patients—a woman something like me, but horrible

289

to look at—pasty-faced, dead-eyed, mouth agape—and I could see I might some day be like that. So, Jack, I never touched it again."

Eva paused for a long time; "But now, with a blue scar on my cheek and my nose broken I will not be afraid. I will go to France. Maybe I can take the place of some better and happier woman, and when the shell comes marked for her, it will take me instead. And Jack," she continued, "you will tell Helmi all of this and ask her to think as kindly of me as she can. She loved me once with all a young girl's adoration."

Jack kissed his sister tenderly with a deep sorrow in his heart. He could not reproach her—there was no need, but his own heart was aching with the sorrow of it all. Sin and sorrow—the age-old partnership—sin and sorrow! By one man sin came into the world, and death by sin; but the one who sins is not always the one who suffers.

Jack had cabled Keith, his former partner, from Paris to send to London one thousand dollars. But when he reached London he found that no reply had come. The information received there was alarming. Thos. Keith of Winnipeg, could not be found. He had left the city over a year ago, and his creditors had not been able to trace him.

Jack sat on one of the wooden benches in the cable office in London and thought, in a queerly detached way, of what this meant to him. He wondered at his own calmness in the face of such a smashing blow, for the gold mine on the Nehanni, with all the comfort and luxury it would bring him, had been much in his thoughts during the cheerless months of imprisonment. He had planned many generous surprises for his companions, too. . . . And now it was all over. He had been following a false light. . . . He had been warming his hands at a painted fire.

Well, there was about two hundred dollars coming to him from the War Office, and he would be given transportation home. Prisoners who had escaped through a neutral country were not allowed to go back into the army. When the *Olympic* sailed out of the harbor at Liverpool into the muddy waters of the Mersey, Jack stood on the deck looking back at the receding shores of England. Behind him lay many bitter thoughts and much disillusionment; the futility of war; the hideous wastage of young life; the horrible suffering and slaughter . . . and Eva, his only relative! He choked with bitter memories as he thought of it all. Then there came to him, beating up through all this, like a fountain of sweet water in the sea, the memory of Arthur Warner and his unselfish love, and of Helmi, with her clear, sweet soul and her honorable silence.

Jack walked to the prow of the vessel and looked away into the gray distance. Behind him lay the sorrow for the past, with its mistakes and regrets. Before him lay Canada—his own country—Helmi, and the little Lili.

Conclusion

At Arthur Warner's bungalow the flowers were blooming. Hollyhocks stood straight and tall against the house, with their quaint, old-fashioned rosettes in prim rows on the stalks, crimson and cream and white. Arthur had planted them, but had not seen them bloom. The walk from the house was bordered with round clumps of dwarf nasturtiums, orange and red, alternating with mounds of sweet alyssum and candytuft, white as snow, and at their feet in a straight line, marking the edge of the gravel path, ran a line of ground lobelia as blue as the skies above.

On one side of the walk stood a rockery of stones from the river, which Helmi had whitewashed, and from which now grew trailing nasturtiums, in all the shades from creamy pink to scarlet and crimson, peeping out from their glossy green leaves. On the other side was a rustic bench, made gay with cushions, where one could sit and think and dream, watching the changing lights upon the mountains.

Here sat Helmi, thinking and dreaming, this Saturday afternoon in late August. Her family had all gone to Eagle Mines—Rosie and Danny Corbett who were spending the holidays with her; old Sim and young Lili, the latter now an enquiring young lady of two and a half years. The teacher, too, who boarded at the bungalow had gone with them.

Twice a week Helmi sent to town a load of vegetables and fresh fish from the English river, and steadily her savings in the bank were increasing. It seemed a long time since she had climbed into the old buckboard, with Lili on her knee, Cleo close beside her, and the pups in a box behind, and canvassed the neighborhood to see where she could get a cow "on terms to suit purchaser." She had been successful in her quest, and brought the cow home with her; the terms being that she do the weekly washing for the numerous and increasing Peterson family, three miles away.

Helmi thought of her neighbors now with real affection. They had all befriended her, and she was glad that Arthur Warner had learned to know them better. Helmi had told them quite frankly all she knew of him, and when his letters came she made no secret of them. When she made the suggestion that weekly meetings should be held at his house, where knitting and sewing could be done for the soldiers, the women gladly came, and a new spirit of friendliness came to the settlement. Every week a letter was written to him, and parcels sent, and so it came about that, though thousands of miles intervened, Arthur Warner had come to know his neighbors and they him.

No letters had come from Arthur now for several months and Helmi feared that the shadow she had seen upon his face the day she said good-bye to him, had fallen. In her dreams she had seen a luminous figure, all in white, that had walked over to Arthur and tapped him on the shoulder; and he nodded his willingness and went away, and the same night Cleo had fretted and cried all night and would not be comforted.

But the boxes went every week, for Helmi and the women knew that some poor soldier would be the happier for them.

Of Jack she had not had a word, and in the midst of all her happiness and achievement there was the one sore thought which sometimes required all Helmi's faith to drive away. Jack's face, so sad and drawn, drifting away from her on the slowly moving train, fell across her happiest hours. But Helmi had not forgotten the experience she had the night of the storm, when her soul was lifted high above the mists of earth.

The hearts of the women were knitted to Helmi's because she had a way of comforting them in their troubles. There was strength in the touch of her hand, and healing in her presence.

"Look what she's done for me," old Sim would often say, "when I got crippled for good and couldn't do my work in the mine any more. 'Come to me, Sim,' she said; 'I am all alone except for little Lili and the dogs, and I need you Sim,' she says, 'for company'—makin' out I would be doin' her a favor. Look what a home she has given me."

It was Helmi, too, who discovered the seam of coal a little farther up the river, shining and hard, that burned with a blue flame and gave off more heat and burned longer than any other coal she had ever seen; and it was like her to tell all the neighbors about it and urge them to come and get all they wanted for their winter fires.

The peace which comes to those who work hard and have a clear conscience was Helmi's that afternoon as she listened to the waterfall behind the house, and through her dreaming came the happy consciousness that her family would soon be home hungry from town and she would need to go into the house and get supper ready.

The valley before her was beginning to show the purpling tints of evening as the sun wheeled its way over the mountains. A car came quickly around the turn of the hill, its wheels making no sound in the dusty road . . . He was half way to the house before Helmi saw who it was . . .

That night, after the others had gone to bed, Jack and Helmi sat long before the fire. Little Lili in her pretty white nightdress was fast asleep in her father's arms.

"Let me lay her down, Jack," said Helmi. But Jack could not part with her. "Remember I am two years and a half behind," he said. Helmi bent over him as she tucked the shawl around the little girl. "You won't leave us again, Jack, will you—not even to go for gold to the Nehanni?"

"Gold from Nehanni!" Jack repeated after her. "I should say not! What do I need of Nehanni gold?" Then drawing Helmi's face to his he said tenderly, "I got my gold from Finland."

Eight years have gone by. The Warner mine is one of the best in the Province, for the coal is a high-grade anthracite. Unlike most mine owners, the Dorans have not moved to the city, but have a large gray stucco house, with a red roof and many windows, on the bank of English River. Behind the house is a large grassy playground, enclosed by a high board fence, where a happy group of children and collie dogs may be seen at play. There is one old dog that walks stiffly, but is plainly the best beloved of all.

Below the falls stands a green and white bath-house, into which the water is piped from the stream. It is called the "Finnish Bath-House," because there is in it a room for steam baths where the steam is formed by water falling on heated stones.

There is a recreation ground across the road, and a white church on the hillside. In the basement of the church there is a well appointed dining-room, where the boys and girls' clubs often meet for supper parties.

The bungalow is a club-house for the miners and their wives, and on the lawn there is a simple white stone with an inscription which reads:—

"Sacred to the Memory

of

ARTHUR WARNER,

who made the first settlement in this valley, and who loved its solitude and beauty.

In 1914

he answered the call of his country;

On January 25th, 1917,
while escaping from a German prison camp, he deliberately
gave his own life to purchase freedom for his companion, who
now erects this stone in the hope that as long as grass grows in
the valley, and water runs in the English River, the memory of
ARTHUR WARNER may not fade."

THE END

Afterword

In the second volume of her two-part autobiography, *The Stream
Runs Fast: My Own Story* (1945),[1] Nellie L. McClung describes
the process by which she came to write *Painted Fires*. While
serving as a Liberal member of the provincial legislature in
Alberta from 1921 to 1926, she spent "many pleasant hours in the
Library of Parliament Buildings in Edmonton" (236). Inspired there
by the "industry" of North West Mounted Police memoirist Sir Cecil
Denny, whom she saw at work among "reports and records" (236) as he
prepared the book that would be published as *The Law Marches West*
more than a decade after his death,[2] McClung undertook "to do some
serious reading while [she] had the Provincial Library at [her] elbow.
For years," she says, "I had wanted to write an immigration story in
the form of a novel. I wanted to portray the struggles of a young girl
who found herself in Canada dependent upon her own resources with
everything to learn, including the language" (237). That "immigration
story" became *Painted Fires*, a narrative account of seventeen-year-old
Helmi Milander, who comes from Finland to join her Aunt Lili in
North America only to find herself alone and besieged at every turn
by what McClung represents as systemic racism and sexism and a
bureaucracy staffed by self-serving and largely corrupt officials.

First published in 1925 in Toronto under the imprint of Thomas Allen, *Painted Fires* is McClung's fourth novel and the last one she would write. Although it is also the only one that is not part of the Pearlie Watson trilogy that includes *Sowing Seeds in Danny* (1908), *The Second Chance* (1910), and *Purple Springs* (1921), *Painted Fires* is not unlike the Pearlie Watson books. It shares with the trilogy a focus on the coming of age—or, more specifically, the coming to reproductive femininity[3]—of a young girl in western Canada in the context of expanded settlement during the first quarter of the twentieth century. It also shares with the trilogy and, for that matter, with McClung's two novellas, *The Black Creek Stopping-House* (1912) and *When Christmas Crossed "The Peace"* (1923), the didactic principles of a narrative that works to enact (to model and to effect) social reform in the North American west. Like most of McClung's fiction, *Painted Fires* is a story devised to expose a particular problem and to show the way to fix it. It was specifically intended, McClung suggests in *The Stream Runs Fast*, to "lay down a hard foundation of truth as to conditions in Canada" for new migrants seduced by "the false flattery which ha[d] been given to our country by immigration agencies in Europe, anxious to bring out settlers for the profit of steamship and railway companies" (241).[4] This "false flattery," which Doug Owram and other historians have shown to be pervasive in the representation of the Canadian west from the end of the nineteenth century into the twentieth, is what McClung suggests in 1945 underpins the book's title, taken, she notes then, "from the fragment of a poem which stuck in [her] mind": "We cannot draw from empty wells, / Nor warm ourselves at painted fires" (241).[5]

Mary Hallett and Marilyn Davis have suggested that *Painted Fires* is McClung's best novel (221). An unsigned review of Randi R. Warne's 1993 book *Literature as Pulpit: The Christian Social Activism of Nellie L. McClung* in *Resources for Feminist Research* describes the novel as "more complex" than her others (Rev. of *Literature as Pulpit*). Warne herself describes it as "McClung's most difficult [and] certainly

[her] most complicated" (58), citing "[o]ne reviewer" who "note[d]
that critics in the United States and Canada 'invariably agree' that
Painted Fires was McClung's best effort" (Warne 56–57),[6] and another
who suggested it was "the first wholly imaginative novel from Mrs.
McClung. There is no question that with the freer scope thus gained
she has written a bigger book than 'Sowing Seeds in Danny' or 'Purple
Springs'" (qtd. in Warne 57). A review in the Toronto *Globe* described
it as a "book worthy to be in every library" (Peggy). By 1945, McClung
observes, *Painted Fires* had "gone through many editions, been serial-
ized many times and [wa]s still in print" twenty years after its first publication. "The year after its publication in Canada," she points out, "it
was translated into Finnish and published in Helsinki" (241). This new
edition makes *Painted Fires* only the second of McClung's longer works
of fiction to reappear in print in recent years: in 1992, a new edition
of the 1921 suffrage novel *Purple Springs*, third in the Pearlie Watson
trilogy, was published by University of Toronto Press with an introduction by Warne.[7] McClung is not well remembered today as a writer
of fiction. As Hallett and Davis point out, her fiction was "extremely
popular . . . in her time" but since the first half of the twentieth century
has often "been ignored or overlooked" or else dismissed as "merely
didactic" (228). This new edition of *Painted Fires* is an occasion for
a new look at her fiction—or, at any rate, at the novel that has been
"invariably" considered to be her "best effort"—and an opportunity to
reconsider what made *Painted Fires* interesting and engaging at the end
of the first quarter of the twentieth century and what makes it "complex" and compelling now in the first quarter of the twenty-first.

Nellie L. McClung was born Nellie Letitia Mooney (thus the "L" she
kept in her name for her publications) in the village of Chatsworth,
Ontario, in 1873. Her family headed west to Souris, Manitoba, in
1880. In 1896, she married Robert Wesley McClung, who worked in
the early years of their marriage as a pharmacist. The McClungs lived

in Manitou until they moved in 1911 to Winnipeg, where McClung, who had by then already published her first novel, *Sowing Seeds in Danny*, began to direct her considerable energy toward social reform, notably to temperance and to woman suffrage. As Hallett points out in an entry on McClung in *The Canadian Encyclopedia*, McClung "played a leading role in the 1914 Liberal campaign against Sir Rodmond Roblin's Conservative government, which had refused women" the vote, establishing herself as an accomplished speaker who would be much in demand in Canada and the United States through the 1910s, when women in both nations were struggling for voting rights. By 1915, the McClungs moved farther west, to Edmonton, where McClung continued to work for woman suffrage, which was granted to non-indigenous women in Canada in 1920 at the federal level in no small measure through the work of McClung and her colleagues across the country.[8] In Edmonton, she was elected to the provincial legislature from 1921 to 1926. During these years, McClung intensified her temperance work, and she may have lost her seat in 1926 at least in part because her insistence on prohibition as a necessary measure for what reformers of the period often characterized as "social hygiene" had come by that time to be much less popular. By the time of the 1926 election, the McClungs had moved to Calgary for Robert Wesley's work—this time in insurance rather than pharmacy—and this shift to less familiar territory may have contributed to the loss of the seat in the legislature. The 1926 election was a crucial moment for McClung: she did not write any more novels after that point, although she continued to produce short fiction and essays. After moving to Victoria, BC, in 1932, she took up new work in radio and in a syndicated newspaper column. She died in Victoria in 1951.

Although she did not produce any more novels after 1926, McClung was a prolific writer her whole adult life. Beginning with "brief editorials, verse, and short narrative sketches" in "Methodist and Presbyterian Sunday School publications" in the early 1900s, as

Hallett and Davis suggest (229), she was soon producing more than the Sunday-school-paper editors could manage.[9] By the late years of the first decade of the twentieth century, she "was receiving requests for stories from American [and Canadian] magazines" (Hallett and Davis 231).[10] *Sowing Seeds in Danny* was followed by a book—fiction, suffrage polemic, creative non-fiction, essays—every two or three years until 1945, when she published the second volume of her autobiography. The sixteen books in total represent only one part of her body of work, however: she also wrote numerous short pieces, not all of which are collected in her volumes of essays,[11] as well as many speeches and some radio work. McClung's fonds in the Provincial Archives of British Columbia comprise 7.3 metres of textual records, a significant portion of which is composed of boxes of scribblers and loose-leaf paper covered, often on both sides of the page, with McClung's handwriting. The manuscript of *Painted Fires*, for instance, is contained in more than a dozen scribblers.

McClung's publications, manuscripts, and ephemera are noteworthy not only for the sheer number of pages she produced but for the fact that she generated this writing while doing many other things at the same time. She and her husband had four children, for whom McClung, like most women at the end of the nineteenth century and the beginning of the twentieth, was the primary caregiver. During the years of the campaign for the vote for women, she travelled through Canada and the United States on whistle-stop tours to promote the suffrage cause. In addition to serving as a Liberal member of the provincial government in Alberta from 1921 to 1926, she was instrumental, with four other women (Henrietta Muir Edwards, Emily Murphy, Louise McKinney, and Irene Parlby), in the "Famous Five" campaign to have women recognized as "persons" through the affirmation of their constitutional right to serve as senators. The Persons Case was successful in its appeal to the Judicial Committee of the British Privy Council in 1929. McClung represented Canada at the League of Nations (forerunner to the United Nations) in 1938, and she served on the first board of governors for the Canadian Broadcasting Corporation, the first woman to do so. With many other women, she demonstrated the possibility of balancing children and career to the detriment of neither. As many critics have observed, McClung's legacy is not without problems: her support for eugenic legislation in Alberta's 1928 Sexual Sterilization Act is well known, and the fact that the granting of woman suffrage did not extend to First Nations women until 1960 represents a matter that should have been addressed in the context of the struggle for the vote. These are important matters whose consequences are still evident in twenty-first-century Canada and, while they cannot be justified, they can be seen in part to be indexical of the ideological context of early-twentieth-century Canada within which McClung was working: her vision was limited in ways that are evident in retrospect.

Painted Fires is arguably, despite the obvious connections between McClung and Pearlie Watson, the suffragist and "woman orator" in the earlier books, the work that is the most compellingly McClungian. Like all her longer fiction—and much of her shorter fiction—*Painted Fires* is foundationally (although not merely) didactic and was unabashedly intended to draw attention to social conditions that McClung saw to be in need of improvement and to make suggestions on how best to achieve that improvement. It is thus a work of feminist social reform and what Warne has characterized in the subtitle of her book as McClung's "Christian social activism." Although the novel must thus be situated in the context of McClung's political and social work, it is not without counterparts in the canon of early-twentieth-century English-Canadian fiction, a context from which it emerges and in which it signifies, at least with reference to white settler culture's fiction of Protestant social reform. Like her best-known English-Canadian contemporaries in the field of popular fiction, L.M. Montgomery (1874–1942) and Ralph Connor (the pseudonym of Charles William Gordon, 1860–1937), McClung developed a practice of writing that, at least in part, took the popular genre of nineteenth-century Protestant "Sunday School" stories[12] and turned their gesture of instruction through uplifting narrative to the imperatives of white setter nation-building, notably in the construction of new white Canadian subjects and their work to build new communities. As Laura M. Robinson has observed, Montgomery's first novel, *Anne of Green Gables*, published in the same year as McClung's *Sowing Seeds in Danny*, operates in this way to affirm her identity as a "born Canadian" (19), with its heroine moving, over the course of eight novels (or at least the first six), from orphan to "mother of the race," and from the outside into the very heart of the Cuthbert home, the village of Avonlea, and the province of Prince Edward Island. Montgomery's Anne Shirley and McClung's Pearlie Watson follow similar narrative trajectories to marriage (both to doctors) and to what is represented as a better motherhood (or, at least in Pearlie's case, incipient motherhood) and both making their communities better as they go (see Devereux, "Writing"). Anne's and Pearlie's narratives are stories of improvement (their own, their community's, their world's), and the novels in which those stories are told are themselves comprehensible as instruments of improvement through their modelling of the better subject and the better space.

Like Connor's—although perhaps less like Montgomery's (despite or perhaps because of her proximity to the Presbyterian ministry in which her husband Ewan Macdonald worked)—McClung's fiction tends to work along the axis of a cautionary conditional that, in addition to operating as a Sunday-school story of the kind that circulated widely through Anglo-imperial locations through the nineteenth century and early twentieth, owes something to the sermon as a genre: that is, it is a story of what could be without intervention, of what might happen without restraint or assistance. In Connor's case, the sermon is of course an unsurprising point of discursive engagement. He wrote his fiction under the *nom de plume* Ralph Connor but performed his public work as a Presbyterian and then United Church minister under his birth name, Charles W. Gordon. His published writing—again, not surprisingly—includes material explicitly framed as sermon. His *The Angel and the Star* (1908), subtitled "a sermon preached in St. Stephen's, Christmas, 1907," is one index of the contiguity in his writing between the registers of fiction and homily. McClung emerged in the suffrage years as an accomplished speaker—witty, engaging, and persuasive, she was called a "great woman orator" by one commentator (see Fiamengo 177)[13]—and because her politics were foundationally embedded in a Protestant theology and an ideology of "muscular" Christianity that is not far from what Daniel Coleman has shown is Connor's, she developed a practice of writing that undertook to achieve the same effect for readers as would a good sermon for an audience.[14] *Painted Fires*, which leans less heavily on the metonymic figure of the "woman orator" than do the Pearlie Watson books, is arguably more compelling, at least at one level, in its homiletic but less overtly sermonizing telling of a story that would draw attention to social problems in contemporary Canada while operating as a "complex" fiction.

McClung's description of *Painted Fires* as "an immigration story in the form of a novel" situates it alongside a good deal of fiction produced in Canada and the United States through the years of settlement and expansion that began more or less in the late eighteenth century and continue into the present. Arguably, settler nations such as Canada and the United States are saliently represented by fictions of immigration, migration, settlement, and displacement, and the history of the massive shift of non-indigenous population into the North American continent is a story that is still unfolding. *Painted Fires* focuses on particular problems of the early-twentieth-century Canadian west: an increased influx of European but not necessarily Anglo-imperial settlers in the context of the treaties' "opening" of the west and the annexation of the western territories to the Dominion of Canada;[15] imperial anxiety about filling up the west with non-indigenous bodies at least in part through what Coleman notes was Minister of the Interior Clifford

Sifton's "aggressive campaign to recruit eastern European farmers for the newly annexed prairies" (133; see also Palmer 22); a rise of nativism characterized by recently new Canadians maintaining a superior right of belonging and, as elsewhere in Canada, by a sense of Canada's proper destiny as an Anglo-imperial nation. Howard Palmer notes that the "predominant nativist cry" in Canada in the early twentieth century "was that non-Anglo-Saxon immigrants would subvert Anglo-Saxon institutions and racial purity" (98). Although her politics of race are as complicated as any early-twentieth-century writer's and her involvement in the development of "race" preservation and eugenic practices in Alberta has been widely criticized, and although this novel does not escape early-twentieth-century racist representation of Asianness (Sam speaks in the clichéd Chinese patois that was mobilized in so much contemporary writing and film), McClung, as *Painted Fires* wants to demonstrate, was herself deeply critical of such nativism. While her politics of "home mission" care and, sometimes, the actual and metaphysical cleaning of "foreign" bodies are clues of the ideologies of racial hierarchies in which her work certainly operates (see Devereux, *Growing* 113–36), her interest in "naturalizing" such bodies for the good of the nation is driven by a sense that the nation is not weakened but is made better by what Veronica Strong-Boag characterizes as her "confidence in cultural assimilation" (xvi) and what would later be called (and officially legislated) as multiculturalism.[16]

Indeed, in this novel as in her other fiction, McClung draws attention to the ways in which the west was *not* pervasively imagined as imperial space and the British Empire was not seen to be the ground and the centre of the work of new settlement. The largely American settlement of Eagle Mines does not respond to the declaration of war in the same way as does the Englishman Arthur Warner. His voice "quiver[s] like a violin string" when he proclaims that "[t]he British Empire is [his] country" and his "mother" (173), but his is a solo performance: he is the only subject who self-identifies in this way.

Warner is not idealized: a bit odd, an outsider (although he comes to regret his failure to connect with his neighbours), he is represented as being essentially good but hidebound by a sense of superiority that McClung represents as the tragic flaw of the Briton in the Canadian west. McClung suggested a similar sense in the Englishman George Shaw in her 1907 short story "Babette," in which a young Metis woman is able to show how deficient Shaw is as an Englishman and as a new Canadian and how the slipshod operation of his home stands as a metonymic figure for the empire he is to be promoting but is actually undermining (see McClung, *Stories* 49–53; see also Devereux, *Growing* 125–28). In *Painted Fires*, moreover, Englishwomen are not configured—as they are in so much imperial adventure fiction of the period—as superior to other women in the Canadian context. Martha Draper, who works alongside Helmi in the kitchen of the Yale hotel, is described as slovenly and lazy, like Shaw, taking for granted what Helmi shows a desire to work for. When Helmi clunks Martha over the head with her tray to express her outrage over her poor dishwashing practices, her temper is "Finn" but the sloppy dishwashing and, importantly, the notion of racial superiority are "British": Martha, we are told, "had the British tradition—foreigners were dirty and ignorant, and certainly 'could tell her nothink'" [*sic*] (18). Martha's dishwashing, as an index of her failure to maintain social hygiene, is linked in the novel to the politics of the arrested sex worker Babe Summers, with whom Helmi shares a cell. In its representation of Martha and Babe as the only female representatives of the "mother" country, *Painted Fires* does not argue that Canada should abandon its imperial history but does suggest that the "best" settler is not necessarily British at all. Indeed, according to this novel, Britons can essentially disappear from the western expansionist scene (as they do here, except in the memorial erected by Jack for Arthur Warner) without diminishing it.

Given its conversion of the British imperial presence to a historical event, it is noteworthy that *Painted Fires*, in addition to drawing on a Protestant discourse of instruction in Sunday-school novels and the genre of the sermon in its telling of Helmi's "immigration story," is also aligned with the genre of imperial adventure stories. Helmi's story of travelling through "new world" space is not far from the kinds of narratives that had proliferated since the late years of the nineteenth century, in which young Anglo-imperial boys and girls travel around the British Empire, encounter adventure, and "win through" adverse and hazardous conditions to establish themselves as benevolent colonizers. What Warne notes was one reviewer's response to the novel as "overblown and irrelevant"—"Surely," the reviewer asks, Helmi's "experiences cannot be typical of all immigrant girls?" (qtd. in Warne 58, 57)—is not unusual in the sphere of imperial adventure. For instance, the novels of McClung's English contemporary Bessie Marchant (1862–1941)—who was sometimes called a "female Henty" (Nevinson 569) and who, with around 150 books, was one of the best-known and most prolific writers of imperial adventure stories, mostly for and about girls—are, if anything, more overblown in their representation of the "typical" experiences of "immigrant girls" in Canada and elsewhere than is McClung's of Helmi. Indeed, the point is made in Marchant's *Times Literary Supplement* obituary in 1941 that "few of her girl readers can have had, or hoped to have, the Amazonian life of a Bessie Marchant heroine—riding the wilds, shooting, and dominating ferocious tribesmen or backwood desperadoes" (Nevinson 569). The same might be said of *Painted Fires*, in which, among the "vicissitudes of plot" Candace Savage has observed, "the villain is struck dead by lightning just in time to prevent the hard-pressed heroine from doing him in" (169). But it is also clear that McClung was writing an adventure story that undertook to expose and address a problem she saw as a *real* one—of young women emigrating to Canada and encountering, as they travelled, not only racism but a complicated and ubiquitous system that was based on a traffic in women and that presented danger to women and girls travelling·alone.

Comprehensible as a tale that crosses the genres of Protestant social reform, imperial adventure, and corrective western Canadian immigrationism, Helmi's "immigration story" can also be seen to engage with the genre of the "white slave" narrative (see Devereux, *Growing* 88–109). That is, Helmi's story draws upon the conventions of a genre that had begun to circulate in the context of intense anxiety in the late nineteenth and early twentieth centuries about the entrapping and sexual exploitation of young girls and women. Concern about the possibility of a traffic in white women's bodies had begun to appear in reform discourse by the 1870s and early 1880s (see Dyer). British social reformer Josephine Butler had begun her "great crusade" against the traffic in young girls, a work that was first documented in James Stuart's 1876 publication, *The New Abolitionists: A Narrative of a Year's Work*. In 1885, *Pall Mall Gazette* editor W.T. Stead, in part at Butler's urging, published what was widely regarded as a sensational exposé of the white slave traffic. "The Maiden Tribute of Modern Babylon" was released in instalments over several days in July, travelling quickly through the relatively new technology of cable and making international headlines. Documenting the fact of a trade in which young girls and women could be bought and sold into a sexual servitude from which they would be unable to escape, Stead's account established the terms of a genre that would proliferate after 1885 and would continue to flourish well into the twentieth century. White slave narratives, communicating the range of possible conditions under which women might be vulnerable to the agents working for the trade, began to appear in print at the end of the nineteenth century as cautionary tales (see Devereux, "'Maiden'").

Helmi's story—"an immigration story in the form of a novel"—is such a cautionary tale, drawing on the conventions of a genre that, in Canada and the United States, frequently represented white slavery as an immigration issue and its control a matter both of stemming the tide of what was seen to be European vice and of protecting potential new

Canadians and Americans from being brought into the trade—and thus of protecting the "new world" itself.[17] *Painted Fires* does not lead to the usual conclusion of the North American white slave narrative: it is not a story of "the girl that disappears," as anti-white-slave crusader and New York City Police Commissioner Theodore Bingham put it in his 1911 account by that title. But the trajectory of Helmi's story and of many of the events and conditions represented in the novel would be recognizable to readers who had by 1925 come to be familiar with the genre of the white slave narrative in popular culture, in print, and, increasingly through the second decade of the century, in film. Indeed, they were so familiar, in western Canada, as elsewhere in North America, that it is difficult to imagine that McClung was not deliberately invoking this narrative. The immigrant girl who falls prey to wicked men when she arrives, the girl who works in a hotel, the girl who loves finery and her own reflected image, the girl who is induced to go to an opium den, the girl who travels by train, the girl who marries a man without regard for the authenticity of the papers, the girl who works in a Chinese restaurant, the girl who goes to movies: Helmi is at one time or another all these girls, all of whom figure prominently in white slave narratives in print and film, and all of whom would be understood to be on the brink of entrapment by the white slave trade.

White slavery makes a frequent appearance in western Canadian newspapers through the 1910s and 1920s, and the point was frequently made that the traffic in women and girls was as evident in Canada as it was elsewhere. For instance, the *Didsbury Pioneer* of 14 July 1909 noted the assembly in Toronto of "[t]he forces arrayed against the white slave traffic" to "deal as vigorously with the objectionable conditions in far distant Yukon as in the central cities of the Dominion" ("Open"). On January 19, 1910, under the headline "The 'White Slave' Traffic" and a subheading referring to "A Warning Cry to Young Girls and to Parents in Rural Canada," the *Red Deer News* announced that "[t]his unspeakable traffic is carried on in Canada, and has been discovered in Halifax, Montreal, Toronto, Hamilton, the West, and the Yukon, as truly as in New York and Chicago" (2). The text of this *Red Deer News* article was taken from a report by U.S. District Attorney E.W. Sims, published in the American magazine *Woman's World* in 1910 and widely circulated in pamphlet and reprint such as this one. Later in 1910, advertisements began to appear in papers such as the *Bow Island Review* for Ernest A. Bell's book, *War on the White Slave Trade* ("War on the White Slave Trade"). On 9 July 1913, the *Red Deer News* used the title of Bell's book to headline a report: "The House of Commons gave some attention to the question of the white slave traffic before adjournment, and definitely declared war on it. . . . [A] brief discussion arose when Mr. Andrew Broder urged that steps should be taken by the Government to prevent the operations of white slavers on the trains and among young girls who came into the country under the auspices of the Immigration Department" ("War on White Slave Trade" 5). The *Edmonton Daily Bulletin* of 8 November 1913 noted "[t]he fact having been established that 'white slavery' has been carried on in Edmonton" ("'White Slave' Case" 4). McClung, a dedicated reader of daily news-papers and a close observer of conditions for women in the Canadian west, as well as a close friend of magistrate Emily Murphy, who sat in the women's court in Edmonton, was, of course, as aware of these reports as anyone—although she did not need such proximity to bring the anxiety about white slavery to her attention. The "panic" that had begun in the 1880s was expanded significantly through the production and circulation of films that built upon the conventions of the white slave narrative.

During the 1910s, as Shelley Stamp Lindsey has pointed out, a "rash of sensational and—for the time—sexually explicit films on white slavery" began to appear (1). "With lurid titles like *The Inside of the White Slave Traffic* (1913), *Smashing the Vice Trust* (1914), *House of Bondage* (1914) and *Is Any Girl Safe?* (1916), the films fueled an already raging nationwide panic" (1) in the United States and Canada.

In addition to "fuel[ling]" the panic, these films would significantly supplement it by framing the ways in which technologies of mobility could be seen to drive the traffic in women. Kristen Whissel has suggested of the 1913 film *Traffic in Souls* that

[i]t is no coincidence . . . that one of the earliest American long features not directly derived from a literary source dramatizes the technological mobilization of bodies between Europe and the United States, the country and the city, public space and private space, and the home and the brothel. *Traffic in Souls* makes clear connections between various kinds of traffic and the everyday, urban experience of technological modernity. The film is based on the simple premise that to participate in modern life is to be absorbed into traffic. *Traffic in Souls* therefore organizes its narrative around the unceasing mechanical mobilization of bodies through space. (167)

At the heart of the white slave narrative, as Whissel's analysis shows, is an anxiety that is specific to the territorial expansion of the late nineteenth century: on one hand, the mobility of women's bodies in and through the technologies of expansion and travel, and, on the other, and crucially, the implications of this mobility for the home and for the nation, both the home nation and the "new world" settler culture. The cautionary tale presented by *Traffic in Souls* is comprehensible, Whissel observes, as a work of "regulating mobility"—what Lindsey describes as white slave films' "alarmist storylines [as they] sought to curtail the latitude women were just beginning to enjoy in urban culture" (15). While it does not necessarily want to "regulate" Helmi's mobility, *Painted Fires* nonetheless demonstrates how it is in mobility that she becomes vulnerable to the traffic in women that this novel, like and with all white slave narratives, undertakes to affirm as a reality. In its construction with reference to white slave narratives,

Painted Fires undertakes not so much to warn women to stay at home, to refrain from travel, and not to be independent—arguably a central motive in white slave narratives generally—but rather to affirm a systemic problem that can be seen to underpin a traffic in women. In other words, McClung's novel is less about the potential for women to be victimized than about the problem of a patriarchal culture that refuses to allow women to earn enough to support themselves, that does not recognize the value of their work, and that pushes them into different versions of sexual and economic servitude.

If *Painted Fires* is compelling in its negotiation of "new world" popular print genres, it is arguably most innovative and interesting in its engagement with cinema both as a cultural context and a narrative system. In 1920, according to *Henderson's Edmonton City Directory*, there were thirteen "[t]heatres and places of amusement" in Edmonton (718). In Winnipeg, according to *Henderson's Winnipeg City Directory*, there were an astonishing forty-eight by 1921 (1505–6). Some of the theatres in these cities were primarily focused on live entertainment, but cinema, which had been figuring in and between live shows in theatres increasingly through the first decade of the twentieth century, was coming to occupy a more prominent place in the "places of amusement" in both Edmonton and Winnipeg, the two urban centres that are prominent in this novel, as it was in other cities. As Lawrence Herzog suggests, the Empress Theatre on Jasper Avenue in Edmonton showed moving pictures as early as 1912, and, from 1915 on, the Princess Theatre in south Edmonton "offered a program of 'high class moving pictures varied occasionally with high class musical vaudeville or musical concerts'" ("Alberta"). From 1918, the Allen Theatre (later the Capitol Theatre) in Edmonton showed silent films ("Fort"), and by the 1920s at least three theatres in Edmonton were showing films. News of cinema and of movie actors had begun to appear in western

Canadian newspapers alongside "theatre" news, and film had begun its shift to the centre of popular culture in North America.

Painted Fires draws early attention to its engagement with film. We are told that "Mrs. St. John," the opium addict who is responsible for Helmi's arrest in the raid on the Shanghai Chop Suey House and for her "escape" from the Girls' Friendly Home to Eagle Mines,

> took her once a week to the Moving Pictures Theater, where Helmi sat spell-bound and dazzled. From the time she entered the enchanted place until she came out again into the sunshine she knew nothing of the real world. Watching the pictures she came up the aisle seeing no one, conscious of nothing, stumbling on the steps without knowing there was a step, or that she had stumbled, following her friend vaguely to a seat, and sitting perched on the edge until some indignant person behind her told her to sit down and let somebody else see, with an impatient "What is the matter with you, anyway?" (45)

As Helmi begins to define herself as a new Canadian, she depends heavily on the ideology of incipient imperial maternalism conveyed in the motto of the Canadian Girls in Training (CGIT):[18] "Cherish health; seek truth; know God; serve others" (50). Indeed, her ability to read English is measured in the novel by her mastery of the text of the Blue and Gold book that is the handbook of the CGIT. But it is also in the context of the cinema that she forms her identity in and through language. The words Helmi uses to define and situate herself in the "new world" are drawn from film—thus the "list of words pinned over the sink" that she practises "while she washed dishes":

> The lady is beautiful.
> She has an elegant coat.

Will you go for a drive?

Have a chocolate?

I adore chocolates. (46)

Helmi rejects the phrases provided by Miss Abbie Moore—"Honesty is the best policy"; "Civility costs nothing" (46)—thus rejecting a kind of everyday and homespun femininity for what she sees in the cinema. Far more compellingly than the women around her—even Mrs. St. John—cinema operates as the location for the formation of the adult femininity Helmi is working to reproduce in her own body in and as the image she sees projected on the screen:

> The world Helmi entered through the green plush doors, laid hold on her impressionable young heart. She saw lovely ladies in trailing beaded dresses and shining jewels, leaving their elegant homes to go with their lovers, and smart young stenographers wearing seal coats and hats they could clap on their heads and always look just grand, and who married the old man's wayward son and saved the old man's business from ruin by listening at the door when the bad men were plotting. . . . Further attendance at the pictures brought home another fundamental truth—the lovely lady is always forgiven—indeed, she can do no wrong. She may appear to do wrong, but some one else is really to blame. . . . She would be a lovely lady! And the words and sentences which appeared on the wall were tinctured with this resolve. (45, 46)

Helmi's identificatory relationship to film is comprehensible with reference to what Lindsey characterizes as "specular mobility": Lindsey cites Giuliana Bruno's point that "the female subject's encounter with the cinema constructs a new geography, gives license to venturing. . . . Female spectatorship triggers, and participates in, women's conquest of the sphere of spatial mobility" (qtd. in Lindsey 15). Female spectators experienced, Lindsey suggests, an "imaginary locomotion" that, as she notes Miriam Hansen observes, "opened up a [social] space . . . as well as a perceptual, experiential horizon" (qtd. in Lindsey 15). Lindsey suggests that white slave films were particularly ambiguous for female spectators precisely because they

> offered [women] the possibility of circumventing prohibitions against both their physical mobility and their visual license. They might watch unseen as procurers spied upon intended victims, crack codes used by the nefarious slave rings, and, most significantly, traverse hidden regions of the nation's sexual geography in cinema's screenscape. (15)

McClung, who does not specifically invoke white slave films in the novel, nonetheless draws attention to this same condition of moral ambiguity in and around cinema, which is represented as both the primary location for the constitution of adult femininity for Helmi and as a space where she must see herself to be in danger precisely because of the "specular mobility" that opens the way from domestic space. Like Sam's opium den, cinema is suggestively here a portal to danger and a space within which femininity could be seen to be compromised. One of the bad male magistrates in the novel makes this point when he says, "Women and girls have too much liberty these days, and that's why they are going to the devil. They don't work any more—they just gad around to picture shows and get into trouble, and the women's organizations encourage them instead of trying to restrain them" (64). Mrs. McMann of the boarding house where Helmi finds work in Eagle Mines says something similar when she explains why it is so difficult to keep female workers at the boarding house: girls "get lonesome. It's too far from Jasper Avenue and the Allen Theatre" in Edmonton (114). Cinema's "specular mobility" works, in effect, against domesticity.

Mrs. McMann and the bad magistrate highlight cinema's condition of ambiguity as it is exploited by Eva St. John, who engineers Helmi's "escape" from the Girls' Friendly Home:

> The plan was this: She would bring the "Merit Class" to see a picture at the "Grand." She had done this, so it would excite no suspicion. When they were all seated and the picture was absorbing everyone, she would whisper to the girl next to her that she had suddenly remembered that she must meet a friend at the afternoon train. Helmi would come with her. Her story after would be that she left Helmi sitting in the car while she went to greet her friend who was passing through. When she came back Helmi was gone. She thought, of course, Helmi had grown tired of waiting and had gone back to the theatre, and when she went back in the darkness she did not notice her absence, believing she had found a seat in some other part of the building. . . . (98)

In this sequence, Eva St. John in effect precipitates Helmi into mobility and into the cinematic, putting her into the circuits of traffic: not only is it she who first brings Helmi to the "Moving Pictures Theatre" (45), but she also leaves her "in the car," puts her on the train, and provides her with the kind of narrative of the mobile "lovely lady" (46) that fires Helmi's imagination. The novel's complexity arises in part through the friction created by the simultaneous pull to bring Helmi back home—to "settle" her—and to protect her when she is in motion, or, as Lindsey has shown of white slave films, to represent and to curtail her sexual danger. It is in this friction that *Painted Fires* is most like film and its narrative most evocatively cinematic.

While McClung suggests that the title's "painted fires" refer specifically to misleading immigrationist rhetoric that, in this case, has led Helmi to Canada, the image of the "painted fires" is also a recurring motif in the novel, naming any kind of guiding illusion. In Helmi's case, it is not rhetoric per se that is shown to have misled her, but the soap company picture Aunt Lili brings her while she is still in Finland that stands in for false advertising. We are told that "[t]he resolve to see this wonderful country for herself was definitely taken when she saw the beautiful picture" (4). Indeed, the point is made that "Helmi believed the title literally, and wondered how her Aunt Lili could leave such an enchanted place even to come for a visit to the old home" (4–5). Helmi's "painted fires" index a failure to separate the image from a "real" referent or to see that the image does not necessarily have a counterpart but is only itself. But hers are not the only "painted fires" represented on these terms in the novel. For example, anti-capitalist Anna Milander, when she is arrested for heaving a stone at a police officer during a labour demonstration, sits in her cell "a prisoner before the law, but not cast-down or desolate. She, too," we are told, "had her own little painted fire, and she had not yet found out that there was no heat in it" (16). Jack, similarly, whose "imagination" has been "fired" by "the glint of yellow gold" (222), comes to the recognition after his partner vanishes that he "had been following a false light. . . . He had been warming his hands at a painted fire" (290; ellipsis in original). Helmi, who abandons mobility and comes home, where Jack will find her in the end, must likewise see the "false light" of the figure of the luminous "lovely lady" of cinema, perhaps the most compelling implication of the title's "painted fires," and settle down.

Katja Thieme has observed that, in its concluding affirmation of Helmi and Jack's reproductive future and the prospect of a family, *Painted Fires* "offers a tale of how the Canadian nation can be redeemed morally" (112). While this tale is conventional enough, the novel works to develop what is presented as a new world popular fiction that moves across the registers of Protestant reform (Sunday school novels, sermons), "immigration story" (McClung, *Stream* 237), imperial adventure, and white slave narrative. In its engagement with cinema, *Painted Fires* importantly draws attention to the ways in which popular fiction in North America develops in the early twentieth century in complicated imbrication with film, and raises questions of the implications for print narrative of its relationship with visual media. In its representation of the "strong female character" (Savage 169) of Helmi Milander who must find agency and subjectivity in and against the "painted fires" of film, the novel puts the story of moral redemption in the hands and bodies of women who might be imagined, in McClung's vision, to be making a world in which they could move freely.[19]

CECILY DEVEREUX, *University of Alberta*

Notes

1 The first volume of McClung's autobiography, *Clearing in the West: My Own Story*, had appeared in 1935.

2 Sir Cecil Edward Denny (1850–1928) is described by Alan B. McCullough in the *Dictionary of Canadian Biography* as an NWMP officer, Indian agent, author, and archivist. McCullough's account suggests that Denny may have been complicit in starvation practices and other controls exerted by white settler culture on First Nations communities in the west.

3 For more on these books, see Devereux, "Writing," as well as chapter 5, "Pearlie Watson and Eugenic Instruction in the Watson Trilogy: How to Be a Maternal Messiah of the New World," in Devereux, *Growing* 63–74.

4 For more on the rhetoric and representation of the Canadian west, see Owram; Owram and Moyles; Francis and Kitzan.

5 McClung indicates in her autobiography that she does "not know from what source" these lines are taken (241); the source remains obscure.

6 Warne cites reviews of *Painted Fires* kept as clippings by McClung and found in her papers at the British Columbia Archives (81).

7 Prior to this, McClung's 1915 suffrage manifesto, *In Times Like These*, was reissued in 1972 with an introduction by Veronica Strong-Boag.

8 As Kelsey Wrightson notes, "The vast majority [of First Nations people in Canada] could not vote in federal elections until ... 1960."

9   As Hallett and Davis remark, "At times, in the early 1900s, Nellie was so prolific that she inundated Dr. W.H. Withrow, the Canadian Methodist Sunday School paper editor, who occasionally managed to send her two dollars for her voluminous efforts: 'I do not know that I can use all of your articles' and, perhaps with exasperation, 'I have enough on hand for some time'" (230; see also 321n5).

10   See also chapter 10, "My First Story," in McClung, *Stream* 75–85.

11   The published volumes of McClung's shorter works include *The Next of Kin* (1917), *All We Like Sheep* (1926), *Be Good to Yourself* (1930), *Flowers for the Living* (1931), *Leaves from Lantern Lane* (1936), and *More Leaves from Lantern Lane* (1937). The pieces in these volumes shift between fiction and creative non-fiction, story and essay. Short stories are also included with the title novella in *The Black Creek Stopping-House and Other Stories* (1912).

12   See, for example, the "Pansy" books published in the United States between 1865 and 1929 by Isabella Macdonald Alden (1841–1930) and the "Elsie" books published between 1867 and 1905, also in the United States, by Martha Finley (1828–1909). English-Canadian writer Agnes Maule Machar also wrote novels of Protestant reform that are grounded in Sunday School genres, including *Katie Johnstone's Cross* (1870) and *Marjorie's Canadian Winter* (1893).

13   On McClung's public speaking, see chapter 6, "Nellie McClung and the Rhetoric of the Fair Deal," in Fiamengo 177–208.

14   See chapter 4, "The Muscular Christian in Fictions of the Canadian West," in Coleman 128–67.

15   Treaties 6, 7, and 8 in 1876–98, 1877, and 1899 had made it possible for the Canadian government to identify and allocate land for settlers, whereas the completion of the Canadian Pacific Railway in 1885 made transcontinental travel and transport a possibility for Canada. First Nations and Metis resistance to both the acquisition of land and the development of the railroad had been fiercely countered by the Canadian government in 1869–70 and 1885, culminating in the latter year with the hanging of Metis leader Louis Riel.

16   Multiculturalism was adopted as an official policy in Canada in 1971. The Canadian Multiculturalism Act was passed in 1988. To suggest that McClung anticipates official multiculturalism in Canada does not minimize the novel's problematic representation of identity as saliently racial. McClung is not making a case in this novel for an identity politics that is not constituted with primary

reference to race, but for relativity, connection, and, although it is also an index of a complicated ideology of racial division, what would have been characterized throughout much of the twentieth century as "intermarriage."

17 In 1911, a U.S. Immigration Commission, first convened by Congress in 1907, noted in its forty-one-volume report that "[t]he importation and harboring of women and girls for immoral purposes and the practice of prostitution by them—the so-called 'white slave traffic'—is the most pitiful and the most revolting phase of the immigration question" (qtd. in Cordasco with Pitkin iii).

18 The CGIT "was founded in 1915, as an alternative to the burgeoning Girl Guides movement.... By the end of its first decade, 75,000 girls had received ... training" in this organization ("Canadian"). The Blue and Gold book Helmi reads may have material in it based on a CGIT pamphlet first published in 1915 with, as its subtitle indicates, "suggestions for the mid-week meetings of Sunday School classes, clubs, etc., for teen-age girls" (*Canadian*).

19 For resources for further study of this novel, see Devereux, *Growing* 89–109; Hallett and Davis 228–69; McClung, *Stream* 234–42; and Warne 55–84.

Works Cited

I. Archival Sources

Nellie McClung fonds. British Columbia Archives, Royal BC Museum, Victoria, BC.

II. Books, Periodicals, and Electronic Sources

"Alberta Register of Historic Places: Princess Theatre." *HeRMIS: Heritage Resources Management Information System*. Government of Alberta, 1995–2013. Web. 17 July 2013.

Bell, Ernest A. *War on the White Slave Trade*. 1910. Toronto: Coles, 1980. Print.

Bingham, Theodore Alfred. *The Girl That Disappears: The Real Facts about the White Slave Traffic*. Boston: Richard G. Badger, 1911. Print.

"Canadian Girls in Training." *Wikipedia: The Free Encyclopedia*. Wikimedia Foundation, 28 May 2013. Web. 31 July 2013.

Canadian Girls in Training: Suggestions for the Mid-week Meetings of Sunday School Classes, Clubs, Etc., for Teen-age Girls. 2nd ed. N.p.: The Committee, 1916. Microfiche. CIHM/ICMH 78302.

Coleman, Daniel. *White Civility: The Literary Project of English Canada*. Toronto: U of Toronto P, 2006. Print.

Cordasco, Francesco, with Thomas Monroe Pitkin. *The White Slave Trade and the Immigrants: A Chapter in American Social History*. Detroit: Ethridge, 1981. Print.

Denny, Cecil E. *The Law Marches West*. Toronto: Dent and Sons, 1939.

Devereux, Cecily. *Growing a Race: Nellie L. McClung and the Fiction of Eugenic Feminism*. Montreal: McGill–Queen's UP, 2005. Print.

———. "'The Maiden Tribute' and the Rise of the White Slave in the Nineteenth Century: The Making of an Imperial Construct." *Victorian Review* 26.2 (2000): 1–23. Print.

———. "Writing with a 'Definite Purpose': L.M. Montgomery, Nellie L. McClung and the Politics of Imperial Motherhood in Fiction for Children." *Canadian Children's Literature / Littérature canadienne pour la jeunesse* 99 (2000): 6–22. Print.

Dyer, Alfred S. *The European Slave Trade in English Girls: A Narrative of Facts*. London: Dyer Brothers, 1880. Print.

Fiamengo, Janice. *The Woman's Page: Journalism and Rhetoric in Early Canada*. Toronto: U of Toronto P, 2008. Print.

"Fort Edmonton Capitol Theatre." *Municipal Affairs*. Government of Alberta, 1995–2014. Web. 17 July 2013.

Francis, R. Douglas, and Chris Kitzan, eds. *The Prairie West as Promised Land*. Calgary: U of Calgary P, 2007. Print.

Hallett, Mary, and Marilyn Davis. *Firing the Heather: The Life and Times of Nellie McClung*. Saskatoon: Fifth House, 1994. Print.

Hallett, M.E. "McClung, Nellie Letitia." *The Canadian Encyclopedia*. Historica Foundation, 2008. Web. 17 July 2013.

Henderson's Edmonton City Directory. Winnipeg: Henderson Directories, 1920. *Peel's Prairie Provinces*. University of Alberta Libraries, 2003. Web. 17 July 2013.

Henderson's Winnipeg City Directory. Winnipeg: Henderson Directories, 1921. *Peel's Prairie Provinces*. University of Alberta Libraries, 2003. Web. 17 July 2013.

Herzog, Lawrence. "The Lost Series: Edmonton's Lost Theatres." *Herzog on Heritage*. Edmonton Heritage Council, 3 Nov. 2011. Web. 17 July 2013.

Lindsey, Shelley Stamp. "Is Any Girl Safe? Female Spectators at the White Slave Films." *Screen* 37.1 (1996): 1–15. Print.

Rev. of *Literature as Pulpit: The Christian Social Activism of Nellie L. McClung*, by Randi L. Warne. *Resources for Feminist Research / Documentation sur la recherche féministe* 23.4 (1994–1995): 72–73. *ProQuest*. ProQuest LLC, 2013. Web. 17 July 2013.

Machar, Agnes Maule. *Katie Johnstone's Cross*. Toronto: James Campbell, 1870.

———. *Marjorie's Canadian Winter*. Boston: Lothrop, 1893.

McClung, Nellie L. *All We Like Sheep*. Toronto: Thomas Allen, 1926. Print.

———. *Be Good to Yourself*. Toronto: Thomas Allen, 1930. Print.

———. *The Black Creek Stopping-House and Other Stories*. Toronto: William Briggs, 1912. Print.

———. *Clearing in the West: My Own Story*. Toronto: Thomas Allen, 1935. Print.

———. *Flowers for the Living*. Toronto: Thomas Allen, 1931. Print.

———. *In Times Like These*. 1915. Introd. Veronica Strong-Boag. Toronto: U of Toronto P, 1972. Print.

———. *Leaves from Lantern Lane*. Toronto: Thomas Allen, 1936. Print.

———. *More Leaves from Lantern Lane*. Toronto: Thomas Allen, 1937. Print.

———. *The Next of Kin*. Toronto: Thomas Allen; Boston: Houghton Mifflin, 1917. Print.

———. *Purple Springs*. 1921. Introd. Randi L. Warne. Toronto: U of Toronto P, 1992. Print.

———. *The Second Chance*. Toronto: William Briggs, 1910. Print.

———. *Sowing Seeds in Danny*. Toronto: William Briggs, 1908. Print.

———. *Stories Subversive: Through the Field with Gloves Off*. Ed. Marilyn I. Davis. Ottawa: U of Ottawa P, 1996. Print.

———. *The Stream Runs Fast: My Own Story*. Toronto: Thomas Allen, 1945. Print.

———. *When Christmas Crossed "The Peace."* Toronto: Thomas Allen, 1923. Print.

McCullough, Alan B. "Denny, Sir Cecil Edward." *Dictionary of Canadian Biography* vol. 15. University of Toronto/Université Laval, 2003–2013. Web. 17 July 2013.

Nevinson, H.W. "Bessie Marchant." Obituary. *Times Literary Supplement* 15 Nov. 1941: 569. *News International Associated Services*, n.d. Web. 15 Dec. 2012.

"Open White Slave War." *Didsbury* [Alberta] *Pioneer* 14 July 1909: 5. *Peel's Prairie Provinces*. University of Alberta Libraries, 2003. Web. 17 July 2013.

Owram, Doug. *Promise of Eden: The Canadian Expansionist Movement and the Idea of the West, 1856–1900*. Toronto: U of Toronto P, 1980. Print.

Owram, Doug, and R.G. Moyles. *Imperial Dreams and Colonial Realities: British Views of Canada, 1880–1914*. Toronto: U of Toronto P, 1988.

Palmer, Howard. *Patterns of Prejudice: A History of Nativism in Alberta*. Toronto: McClelland and Stewart, 1982. Print.

Peggy of Day Dreams. Rev. of *Painted Fires*, by Nellie L. McClung. *Globe* 6 Mar. 1926: 20. *Globe and Mail: Canada's Heritage from 1844*. Micromedia ProQuest, 2002. Web. 28 July 2013.

Robinson, Laura M. "'A Born Canadian': The Bonds of Communal Identity in *Anne of Green Gables* and *A Tangled Web*." *L.M. Montgomery and Canadian Culture*. Ed. Irene Gammel and Elizabeth Epperly. Toronto: U of Toronto P, 1999. 19–30. Print.

Savage, Candace. *Our Nell: A Scrapbook Biography of Nellie L. McClung*. 1979. Halifax: Goodread, 1985. Print.

Strong-Boag, Veronica. Introduction. McClung, *In Times Like These* vii–xxii.

Stuart, James. *The New Abolitionists: A Narrative of a Year's Work*. London: Dyer Brothers, 1876. Print.

Thieme, Katja. "'The Grim Fact of Sisterhood': Female Collectivity in the Works of Agnes Maule Machar, Nellie L. McClung, and Mabel Burkholder." *Diversity and Change in Early Canadian Women's Writing*. Ed. Jennifer Chambers. Newcastle upon Tyne: Cambridge Scholars, 2008. 100–17. Print.

Warne, Randi R. *Literature as Pulpit: The Christian Social Activism of Nellie L. McClung*. Waterloo: Canadian Corporation for Studies in Religion/Wilfrid Laurier UP, 1993. Print.

"War on the White Slave Trade." Advertisement. *Bow Island Review* 29 Oct. 1910: 1. *Peel's Prairie Provinces*. University of Alberta Libraries, 2003. Web. 17 July 2013.

"War on White Slave Trade." *Red Deer News* 9 July 1913: 5. *Peel's Prairie Provinces*. University of Alberta Libraries, 2003. Web. 17 July 2013.

Whissel, Kristen. *Picturing American Modernity: Traffic, Technology, and the Silent Cinema*. Durham: Duke UP, 2008. Print.

"The 'White Slave' Case." *Edmonton Daily Bulletin* 8 Nov. 1913: 4. *Peel's Prairie Provinces*. University of Alberta Libraries, 2003. Web. 17 July 2013.

"The 'White Slave' Traffic." *Red Deer News* 19 Jan. 1910: 2. *Peel's Prairie Provinces*. University of Alberta Libraries, 2003. Web. 17 July 2013.

Wrightson, Kelsey. "First Nations' Enfranchisement in Canada." *Women Suffrage and Beyond: Confronting the Democratic Deficit*. N.p., 7 Jan. 2013. Web. 1 May 2014.

Books in the Early Canadian Literature Series
Published by Wilfrid Laurier University Press

The Foreigner: A Tale of Saskatchewan / Ralph Connor / Afterword by Daniel Coleman / 2014 / x + 302 pp. / ISBN 978-1-55458-944-9

Painted Fires / Nellie L. McClung / Afterword by Cecily Devereux / 2014 / x + 324 pp. / ISBN 978-1-55458-979-1

The Traditional History and Characteristic Sketches of the Ojibway Nation / George Copway / Afterword by Shelley Hulan / forthcoming 2014 / ISBN 978-1-55458-976-0

The Seats of the Mighty / Gilbert Parker / Afterword by Andrea Cabajsky / forthcoming 2014 / ISBN 978-1-77112-044-9

The Forest of Bourg-Marie / S. Frances Harrison / Afterword by Cynthia Sugars / forthcoming 2014 / ISBN 978-1-77112-029-6